STORMY SEDUCTION

"Oh no, my dear, sweet Mona," the dark stranger whispered. "You will not escape me now."

Monica shivered as his hard fingers massaged her shoulders. Was this the touch that had filled all her dreams? Determined to resist him, she struggled and lashed out, but in vain. He covered her damp face with soft, sensuous kisses while she moaned aloud in newly awakened desire.

"Do not play the innocent with me, Mona," he said, his voice harsh. "I'd much rather you be the lovely coquette that you really are."

If Monica had been more alert, she would have noticed something familiar about that deep voice, but as it was his identity remained unknown to her drugged senses.

His lips fastened to hers again, he kissed her in a sweet, ardent fashion that carried her almost to the point of abandonment. Almost.

He pressed her deeper into the smothering folds of the bedclothes and Monica felt herself weakening. She was past the point of struggling or thinking; she was aware only of his lean body bearing down upon her while his lips held hers captive, and her own wanton passions sealed her fate. . . .

MORE RAPTUROUS READING

WINDSWEPT PASSION (1484, $3.75)
By Sonya T. Pelton
The wild, wordly pirate swept young, innocent Cathelen into an endless wave of ecstasy, then left with the morning tide. Though bound to another, the lovely blonde would turn one night of love into a lifetime of raging WINDSWEPT PASSION.

BITTERSWEET BONDAGE (1368, $3.75)
by Sonya T. Pelton
In sultry, tropical Morocco, Rosette would forget the man who had broken her heart. And forget she did in the tantalizing embrace of mysterious, magnetic Mark — who knew he'd always keep her in BITTERSWEET BONDAGE.

AWAKE SAVAGE HEART (1279, $3.75)
by Sonya T. Pelton
Though Daniel craved tantalizing Tammi, marriage was the farthest thing from his mind. But only Tammi could match the flames of his desire when she seductively whispered, AWAKE SAVAGE HEART.

THE CAPTAIN'S VIXEN (1257, $3.50)
by Wanda Owen
No one had ever resisted Captain Lance Edward's masculine magnetism — no one but the luscious, jet-haired Elise. He vowed to possess her, for she had bewitched him, forever destining him to be entranced by THE CAPTAIN'S VIXEN!

TEXAS WILDFIRE (1337, $3.75)
by Wanda Owen
When Amanda's innocent blue eyes began haunting Tony's days, and her full, sensuous lips taunting his nights, he knew he had to take her and satisfy his desire. He would show her what happened when she teased a Texas man — never dreaming he'd be caught in the flames of her love!

Available wherever paperbacks are sold, or order direct from the Publisher. Send cover price plus 50¢ per copy for mailing and handling to Zebra Books, Dept. 1602, 475 Park Avenue South, New York, N.Y. 10016. DO NOT SEND CASH.

Forbidden Dawn

Sonya T. Pelton

ZEBRA BOOKS
KENSINGTON PUBLISHING CORP.

ZEBRA BOOKS

are published by

Kensington Publishing Corp.
475 Park Avenue South
New York, NY 10016

First printing: June 1985

Printed in the United States of America

For the Drummer:
John H. Pelton II
(Jonathan Rockenfield)

Burn on, O Fire of Love,
O shimmering spire!
Burn on, presence of
Sweetness, blood-red,
Essence of liquid fire.
Burn deep within, consuming
Love's glory fed.
Burn deep within my soul!
And so steal my name—
O Defiant Heart,
destruction of the Flame.

Part I

Steven

1

Yerba Buena, California, 1844

A tall, still man with a wariness about him stood apart watching the *Don Quixote* sail up the California coast and majestically enter the bay where sister ships were juxtaposed with one another under the summer blue sky. To those who knew the man's reputation and skill, he was limber as a whip, just as fast with gun and blade, and tough as well-seasoned rawhide. Though here, he was mostly among strangers.

Steven Hawke was not dressed in the usual mode of the village, but wore instead a white cambric shirt, open midway to his waist, and tight-fitting black breeches of broadcloth, the ends tucked into dusty, worn jackboots. His thick black hair was worn carelessly long at the nape of his neck while the front feathered back from his aristocratically high forehead.

Steven's white smile twisted laconically in his

bronzed face, and to those milling near him he seemed to be a well-dressed gunslinger as he stood, boots planted firmly apart on the boardwalk, Indian-black eyes set between cheekbones slashed high and lean, and scanned the bay for new arrivals.

The party in honor of the spanking new trading post had already begun to bore Steven. If the party livened up a bit now that the company of performers were coming to play for the dancing, he just might stay.

"Maybe," Steven said softly to himself, watching a sailor drowsing comfortably in a chair tilted against a crude adobe wall, "just maybe."

On the other hand, now that he had collected the prize money from the horse race he had just won with his swift black, he was of a mind to find Jess, his younger brother, and head back to *Hacienda de los Caballos*.

Maria del Consuela, his adoptive parent, would be waiting back at the rancho for their return by now. Before the raid the Apaches had staged years ago on his father's village, in which the lives of his parents and of numerous others had been lost, Steven and his brother had been sent to the safety of the rancho where Suela at once had taken them in.

An iron smile now touched the corners of Steven's mouth. His skin had become darker, deep copper, even in the small crinkles that had appeared about his eyes due to peering against strong sun and along the barrel of a gun. Steven had deduced long ago that they had been whisked to the safety of the rancho because of their father's premonition.

Suela had spent lavishly for Steven's education even though his mother, Leah, had already taught him English, French, and a smattering of Spanish. Suela had worked on the Spanish with him and now he spoke Andalusian fluently.

Jess, on the other hand, had had no desire to cultivate his mind and had clung to the Indian Way. But Jess did not need much persuasion to come and flirt and dance with the Spanish beauties, and that was where Steven would find him right now, waiting for the dancing to get under way.

Indeed the party was well under way at the trading post and the feasting and dancing would go on for three whole days, although Suela had stayed on at *Hacienda de los Caballos* to tend to the birthing of a black's new offspring.

All the prominent California families from the village as well as folks from faraway ranchos were steadily flowing in. Some came on horseback, some by oxcart, and those from the north shore were being ferried across by schooner. The fife and drum corps from the *presidio* was now making a lavish appearance, along with Captain Hinckley and his ship's orchestra.

Steven found a seat on a low bench near a squat adobe store, lit a slim cheroot, and shifted the J&S Hawken pistol in his wide leather belt. The pistol was massive, a single-shot percussion arm of large caliber like his rifle.

Often alone in hostile country, Steven could not

trust his life to the one shot in his rifle. A pistol doubled his firepower, giving him a reserve weapon if there was not sufficient time to reload. So far on only one occasion had Steven used it to save his life. That had occurred when a burly trapper challenged him to a duel. The trapper had picked on the wrong lad, for Steven's pistol had lifted his antagonist right out of his saddle because of the tremendous impact of four hundred grains of soft lead. He could have fought the man barehanded, sure, Indian fashion, if the man had not been in such a hurry to kill Steven first.

Steven expected no trouble in the indolent village. But then, he had learned at an early age that one could never be too cautious or unprepared in these raw settlements where new bands of hunters and trappers and traders kept arriving, having followed the trail between Santa Fe and Mission San Gabriel.

Of late, Steven found himself craving something more than just raising horses, something with more of a dash to it. Like the sea, he was thinking now. Ah, there was daring, adventure. Although he wasn't quite sure just what it was he wanted to do, he was determined to become a wealthy man, perhaps a merchant captain. How to expedite his expectations, to set into motion the wheels of fortune, was his main concern.

A dusty old-timer came up leading a tired-looking horse and said, "Care fer yer horse, *hombre?*"

"Sure," he said, "right over there. Can I trust you?" he went on, a smooth and deadly look in his black eyes.

"Me? Ever'one about these parts knows of me—name's Jarvis."

Steven nodded. "Jarvis. Everyone knows of me too, and I'd better be able to trust you with my horse."

"You kin." He looked down at Steven's pockets. "Pervidin', o' course, that you've the cash, *hombre*."

"I do." Steven handed over several coins and old Jarvis led the black away.

Flicking the half-smoked cheroot off into the water, Steven watched it sizzle and then go out. Gay music reached his ears and he knew that the young folks would already be weaving back and forth in the intricate movements of the fandango. Hell, he might as well join them and find a spot on one of the benches against the rough wooden walls of the store until a lovely *señorita* caught his eye.

Steven was just making his way up to the structure when a buckboard rumbled down the dusty, rutted street. The driver, apparently in a great hurry, sat ramrod straight and wore a black scowl. He stopped near the trading post and swung down to tie up the lathered and sweating horses. The man, who appeared to be English, stood for a moment looking over the group of men gathered near the structure and then strode briskly toward one who appeared mighty surprised at his coming.

From beneath the wide brim of his hat, Steven caught a flash of blue. He turned his head a little and it was then that he noticed the young girl on the buckboard just moving to straighten the bonnet that was askew over her honey brown curls.

"Damn sight," Steven breathed through barely moving lips.

Her peaches-and-cream complexion was no doubt heightened from the jolting ride; her petticoats that provocatively peeped out were splattered with mud. Every shifting shadow below her bonnet, every falling tendril caught his eye, and he almost stumbled as he walked in a complete circle to survey this lovely creature.

The girl removed the bonnet heatedly after several attempts to set it aright. Steven laughed low at her efforts and could swear her softly pouting lips moved to invoke curses on her recalcitrant headgear.

Steven unconsciously continued to gape at her. Her tawny hair caught the sun's bright rays and coruscated in every shade of gold and brown he could think of, casting a fiery halo all about her pretty head. Just then a salty breeze issued off the sea and whipped up the hem of her dainty dress, giving Steven a full glimpse of a slim, well-turned ankle.

Leaning up against a building, Steven pulled out a slim cheroot but only chewed on the end of it as he pulled his gaze reluctantly from the gentle sight of her to appraise the goings-on. He unconsciously fingered the hawk band on his wrist, tracing the tooled leather. The colorful beads were all gone now from years of rough-and-tumble wearing, but the leather was yet soft and the memory of the one who had given it to him alive in his mind as ever. Leah, his mother, the only woman he had ever loved in this world.

Steven shivered for a moment and felt the rush of blood rising to his skin. Who is she? he wondered. His Indian-black eyes were still curious as he turned her way again. The girl touched something inside him, and although he wanted to ignore her presence, he was having a hard time of it.

Reluctantly his gaze returned to her. Apparently they weren't staying for the festivities, for the girl remained seated demurely atop the buckboard. Steven thought she looked a bit agitated and disheartened as if she had just been informed that this was exactly the case—they wouldn't be staying the three days. Between her eyes, a trace of a frown came and went, but she never shifted a muscle now that she had laid the bothersome bonnet aside.

Then, quite suddenly, tawny lashed eyes lifted and Steven's breath caught at the sight of jade green eyes boring squarely into his own. Despite her obvious youth, Steven thought her the most ravishing beauty he had ever set eyes upon. Not that her golden look was unusual, for there was a plentitude of fair-haired women about the settlements. The Swiss, the English, and the Dutch had come to partake of the opportunities the new land offered and most of them had stayed on. This one could be English by the looks of her, Steven thought. But there was more, he decided, as he studied her creamy peach skin. Perhaps Spanish or French ancestry.

Above all, the many-colored lights in her hair caught and held his eye. Golden strands shimmering

17

among tumbled and opulent curls, she looked like a princess from a faraway land, long ago, almost out of place in the rawhide settlement.

Having caught the black gaze that measured her, she shifted and turned her attention elsewhere, as if to say "Take your eyes off me, stranger, and look where you're going." Steven chuckled low at where his thoughts, not his feet, were taking him.

Monica sat in a rigid position on the seat of the buckboard. After the long, dusty ride into town her posterior felt battered and tender. She could blame her ugly-dispositioned stepbrother, Alex Bennington, for her discomfort. He had driven the team like a madman hellbent on bruising her poor backside.

She would not have come to town at all if she had known Alex was going to drive instead of the stablehand.

Light dust floated in the air and settled like a gossamer coating of angels' mist in Monica's hair. The silky strands were already damp at the back of her neck. She felt hot, sticky, untidy, and it never would have occurred to her that there were those who would find her dishevelment charming and easy to look at.

Monica lowered her gaze suddenly. She had the strangest feeling that her destiny path had just crossed someone else's. From the moment she had stared across the way at the handsome stranger, inexplicably and startlingly her cheeks had become flushed and hot. At first she had thought him unreal and had almost deemed this splendid male specimen a figment of her creative imagination.

Monica had been left in little doubt of what this male's feelings were, for she was not so innocent that she did not comprehend them. His gaze had traveled slowly and intimately over her body. She could feel that he hardly took his eyes off her. She would know precisely when to look up again, for the warm floating feeling would leave her when he looked away.

Monica felt instantly drawn to him. It was a frightening moment of self-discovery the first time these intense conflicting emotions had swept over her, and it was confusing that the tips of her breasts grew hard.

Enraptured, for the briefest space of time, she studied the stranger when he looked away. Clad in a contrasting white cambric shirt, which he wore shockingly open against lean, muscled ribs, and tight, black breeches that were molded to the sleek muscularity of his legs, and tall well-worn boots, the bronze-countenanced stranger was the most handsome man Monica had ever seen.

The man's male beauty and virility made all the wildest dreams of a young and impressionable girl come to life. She hadn't been able to see into his eyes, but in that briefest of glimpses she had noted they were fringed with long black lashes that matched his eyebrows and gleaming hair. His bold presence frightened and excited her at the same time.

Monica looked away. She fought her heart and flesh with every honed female weapon at her command. But she was so young and inexperienced. She was thankful that the black-haired stranger was walking away from her with a pretty Mexican girl, leaving Monica almost weak with relief. But she felt strangely disconnected from the world when he disappeared into the crowd.

Monica stared at the dusty street, at nothing in particular aside from hues and shades of gray and brown. Dust swirled before her eyes and she blinked.

And now Monica's preoccupation with the return trip left her little time to think about anything else. She heard Alex laugh sinisterly across the way. She wished she had never come along for the ride. Her stepfather had said she was too young to be here unchaperoned and neither he nor Alex had time for her. He had made it quite clear that he did not trust Tina Maller to be in charge of her. It would be different if he were to be in town for the duration of the festivities, but he would not. So Alex was taking her back as soon as his business with Branville and the others was completed. In a day's time Alex would return for his stepfather.

Alex laughed again. Oh, Monica thought, for just one glorious day I would love to become a man, rippled with muscle from head to foot, so I could squash Alex down to the size of a steaming dung heap. She gritted her teeth, wishing, If only I were stronger, like Hercules, or little David in the Bible.

Alex would soon be returning to the buckboard.

She had little time left before she had to tolerate his presence beside her. He was looking her way, she knew, but she just smiled a secret smile straight ahead. Suddenly the sun was a brighter yellow, the sky seemed more blue, and the dusty gray and brown street of Yerba Buena had never had such vivid color.

So long, golden girl, Steven was saying to himself as a pretty Mexican girl sidled up to where he stood, now in a dumb trance, and nudged him shyly with her elbow. "Like to dance, *hombre?*"

"Not just now, *querida*," Steven answered languidly. "But I'd like to try some of that *aguardiente* I saw you and your friends hiding over yonder by that table. Join me?"

"*Sí, sí,*" the dark-haired girl said excitedly, snatching Steven's hand to guide him to where the liquor was concealed.

Steven couldn't resist throwing a last glance over his shoulder to where the golden girl still sat staring at nothing, a fixed look masking her emotions. Steven shook his head, chuckling at this feeling that was rolling in his gut like seasickness. Just looking at her had provoked an unwelcome response in his groin and he decided he was going to have to do something about that—and soon.

"*Hola, Esteban!*"

Jess slapped his preoccupied brother hard on the back as he passed with a wild-looking Spanish girl who shot Steven a flirtatious glance with her dark liquid eyes. His own eyes rolling, Jess took up the girl's hand possessively and walked her right on past his brother and down toward the bay.

"I'll be damned." Steven caught their gay laughter as, hand in hand, they swung along the wooden planks, and he couldn't help grinning and wondering what the outcome of that tumble would be. Perhaps a little *bébé*. Jess was reckless in love affairs to say the least and possibly, just possibly, Steven would see him shotgun wed before the season wound out.

Yet Steven found humor in his brother's ways, for Jess was wily for one whose mind was uncultivated. At the tender age of eighteen Jess searched for the ideal situation—to get one of the dark-haired *niñas* of his choice plus a large gift of fruitful land. Jess knew that as soon as a Spanish girl wed she would become a citizen of California and receive a large grant of land from the government. California families were large and sometimes there were as many as twenty children to one family. They were easygoing, pleasant, but Steven found them somewhat indolent. He had assured his brother—warned him—that he would inherit more than just land to raise horses on, that if he didn't watch it he would find himself saddled to a fat wife and raising a bunch of Spanish-Indian brats to boot.

"Crawling in bed with a pretty *niña* for a night is one thing," Steven had instructed, "wedding one is getting more than one bargained for."

Jess sobered at once at the stifling words, then

22

grinned wickedly. Jess, in turn, told Steven that if *he* kept up like the stud horses back at the rancho it wouldn't be long before he would be forced into the same *aprieto*, predicament.

"*Touché*!" Steven had laughed, assuring his brother at the same time that there would be no shotgun wedding for him because it was not his habit to bed vestal virgins.

No, Steven thought now as he had then, a more experienced woman, one educated on such matters, would be more careful than a fluffy-headed dull maiden.

"Anyway," Steven had added with a deep chuckle, "who would desire bedding some *niña* inexperienced in the art of love? I would much rather take one experienced than a giggling maid who only has marriage in her mind."

Ah, there was no sense arguing with Jess. If he wanted such a chubby *niña*, and the land grant with her, then he would just have to suffer the consequences.

The Mexican girl was offering him a cup of *aguardiente* and her dark eyes had a question in them as she asked, "Your brother, *sí*, Esteban?"

"*Sí*, my brother," Steven sighed. "And a reckless young devil I might add." Then, "Who's the girl?"

"Pilar," Louisa said quickly, thinking he'd meant Jess's girl.

But Steven's gaze traveled to the golden one still seated on the buckboard and growing mighty impatient judging by the tapping of her light brown, fancy-stitched boots. "Pilar?" he questioned Louisa, doubtful about the name. But then, who could tell?

The Mexican girl's lower lip jutted out as she followed Steven's ardent gaze to the buckboard. "Oh, that one!" She shrugged. "I do not know. But I tell you my name. It is Louisa."

"Her name is Monica."

A bombastic voice declared close behind Steven, and he turned to the owner of it, one hand closing around his pistol with the speed of a cougar. The man was indifferent to Steven's reaction and went on.

"Her last name is not important because you will never see her again. She's much too young and innocent for the likes of any of you *hombres* here. And I might add, she is already promised. So set your sights elsewhere, *muchacho*."

"*Muchacho?*" Louisa laughed in the man's thin face. "Esteban is not a boy! He is a man!" she said defensively.

Steven had stiffened at the warning, but before he could reply the tall, thin man sauntered over to a group of richly garbed gentlemen who were engaged in a heated discussion. The one that had alighted from the buckboard acknowledged the presence of the thinner man and drew him into the discussion.

"That one is Alex, *the mean one*," Louisa was saying, hatred in her voice. "He is what they call here a poli . . . polic— Ah, *maldita sea!*"

"Politician?" Steven furnished the word for her, watching the gathered men with renewed interest.

"*Sí, sí*, a *político*. Esteban, you drink now?"

24

"In what way is this Alex so mean, Louisa?" Steven's gaze went once more to the small figure on the buckboard as if she were a mirage he did not want to vanish. He was wondering at the same time what authority the man called Alex had over her. He'd said she was innocent, so he could not be her husband.

Louisa thought deeply for a moment, groping for the right words to explain. Then she blurted out what she knew.

"Government give mission lands to Indians. Indians gamble, drink much, and many, many die. Men like Alex and his friends take it all away then."

Steven pondered her explanation for a moment. So, the Indians unused to their new freedom were at the complete mercy of these unscrupulous politicians and soon lost their lands to them. Yes, and these same men were content to live easy lives, letting Indian servants do the hard labor for them while they sat back on their backsides and became fat.

As Steven unceremoniously strode away—much to Louisa's dismay—he was pondering how he would love to put a nice big hole in the head of each of those men. Maybe that day was not too distant—for Alex anyway. Steven already hated the man thoroughly.

2

Not one person in Yerba Buena knew the man Alex's last name, or they just weren't in the habit of giving out any information about him. Steven Hawke could discern that this Alex was feared by all, himself being the exception. Steven feared no man.

For two more days the guests lingered on, in rancheros that stretched for miles along the fingers of the Bay, or, like Steven, stretched out on the ground near the adobe huts, wrapped in saddle blankets under the midnight moon and the stars that shone from the dark blue sky.

Steven hadn't set eyes upon Jess since the lad had disappeared with his dark-haired *niña*. And Steven was becoming more than a little concerned.

"Damn *aguardiente*," Steven hissed, awakening with the sun fully over the horizon. He had been at a little party the night before with Louisa and her friends and, Lord, was he sorry—for the big head this morning, not for the pleasure Louisa had given him.

Jess's mount was still tied up next to Steven's black

and that was another thing that perplexed him. Jess was not in the habit of leaving his brother to see to the care and feeding of his own mount. Nor did he have cash to put the mare up as Steven had the first night here in Yerba Buena.

Steven made inquiries as to his brother's whereabouts, even down to describing the girl he had been with. Yes, they knew of the girl Pilar, for this very day she had joined the others riding to a point south of town for a picnic. And yes, she was alone. That is, no *hombre* that fit Jess's description accompanied her.

Later, he questioned Pilar who blushed profusely over some matter Steven could well understand but who supplied Steven with little information to go on.

"After he leave Pilar two nights ago, he did not come back. Say he have to go meet his brother. You his brother, *si?*"

"That's correct," Steven answered, his black eyes even blacker than usual, like a void.

"That is all, *señor.*"

Then Pilar's dainty huaraches padded along the wooden planks, leaving Steven to stare vacantly after her, no light of hope alive in his deep dark eyes.

Days stretched into weeks as Steven combed the surrounding areas, packing his old blanket roll and riding the hills furiously from dawn to dusk. There was not a soul for miles around who knew what had happened to Jess Hawke. Either that or they just weren't talking. Being birthed according to the Indian Way did not assist Steven in his ineffectual tracking. This vast land and its winding green trails were unknown to him; he was a red man in a white man's land.

One day Steven drew his mount to a halt, the horse's mouth opened by the pull of the Spanish bit as he reined in atop a steep incline. Gazing down over the vast unchanging wilderness of green, Steven knew an aching forlornness that had never washed over him this strongly. An unheeded vision of the golden girl loomed up before him, and his eyes narrowed to a velvety darkness as he thought of her. She burned in his daydreams and in his thoughts at night under the moon and stars. He'd dreamt wildly of her just the night before; in the morning he'd found himself drenched in the liquid of love.

"Women!" Steven snorted. They always managed to take up the better part of a man's life. Like now, when he should have his mind solely on finding Jess. Even Suela, beautiful, even though well past the prime of her life. True, she had taught him that love could be wonderful, but Suela never seemed to be fully satiated. She had always come between him and Jess, turning them against each other. He decided he would remain a bachelor.

Perspiration streamed down his coppery face, but Steven was almost glad of the heat for now. It helped to cure the ache of his heart. One flash of a glorious angel. The desire for such a woman was not only in his body but in his very soul also. Every line of her face seemed drawn by an artist's hand, her every slight movement filled with lightness and grace. *Ah*

Dieu, if he did not stop this madness he would go in search of that angel and murmur sloppy and affectionate words he would regret by the next morning. What was he thinking? This Monica, the angel, was a mere child and children were not for the taking.

Steven rode on and strove to make himself forget.

His rampant thoughts swung back to his brother. Perhaps Jess was better off, even if deceased, than living out the remainder of his fledgling days in imprisoning wedlock. What the hell did Jess want to go and get hitched for anyway? To Steven, land was not all that important, but maybe it was to someone like Jess Hawke who was, in truth, all Indian in his brainwashed mind.

Finally, when the hot sun was well over the treetops and the air sultry, Steven made his way, on a weed-bordered path, back to the rancho.

The sea seemed to call him back, the scent of salty air beckoned him to return. But his thoughts were now of a different nature; he hoped despite his fears that he would discover Jess waiting at the rancho.

Up ahead the mountains loomed lonely and black, yet as he rode in, hot and dusty, with Jess's head-down mount lagging behind on a rope, Steven knew beforehand that he would never set eyes upon his younger brother again.

3

With the morning sun just a hazy ball of citron above the sea's horizon, dim streaks of red and gold steadily worked their way through the mist that hovered over the coast of Monterey.

The spacious harbor was dotted with anchored craft, most of which were sagging and in poor repair. On shore, stocky dark women lumbered along, toting pails of water into small cookhouses which were separated from the main dwellings. Most of the servants here were Indians. Even the poorest of families in Monterey was able to keep at least one Indian.

The servants paused in their labors to survey the two men tying their mounts to the doorpost of the little cottage, these strangers watching the harbor for an approaching vessel.

"Ahh, there she is, Étienne," Antoine Lyons said proudly to the young man he had signed on as first mate.

Even though Steven Hawke knew naught of ships

and sailing, Antoine was confident Steven would learn quickly, for the love of sailing was all one needed to begin. Meeting Steven Hawke at Consuela's rancho had been fortunate indeed. Steven had had his fill of ranching and his three-year search for his brother had proven futile so he was ready for a new and different venture, even after buying the California house.

A ship's proud sail glided majestically into view, out from behind the black fingers of rock that jutted out into the bay. Behind the two men, highly excited voices exclaimed as the tall-masted square-rigger, moving as if she rode a heavenly cloud, took a tack to make her awe-inspiring entry.

"Indeed, she is all that you said, sir," Steven commented approvingly, his eyes brilliant ebony in his excitement to be aboard the vessel, "and more."

Then Steven's heart gave a bound as the tall queen of the seas drew closer. He felt excitement feed into his blood, giving a lift to his heart as well as his heels. He wanted to run abreast with the beautiful winged creation of God and man. At that moment in time Steven sorely missed his brother now that he was leaving America, and a lonely sick feeling tore at his gut. He squashed it down, as he had on many previous occasions, and looked toward the future.

The *Mañana* was anchoring and already the crew was beginning to lower a longboat to pick up their captain. Antoine Lyons pulled hard to savor his cigarillo, making the tip glow red as he inhaled. He was nearly as tall as Steven, slim-hipped, and he

31

sported a rich waistcoat that fit snugly across the broad shoulders he held straight as a ramrod. His graying dark hair swirled about his ears and his sideburns were long. Two dangerous-looking revolvers were tucked neatly into a Spanish red sash. His lacy jabot was open, displaying a strong furred chest, youthful in its muscle and taut golden flesh. He wore over his waistcoat a black swinging cloak, a mark of rank and of the wealth of the owner. Despite his rich garb Captain Lyons looked like a daring pirate, not the wealthy merchant captain he really was. Despite his fifty-some years he could slip in and out of slim white arms as easily as he could shuck an unwanted *amour.*

Sailing down from Yerba Buena, where the cargo of trade goods had been unloaded, the silks that Captain Lyons was noted for, the crew of the *Mañana* was now picking up their captain to make the return voyage to France. Pitt Dailey, for all his crude ways was one of Antoine's best hands; he took care to secure the California bank notes and, no doubt, picked up a few pretty, lively, dark-haired *señoritas* to please his captain and the crew at the onset of the long voyage. Captain Lyons was one captain who did not believe women on board brought bad luck to a ship and its crew.

Nearing the vessel while seated in the longboat, Steven could make out a dozen women aboard, some of whom were dressed in gaudy velvet skirts and lacy white blouses. One of them, slender and full-blossomed as a peach, watched Steven closely as the longboat approached.

"*Hombruno*," she purred for only the women's ears.

The breeze molded her skirts to her long-legged figure and Steven caught his breath in the tunnel of his throat as she leaned forward, her full breasts all but spilling out of her far-flung bodice.

Steven whistled softly—a wolfish sound—once, and made up his mind which one he would entertain, or the other way around. He was easy to please.

For three whole nights the vessel rocked and rang with song, laughter, and wild merrymaking. If Steven didn't know that his captain would not be long at this sport, he would have believed himself to be aboard a pirate ship.

On deck, taking his turn at the helm, Steven lifted his face to the ocean of sky and sang lustily for the joy of living and of being in sound mind and health. The *Mañana* followed her course easily, free-spiritedly, her golden sails shining in the sea-misted sun. She sailed just a few miles out from the coast now, and soon, Steven learned with some disappointment, the women would be dropped off at one of the villages before they reached the Cape.

Getting his sea legs, Steven studied and worked hard at his new profession, learning the things essential to a merchant captain during the day, and in the brisk evenings enjoying the devil-may-care revelry. Steven found that the *Mañana* sailed with regularity between France and North America, sometimes to China. She carried the usual cargo of silks from Lyons' silk industries—and passengers. Sessions of drinking and dicing alternated with wenching and at times Steven had the feeling he had taken up with an unrepentant band of buccaneers.

On the third night out, Steven came out of his tiny cabin for a breath of fresh air, leaving his long-legged, full-bosomed partner asleep in his bunk. Alicia had amused him for a time but he was already becoming bored with her silly chatter. Granted, she was a beauty with a curvaceous body, and a wild creature in bed to boot, never satiated.

Satiated now, Steven was prepared to muse awhile on becoming a very wealthy man. He chuckled. He was learning about navigation, the winds, the tides, and the stars. "And *women*," he said aloud into the wind.

Steven had sold all his breeds and had invested all of his funds in the ship. He was now part owner of the *Mañana*. A very small interest, of course. But he was determined to have her for his very own someday, as Antoine already had his eyes on a newer and larger vessel that well suited his own growing demands.

Steven lit a slim cheroot now and leaned against the rail. The night was ink black, and the red glow of a cigar approached him in the purplish dark.

"Ah, Étienne," Antoine shouted rakishly. "I see you have need to refresh yourself also. Gets a bit stuffy in the cabin eh?"

"Stifling is the word, Antoine. Mind you, I'm not complaining about the bit of fluff in there. Alicia is just about the liveliest bit I've ever had the opportunity to make love to."

Antoine threw back his head and indulged in a loud burst of laughter.

"Hah! If you think that Alicia is lively, my friend, wait until I introduce you to my cousin Juliette. Knowing her, she'll have your face covered with kisses before you even cross the threshold to her château."

Steven's dark brows lifted, wondering as he was about this cousin of Captain Lyons.

"Juliette's lovers follow each other out the door, discreetly, of course"—he chuckled—"in rapid succession."

"Tell me more about this cousin of yours?"

"Cousin, *oui.*"

"Is she also beautiful?"

"The most—ah—attractive *demimondaine* in all of France. Take heed, my friend for she is a duchess."

"Well then . . ." Steven shrugged, wondering what Antoine was up to.

"But, that does not stop her from collecting dashing young swains." Antoine grinned. "It does caution you, though, for the Duke of Fitz-James is very influential, especially from Bordeaux to Lyonnais. I have my factories in Lyonnais, not connected in any way with my name and just a coincidence, you see. Actually these factories are conducted in most of the dwellings of the people. After we establish you in business there you may, if you so desire, procure the lovely villa that is soon to be up for bidding."

"I will owe you, Antoine Lyons," Steven commented drily.

"You will work damn hard, my friend!" Antoine thundered.

"Mañana," Steven said reflectively after a lull in the conversation, "Spanish for tomorrow."

Antoine nodded indolently. *"Oui,* and all my *mañanas* have been rich since I christened her with that name. I'll be sorry to see her go, but she'll be in good hands. My next one will be *Mañana II,* larger and just as serviceable I might add."

"Perhaps more so."

"Perhaps."

Steven nodded and they continued to smoke, listening to the night sounds of sea and ship, water lapping against the hull and the creaking of timbers. Antoine was reflecting that all his dreams of wealth had come true. Indeed, all but one. The love of a woman whom he loved. He had dreamed of having a fine son one day with her. True, she had given birth to a beautiful daughter with hair as bright as her own. But the eyes . . . Ah, the eyes of the child, like the sea, stormy one minute, sea-green calm the next. How long, he pondered, had it been since he had last looked upon that lovely pair of females. Ten years? No, more like fifteen. The child would be a young woman now, perhaps nearing her eighteenth or nineteenth birthdate. His dream of being loved by his wife had dissipated when Victoria had left him for the arms of another.

One day she had just gathered up the child—Monica yes. Then Victoria had packed her many belongings. Her last words still rang in his ears: "I think, Antoine, you will be overjoyed to know that I shall not be returning this time. You can be a pirate of the seas, or whatever men like you who flit from port to port call themselves!"

How lightly he had taken this. Had he been a complete idiot to let his pride interfere so readily? Let her go, he had thought back then. She will be back, but she hadn't returned. The last he'd heard Victoria had married again. Hadn't even obtained a divorce for all he knew.

The wind had changed and now there was an occasional flurry of rain as the two men made their way to their separate cabins.

Offshore in predawn grayness, gentle swells lapped against the sides of the *Mañana*, raising and then quietly lowering the ship in slow succession. Along the coast of the great Atlantic seaport of southern France other small swells spent themselves on the land, lapping it softly in a rhythmical series of sighs, while nearby onshore to the people in the Public Gardens Steven Hawke was obviously a stranger.

Steven waited on the finest promenade of the city with Monsieur Lyons while the local inhabitants paraded by to stare at them with a mixture of curiosity and awe. The younger man, they were thinking, looked like a genuine pirate with his black beard and long sideburns, certainly not a servant.

"What can be keeping them?" Antoine strode back and forth, puffing on a cigarillo until the tip glowed hot red. "I sent word ahead hours ago!"

The rising sun cast the brown brick of the main buildings in vibrant hues of red and gold, and Steven pondered at the early morning risers. He listened to the rustle of silk petticoats and caught the sparkle of an eye beneath the scoop of a becoming bonnet. Choosing to let the warm air whip through his black hair, Steven doffed his wide-brimmed hat and whirled it about in his lean, tanned fingers, matching Antoine's impatience by this time.

Steven let out a shrill whistle then, startling Antoine. A murmur went through the crowd as a phaeton and pair of high-stepping mares careened into the square, coming toward the sound.

"Ah. At last," Antoine said. Then giving his young business partner a smiling sidelong glance, he added, "Very good, Étienne, very alert. I like that in a man."

The Château Sauville on the outskirts of Bordeaux was settled mostly in moorland, the sweeping wilderness giving way to great winehouses along the way. Steven peered out at the gray towers looming up ahead as the horse-driven phaeton sped swiftly up a narrow drive lined with the yellow pussy willows that gave the place its name.

Antoine interrupted Steven's thoughts. "We will rest up here for a few days before we make our journey to Lyonnais. Give you time to become

38

acquainted with the Duchess and Duke of Fitz-James. Juliette is not as young as she appears, all that cosmetic gook women apply to their silly faces. Do not let her fool you, friend, she's well over thirty-five, and as shrewd as a general."

Steven laughed heartily, knowing Antoine was not jesting. A woman without all that feminine warfare was hard to find nowadays, especially in France he was told. Even Alicia was wont to apply all that "gook." He shook his head. It all came off in due time anyway, so why all the fuss? The only women he knew who were *au naturel* were the Indian women of the Ute tribe that he'd grown up with.

"If it is more convenient to stay on the two nights, I will quite understand," Steven began. "And I promise you, Antoine, that I'll try to resist Juliette's charms and will certainly do my best to discourage her from seeking out *my* attentions!"

Antoine laughed just as heartily, slapping Steven hard on the back. "*Oui*, Étienne, that you will, that you will!"

A twinge of nostalgia rode Antoine's memory hard as they neared the façade of the château. Almost a space of two decades had lapsed since Antoine had come with his bride to spend the remainder of their honeymoon here. He had watched his twenty-year-old cousin stiffen with jealousy when he had introduced Victoria as his wife. There had been no doubt that Juliette had instantly hated the golden beauty. He recalled Juliette's words as if they were spoken yesterday. "My dear, do you add color to your hair, or is it naturally that—*bright*?" Victoria had smiled sweetly, and replied in kind that it was indeed, quite natural. "Oh, really? The women in Paris and London change the color of their hair five or six times a day." Juliette had said matter-of-factly to which Victoria had returned a "How nice for them!"

The groom now swung the matching pair and smart phaeton in a wide semicircle that brought them close to the double set of doors. Just then a voluptuous brunette with sultry green eyes slipped from the portal, alone. One side of her hair was brushed behind an ear in a sensuous style and caught up with a golden leaf comb, while the other caressed her shoulder in a large sausage curl. She wore a green velvet Parisian gown of the same emerald shade as her eyes. Generous mounds of creamy-looking flesh pushed up from her lacy bodice.

Swinging the carriage door open Antoine leaped out first and reluctantly held out his arms as Juliette dashed the few yards into them, overwhelming Antoine with a strong-scented eau de cologne. Holding him at arm's length to look him over, Juliette fluttered such long lashes that one might pause to speculate on their authenticity.

"In a few more days, *monsieur*, I would have had cause for alarm, thought you to vanish into the sea," Juliette murmured in a half-scolding tone. "What have . . ." Her red mouth fell agape in midsentence as she gazed at a pair of extremely long legs emerging from the carriage, followed by a bearded and

40

handsome young man with the blackest of eyes. Her heart fluttered like something fully untamed as she gaped boldly at the most savagely virile male she had ever set eyes upon.

"Mon Dieu," she whispered under her breath, feeling the heat rising in her.

4

Steven straightened his cravat before donning a waistcoat of dark blue brocade and ran his lean fingers through ruffled black hair. He preferred to do without the tangled, cocked hair that was so fashionable in Paris this year and would, no doubt, be in fashion for some years to come.

Monsieur Étienne Hawke was becoming increasingly wealthy, but he was also becoming thoroughly bored with life and an enlarged bank account. The first half of the year had been nothing but hard work, now it was all too easy. Even the trips he made to far ports with cargoes of silks were without complication and mishap. In fact, his life had become somewhat soft, and he longed to experience more, something he could not put his finger on.

He divided his time between the factories and his Villa El Corazón, the stalls and boxes at the operas, salons, or of late at swordplay. In short, he patronized all the exclusive haunts of fashionable men and women of France.

But that was before he received the letter. Now he seemed to be a different man. The letter From San Pablo Mission had occupied his mind completely for two weeks. He had to get back to America without further delay and the *Mañana* was almost ready to take him back to pick up the lost threads of his life there. His brother Jess. He couldn't believe it, after all these years. Alive! the missionary had said in the letter. His only flesh and blood, existing somewhere in the growing land he had left behind shortly after purchasing a house in Yerba Buena. He had gone back with a load of silks for only the briefest of visits.

Looking in the mirror, Steven had the feeling of being alive again too, painfully and yet joyously aware of it. The letter Pitt Dailey had delivered to him one morning past was scrawled in bold letters, yet he could barely make out the beginning portion of it. A stranger, unwilling to mention his name, left a verbal message at the mission stating that he had information about a certain young man by the name of Jess Hawke. This stranger had knowledge as to the whereabouts of Jess and wanted it kept secret until Steven Hawke could be reached. Steven, before leaving America, had left a note at the mission as to where he could be contacted—just in case there was any news concerning his brother. It was a dangerous situation, the letter stated, and he was to come to the mission where this stranger would meet him after the contact was made. From there he was to go to New Helvetia Fortress.

"By the time I reach the coast of California,"

Steven mused out loud, "a whole four months will have lapsed since the letter was written!"

Steven found himself wishing he could sprout wings to hasten his passage to America and his brother. Was he only fooling himself in believing, from what the letter related, that his brother Jess was truly alive and well in California?

Steven hoped not, if not for himself, then for the one who had sent him the letter. There would be hell to pay if it was only a trick, a ruse to get him back to California. But why, for God's sake?

A deep sigh came from Steven as he thought of one other who could lure him back to America. She had been a golden angel that day in Yerba Buena four years ago when she had caught his eye instantly. No words had emerged from her lips that were like ripe, red cherries. There had been no need for words; Steven had caught the flame that darted between them, even if the young beauty had not noticed it.

Monica . . .

Indeed, Steven thought, he might just find himself enjoying California for the first time in his life.

Part II

Monica

5

Sonoma Valley, California, 1848

Recklessly two girls galloped their mounts down the sun-dappled wooded path leading from behind Temloc into the dense forest of towering pines and firs. Twigs snapped sharply under their spirited mounts, the horses' snorts sounding like soft thunder in the primitive stillness. As the two huge shadows left the deeper shade where the trail emerged from the pines and came onto a sunlit clearing, the radiant beams descended on one who was fair and on another who was Amerindian.

"I beat you, Maya!"

"You did not!"

Monica tossed her long sunlit brown hair and laughed with the pure pleasure of being alive. Alive yes, when she was not in the presence of her stepfather or his son Alex. She could be herself at times like this, alone with Maya or Tina, not guarded as she must be when Alex or Branville

47

was about.

Four years had passed since that day in Yerba Buena when by some luckless fate her stepfather had informed her that "business" made it quite impossible for them to stay on for the festivities. Monica knew that that "business" had to do with collecting yet more Indian slaves for his kingdom. Oh yes, Branville and Alex, plus their band of trusty vaqueros rounded up a good twenty more unfortunates that had gotten drunk that week of the festivities.

Monica pulled a long face now as she remembered: Branville was always promising her something and then going back on his promises. Well! this was one day, like some others in the past weeks, that he was not present and she would not be the object of her stepfather's enmity. She knew that that enmity had to do with her mother's leaving him.

Branville Bennington, Monica's stepfather, had left again, but this time for two whole glorious months. To purchase cattle from General Vallejo, so Branville said. However, Monica knew better. One night in his salon she had overheard his conversation with Alex when he'd said they would be among those present at the meeting in Jacob Leese's store. Monica, not caring that she'd eavesdropped, had heard Bennington saying that when the people learned Comandante Vallejo had moved his whole family to the *presidio* at Sonoma, everyone would be afraid. The people in Sonoma Valley were no longer pleased to see new faces arriving from the ships in the Bay.

Nor were they pleased, she knew, to see Alex and Branville coming.

From her mount, Maya studied her friend. Monica had changed from a lovely young girl into a breathtaking beauty, one that attracted every male for miles around Sonoma Valley and made them ache with desire for her. Maya could see this in the young men. It came as no surprise to the servants at Temloc mansion that Bennington barred his doors to all the young gentlemen who came calling, for Monica was unobtainable, and promised, he had *said* on many occasions. Just who Monica's stepfather saved her for was a mystery to everyone still. Even Monica did not know who her future husband was to be. She doubted Branville Bennington even knew himself. She thought he was just fishing for the right one to come along—the one with weighty pockets. Probably some wealthy old politician, or even worse, Monica quailed at the thought, perhaps he planned to marry her off to his son, Alex Bennington.

Monica despised Alex with every fiber of her being and she didn't have to search for reasons for her intense dislike of the man. He supplied her with more than enough.

"Come on, Maya, I'll race you again!"

Monica was breathless now, her firm young breasts rising and falling with the exertion of the bracing ride. Days in the sun had made her riotous tresses seem even more golden, a delicate honey brown that framed and entranced her sun-tanned countenance. Monica thought her tresses rather mousy and dull, yet when the sun struck her hair as it did now, without her knowing it the shimmering tones of yellow, scarlet, and russet—even magenta—came alive and shone like watered silk. Monica believed her only claim to loveliness was her eyes, neither green nor blue, but a jade that changed colors like the stone itself. She would not acknowledge that her eyes were catlike, even though Tina pointed this out to her while helping her dress for the day.

Maya, Monica's companion and maid of all sorts, accompanied her on these everyday outings. They complimented each other, Maya with her blue-black hair tickling her waist, her smoky brown eyes, and coppery skin; Monica with her golden look and lips like ripe red cherries.

Bennington just dragged Maya in one day and almost threw the poor girl at Monica and Tina who was the downstairs maid and Monica's personal maid. Tina just stared at Bennington, bewildered and afraid of the man.

"See what you can do with this one," he snapped. "Well, don't just stand there looking stupid, train her, dammit!"

In the months to come the Amerindian told Monica many tales from when Maya was just a small girl, tales the storytellers of her camp were wont to recite of giants and ghost spirits, of feats of bravery, of cleverness and magic. Maya shared one of these tales with Monica now as they rested under the shade of towering pines, picnicking on a cold lunch of pink ham slapped between freshly baked bread, and pinkened lemonade.

Maya said between bites, "White Swan, she was struck down one day by evil curses. White Swan, she turn red, become Red Swan. Red Swan go forth in Moon of Falling Leaves, to seek for brave and promise to be wife of him who bring back father's Magic Headband and bring back to Red Swan father. Dark Hawk then marry Red Swan and soon they have many daughters, most handsome women of tribe who have many sons." Maya giggled then. "You White Swan to me, with hair like Moon of Falling Leaves and skin like golden wheat."

Monica laughed happily, reflecting Maya's humor. "I may be White Swan, Maya, but to tell the truth I would find it most distressing to be struck down by an evil curse. Red?" She shook her honey brown hair all about her shoulders, loving it loose and free in the wind as it was now.

Maya grinned, exposing large white teeth, and shrugged. "Just, what you call it—fairy tales?"

"Yes, Maya, a fairy tale. But, there could be some truth in it I suppose, like the daughters who bring forth many fine sons. I would like to have sons someday, but first I shall have to find a husband." Her odd-colored eyes twinkled. "And I am not sure about the Dark Hawk." She laughed.

Maya shrugged again. "Just fairy tale."

Monica sobered then. "What was your Indian name?"

"Maya mean earth. Mine name Earth Eyes in village." She stiffened. "What is that? You hear?"

"What is it, Maya, what did you hear?"

"Someone is watching us," Maya breathed, liquid brown eyes peering about while her head remained frozen. "I feel, too."

Monica felt a sudden stab of alarm in the pit of her stomach as she scrambled to crouch upon one knee. "Are you sure?" she asked her friend.

Maya sucked in a deep breath, nodding her head. Both girls listened now as the crunching of pine needles and the snapping of twigs reached their ears, growing louder and closer every moment.

"Oh!" Maya and Monica exclaimed at the same time.

Just then a huge, grisly man stepped out into the clearing. Crossed bandoleers stretched the wide expanse of his massive chest. His black eyes were squinting in the sun as, ominous in size, he took in the scene like a hungry bear about to devour them.

Fear was mirrored in both Monica's and Maya's eyes. If that look in his eyes meant what Monica thought, then heaven help them, for they would never be able to fight such a bear of a man off. Maya would never turn coward and leave Monica alone. Monica straightened. Bold as a lioness guarding her cubs, she squared her small shoulders. Maya was more frightened than her lovely friend was, but took courage from Monica's bold front and something about the glint in Monica's eyes made Maya's blood run cold. She was afraid her friend was going to do something foolish.

"Go away!" Monica warned. "You do not belong

here." She searched for a word his kind would understand, for he was tilting his head in her direction as if he were in some kind of trance. *"Tenga a raya! Dejar!"* she shouted in her fumbling Spanish. "Keep back! Leave! This is private property," she added to the warnings.

Monica didn't even stop to consider that this bear of a man could be one of the vaqueros her stepfather hired on to work at Temloc, one of the many hands. Of a certain he couldn't be one of the Indian slaves Alex used ruthlessly to move tons of dirt for the excavation of the lush new gardens Branville planned. No, this beastly man surely appeared to be a stranger!

"Bella," he grunted back to her in Spanish. *"Angélica."*

Just when Monica thought he was on the verge of attacking he turned about to reenter the pines, his huge frame swallowed from view, pine needles crunching, twigs snapping.

"He is certainly not very quiet about his comings and goings," Monica said, and when she and Maya could no longer hear the sounds of his departure, they simultaneously mounted and returned to Temloc at breakneck speed.

"He said something about a beautiful angel," Maya said after they had stabled their mounts. "He must mean you, Monica. I am too dark to be angel." She laughed to lighten their mood.

The excavation of the gardens was well under way the following week, and with Branville gone, Alex took full command. He was cruel, inhuman to the Mexican and American Indians laboring in the scorching sun. If one should falter from exhaustion, Alex mercilessly slashed the heavy whip he always carried across an already sunburn-pained back and made the object of his cruelty cry out in a deep racking sob.

"Someday, I vow," Monica told Maya and Clara, "that cruelty is going to come back on Alex Bennington!"

There was one man, though, Monica noticed, who never so much as paused to wipe the sweat from his dripping wet brow. He had caught Monica's eye countless times, yet he never once glanced up to acknowledge her presence or anyone else's for that matter. He was magnificently built, long and lean and muscular with blue-black hair swinging against his strong shoulders. He was one of the biggest, most handsome of the Indians Monica had ever had the occasion to set her inquiring eyes upon. The leather medallion encircling his dark neck had caught her attention many times, causing her to wonder what sort of animal or bird was tooled into its soft, age-worn beauty. Maya said one of the vaqueros thought it depicted a *halcón*, a hawk. He fascinated Monica, and he was somehow familiar. His name was Jess.

6

Branville Bennington continued to use Indian labor although the other ranchers and landowners had replaced the Indians with hard-working Chinese coolies. He reduced all of the Indians' privileges, made them slaves, and kept them prisoners in the dank, dark caverns below the mansion. Any who attempted escape did not get far for the loyal vaqueros swiftly hunted them down and meted out savage punishment. Usually Alex himself did the punishing and then the escapee was returned to the caverns without even bread or water.

Branville was tall but not as reed thin as his only offspring. Yet father and son had the same colorless gray eyes that bespoke their cold, cruel natures. The sire was sneering and dictatorial, and he frequently and harshly denounced everyone about him—except his son Alex. Both men had cold countenances and no friends, at least not for long. The vaqueros were paid handsomely and remained loyal, but they were not close to the Benningtons.

Tina, the downstairs maid, had been with the Benningtons for years, even before Victoria, Monica's mother, had seemingly vanished into thin air. Everyone employed in the household knew better, though; they knew Victoria had left Branville to go in search of her first husband, Monica's father.

"If it weren't for Monica, I would've left long ago," Tina often said to the cook Clara. "He's gotten worse in the last ten years. Why Monica's mother left her with Bennington I'll never know. He's become a cruel man. Sure and that evil's eating away at him— worse now that Victoria left him. He's possessed by that and he's taking it out on Monica. He's got something on his mind for that poor child, and if I could get away with it, I'd take her away from here myself." Tina sighed. "It would be like trying to take away one of Bennington's most prized possessions."

"Sure and he is a vicious man I've never known the likes of before I set eyes on him," Clara whispered. "Two years now I been here and it's leavin' I'd be doin' too if I had me somewhere to go."

Really, where would Clara go? Clara Simmons remembered fleeing from starvation when the potato crops had failed and she'd come with her brother and the other Irishmen who filled the westbound ships. Government, private philanthropy, and landlords anxious to be freed of the weight of human misery which bore heavily on local taxation, all three contributed to sending Irishmen fleeing by the thousands to America. Even when the "pot of gold" at the end of the New World rainbow turned out to be a delusion.

Tina spoke more gently now. "I remember the last words Victoria spoke to Monica before she went away. 'Now you have to be a good girl, luv. Do not anger your stepfather, and if you do as he tells you, everything will be fine. It shan't be too long before I will come back for you, darling.'"

But that was some ten years back, and Tina doubted that Monica would ever see her lovely mother's face again. Tina remembered the earlier sunlit days with nostalgia, the years at the old rancho when Monica and her mother rode the green hills together before they'd moved to the cold, ugly mansion which Bennington had ironically named Temloc. An Indian name, which was strange, for Bennington hated Indians with a passion that knew no bounds.

It sometimes frightened Tina that Monica and her mother were so much alike; they had seemed to share an awareness of each other's thoughts, as young as Monica had been then. Even their luxurious tawny hair and jade green eyes were the same. They could have passed for twins but for the age gap. Victoria could ride and mount a horse as well as any man and Monica soon had matched her mother's skill. Victoria also saw to it that Monica was fully educated by tutors. Monica had learned to stitch beautifully when it had become known to her that Branville's penny-pinching ways made it necessary for them to make their own gowns and frocks, mostly of muslin and of cambric.

Monica now stood scrutinizing one of her old dresses in the mirror. The reflection was that of a plain, faded green muslin that had seen many washings. The dress was so tight that Monica could scarcely breathe nor could she keep from pouting while she gazed at the bodice that crushed her nicely pointed breasts to near flatness.

"Oh, I hate it!" Monica said to her reflection. "I simply hate it!"

Although she had let out the bodice there was not even an inch of material left to alter it one more time. She would have gone to Branville requesting to purchase some material to stitch new clothes, but he was always so preoccupied with some new undertaking or other that he hardly even noticed she was alive. Or did he? Monica wondered now.

"Ha. Maybe it pleases him to see his stepdaughter clothed like a peasant!" She made a *moue* pretending it was Branville before her instead of her own reflection.

Perhaps this pleased him or perhaps he gloated when he saw that she was pressed to don the larger frocks Victoria had left behind for her. Victoria no doubt had worn them when she was heavy with child. Monica was slow to realize that Victoria had left them behind because she hated the dresses so. But she knew that now.

"Mother, how could you? . . ." her voice trailed off. She could not even put the question to her mother's memory.

She should be somewhat grateful. For there was

one, only one of her mother's frocks Monica cared for—a yellow-gold affair with a low, scooped neckline edged in russet lace. Monica had kept it, why she still didn't know.

"I can only wear it at special times," she told herself and then felt her shoulders sag as if of their own accord.

Her youth seemed to have fled ever since her mother had gone away. Indeed, she was eighteen now! But social affairs were few and far between, Branville grudgingly allowing her to attend only an occasional party or dance. Even then, either her stepfather or Alex constantly chaperoned her, leaving her no freedom whatsoever in her movements. They were always so proper and formal, stifling, and they never once gave her room to mill about and become acquainted with even one lad. Monica yearned to join in the gaiety of other young people, to dance and participate in their games and laughter. To be free from so many restrictions!

Perhaps it was borne in her blood, this yearning to be a creature wild and free, a free spirit just like her mother. Back in England Victoria Clivedon had grown from childhood to a young woman without a stroke of discipline. Lord Clivedon, fifth Duke of Devon, and Victoria's father, had permitted her shocking behavior and she had become like her father, the scandal of London society. They were of a piece, father and daughter, for His Lordship in his younger days had fallen prey to the ills that flesh is heir to.

Monica had no desire to become wild and debauched as her mother and grandfather had been—just up to a certain point. She knew she had the ability to tease a man and to leave him wanting, that she could walk away unscathed by the flirtatious encounter.

Looking over her threadbare wardrobe once more, Monica removed the dress and, seething with disgust, tossed it aside. She then donned one of Victoria's gray riding habits. This one would undoubtedly be a bit more suitable for today anyway, she was thinking, even though she disliked gray intensely. Her stepfather would be returning later in the day, and with Alex riding herd she was determined to make the most of her freedom by riding until the sun set!

Monica gazed out the window, hating the oppressive mansion constructed of homely, gray stone inside and out. "Gray!" How she hated the color, even people with cold gray eyes made her cringe.

The only warmth Monica found in the mansion was the solid oak flooring—and this room, her bedchamber. It was the only halfway cheerful room in the ugly dwelling, and it contained all the items from her happy childhood. A tortoise-shell comb and brush set her father had given her was her most treasured item.

"Father." The word sounded almost strange as she was in the habit of calling her stepfather by his given name. Monica realized she couldn't even remember her last name but that it had a feline ring to it. She had gotten so used to everyone calling her Monica

Bennington, and how she hated it! She would rather use her mother's last name, Clivedon, but Branville expressly forbid the use of it. He would not even help her to recall her father's last name and no one else dared to say it.

As a large dinner was planned for that evening upon Branville's return, Maya was ordered to join the others in preparing the feast. Monica nabbed some side pork and bread to munch, seating herself at the farthest table in the kitchen to survey the preparations for the meal and to be out of their way.

Clara was just brushing melted butter over the crusty brown tops of freshly baked bread when she noticed with interest the vision of breathtaking beauty Monica made as she sat quietly near the open window, her long hair whispering against her pointed bosom. She looked ethereal in the morning light filtering through the kitchen window, the birds chirping outside as if to serenade the lovely Monica.

Sighing dreamily Clara went to the fire, tipped a large kettle of steaming coffee into a heavy mug and then brought it to Monica, placing it on the table in front of the girl and standing back.

"'Ere you are, lass. It's freshly ground, too," the older woman said, smiling hugely.

"Mmm, smells delicious, Clara. Thank you."

Monica flashed perfect rows of tiny white teeth at the cook. "Clara, has Alex been down to breakfast yet?"

"Oh, yes, lass. He's been down and took his breakfast a long time ago. Sure and he's done gone out to herd the cattle," Clara answered in her heavy Irish brogue. "Best stay out 'o his way, lass. Must tell ya, a ugly way he's 'boot this day. Brrr, no good'll come 'o it."

Monica nodded, rising to her feet while taking a last sip of coffee. "Thank you again, Clara. I'll keep a distance from Alex as I do not wish anything to spoil such a perfectly lovely day. I want to ride until Dancer and I are plumb tuckered out!"

Monica laughed, cocking her bright head pleasantly to one side. Then, planting a kiss on Clara's blushing cheek, she turned and departed, going out with a gay twirl.

Dancer was already saddled when Monica entered the stables. She breathed deeply, enjoying as always the smell of hay, leather, and horses. Bob, the stableboy, handed the reins over to her and patted Dancer's white neck. Bob Warren was short and rugged looking, with blue twinkling eyes.

"You are a luv, Bob," Monica said, genuinely pleasured by his company, short as these visits were.

A dwarfed young man of eighteen, Bob showed no promise of becoming taller. Bob was well aware that Monica possessed a most uncommon beauty for her gentle age, and he was very careful to touch her only briefly lest she become mindful of just how much she shook him. Bob was also heedful that the Benningtons, either of them, did not learn just how many times she rode out.

"Now, you be sure to keep a ways from Alex,

Miss. Also heard Bennington's coming back later in the day. Better be back way before he shows, Miss Monica." Bob frowned slightly, his blue eyes flashing a warning she knew only too well.

"I plan to do just that, Bob. And if Branville ever discovers I rode out every day of his absence I'll just inform him that I slugged you over the head and readied Dancer all by myself." She smiled at her simple jest. "Thanks, Bob."

Monica mounted. Moving at a quick pace along the grounds she held her breath when Dancer, with easy grace, cleared the wooden gate, then as soon as Monica was in open country she gave Dancer full rein. They flew like the wind, free, without the restrictions she hated.

Bob Warren had second thoughts as he watched her go. At the last minute he tried to warn her that there was a ragged band of *bandidos* scouring the countryside, but Monica was already out of earshot and was now clearing the white gate.

Bob watched her until she was just a white blur clipping across the open meadow. He chided himself for even saddling up for her. Yet, there was no arguing with Monica Bennington for she was a strong-willed girl. In fact, she had grown into a beautiful woman, a child no longer.

"Yeah, and she just might've slugged me over the head and then saddled that white mare herself. Gad, how'd I ever get into workin' for such a crazy mixed-up family!"

Then Bob comforted himself with the understanding that if them Mex soldiers who stole and killed as they pleased were to be confronted with Monica head-on, she would no doubt meet them with all the ferociousness of a sharp-clawed tigress!

Monica felt that only by traveling very fast could she put the greatest possible distance between herself and Temloc. Her gay mood was fast altering, however, as she thought ahead to Branville's return later in the day. She pushed aside all thoughts of that meeting then and imagined that she was escaping, never to return to the ugly gray mansion.

The expression in her jade green eyes was wild, free, and beautiful as Monica fantasized she was going to meet her lover. He would have dark eyes, the blackest she had ever seen, with sun wrinkles at the corners of them and jet black lashes shading the desire he felt for her. Monica whipped Dancer to greater speed, feeling as if she were a part of the sky, the sun, the clouds. There was nothing else but herself and Dancer, her horse that she pretended was Pegasus, taking her above and beyond. Her lover's midnight black hair would be blown wildly by the wind and his lips would become full and sensuous in parting to take her own. She would arouse in him a passionate desire for her, excite him with honeyed words of love and make every movement of her lithe body drive him wild. She would be seductive, a woman of the world instead of the untouched maid she was.

Monica arched her neck, letting Dancer take her where he would. Above all, her darkly handsome lover would be persuaded to take her away from Temloc. Suddenly her eyes flew open. Had she only dreamed of him? Or had she truly looked upon this same countenance a long time ago?

She could not be certain of this, but she knew with a sudden quickening of her heartbeat that she would someday soon come face to face with this man. This was as inevitable as a new tomorrow.

"Whoa!"

Suddenly Monica noticed that she had ridden all the way to the south pastures where Alex was supposed to be herding cattle into the newer grazing lands they had just purchased. She reined Dancer into a graceful prancing of long limbs. The magnificent animal gently swished its tail, and its mane lay flat against its velvety moist neck.

Monica narrowed her odd-colored eyes, like dull flat stone now. Purchased or *stolen*, she thought, from the Indians who were issued large land grants to raise horses upon. The new governor did not seem inclined to help them one bit, those hapless Amerindians. Branville Bennington, no doubt, got Maya the very same ruthless way. Just up and plucked her from her homeland as one would thoughtlessly transplant a pretty flower, minus roots or humus soon to wither and die.

Monica was hoping against all odds that perhaps Alex had not seen her as she reined to a complete halt near the enormous lone oak. The low, overhanging branches all but concealed her from view. She was shaded from the sun—but from Alex Bennington's eyes?

Monica would have spun her mount and headed back to Temloc but for a sudden feeling of uneasiness which she could not dismiss. Something was amiss here, and she paused, mesmerized by the torrid air and by the strange feeling that something dreadful was about to take place, something she must see because of her hatred of Temloc and its lords— something that might make her run away.

Clearly Alex was in a particularly monstrous mood, Monica decided as his booming voice, ripping out a string of ear-burning curses, carried to her. The profane animosities were directed toward the one Monica knew by the name of Jess, the handsome slave whom Alex, of late, seemed to blame for all his personal problems. Monica had overheard a woman's name enter their heated conversations on countless occasions.

What took place presently happened so fast Monica barely had sufficient time to blink twice before it was over. Nor did she notice the dark, ominous clouds swiftly rolling in low.

Held by the scene about to unfold, Monica watched as Jess dismounted, opened wide the wooden gate for the cattle to enter, then swung easily back into his tooled leather saddle. Startled, Jess looked up as all of a sudden Alex galloped his mount out of the swale and charged into Jess with such force the attack brought the slave's horse to its knees.

"Damn you!" Alex expostulated. "I told you to wait, that I would personally open that gate!"

Mesmerized and shaking from head to foot, Monica saw handsome Jess spit on the ground close to Alex's mount and that infuriated Alex further. Alex tried to nab Jess from his mount, but the swift lad whipped Alex's horse away with his reins, looking at him resentfully and hatefully.

"Lord, no," Monica said, nipping the knuckle of her soft leather glove.

Again Monica gritted her teeth as she saw Alex whirl again to ride into the slave. Her eyes grew even wider, like deep pools of eddying water with horror at the center, when this time Jess slashed out viciously with a long curved Green River blade, leaving a thin line of red blood trickling down Alex's throat. Alex then made as if to retreat, riding away as if he had finally had enough and had given the game to the winner. Then he surprised everyone by whirling again. Looking like the devil himself, this time he drew his gun and at close range fired point-blank into Jess's forehead.

The horror in Monica's eyes surfaced drawing her every expression into them and mirroring her shocked disbelief at the murder taking place. It was as if a leprous black canker had suddenly rotted the flesh on the slave's forehead. The wounded man lurched sickeningly, his torso and arms rendered useless as a marionette's; then his whole body slumped slowly off the horse's haunches to the ground.

Only a flicker of emotion played across Monica's face. She went cold all over, weightless, as if she, too, had met death on the sunbaked earth with handsome Jess.

7

Long before Monica opened her eyes she heard the rain and the rattle of thunder against the bulk of Temloc. Her eyes felt heavy and swollen though she did not cry.

She lay there unmoving, cold of heart and spirit, and weary of mind. The mindless, cold-blooded murder she had witnessed just a few short hours before would forever be etched in her mind. At that moment she felt that she hated men, all of them, and especially Alex Bennington. She had found an enemy in her own stepbrother.

Monica had fallen asleep, but no tears had stained her pillow. Now she eased herself to the edge of the bed, her hair falling over her shoulders. She noticed as she looked down that she hadn't even removed the gray, now-crumpled riding habit.

Monica moaned. Her hair hung about her in wild disarray. What did it matter how she appeared when she went down for dinner? A plan swiftly began to form in her mind.

Somehow, someway she was going to leave Temloc and never return!

Outside a wet dusk was quickening, casting an eerie glow into her bedroom. She tensed her muscles as a shuffling sound made her sit straighter. It came from just outside her door.

Unceremoniously the door was flung wide and in the purple shadows Monica could make out the tall form of her stepfather. Even in the dimness she knew his colorless eyes rested on her in her disheveled state.

"Monica!" Branville shouted. "What the hell? Why weren't you downstairs to greet me?"

She shrugged, lifting cold eyes. "Did you want something, Stepfather?" she said acidly.

"Never mind." He turned his head to look with disgust at her dusty boots. "So, you have been out riding again, eh, without my permission?" He questioned harshly, and her definite nod of response unnerved him. "And I suppose you have been out roaming the countryside from morning till sunset, am I correct?"

Even her disheveled hair and her paleness did nothing to detract from her beauty, he was thinking.

Again Monica only nodded, plucking a fold of her shirt busily.

"Well, we shall dismiss it for now. I'll give you half an hour to bathe yourself and change clothes. Then over dinner we will discuss something of great import."

"Yes, Branville," she said sharply, her eyes slitted.

"And stop calling me Branville! You might as well

get used to calling me Father, Monica!"

He slammed the door hard. His voice resounded in the bedroom, leaving Monica to stare at the insulting portal that seemed to echo his inappropriate words.

Monica didn't have the opportunity to ponder further on his odd statement for just then Tina entered, towels draped over her arm, to inform Monica that her bath had been readied.

"Monica," Tina spoke low while Monica stripped off the dusty garment. "Better wear that yellow-gold frock your mother left you, the only one of them that fits you."

"Fits!"

"Well, almost. It's better than some of the others."

Tina turned, holding the soap she had gotten from the drawer beside the bed. "Did your stepfather tell you there's a stranger downstairs?"

"No, he did not."

"Of course."

Tina Maller's black hair was just beginning to be streaked with silver at the temples. Her sweet face and her hazel eyes were always tinged with merriment, despite the fact that she, too, disliked her surroundings. Yet, there was more hatred in Monica suddenly, hatred of almost frightening proportions.

Tina regarded Monica's back while she brushed out the silky hair that was full of windswept tangles. Monica was tense, full of turmoil. Tina could sense that the girl had a tendency toward being secretive but did not tell her so. Tina kept silent, wondering if the girl's mood was just due to Branville's return, or if something had happened out there today, something that had provoked this sudden change in Monica.

"Now," Monica turned, "tell me about this stranger downstairs before I go bathe. Is he one of those old, withered politicians?"

"His name is Mister Brewster. He carries a—a lace hanky."

"Ugh! He sounds just awful, Tina. Why, just once, could Branville not bring someone home who is dashingly elegant." Monica caught herself. She did not want anybody, no, not anymore!

Tina shrugged. "Now, go and get your bath, pet. Maya will be up to help you to dress shortly."

"No, Tina. Not this time as I want to be alone for a time before I go down. Tell Maya to go rest, she must be bone-weary after all the preparations."

Tina complied. On her way downstairs Tina's eyes lost their tinge of laughter and she shook her head sadly. She said under her breath, "Where are you, Victoria? Lord, your baby needs you."

Monica, after bathing, was of two minds about donning the yellow-gold frock.

"Well, I might as well suffer gracefully if that's what I'm about tonight." She sighed deeply.

Laying the dress carefully across the bed she crossed the bedchamber in her thin chemise. Picking up the tortoise-shell comb she ran it through her hair until it had been dried sufficiently and shone like sparkling sun on water.

The rain had ceased and the terrace doors had been

left ajar to air out the room. The old red drapes swayed and billowed in the light breeze that stole from the open terrace. Two lamps had been lighted on the walls, and they glowed in their separate corners while Monica finished donning the frock and completed her toilette.

Like one in a trance, Monica searched for the gold-colored slippers that would complement the frock. She was looking under the bed when a scraping sound met her ears and she halted in her search. The sound had come from the direction of the terrace, but she decided it was just the noise a shrub made against the windows below. Nothing more.

Discovering the lost slippers, she sat down on the far side of the bed to fit them onto her dainty feet, her back to the terrace doors now.

"What? . . ."

Icy fingers of fear ran up her spine as she felt rather than heard a rushing movement behind her. Before she could twist about, the bed dipped with weight and a hard hand clamped over her mouth. Monica tried to scream, but she couldn't even open her mouth against the insistent pressure. She could not even see the face of her attacker for he held her neck stiffly with a dark copper-hued hand. Her heart pounded so wildly Monica thought surely she would faint from that and from the pressure he—for surely this was a man—was putting to the slim column of her throat.

"I am not going to hurt you," the voice breathed hotly into her ear, "if you keep perfectly quiet when I take my hand away. Understand?"

Oh God, Monica thought wildly, why did I lock the door to dress? Not hurt her! It felt as if her attacker had already squeezed the life from her body. And worse yet, whoever he was, he was probably going to rape her. The terrifying thought shook her because she thought he could very well be one of Alex's stinking vaqueros. But, strangely enough, this man smelled nice and clean, as if he had washed not long ago.

Monica struggled in earnest now, pushing back against the rock-hard chest and kicking at the air with futile movements. His disturbing touch racked her nerves as he slipped an arm about her waist in a tight vice, crushing the life from her struggling form. She felt herself being flung unceremoniously onto her back, his other hand remained clamped over her sore mouth.

Monica tried biting him next, but his hand left her mouth only to slap her hard, returning swiftly, even before she could open her mouth to scream. She tried squirming out from under his grip but was then shockingly straddled by his long legs.

He jerked his head up then, looking wildly in the direction of the door. In that instant Monica chanced a quick look at her attacker. She gasped in pure shock, her mind merely registering the word *Indian*—an Indian the likes of which she had never seen before. Odd, she thought, how dirty he looks despite his clean manly smell.

74

"Hush," he whispered in her face, his head bent low.

For some crazy reason, now that Monica had heard his guttural voice, she was feeling somewhat calmer —if that was possible under the circumstances. Still, she pondered on his intent. Why had he come upon her like this, and what was he planning to do to her?

"You," she panted for renewed breath, "you are hurting me. . . ."

Feeling the lean, muscular hardness of his thighs, Monica grew more than uncomfortable with his granite form atop her. And to make matters much worse, he was the most attractive Indian—at least physically—she had ever set eyes upon. Before this the closest she had ever been to a man was when dancing the waltz.

This, dear God, was mortifying, this position he had her in!

"There is not much time, Monica Bennington," he husked low, sensing the change in her. "I will not hurt you. Is the door locked?"

Swiftly Monica nodded, wondering what was going to happen next. Surely . . . surely he was not going to hurt her? If he had wanted a woman, why hadn't he sought out his own kind? It was highly unlikely for a white woman to be attacked by an Indian—much less in her own home!

"Good. I will take my hand away now. You be quiet."

Not too afraid any longer, Monica again nodded

obediently. When he did as promised she breathed deeply, sucking in great gulps of air, watching as she did so his every catlike movement.

Only a few minutes had passed, Monica deduced, since she had first heard the scraping sound out on the terrace. He had moved so quickly, dear God!

What he did next thoroughly surprised her. He left her alone and lifted his tall dark frame from the bed, the boards creaking ominously as he went to listen at the door. Monica, still breathless as a nestling in summer's heat, watched him curiously and noticed that his motions were easy as a tom cat's.

He sprung back and Monica gasped softly, taking note of his blue-black hair circled by a sweat-stained blue headband. His hair was cropped shoulder length and he had the strangest eyes for an Indian. Not gentle brown as most she had seen, but black—penetrating, glittering, above a nose long and straight. Even through the dirt she could detect he was unlike his ethnic caste. What would he do now?

Steven Hawke paused a moment to survey the pale beauty who tensed and relaxed in turn, depending on the movements he executed. He could not imagine what his Golden Girl was thinking now, her full, pointed breasts rising and falling with each deep pull and release of breath. How lovely she had come to be, he thought, since the first day he had laid eyes upon her in the buckboard. She had been lovely then, but now she was like a glorious white flame burning into his very soul. It was too bad, Steven regretted, that he had no time to get to know her *physically*.

He continued to study her. She was silent. She was angry; it showed in her beautifully slitted eyes that reminded him of a mountain lion he had cornered once with his brother to tease. She faced him squarely, just like that lion with her ears pinned back, and Steven thought for a moment Miss Bennington would hiss and reach out to try and claw him as the lioness had. Steven had chased the beautiful cat off, but his brother Jess had hightailed it out of the woods and Steven had found him shaking in the branches high at the top of a scrub oak.

Monica stared at the big Indian who had gone still as stone. "Have you finished with s-scaring the daylights out of me now?" she snapped, but completely missed his amused grin at her irritated profile. "If so, my presence is awaited downstairs, and if I do not appear soon my stepfather—"

"You are not afraid of me, are you?" he said, in his voice a note of respect and another emotion with which she had not yet become acquainted.

She stabbed up her chin. "I am not, but—"

"One day soon," he interrupted softly, "what I want you to do is go down to the caverns and look for a young man by the name of Jess. The vaquero there will already be out like a light." At least, Steven hoped his friend could get that far. The bear of a man did move a bit noisily; they would have to work on that.

Monica gasped. "No—never!" Her eyes glared angrily at him, matching the tone of her voice. Now

77

she realized fully his intent. He meant to escape with one of the Indians—*Jess*! "That is impossible!" she tossed up at him.

"Why is that?"

She trembled inwardly as his eyes narrowed in the dimness of the room. "Y-You'll never get away with it, that is why."

"Listen to me!" he hissed in a tone just below a whisper. He pounced and whirled her about, grasping her arm with hard clamping fingers meant to punish. "I want you to help me get a man out of that stinking rathole cavern. Do you hear?"

The night grew strangely hushed as for one suspended moment in time the Indian stared, lowering his obsidian gaze to her lips. Suddenly he seemed mesmerized. For a second, a pulsing warm excitement flooded her being and then was gone as quickly as it had come on.

She had to bluff, for the young handsome Indian he sought was *dead*.

"If you know your way around here so well," she began, a quaver betraying her new fear, "then why is it that you don't get him out yourself?"

"Because, Mona the Cat, I do not belong here."

Monica frowned and tried pulling herself free of his grasp but he held and squeezed all the harder. "Ow, you are really hurting me now! *Stop it*."

His black brows drew together and for a moment Monica imagined the whites of his eyes went that same shade of glistening black.

"I mean to hurt you even more if you do not do as I say."

There was a promise of things to come in his eyes. It was shocking and exciting at the same time, almost as if she were being pulled back in time to another place where those same eyes had surveyed her, held her in a moment of eternity in which he possessed her. She only wished she could make out his shadowy features better . . . *he is so dirty.*

He made a sudden derisive snort that caused Monica to start and search his face for the meaning.

What was it, she wondered? Why was he looking at her like that? Had he already guessed her lies?

Eyes flashing a dark warning, he pressed long fingers into her palm and Monica trembled against his touch, wondering why he was touching her this way. She flinched as tingles of shocking pleasure ascended her arm, for now he was tickling her palm with two fingers. He appeared surprised at her bewildered expression, but this expression, too, soon fled from his stone-hard countenance.

"I-I don't like that," Monica said, slowly tugging her hand from his fingers that had been gently mating with hers.

Glittering orbs of black flicked her from head to waist, and he seemed almost to read her mind. Monica shivered as it occurred to her, despite her trepidation, what it would be like to be kissed by such an excitingly handsome, dangerous young man. She could remember with intense revulsion the lips of older men who had pressed moist lingering kisses into her palm, their fingers that fumbled for her hand reminding her of unbaked bread dough. Not so this man's, his fingers were hard and strong, identically like a finger of petrified wood she had gotten from an old Apache Indian who dwelled in a long-forgotten mine shack near the Sacramento River.

"What do you hide from me?"

"N-nothing," Monica said hastily, feeling his eyes boring into her skull. "I cannot help you. I am sorry."

"Sorry?" He tilted his head. "Oh, that is too bad. I will never forget this—"

He bent close to her mouth, warm breath coming from his flared nostrils.

"Someone is coming!" Monica warned, the words spilling fast and breathless, her lips so near his and then so far away the next moment, wrenched away when she looked quickly to the door.

Whirling back, Monica saw with some weird kind of regret that he had already vanished, the only indication of his going the soft rustle of the red drapes.

"Monica, aren't you ever coming down?"

Tina's words stopped; she listened.

As much as she hated having to lie to Tina, Monica did just that. "I had a headache, Tina, but it—it's gone now."

"All right then. But you'd better hustle."

Something across the room caught Monica's eye. It was on the very spot where her stepfather had stood

earlier. She went there and bent down to pick it up—
a tooled leather medallion with a perfect hawk carved
into it, the very same medallion that the slave Jess
had worn.

Jess. Oh, dear God.

Monica turned the medallion over. It was stained
with fresh blood and she shivered all over just
holding it and remembering who the band had
belonged to and what had become of him. Her eyes
almost bulged then. Oh . . . it came to her now, that
for a second in time when the Indian had come to her
she had at first thought him to be Jess, the one this
man had been searching for, *the dead one.*

She crushed the medallion in her palm and tossed
it aside where it slid beneath her dresser. She never
wanted to look upon it again, ever.

Monica knew she would never forget this day, but
she *would* forget the Indian. Her heart sank at that—
she would try to, then.

"Monica!"

"Yes, yes, right now, Tina."

Monica ran trembling hands down over her frock
to smooth it and walked on limbs that had the texture
of jelly. She tried hard not to relive the pressure of, of
his body, the sheer animal heat of his youth and
strength. The white-hot embers of memory cooled as
she unlocked the door and Tina surveyed a pale
white face for the second time that day. But this time
two mysterious circles like patches of ripe straw-
berries shone on Monica's cheeks.

Tina chewed the corner of her lip, looking around

the room curiously, then asking, "You alone, Mony?"

Heart thumping wildly as she turned her slim back to Tina who was looking in the direction of the red drapes, Monica said:

"Of course."

8

Only minutes later Monica was pausing at the portal of the dining room, gathering her wits about her the best she knew how. She listened for a few moments before entering.

"Mexico has again replaced its governor. This time it is a man by the name of Alvarado. He is trying his best to get those gringos, he calls 'em, to leave the country. But those foreigners give 'em more trouble than anything. Better keep an eye out, Branville. Them foreigners are up to rustling cattle nowadays, even way up here."

That must be Mr. Brewster, Monica thought, feeling disgust at just the sound of his slightly slurred voice, and already envisioning his doughy countenance.

"Yes, I have that knowledge, Mr. Brewster. These people really feel that the land they seize belongs to them and it's high time they were forced off."

Branville gave Alex a sidelong glance before he caught a movement just outside the door, a flash of yellow gold.

"Monica!" Branville bellowed. "Do not dawdle for dinner is about to be served. And"—he cleared his throat—"I want you to meet a very good friend of mine. He has taken time to travel with me from Monterey—just to meet my lovely daughter."

Stepdaughter! Monica wanted to scream at the top of her lungs.

Monica was already standing at the foot of the elegantly set table when Branville Bennington finished addressing her. Already empty glasses and bottles stood on the table, she saw, and stiffened visibly when Mr. Brewster stood up, dabbing at his protruding lower lip with a lace handkerchief. She wanted to laugh aloud. Tina, you were so right, she thought. A lace hanky for his doughy lips!

Mr. Brewster came around the long table and Monica felt sheer revulsion run through her at the warm, sweating hand that almost smothered her own. All she had to do was remember another's touch and that he had almost—

"Gad, Branville!" Brewster peered down into the low cut of Monica's bodice, almost drooling saliva onto her breast. "This daughter of yours is simply *gorgeous.* I'm almost tempted not to wait until the wed—"

"Please be seated!" Branville boomed suddenly, giving Brewster a shake of his head, one that Monica missed completely for her thoughts were far away.

"Sit down here next to me, Miss Bennington!" Brewster exclaimed, keeping his eyes trained on her softly flouncing mounds and pulling out a high-backed chair for Monica. He stood behind her, his fat tongue licking at his pink lower lip as those mounds of flesh settled into her bodice and her shoulders rolled back defiantly, her eyes flashed yellow sparks, her lips pursed haughtily.

"Do be seated," she ordered Brewster, tossing a shoulder as if to shoo away a bothersome insect.

Monica sat gingerly, with affected demureness, but a dangerous spark of mischief lurked in the depths of her catlike eyes. Her mind worked fast, making plans, and her lips quirked as she settled on one that she had little doubt would send Brewster fleeing as if from the hounds of Hell.

Mr. Brewster devoured the first course of the meal but the lustful glimmer in his dissipated brown eyes revealed that he fed on Monica's form as well. He hungered not only for food and wine, Monica perceived, cringing inwardly at his unconcealed lust for her.

Dining peacefully came hard for Monica. She was much too excited by what she had planned for Mr. Brewster, so much so, in fact, that she had a hard time not to squirm in her high-backed chair. Alex's colorless eyes fixed on her face, observing the high color dots on her cheekbones. He would, he was thinking, love to see Monica wedded to a man she truly found repulsive. She had always been a burden to his father. But soon, ah, perhaps very soon, they would be rid of this little inconvenience.

"Pass the bottle, Branville," Alex said, smiling

smugly at Brewster's constant rain of inane one-sided conversation.

Alex took sadistic pleasure in knowing he made Monica's flesh crawl by his bold scrutiny. Still, his cool gaze lingered momentarily where the higher curves of her breasts swelled above her lacy bodice. He would love to have her just once, and maybe that occasion would present itself to him sooner than later. After all, Brewster wouldn't always be home once they joined in marriage and were settled in Monterey. The man was always off to one place or another with his highborn politician cronies. Branville wanted Monica to be lily-pure for the marriage he planned, so Alex would just have to bide his time until that event had taken place.

"I'd be delighted . . ." Brewster said, holding out his cut-crystal goblet for another splash of Branville's expensive brandy. Brewster twiddled his pudgy fingers. "Just a little more, Bran. Ah, there, that's it. My thanks." He sighed and sat back to gulp it before attacking the rich fare once again.

Across the table, Alex's lips curled in the specter of a malicious smile and a shudder went through Monica's body. There were no more niceties or subtleties to excuse the man's evil doings. Masking her raging emotions, Monica clenched her hands into tight fists under the table. Murderer! Slave driver! I despise and detest you! she longed to shriek at Alex Bennington.

Endeavoring to focus her attention elsewhere, away from the trio of smothering gazes, she riveted her eyes to the fireplace across the hall where a small orange fire was burning to extract the May chill from the cold salon. To Monica's way of thinking the flames helped not a bit, for the house still gave off the facsimile of ancient Egyptian chambers.

Branville, between bites of food and conversation, feasted visibly on his stepdaughter and was haunted once again by the rankling memory of Victoria. Her golden brown tresses glowed with the same great luster, a riot of tempting curls that hung in a deluge down her proudly held back. He was reminded of long-ago evenings as they sat by the fire, Victoria with a faraway look in her eyes that never ceased to annoy him tremendously. Actually, it was not all that long ago.

Pure resentment kindled anew in Branville Bennington's heart, for as he sat watching Monica with his flinty gaze, he saw that Monica had grown into a glorious replica of Victoria. Monica was a nestling no longer, but a young woman who had blossomed and who had soft, rounded curves that matched Victoria's own. She was a prize worth having, and any man would have to be blind as a bat to not see this. In less than a year Monica would be nineteen, and at that time the secured funds Victoria had left with a trustee would be released to Monica—only in the event that she had found herself a suitor who intended marriage. A dowry so to speak, and a considerable sum of wealth Victoria had hoarded from him.

Branville smiled inwardly. Monica could not

know the plans he had for her, he thought malevolently.

Brewster had already promised to split up the sum with Branville once he had his hands on it and Monica had become Brewster's wife. Branville could already see that Monica pleased the man, that Brewster was unaware of the defiance that was so much a part of his stepdaughter. And Kane Brewster was not such a bad catch, not at all. Brewster possessed an amiable broad face, rather dark, with short side whiskers, but that was not all. He owned one of the largest stock ranches, on which he lived like a miser while he increased his pasture lands to sixty thousand acres.

There was one catch, Branville now concluded, watching Monica. She picked daintily at the tiny peas and onions smothered in a creamy sauce. She was thoroughly bored with Brewster's company. She ignored him almost to the point of impoliteness. It maddened Branville. She contributed nothing to his heavy pursuit of conversation with her. Damn her! Just like her mother. Coldhearted females. But that was what had attracted him to Victoria in the first place. An absolute defiance that had shone in her eyes, eyes that caught a man up like a helpless leaf in a whirlwind.

Branville had awaited Victoria's return for years, had deluded himself, hoped against hope that she would come back for Monica and that he could bind her to him by promises of a better life. He would lavish anything on her: new clothes, the parties she so loved, everything her little heart desired. But that day was never to be, and he would extract from her daughter what he felt was his due, for Victoria's obstinacy.

Aware that she needed to keep her wits about her this night, Monica drank none of the proffered wine.

"I will not!" Monica exploded into angry defiance. "He is old enough to be my father. God, I would rather die than be married to the likes of that man!" More softly, she stated, "Dear God, he makes my very skin crawl."

"*I* am your father!" Branville shouted.

"Ah, so there it is. You really want me to believe that horrible nonsense?"

At that, swept into a fury that knew no bounds, Branville stepped before her and slapped Monica so hard that she thought her frail neck would snap from the force of the blow. Branville stared at the unruly riot of honey brown that had been loosened about her beautiful face, beautiful but for the bitterness imprinted there.

Monica positioned her head back ramrod straight and glared into her stepfather's colorless orbs, her own hot but showing no tears. She would never cower to any man, this young woman.

His open hand hovering, Branville almost flinched at the bold hatred she displayed and to his own amazement he stood aghast now, at a loss as to what to do next. He had the feeling that he had just vexed

SONYA T. PELTON

an angry tigress who was guarding her little cubs and was herself preparing at any moment to pounce on him. He was thinking how like the morning meadows, with their sprinkling of yellow wild-flowers, were to Monica's hair. She was truly magnificent, especially her furious jade green eyes with the mysterious tiny flecks of sun rays in them.

Monica watched with glowing hatred as Branville strode back and forth in the salon, contemplating Brewster smoking with Alex in the other room. Branville went to the portal, then peered out into the dining room to see Alex excusing himself. Brewster sat back in a small yellow gold brocaded couch, relaxing after the huge amount of food he had devoured, his belly protruding between the buttons of his overstretched silk vest.

"Damn the hog!" Branville hissed under his breath.

He eased the door shut and approached his stepdaughter once again, determined to have her see it his way. Still he grimaced, hoping that Brewster would not pop a button of his vest before he popped the question to Monica.

"You shall change your mind, Monica," Branville spoke with a terse warning. "Come down from your pedestal. If you do not, I will see to it that your favorite nanny is discharged and your horse is sold to Ragman immediately."

Branville stared at the sudden wild, haunted look in her eyes, and doubts clashed inside him like nervous swords.

Branville went on: "And perhaps even Maya, hmm, your personal maid will have to be released. But . . . not back to her people. Something more appropriate for her kind." He clucked his tongue. "Those poor, wretched Indians in the caverns below, those that tried defying my word . . ."

Suddenly Monica's lips twitched as if restraining some amusement Bennington could not even guess at. Besides, the barely perceptive movement of her lips was so fleeting that afterward he wondered if they had moved at all.

Whirling about, Monica left her stepfather to stare vacantly at a swish of yellow gold skirts. He gloated with a contented smile then, pouring himself a lavish snifter of brandy. That did it, he was thinking. Then, only maybe . . .

In the dining room Brewster watched as Monica Bennington entered, edged alongside the long table and then approached him smilingly. He licked his full lips while she drew ever nearer, swinging her hips while her odd green eyes flashed with something akin to desire. Oh, it must be desire! he thought with uncontrollable shivers. He felt his blood rise lustfully at the pleasing change in Monica Bennington. Branville must have told her. Gad! she looks ecstatic.

"Come, come." Kane Brewster stood up in anticipation of her caress, his hand smoothing down what most women thought to be his questionable manhood.

Standing like a beautiful siren before him now, Monica could see that Brewster's face was turning from flushed pink, to crimson, and his hands were working at the tight collar of his stuffy shirt. She tossed back her head and purred deeply in her throat, watching him as his look of lustful anticipation, only a wild, fleeting moment long, became one of stupefaction.

"Egad . . ." His eyes went wide as bulging fish eggs.

Brewster had caught the flash of something too late, a thing that had been thrust between his legs, its sharp edge pressing into his testes. The suddenness of the move took Brewster completely off guard and left him weak as a newborn foal.

"Ah, ah, God . . ." He moaned low as the pain shot up from his groin to his belly and a bilious green crept up his throat.

Dazed with pain and looking over Monica's shoulder, Brewster saw the huge oak door to the salon open up. His gaze slid back to Monica, she who stared at him through slitted feline eyes full of succinct meaning. She stood at eye level with the man, and he gulped hard while sweat dipped off his forehead.

Monica's voice was pitched low. "Now. You must inform my conniving *stepfather* that you have had a change of mind, Mr. Brewster. Tell him you have decided not to court me and wed me—ah, something came up." Monica pressed her point home. "Either that, or I'll cut them off!" she hissed. "And if not now, my dear Mr. Brewster, later." Smiling sweetly, she added, "In the dark, Mr. Brewster. I've *cat* eyes, you see."

Mouth slack and eyes mesmerized, Brewster indeed saw that Monica Bennington was correct in what she said. Her cat's eyes were slitted upward, beryline, beautiful, and oh God, so dangerous!

Monica waited. She could hear Branville approach from behind. Brewster gulped convulsively, nodding his head briskly in response to her urgent demand. He was now determined to leave this very night. No thank you, Kane Brewster was not staying on for three days as planned! He was getting the hell out of here tonight! If he didn't, Kane knew he would very likely wake up minus his manhood. He went one step farther. He would probably bleed to death and never know another morning.

"Well, well, what have you two been up to?" Branville questioned lightly, thinking he knew full well the reason why Brewster was flustered, his face one huge tomato carbuncle.

Monica turned slowly about, concealing the sharp fruit knife she had swiped from the table in the yellow folds of her voluminous skirts.

"Mr. Brewster has something ah, *pressing*, to discuss with you, Branville," Monica said very nicely. "Now, if you two will excuse me," she pretended to stifle a yawn, "I think that I will retire. It has proved to be a long day. Good night."

As Monica mounted the staircase she heard Brewster's trembling voice. "I . . . I've been thinking, Branville. . . ." His last hurried words were lost in her giggles as she reached the top stair.

9

Within the depths of the lush gardens the morning sun peeped through the redolent beds of asters, roses, and morning-glories. The drone of buzzing insects spreading pollen and gathering nectar filled the air while here and there flowering shrubs and potted plants graced the garden walks that swept around the base of Temloc.

Upstairs, Monica hummed while she carefully stitched coral-colored rosettes to the bodice of a pink muslin gown. Her voice, fresh and sweet in the springtime morn, sang a snatch of song.

Monica paused, her slim tapered fingers holding the threaded needle taut and high. Had she first heard the tune down by the Bay? Yes, a burly seaman had sung it lustily while rowing a loaded boat to shore. Over and over he had sung the words until other sailors, bent to their tasks, had paused a moment or two to join in, unconsciously persuading Monica herself to pause and listen to the lonesome chant which cast its spell over her. She'd felt as if the singing sailors had tossed a gigantic web over her and held her enchanted forever. The feeling that had washed over her was haunting and she had stood mesmerized, a part of the foaming turquoise sea, a comrade of buccaneers whose deep and lusty voices not so long ago had drifted out over the water like gentle soughing wind.

Sighing now, Monica resumed stitching on the muslin frock. "A fiesta!" her heart sang. She was going to a fiesta!

In a few short days they would be leaving Temloc to make the small journey to New Helvetia. She would even get to see the old mission on the way! How breathtakingly exciting!

Monica often had heard of the Mexican fandangos where Spanish women danced till dawn with handsome soldiers. "You will like Captain Sutter," Branville had told her earlier. "He served under the king of France in the Swiss Guards. The number of Americans arriving overland has increased greatly and Sutter has welcomed many in the New Helvetia lands. There will be quite a crowd at the celebration of the naming of the trading post—New Helvetia Fortress—and of Sutter's becoming governor of the same."

Monica's eyes had sparkled like precious gems when Branville had informed her that she would be going too. He had added that Tina would accompany her as chaperon. Tina had been just as thrilled as Monica to learn this news. It had been such a long time since Tina herself had attended a fiesta.

The intervening days had passed quickly for Monica and at the last minute the pink frock was completed. The day of their departure was scorchingly hot. Monica swept up the sides of her hair and left the rest to swing freely down her back. She selected the yellow gold frock for the journey, although it was worn, because its décolletage would be more comfortable in such heat.

"Monica?"

She turned as Tina poked her head in the door. "Are you looking for something?" she asked the maid.

"No, everything's been packed. It's just that there'll be a delay."

"What is it?" Monica asked, feeling disappointment cloud her day.

"Busted wagon wheel. But we'll be setting out soon. Don't fret. Anyway," Tina said with a sheepish grin, "I've not finished packing the lunch. This will give me time to get it done. Why don't you lay down for a spell? It'll do you good, Mony."

Whirling, Monica faced the wall to hide her great disappointment. A delay! What could happen next? And she didn't want to lie down. Why had Tina assumed that she was so delicate all of a sudden?

"Oh," she murmured, crossing to the bed just the same. She plopped down, not bothering to remove her dress, not caring if it was crushed. She would look a mess by the end of a day's ride in the wagon anyway. Besides who was there to see her that she cared about?

Not realizing how tired the preparations had made her, besides staying up half the night to complete the frock on time, Monica fell fast asleep.

In her dream she was walking through a deep blue mist near a house she had never seen before. A hand appeared before her, the fingers hard as they made contact and pulled her along. He seemed to be without form, but obsidian black eyes turned to stare at her. She gasped as his body appeared, chest bared, wearing only a breechclout, a hunting knife strapped to his thigh. She wanted to run, to flee, but her feet held her rooted to the spot. A strange sensation permeated her, a premonition that was not fearful but felicitous, exciting. The bronzed body pressed closer to her, causing pleasurable feelings to course through her bloodstream, penetrating her very soul. Her dreaming mind whirled with the wonder of the feel of him. His head bent to seek her lips, and it was as if every muscle in her body had a will of its own and moved out to meet his fiery touch. She had never been kissed this way; it was soft and stirringly gentle. She was shocked by his rock-hard maleness and by her own first intimate contact with such a man. Her fingers of their own volition found the sleek and muscular ripples in his back. Fires flared within her, overwhelming her with powerful desire as their bodies melded together. Countless crystalline sparkles moistened the now golden mist which gilded them with a patina, and they were transformed into shining beings. Featherlike darts swirled in her belly as he lowered himself to the fragrant folds of her secret self. "Say my name, Monica. Say it: Steven. Say Steven," he pleaded when she awakened.

"*Steven . . . Steven*," Monica found herself murmuring as her eyelids opened, then flew wide as she saw the awkward sprawl of her legs, her yellow frock hoisted clear to her waist.

Sunlight sifted into the room, lending an opaline quality to the rosy flush that covered her skin. Mystified by the strange but not unpleasant sensations that still coursed through her belly, Monica wondered at the wakening desire she felt. Her breath drew in sharply as she became aware of a strange, gnawing ache that would not leave her. The featureless man of her dreams loomed in her mind, and waves of heat spread over her once again as she remembered the dream and what he had been about to do to her.

Hearing a noise in the hall, Monica leapt from her bed, straightening her frock with guilty motions. Frustration washed over her and she couldn't fathom why, but as she refreshed her toilette she experienced something like a small death.

The road was filled with rocks, holes and uneven patches that caused the wagon to pitch and sway, but the scenery could not be surpassed as they traveled through a truly magnificent land. The panorama of the meadows and trees was breathtaking, a warm paradise much like Sonoma Valley, with forests of giant pines rising to a towering height and thick-trunked oaks growing rich with acorns.

The party passed fascinating villages full of chickens, children, and friendly Indians who ground the oak nuts into food. Some of these Indians wore white men's shirts but were otherwise almost naked.

"Very eye catching," Tina remarked.

Monica laughed. "You could say that," she said, trying not to remember the name of her dream lover yet aware that he could still make her feel that strange, gnawing ache if she dwelled too long on the disturbing dream.

Monica smiled and waved to the Indians and they in turn commented to one another about the young woman with "sun in her hair" and tried to decide if she was an evil omen or a good one. They decided on the latter; no one that comely could be bad.

Tina related some of the history of the area to Monica and the young woman settled back to train her thoughts on what her maid was saying. Otherwise she would be in danger of straying into imaginings that only created frustration.

Lagging behind in one of the wagons, Monica and Tina often wondered just what Branville was carrying in the other two. Probably just supplies to trade with Captain Sutter, Monica thought. How she wished that she could ride astride, she was thinking as she rubbed her aching backside. Already her hair had come loose, so she smoothed the disheveled hank into a demure topknot, allowing a few tousled curls to remain free at the edge of her pink flushed cheeks.

Yes, she could have ridden if it had been up to her.

But Branville, upon leaving, would have none of that. "You will arrive like a lady," he had ordered when she had questioned him about taking Dancer along and another mare for Tina.

"Yes, if you say so—a lady." But Monica had pouted nevertheless.

The wagon creaked and groaned, tossing them from side to side as the wheels passed over deep ruts in the dusty road. Tina shifted uncomfortably and reached behind her to hoist out a picnic hamper loaded down with fried chicken, candied apples, and lemonade.

"We might as well have something now," Tina said. "No telling how long we'll go without victuals once we get to New Helvetia."

Monica accepted a chicken leg and settled back to chew, talking between bites. "I'm sure that quite a table will be laid out soon after we arrive. Heavens, Tina, who wants to eat then? I want to dance and dance." Monica stopped, realizing she didn't know the steps to the fandango.

"Oh, Tina—the dance!"

Tina read Monica's meaning. "It is very simple, once you learn the steps," Tina offered kindly. "the Californian fandango is much easier than the Spanish dances. Once you learn that, you can go on to the fascinating dance of Spain. And you know how to waltz, so that will come easy after a few steps."

"Tina." Monica placed her hand affectionately on the woman's arm. "You never once told me you could dance the fandango. Why, if I had but known I would have had you instruct me long ago."

A sudden movement under the tarpaulin caused both women to start before a dark head popped up with a smiling toothy grin.

"I teach White Swan. Know good!" Maya said a little anxiously, looking from one to the other for understanding of her misdeed.

"Maya!" Monica exclaimed softly. "You shouldn't have done this. Branville decided at the last that you could not come and now he will punish you severely!"

"Mister Bran not find Maya. Hide good all the time. Sneak back under here when go home," Maya said assuredly, filching a piece of chicken back to her hiding place.

Monica moaned and Tina, noticing she had let the reins go slack as the horses wandered off course, took them up once again to follow the road.

"We'll make out somehow, Monica," Tina said. "After all, the girl has never been to a fiesta."

Both heard Maya grunt happily under the tarp.

After a time Monica again broke the silence. "I feel as if something quite wonderful is about to take place, something that will change my life. It is almost as though I have experienced this feeling b-before," she stammered, not looking at Tina. "A sort of *déjà vu*."

Tina nodded and Monica sighed, looking out over the landscape. Suddenly she sat up straighter, straining to see better. "Look. Over there, that rider we caught sight of just a ways back."

Tina's gaze scanned the countryside, settling on a dark rider and horse. It was much too far to discern whether the man was an interloper or just a vaquero of the Benningtons.

"He's probably just one traveling, as so many others, to the fiesta," Tina said matter-of-factly. But Tina often wondered why the stranger kept to the hills and off the main road instead of joining up with the party. Yes, she shivered involuntarily, as if he tracked them from afar.

Night had settled blackly around the party as they camped in the jagged shadows of many oaks. Once in a while Monica would hear soft whistling and snatches of song on the scud of the night wind. The sounds were strange to Monica, and with the fall of darkness her heart had taken on a stronger beat. Who, she wondered, was out there whistling so plaintively? Could it be a bird? No, she decided it was not a bird but more than likely the stranger who had trailed them all day.

Awaking to the wild cacophony of colorful birds, the next morning Monica was refreshed even after a long night under the moon and stars, a night during which the soft whistling had gone on and on until at last the sound had lulled her to sleep.

"Up, up with you now." As Tina roused her, Monica cast a sidewise frown at Maya. Sleeping with the Indian had proven to be more than a chore. Not only did Maya snore, but the blanket often had to be pulled back up to cover them and the task had fallen every time to Monica.

"The Hawk is near," Maya said cryptically as she trained her black eyes on the rolling hills of verdant green.

"What hawk?" Monica said, following the Indian's line of vision. "I see no bird."

Maya shrugged, saying as she dove for cover, "Shhh, boss man coming!"

The landscape brightened with flowers and the cool, clear Sacramento River stretched majestically for miles before them. A natural sideshow for the women, the banks were absolutely golden with the California Poppy, while large live oaks cast abundant shade over the rolling, bumping wagons. Miles later and after crossing the river without mishap, they came in sight of New Helvetia Fortress.

A horse and rider suddenly appeared outside the high wooden gates and came galloping swiftly in their direction. It was Captain Augustus Sutter himself.

The wagons caught up to the outriders who had halted to await the approaching horseman. On closer view he was a short-legged chubby man with a bald head, bulging blue eyes, a yellow mustache, and a goatee. He reeled up before them with a warm greeting, reaching over his horse's mane to pump the outstretched hands of the Benningtons. He then turned and nodded politely to the ladies, not noticing the one hidden beneath the tarp who was peeking out from her concealment.

"Welcome to New Helvetia, my friends. How do you do, ladies."

Monica nodded, smiling into the bright blue eyes of the captain. Despite his warm greeting, Monica detected a pompous attitude in this small man as his gaze roamed down over her once, quickly.

Captain Sutter cleared his throat. "It is sorry I am that you missed the ceremony the evening before when we renamed the place from post to fortress."

He turned his horse then and Monica whispered low to Tina, "What an odd little man."

Sutter was impressive but haughty, Monica noted, even though his height could hardly be much over five feet and he was a bit overweight. He escorted the little group inside the walls of the fortress and off to one side toward his meager residence. Without preamble Sutter dismounted and led the way.

Once inside, Monica took note of the tiny interior furnished with nothing but a few stingy chairs and a rough-hewn table where he took his meals. Monica decided another curtained-off room must be his bedroom. If he slept at all. He appeared very weary, she thought, but it was really none of her business if the man wanted to wear himself to a frazzle.

Alex and Branville remained quiet for the most part, eager to get the formalities over and to see Tina and Monica situated in quarters nearby so that they could get down to the business at hand.

Sutter's reception proved to be very cordial. He proffered refreshments from a side table. The gentlemen stood and the ladies were seated as they quenched their thirst. But Monica and Tina felt uneasy in this man's world.

"I am sorry about the lack of furniture in this, my home, but I never saw the need," Sutter was saying. "We could go into the dining hall next door if you gentlemen would care to, where the ladies would be more comfortable?"

"No, you needn't bother, this will do for now," Branville admonished. "The ladies will soon be taking their leave, anyway."

Monica, nervous and worried about Maya and how she would fare stashed in the back of the wagon, began to ask hurried questions, but these only added fuel to her stepfather's growing frustration and impatience.

For the first time since she had entered the dwelling, and now that her eyes were getting used to the dimness, Monica noticed that a wooden tub stood forlornly in one corner of the room. How she would love to take a leisurely bath. She wondered if there would be a tub in her own quarters.

Tina nudged her, having noticed that Monica's attention had wandered as had her eyes. Sutter was still making his speech and Monica noted, stifling a laugh in the tunnel of her throat, that Branville's gaze was rolling up toward the gray ceiling. Alex, too, shifted his lanky form back and forth, one corner of his cruel mouth indented in a sign of impatience.

Suddenly Sutter surprised her by turning expressly to her and laughing deeply. "Miss Bennington"—it was his turn to be surprised when the young woman

105

flinched at her own name, but he went on as if he hadn't noticed—"your charming presence lends a certain—ah—grace and beauty to my rugged fortress," Sutter complimented her falteringly, as if he groped for the proper words to say.

"Thank you, Captain," she said, wishing they could leave Sutter so that he could secure some rest. He seemed greatly overtaxed, almost ill, she decided.

Sutter cleared his throat noisily. Branville stood up to announce, "We have business to attend to now. Tina, you will chaperone Monica to the courtyard later. And, do not let her out of your sight." His frown said that Tina had better be on her toes this night.

Augustus Sutter raised his blond brows at the harshly meted out command; then he said lightly, "Have a good time at my fiesta tonight, ladies. I'm sorry I'll not be here. But I'll be back in a day or so and I—we—will ride while I show you around. Again, have a good time." He sighed.

Monica caught Branville's stern dark look as she thanked the captain, then turned to leave. Once outside the sun's fiery rays touched them again, and Monica glanced up in surprise, up into the dark eyes of a tall Indian who waited to take them to their quarters.

"Oh, I did not see you there." She backed up after nearly colliding with him. Had he been spying on them? she wondered. Why had he stood so close to the door?

"I am Chaka," the deep voice muttered.

Monica's peripheral vision caught a flash from the wagon which stood next to a low adobe. Maya was pointing furiously at the big Indian, the tarp surrounding her face like a serape, her black eyes bulging with what Monica thought was recognition. It was then that Monica took a moment to study the Indian while trying to see what Maya was all excited about. Monica frowned and then shook her head. No, she must be wrong, this could not be the bear of a man she and Maya had run away from in the forest at Temloc. But then again . . . Monica shrugged. What did it matter, for he seemed safe enough now that she had gotten a closer look at his happy face.

"I will take you to your room now," Chaka said on a cheerful note, obviously having been into the aguardiente already, before the fiesta had even begun, by the smell of him.

Seeming not to have a care in the world, Monica walked before the Indian, her skirts brushing the dusty courtyard. This night there would be a fiesta here, right here where she walked. A new scene began to unfold, a new experience lay before her, and for some inexplicable reason she wanted to jump and twirl round and round beneath the sun's radiance!

Part III

Fiesta

10

Warm phantom arms reached out to her and Monica turned her head to protest but before the words could emerge his lips lowered over hers. The captured kiss was wildly exciting, his tongue thrusting and possessing. Long thighs, lean and hard muscled, pressed intimately against her own, causing deep pleasurable sensations to undulate throughout her body.

Quickly then a wild sweetness began to stir inside of her, whirling at the height of her chest and in the deepest pit of her belly. Warm hands cupped her flesh and the phantom, hot and hard, tested between her thighs. She tensed but not with anticipation. Maidenly fear raked her, and then a gentle whisper caught at her mind:

"Monica. Come. Give yourself to me. It is I, Steven. You have nothing to be afraid of."

She could not yield, for indeed fear held her on a tight leash. Then her phantom grew a face. But it was not human. She cringed at the fierce alertness in the large, dark eyes. She shivered as she saw the strongly hooked beak; long, pointed wings; the black head and great talons. As the winged creature came closer, Monica could almost feel its hot breath against her soft, moist cheek. She whirled after staring into the mesmerizing black eyes, and ran.

Panting heavily, she found herself in a lavender-blue fog, encased in its thick damp folds. Her gown was plastered against her skin and she stopped, pausing to catch her breath, her eyes darting about. Then she saw him. Frozen with fear, she stood still watching the creature speeding behind her in swift, powerful flight. She heard the wing beats closing in on her, each second bringing the clenched talons closer, and she knew as it went into a powerful dive that the creature could kill by impact alone.

Monica's breath caught painfully in her throat as she began to flee again, the thing pursuing her as its prey. It raked the air above her, swift wing beats menacing her, following her efforts to escape. Coming straight for her, she looked up to see it swoop with closed wings . . . down, over her defensive position, her arms thrown up protectively.

The warmth of the blazing black wings covered Monica, but a voice unlike a creature's came to her again, hoarsely demanding:

"Say it, my name, Steven."

Again the male form was beside her, featureless, but now comforting, loving, gentle, kissing every inch of her quivering flesh. Her senses warmed at the gentleness of his voice and she felt herself begin to

112

relax again. Hard, hot fingers touched her to the quick and when she thought she could bear the heat no more, she felt that same hard member stroke her trembling thighs and move gently between them.

"Say it, Monica, say Steven."

"*Steven ...*" the whisper of his name—no creature/thing now—came unbidden to rush between her parted lips.

Monica moaned and twisted, but before the fullest draught of pleasure could burst within her, she awoke, still feeling the heat that was the last rose and gold afterglow of the lingering sunset slanting over the sill and onto her face. Wave after wave of flickering warmth dissolved subconscious dreams into conscious wakefulness.

Only the sun, nothing more.

With a burst of shivering apprehension, Monica bolted upright in the bunk. She stared down, eyes gone wide, believing she would discover a warm, human form in bed with her. Damp and twisted, the rough blanket coiled in and out of her slim legs although most of it was bunched between her moist thighs.

A trembling hand flew to her cheeks, and she felt the hot, flaming feel of herself. She knew a hollow ache within, as with the first dream of—of ... she dared not even think his name. Her anger steamed at the thought of *him*, the creature, half-man, half-beast.

Bounding from the bunk, Monica stood beside it and found herself still trembling with unbidden

113

desire. She was beginning to despise and distrust the dream that came to her so readily just upon falling asleep, the thing in it—and what he could do to her. Her cheeks flamed crimson. My God, to think what shameful deed had almost taken place with a mere phantom of her dreams!

But the unseen presence, like a lingering unwanted aura, was still with Monica when Tina came lumbering into their quarters with a washbowl and fresh towels. First she saw the rumpled damp bed; next she caught sight of Monica, her disheveled, bewildered look; and then she went about her task as if she had never seen the real evidence that her charge was blossoming into full womanhood and beginning to realize the stuff that dreams are made of. But Tina could only guess at a small measure of what Monica was really going through.

"Thank goodness they have a Chinese laundress here."

Monica heard Tina mutter almost inaudibly to herself. As Monica feigned rubbing sleep from her eyes, the dregs of the dream allowing her some measure of peace at last, she remembered Maya and sprang to action, only to be dismayed once she reached the window and peered out.

Monica's heart sank. The wagon was gone! Where was Maya? Where could they have taken the wagon?

Tina cocked her graying head at the girl's strange behavior. She was about to ask Monica what was bothering her when the girl spoke.

"Tina, I've completely forgotten all about Maya.

114

I'm worried. Where do you suppose she has gone? What if? . . ."

"Mony, don't go fretting your pretty head. I have already checked and she's doing fine. Better than you, in fact." Tina shook her head and smiled. "Gone off celebrating with that tall Indian Chaka who she was so afeared of at first. She's hidden well, I promise. He found her one of those things that the *señoritas* use to cover their head and shoulders. A serape, I think it's called. Anyway, she'll be here later, so I guess it'll only be me what's showing you the dance."

Monica's eyes narrowed into bright green slits. "Can we trust this Chaka fully? Are you certain?"

Tina chuckled, throwing her hands to her hips. "That girl can fend for herself!"

Monica dropped the subject, looking eagerly forward to the dancing lesson. Suddenly her eyes lit, her heart pounded in anticipation of the evening to come. Just to think that she could forget all about the disturbing dream seemed like heaven itself. No more Ste— No, she would not even think his name. She must force herself to erase the name from her brain until not one letter of it remained and . . . All at once she received a jolt. The Hawk! It was indeed a Hawk in her dream and just that morning Maya had said that the Hawk is near. What did it all mean? Was it mere coincidence, or were the dream and Maya's warning somehow linked together? Oh, she just didn't know! Nor did she want to . . .

Tina splashed the water in the small oval tub, bringing Monica out of her staring trance. "First let's wash that dust out of your hair and make it shine again." Tina danced a few steps and then stopped, smiling broadly. "I may be a bit rusty on the dance steps but you'll soon catch on—even leave me behind in the dust!"

The throbbing undertones of the Spanish music began, reaching them in the purple twilight while Tina scrubbed the journey's grime from Monica's pale hair.

"Oh, do hurry, Tina," Monica exploded, her eager excitement provoking movement of her dainty feet.

"I'm scrubbing fast as I can. This is not my usual chore you remember." She poured the last of the rinse water over the squeaking clean hair. "There!"

When Monica's golden brown hair was dry, Tina brushed it out to create cascading ripples down her back. For a look of romantic innocence, she expertly brushed sections of the waves up from either side of the head; twining, twisting, and pinning them up, she formed a heavy braided topknot. As a finishing touch she added a small sparkling Spanish comb of red and gold that sat proudly atop a now-glorious, shining mass of shimmering hair. Coiling tendrils escaped and glided in gold rings down past her shoulders.

"How do I look?" she asked Tina, then groaned, "There is no mirror!"

"Beautiful, simply beautiful," Tina answered the question then rifled around in a bag for a small cracked mirror she was certain she had packed. Her hand came into contact with a band of leather and she lifted it, curious as to how it had gotten there. "I don't remember packing this thing. . . ."

Monica's eyes fell to the medallion that Tina's hands were turning over. Shock washed over her. Mesmerized, while Tina curiously watched, she stepped closer to take the round of leather into her own hands, suspiciously aware of how it had gotten there and of Maya's warning just that morning.

"Look," Tina said, interested now. "There's a hawk carved into it."

"I know," Monica said, her eyes large and luminous and suddenly frightened.

The dusty courtyard contained several hundred folk who were milling about and Monica noticed, true to Sutter's word, that every type and color of person imaginable was present in the crowd.

The fiesta was well under way; aguardiente and ale flowed freely. The smells of tobacco and of the grease that the Indian women used on their hair intermingled with the odor of cooked meat and spicy Mexican foods. Long tables groaned with the ponderous weight of various foodstuffs and liquors and ales.

The swaying movements of the dancing partners seemed erotic to Monica as she moved about in the flickering orange light the torches cast over the area. Her pink muslin frock with the coral-colored seed pearls twinkled when the glow shed by the red, green, and blue lanterns fell upon it. All eyes were glued upon Monica and she felt rather than saw the men looking at her in open amazement and some awe. She heard an occasional whisper. *"Bella,* beautiful."

But frequently one of the many dark-haired women cast jealous sidelong glances her way. Still, they could not help but admire her glowing tresses that seemed to be in constant motion. Most of the other women wore gleaming white peasant blouses with full multicolored gypsy skirts that twirled like so many wild butterflies.

When Monica tried to make simple conversation, the responses she received to her efforts at being friendly were glares from dark eyes and indifferent shrugs of bare shoulders.

Monica herself shrugged and moved along, gritting her teeth as she determined to enjoy herself this night. It would be a long time between festive occasions and she might as well make the very most of this one.

The violins and guitars started up again, this time with the rhythm of a Spanish fandango. Suddenly, and to Monica thrillingly, a dark Spaniard was holding out his hand to her. "Dance?" he said simply.

"Oh, of course!" she quickly replied.

She had been staring at the dark-skinned hand he had proffered to her, but now she took it, feeling his hand warm in hers as they moved into the dancing sphere. His black eyes never once left her face as Monica, arms upraised as Tina taught her, moved sensuously to sway her body to the rhythm. The tempo was slow, then quicker, and people clapped simulating the sound of castanets.

The dance was total abandonment for Monica, releasing the tense emotions in her that she had never known until now. Her movements were those of a girl begging to feel the arms of a lover, wanting that which she did not yet know. All the bitterness she had long felt at Temloc disappeared, but she would not—dared not—remember the dream. Yet somehow, in some horrible way, it crept into the dance and was strangely intertwined with the motions of love and desire, of sensuality, of all the things Monica felt burgeoning in her tonight.

"*Steven!*" she felt her heart cry out, and tears threatened to well up in her eyes.

"Oh!" she cried out loud, frustrated and afraid of what was happening to her.

The dark Spaniard brushed close by her, whispering passionately into her ear. "You are a golden gypsy, *querida*."

Monica smiled and twirled her sparkling pink skirts flirtatiously, feeling herself very seductive. When the dance ended, Monica's eyes slowly scanned the crowd. She tensed. What was it? Someone had been watching her, was even now watching her more intently than the others. As if the watching face were inches away, she felt the eyes upon her, devouring her inch by inch. She felt as if a hostile being were closely watching her every move. Yet there was something else, another sensation Monica could not name. It, too, came from the source of those ever-watchful eyes.

"What is your name?" the Spaniard asked for the second time.

"Oh!" She spun to face her partner with a ready smile. "Monica."

"That is all, just Monica."

"Just Monica," she said, still feeling those hostile eyes burning holes into her, but her back now.

"No last name?" he pressed, his eyes hot black coals in his swarthy face.

"For now that is all." Monica appeased his curiosity with a glowing smile. "I am sorry, I was looking for someone."

"You were?" he said. "I did not know." But his eyes shifted to the fringe of the crowd, and catching the black eyes of another, he nodded once swiftly.

"Miss Bennington . . ."

She whirled back to face the Spaniard. "What did you say?" she said in clipped tones. "How did you know that name?"

"Would you care for refreshment, Miss Bennington?" he continued insolently.

She would become the laughingstock of the fiesta if she made a scene, even though this man was arousing her anger. She nodded, reluctantly giving in.

"Ah, good." His eyes came back to her after having wandered off again. "My name is Antonio Alvarez. I work at the San Pablo mission. Have you heard of it?"

"Yes," she curtly replied, feeling as if she were being spied upon somehow. "What do you do there?'' She reversed the situation to see how he liked being interrogated. He was rude and a thorough bore!

"Paperwork," he answered with an insolent grin, "for others in need."

Monica screwed up her mouth, not liking his evasive answer one bit. "I have never heard of such work, Antonio Alvarez."

"And you never will again," he grinned, "I assure you. Now, Miss Bennington, I will get you something and if you are occupied when I return, please save me the pleasure of the next waltz."

Monica's jaw moved backward and forward, but she could not speak she was so vexed by the man's rude manners. What did he want with her, anyway? It was as if he were spying on her. The intrusive Spaniard vanished, as if into thin air, leaving Monica alone and fuming.

"Just who does he think he is!" she uttered under her breath, ready to tear him into ribbons if he showed up with a drink in his hand—or, better yet, if he held out his hand for another dance she would spit in it!

Suddenly a chill raced up her back, raising her hackles, and turning, she was startled as she gazed up into penetrating black eyes, as black as the darkest night in the pits of hell. She stood frozen, transfixed in time, caught somewhere between dream and reality. She could not utter a single word under this cool hostile regard. A deep-seated fear enveloped her when his lips moved to mutter one word, one Monica suspected was not very nice.

"*Puta.*"

Laconic black eyes raked every inch of her, ever so slowly, coming to rest insultingly on the golden mounds of velvet flesh showing above her low-cut bodice. Monica could only gape dumbly, mesmerized at the feral gleam in his eyes. Somehow familiar . . .

She started when he laughed, softly, one side of his lip curling back over straight, white teeth. Monica felt her knees begin to shiver uncontrollably. He was still smiling, but it wasn't a pleasant smile, rather she detected a sneer of contempt on those sensuous lips.

"I—" Monica fumbled for something to say to break the tension spanning the small area that separated them.

His nostrils flared, and it was then that Monica decided she'd had just about enough of this stare-down match. She was becoming confused by the man's rude silence, and her own ire was being fanned by the ominous devouring eyes that slithered over her like some black spitting cobra.

He was finished then, and walked away.

Biting her lip, Monica whirled about so she could not see him return to the fringe of the crowd where she knew he would take up his position and again measure her coolly up and down. She wanted nothing more than to avoid any further assault by the cold vacant eyes that had aroused a tumult in her breast. That hollow ache between her legs returned and she damned it all over again.

So distraught was Monica that she barely heard the

strains of a Spanish waltz beginning, and she was hardly aware of the presence of the Spaniard who proffered her a cup. Gladly she accepted the drink and took a generous sip of the fiery liquid, almost choking on it. She didn't care. Two black-eyed devils had tested her to the limit this night.

"Come, little one, let us shock them all!" Antonio was saying, emboldened by her new reckless air.

He led her through the whirling mass and they eased into the waltz. Over the Spaniard's square shoulders, Monica caught sight of the insolent stranger entering the outstretched arms of the handsome mestizo girl she had heard someone call Elena. She was one of those who had rudely snubbed her. Monica reluctantly noticed that the stranger all but towered over the rest of the males. He was rakishly handsome, and in his dark charro suit trimmed in silver, he was by far the most elegantly garbed man present. Even the beard he sported was neatly trimmed. Long sideburns added to the strong lines of his jaw and of his slashing cheekbones. He reminded her of a well-dressed bandido.

For a time Monica forgot the disturbing intruder, and let herself be swept away by the excitement of the festivities. It helped that she was surrounded by eager males, waiting to dance with her. She was grateful that she was not alone with the stranger.

"You are wonderful, *querida*," Antonio shouted above the music and the loud laughter.

Having no lack of partners, she was soon breathless, giddy from the dancing and the drinks she had consumed. Antonio had disappeared once again and Monica thought she saw him conversing with the *bandido*. Unable to fathom or to control her own actions this night, Monica flirted seductively with all of the men, snapping her trim fingers high over her tumbled, bouncing curls.

More than once she caught Tina's warning look, but she paid no heed and only twirled away before Tina could approach to slow her down. Even Nikolai Abdonovich begged her for the honor of a waltz. Monica chattered gaily with him, flirting outrageously while they danced.

"I cannot believe it," Monica said breathlessly, "a Russian consul here in California. What brings you here, Ambassador?"

Nikolai was aware that she suddenly flushed somewhat with embarrassment at the silly question. He gallantly came to her rescue.

"But of course, you could not possibly know. I should have explained. Let me. The Captain Sutter has been plagued by the local Indians and some Mexicans. He finds it necessary to keep the fortress well protected. It is usually garrisoned with forty obedient Indians, twenty white men. Now that I have brought the cannon, he has the firepower of twelve mounted artillery," he explained.

When Monica replied, Abdonovich was hardly aware that she was speaking to him, so intensely did he gaze at her flashing jade-green eyes and at her tawny hair that shone like silk in the lantern light. She was by far the most beautiful woman he had seen in the Americas, even more beautiful than the young women he had courted in France while visiting there. None of them pleasured his eyes as this winsome beauty was doing tonight.

Nikolai Abdonovich could hardly believe it, when he had observed her entrance into the courtyard. Certainly there were handsome women here, like the exotic Elena with the flowing black hair, who had earlier instructed him in the steps of the fandango. But this one, this Monica Bennington, there were no words to describe her!

There was no chance whatsoever for the ambassador to further indulge himself in her presence for at the moment the music ended a young man stepped up to them.

"Ah-hh, Lieutenant Conners," Abdonovich greeted him reluctantly, knowing the gorgeous young woman would soon be stolen from him.

Monica stepped out from behind the ambassador and gazed into the deepest blue eyes she had ever seen. This man was attired in a dark uniform, as commanding as his bold blue gaze. Monica found his face pleasant, very handsome in fact, and he had tawny hair that waved delicately about his broad forehead. This was the sort of young man she had often dreamed of having for an older brother, if only Victoria had given birth to a son before she had come along.

"I apologize, Ambassador, but this sweet young thing has swept me off my feet and in all probability I will not have another chance to dance with her.

Excuse me."

Conners pulled Monica gently toward him while holding her hand tightly in his big paw. She went gratefully, leaving the ambassador standing there, grinning foolishly as the lieutenant vanished into the crowd with her.

As they made their way to a refreshment table, Monica noticed the tall man in the black charro suit leaning laconically against an adobe structure, and puffing on a slim cheroot. She felt his hypnotic black eyes follow her, and she decided he looked like a sneering beast—damn him—just waiting for the right moment to attack and breathe fire over her. What did he want anyway? He acted as if *she* were a criminal, as if she had done something indecent and must be punished.

Was he angry because he didn't know how to approach her? That was laughable, highly unlikely by the dangerous look of him. And she had watched him dance with several women, all much older than herself, like the exotic Elena.

What is wrong with me? Monica wondered. She was afraid to look at him, afraid of what he might read in her face. She told herself next that the tingle she felt from head to foot was due to the inebriants she had consumed; she just wasn't used to strong drink. Was she fooling herself?

The pleasant voice of the lieutenant broke her contemplation. "Allow me to introduce myself fully. Lieutenant Edward Conners at your service, ma'am. And you are Monica Bennington." He smiled.

"You'd better be, or I have the wrong woman."

"Why, yes I am," Monica answered with affected demureness, having already learned to live in a man's world.

But Monica thought the lieutenant was studying her with an oddly intense expression on his ruggedly handsome face. He made her feel both excited and curiously diffident.

"I'm afraid that I must speak to you alone, Miss Bennington."

"I don't see . . ."

"No, don't get me wrong. It is not what you think, it concerns . . ."

Monica smiled expectantly. "Yes, please go on, Lieutenant."

When he didn't reply at once, Monica thought that he had changed his mind about whatever he had been about to reveal to her.

"Would you care to join me in a drink?"

Before Monica could answer, he guided her over to a bench that lined a stone wall, picking up a bottle from one of the tables on his way.

"No, thank you," Monica said. "I have had plenty to drink, and I am a bit dizzy. I am not used to spirits of any kind."

She had thought that he wanted to dance with her, so where was he taking her? He whirled then, making her gasp softly.

"I must come right to the point, Miss Bennington."

"Please . . . just Monica. I am not used to formalities, either," Monica said with such ease and dignity that Conners was mildly shocked. No coy tactics here, no fluttering of the lashes as he had expected after watching her dance and flirt that night. He came to the conclusion that her act had been solely for the benefit of another.

"Come right to the point then, Lieutenant."

Conners cleared his throat. "Your father and—"

"My *stepfather.* Go on."

He stuck a finger in his collar as if he was mighty uncomfortable with what he was about to say. "Your stepfather and Alex, it seems they've had some dealings with a horse thief we've been having trouble with lately."

When he didn't go on she said, "And?"

Again he cleared his throat. "Your party is to remain here with us for a week or so, at least until we get this matter cleared up. Uhmm—as prisoners."

"Prisoners!"

Monica was aghast. That meant that she and Tina would be considered prisoners too. Dear God, why?

"I'm afraid so. A Mexican officer was apprehended just a short time ago. Did you know anything of the dealings your father—I mean stepfather—had with a Tom Hunter?"

"Lieutenant Conners! I know nothing of my stepfather's dealings—with anyone. What he does is his business! Now, if you'll excuse me." Monica pushed past him.

Lieutenant Conners watched Monica weave in and out of the crowd. He groaned. She must be made to realize he was only acting under the orders of Comandante Vallejo. As for the horses, that was another problem yet to be dealt with. He would have to discover their whereabouts, bring them back. Conners was contrite for having had to question Monica Bennington. But he must do his job. Those stolen horses were being used in the campaign to turn the settlers out.

Conners spun on his heel to follow Monica. "Damn!" he muttered as he saw her and another woman disappear behind the door to one of the quarters. He paced up and down in front of the building, puffing hotly on a cigar. She was an enchantress, a *bruja*, but he wanted Monica Bennington and by God he would have her soon!

11

The day following the fiesta passed without much incident. So far, anyway, Monica was thinking no mild disaster had befallen them as yesterday.

Yet, as the hours passed Monica became increasingly uncomfortable, and she asked herself over and over these questions: Where was Edward Conners? Where would she go from here? Last night she had felt so sure of herself but now . . . prisoners!

Tina interrupted her reflections when she entered bearing a tray of bacon and beans. The crude fare smelled delicious to Monica for she had neglected to eat last night due to the intrigue and excitement.

Tina's usually bright countenance was sober, and a slight frown puckered her low forehead. "I talked to one of them military men outside just as I was coming from the cookhouse. A Sergeant Esteban ah—something-or-other asked for you. He mumbled his last name so I couldn't hear it very well."

"Then?" Monica said.

"I told him you were still abed," Tina said with a

sheepish look, forking out the still steaming beans.

"At this time of day?" Monica gasped.

Tina only shrugged.

Monica was truly vexed now. "Oh, no, Tina, you should have let me talk with him. He might have had a message from Edward." She rose to comb out her long honey brown hair, unaware as Tina was that she had used the lieutenant's name in so familiar a fashion.

"Wait a minute. I did ask him if he had a message from the lieutenant."

"Why didn't you say so!" Monica slammed her brush down hard on the small gray table that resounded as if it were fashioned of nothing more than tin.

"Let me finish—he said 'No'."

"Oh, you should have said so."

Tina only shook her head in exasperation as she sat down to her pork and beans. Monica sank back down onto her bunk, her face a portrait of golden-hued boredom. The sun, already sinking low to the west, had cast a lemon yellow light on the homely gray walls above her bunk. She sighed.

Tina shuddered after swallowing a forkful of beans. "Aren't you haven't any?"

"Not if they are that bad."

"They are not so bad," Tina said taking some more onto her fork.

"Why did you shudder then?" Monica asked, not really caring.

"Oh, that sergeant—ah—Esteban he looked to be

131

the devil himself with his straight hank of raven hair and cold black eyes to match. He penetrates my soul, that one. Wonder why he walks around looking so nasty. I just bet something is eating away at that one, he has a single-minded look about him and no good will come of it. At least if . . .''

Monica sighed, not listening to the rest of Tina's jabber. In a daze now, she nodded absently at the one-sided conversation, but inwardly she was shivering. She tried to calm herself while she wondered what sort of ailment she was coming down with. Surely not her time of the month. Not here, not now. No, the timing of the flux would be off. It was something else and she couldn't put a proper name to it otherwise she might be able to deal with whatever plagued her night and day. Especially at night.

The activity of the day was finally subsiding. The soldiers who had been rushing about were heading for their quarters to rest, and the Mexican women returning to Yerba Buena were just about gone. Monica watched, moodily gazing through the grimy window and surveying the grounds. Her eyes scanned the compond for some sign of Conners. She could have gone in search of him but that would not be the most ladylike thing to do. She had taken a liking to the lieutenant and she felt safe and protected with him nearby.

Tina's voice brought Monica out of her daze. "It is almost as if he knows something is going to happen soon and will even be a part of it."

"Who, Tina? Who are you talking about?"

"Why that dangerous-looking sergeant of course!" Tina said as if Monica hadn't learned her lessons well.

Impatiently Monica sighed. "Just what *did* he tell you?"

As she wiped her hands on her apron, Tina turned to her charge. "Nothing. It seems he was just going about guarding the fort, waiting for something," she shrugged, "or someone." Tina would not say that he might just be waiting around for Monica to step outside where he could snare her like a wolf. She wouldn't put it past the likes of that one!

"You mean you think this sergeant will come back?" Monica said, hope in her voice. "He must have a message for me, Tina, I am going out. Help me get ready."

Happily, Monica rid herself of the sweat-dampened dress she had worn all the day. She drew her rumpled white cotton, an old frock that had seen many washings, from her meager baggage. The dress was too small for her actually and revealed too much of her golden flesh, pushing it up much too far for decency's sake.

Tina's face clouded as she stared at Monica, not seeing a single flaw in the overly small frock she herself had mended lovingly on several occasions. "You look just like Roxanna out of Arthur's time, with your hair flowing down your back and sparkling like so many jewels. Did you know that when the light hits your hair just right it shines all different colors but black?" Tina smiled at Monica's gentle shake of the head. "I know, I've said it before."

"Oh, Tina, don't go getting sentimental on me now." She laughed. "Arthurian princess I may be, but what a setting for such a one!"

"If I were you, Mony, I wouldn't go outside alone, not with . . ." She grabbed up her shawl. "Better I go with you." Suddenly she had been reminded of that sergeant's penetrating stare right from a Stygian night.

"Tina, please." Monica held up her hand to stop the other woman. "I would much rather go alone." She pressed Tina's hand affectionately.

Before going out the door Monica shook her mane to make it fall down her straight back in shimmering golden warmth. She smiled as she backed out the door, leaving Tina with an extra plate of pork and beans and a carelessly strewn bunk of clothes.

Now that the sun had left California to a new ebony night, Monica was enveloped in its velvet folds as soon as the door closed beneath her hand. She shivered stepping off the boarded walk onto the dusty ground. Without the light of so many twinkling lanterns it was darker at the fort than Monica had expected.

Clouds suddenly appeared from the east to scud across a frail yellow sliver of moon which she had viewed from the window before the sun had given way to purple dusk. She shivered involuntarily as a tentative breeze lightly played over her shoulders, almost like a lover's gentle caress, and teased her into regretting that she'd forgotten her shawl. A few

134

blinking lights shone from the men's quarters and occasional laughter drifted to her. A dog howled at the haunting segment of moon.

All at once a small frown tugged at Monica's forehead. It seemed an eternity had passed since the afternoon of Alex's evil deeds. The events up until now had caught her up and freed her of those tormenting memories. Now they all rushed back as if they had grown soft wings and her very worst fears had been realized. She had knowledge of two murders, possibly more, and she could not do a thing about it!

Indeed, where would she go from here? Oh, she had been so certain that something wonderful would happen, something that would free her from the nightmares of blood and lust. She could think of her dreams as nothing but that, for they could not be called dreams of desire. Desire was what a man and woman felt for each other when they were in love; it was not lust for an unknown. She had never seen the face of her night tormentor!

"Ah, l'amour à la belle étoile."

Startled out of her wits, Monica whirled to see nothing more frightening than Lieutenant Conners striding toward her and adding rather fuzzily, "A white swan among all the thorns. You are beautiful tonight, again." He gazed at her with open admiration in his glittering blue eyes.

Monica had never seen such a handsome man. He was like a Greek statue carved out of marble, hard and unbreakable. Impressed by his flowing French,

SONYA T. PELTON

she said, "What was it you said? It was lovely."

His deep laugh was strong but somewhat be-fuddled as it rang in the velvety night. "I only said: Love under the stars, in the open air!"

Dropping tawny lashes, Monica hid a slight frown from Conners. She was wondering if he had been imbibing strong drink since he seemed so familiar with her and they had only just met the evening before. She hoped he was not going to create a scene that would make her forget she was a young lady. She would not relish meting out some form of punish-ment for his advances.

Edward reached out to brush her cheek gently with fingers that slightly shook. "Are you cold, my dear?" he asked her softly. "I could go to your quarters and get your shawl."

"That won't be necessary." Now that he was here and she had some company, she had no desire to be left alone with wisps of nightmares. Besides, he was so kind and was being the gentleman.

Edward's hair appeared burnished by the moon-light as his incredibly handsome face drew close to hers. She sensed that he was going to kiss her, and she experienced a feeling of anticipation. Then, he was moving closer, his lips were moving gently over hers!

Strong hands massaged her back and Monica was wrapped in the enchantment of the moonlit kiss, in the romance of being young and alive, free from dreams of *that one*!

Edward moaned, desire swelling in him. God, he thought as he kissed her thoroughly, he could take

136

her into that wagon over there in the shadows and . . . Would she protest? The manner in which she had danced and flirted last night . . . Why she had responded to the men like a woman of studied passion. He might as well . . . his hand crept up to cup her breast.

"Ah," he said lifting his lips from hers, while his hand captured a perfectly formed breast. "Lovely."

"Remove your hand, Lieutenant Conners, or lose it at the wrist!"

He stepped back, blood pounding in his veins. He coughed. "I must apologize for taking such liberties, Miss Bennington. You see, a few of the fellows and me, we had a couple of drinks and—"

"You just didn't know your own mind," Monica finished for him, suddenly realizing she had met his kind on countless occasions before this night. Still, she liked him, and she wasn't going to hold a stolen caress against a man who had had a little too much to drink.

Damn! How beautiful she is, Conners was thinking and he silently chastised himself for being such a dolt. He hesitated for just a moment before wrapping his arm about her waist.

"Come, I'll walk you to your quarters and tomorrow, if you like, we'll"—he coughed—"have a normal walk without me seeing the fellows first."

Monica smiled wistfully. Suddenly she knew Edward Conners was not the one for her, nor could he ever be one-half the man she was hoping to meet . . . someday, but not now, not tonight. She broke away from the possessive arm still holding her wrist.

"I can manage to find my way back alone."

He nodded, thinking for now he only wanted to get back to his buddies and drown himself in sorrow—and a few more cups.

Monica watched him walk away, his broad shoulders hunched dejectedly. Poor Edward, he had a long way to go before reaching full manhood, but Monica decided he could be her friend during her stay at the fort.

After this damper had intruded on her evening walk, she thought it best to return to her room and ready herself for bed, though she did not relish the thought of what sleep might again bring to her.

Hard fingers seized her wrist, and she was preparing to scream when another hand was clamped over her mouth. She struggled, in earnest, for her life, shaking with a terror that could not be denied. Then a deep voice hissed in her ear as she was being bodily dragged over to the wagon in the shadows. The living nightmare had only begun.

"I'm not going to hurt you," the voice ground out. "Dammit, just hold still!"

She struggled to break free, but he was too strong, much more the man than Conners had proven himself to be. He spun her about to face him, one arm still clamped about her neck, his hand spread over her mouth that was trying to release a scream. The sound died in her throat as she looked up at the dark face looming above her, menacing and hostile.

"I just want to talk to you!"

She knew she had heard his voice before, but all she could do was stare at his bronzed face, illuminated softly by the moonlight, and nod. She was mesmerized by the savage look in his cold eyes, eyes that were vaguely familiar. Ever so slowly she felt his hand being lifted from her bruised mouth.

"You h-have a strange way of talking to people," she found herself stammering out, tendrils of hair escaping across her face, her great pale green eyes misted over with fear. She swallowed convulsively, trying to go on, "I . . . I . . ."

But his face was dark with some untamed fury and his hard fingers had slipped to grasp her shoulders so hard that she cried out. She was surprised to find him shaking her roughly then, and she retaliated by kicking out at his shins.

"*Basta*! Enough!" he snarled into her face. "I said I would not hurt you."

"You lied," her eyes dropped to his lapels, "Sergeant!"

"*Bruja*, witch, you weren't afraid a short time ago when the lieutenant apparently was about to have his way with you. I have knowledge you have only known him a short time!"

In a voice more like a squeak, Monica protested, "B-but I have never . . . never laid eyes on you before. Why do you attack me out here in the dark like . . ." She choked back her next words, about to say: like a beast. Dear God, her nightmare was with her and she wasn't even asleep!

His relentless fingers tightened on her arm and pinched her soft flesh. "Tell me you have never laid eyes on me before. Or do you forget so easily—the fiesta?"

"But I do not—"

"*Silencio*!"

He shook her again and Monica could not believe this was happening to her. Her dream must have been a forewarning of this devil who had come into her life to torment her!

"I have never seen a woman flirt as outrageously as you did, *puta*!" His eyes flashed into her astonished face. "You little tease, you almost got yourself in a state of undress, did you know that? I even thought of accomplishing the task myself before that idiot of a lieutenant rescued you!"

Why of course! Why hadn't it occurred to her before now? The sardonic *bandido* leaning up against the stone wall, smoke curling up around his black hair from his cheroot. The very same who had called her a name she could not recall now, but the word had been tersely spoken in Spanish and she had suspected it was not a very nice one. He had been dressed differently then, like a Spaniard in a dark charro suit. But the eyes, how well she remembered them, black as ice on a midnight pond, the muscles below them twitching maddeningly in his high slashing cheekbones. He had shaven off the beard too. She had been most relieved that he had not asked her to dance. Now, he appeared, like a villain. Yes, still the *bandido*, but disguised in a soldier's costume.

Finally composing herself but still outraged she accused him, "Are you out of your mind, Sergeant! Or do you always go around attacking helpless women in the dark?" She dug her sharp nails into his forearm when he would not release the biting hold to her wrist.

He muttered savagely, his eyes flashing anger as he seized her neck between cruel fingers and forced her arching head back to the frame of the wagon. "Are you through, *muchacha*? Or do you have more flaming insults to throw at me?"

I would love to carve out your black heart with a knife, she kept to herself. He'd insulted her first, anyway! What now, had he decided to rape her next?

He began to study her face with interest now. She, too, thought he seemed some way familiar to her. His relentless fingers were slackening their hold and sliding down to clasp her upper arms. Again she tingled all over, but of course he couldn't know this and she was thankful for that one thing, if nothing else this night.

Under the sailing kite of a moon his ebony hair had a silvery cast. "That's better," he said coolly, but Monica still noted the strange hard bitterness in his voice.

Hypnotized by the maleness of this man, Monica lifted her eyes and met his cynical face. He was not hurting her now, but she had an overwhelming desire to escape from this frightening man. What did he want with her? Did his ruthless manner have something to do with those horses Conners had said were stolen? Did he think she was involved with such a crime? It was unthinkable. She was just about to put this into words when he broke the silence first.

"Jess Hawke," he drawled harshly. "Does that name mean anything to you?"

She lowered her eyes swiftly to veil the anxiety she knew had leapt into her eyes, but was at once sorry. His dark trousers gleamed in the moon that had gained strength in the last half hour, the material molding to his lean hips and thighs and emphasizing his tall legs and frame. Her heartbeat stepped up and sent the pulse in her throat to pounding.

The muscles in his jaw tightened again, and the black coals of his eyes blazed into hers as she lifted her gaze defiantly. "You little fool!" He grabbed a handful of her loose silken hair and yanked until her head was forced backward. "Maybe you can answer me this then: What do you know of the slaves your bastard of a father keeps at Temloc? That's your home, right?"

She could only nod a little beneath the steady pull of his hand.

"Does Bennington kill off Indian slaves when they get out of hand?" He tipped his head to watch her with catlike alertness. "Where are they now?"

"Release me, you animal!" she spat and struggled wildly to get away. "How many are there like you, anyway?"

Flat, black eyes watched her futile struggles, lifted to burn into her face, then scorched a trail down to her lips that were moist and trembling, to her breasts that rose and fell as she panted with her exertion.

"I-I have no knowledge other than he keeps them there, they w-work for him. . . ."

"For who?"

"My stepfather!"

"Bennington then, he is your stepfather," he stated in a low, angry voice.

"Yes! Yes!"

Dear God, just who is *this* man? Had Branville's slaves been *his* slaves, stolen from him by her ruthless, cunning stepfather? Her mind reeled in shock at the thought that Jess could have been *his*—was possibly even related for the coloring was there. She was beginning to believe this man, this animal, would slay a woman had she done anything to cross him. But she had had nothing to do with her step-father keeping those slaves. All she'd done was try to live peacefully. Still, this sergeant would never in a million years believe she hated her stepfather as much as he seemed to. It was true. More than one man had perished under Branville's relentless hands because of misbehavior.

"Where does your *stepfather* keep the slaves, Miss Bennington?" He smirked. "*Monica*, is it?"

A tremor passed through her when he said her name, leaving her dizzy, for no man had ever quite said her name like *that*. He had seemed to be purring it, deep in his throat, but then the question had ended on a harsh unfeeling note.

Now he was angered all over again. "Dammit, bitch, tell me!"

"In the caverns," she blurted without thinking,

"below the mansion."

Steven Hawke sighed impatiently. "Oh for Christ's sake, I know that!" He shook her again. "The ones that cannot be accounted for, where are *they*?"

"Don't hurt me any more," she hissed. "I tell you I do not know! As I told the Indian before you . . ."

He leaned into her, his hard frame brutally smothering her soft slim one. He pressed even harder, with one knee pinioning her skirts against the wagon between her legs and making blackness reel in front of her eyes so that she had to grab his arms to keep from falling backward into the wagonbed and perhaps breaking her neck in the process.

Monica's slow moan caught in her throat. The male scent of him, so close this time, filled her quivering nostrils. Waves of feeling close to those she had experienced in her dreams washed over her, and she shot forward, accidentally brushing his lips. He held her firm in that position. She tingled as his breath rushed against her lips, and she cried out when his tongue, without their lips touching, thrust humiliatingly into her moist pink mouth. Then they stood, suspended a moment in time, as their lips merely wavered close. It was like being tickled by a feather Monica thought for one crazy moment before he frowned darkly and cast her roughly away.

Monica fell to the hard-packed earth and then staggered to her feet, staring up at this beast with gleaming green light of hatred. He returned the look, twofold. As she stood, quite calmly under the tumultuous circumstances, his eyes caught hers,

144

promising before he strode away that they would meet again, alone.

Suddenly he was gone, like a huge cat. She paled then as the revelation struck her. Not a cat, a *hawk* on swift silent wings swooping into the dark. She had found her nightmare to be a living reality!

She stepped toward Tina's voice calling her anxiously. Monica hurried toward the comforting sound. What if, and she almost gasped at the thought, what if his name turned out to be Steven?

12

Hawke strode briskly past the main building that was the headquarters of the fortress. Standing near the center of the enclosure, it was a rectangular, two-and-a-half-story structure with outer walls fashioned of adobe bricks and its floors, partitions, and roof supports were made of timber hand sawn from the trunks of great oaks that grew all about Rio del Sacramento.

For a moment the Indian sentry stationed beside the cannon near the main gate said nothing as Hawke slid down next to him. Chaka preferred not to look into the perturbed dark face of the new friend he'd met just outside San Pablo mission before coming here. At the mission he'd had a meeting with Antonio Alvarez, something about a letter. Now Chaka had learned what that letter contained.

The Spanish-speaking Indians chose to call Steven Hawke Sergeant Esteban; Esteban, Spanish for Steven. But Captain Sutter knew him as Sergeant Steven Hawke and had sent him out not long after his

146

arrival to track the Benningtons to the fort—*escort* from afar. One could not be too careful. This had been exactly the mission Hawke had been waiting for.

Sutter had found Hawke very useful during the two weeks of his appointment as sergeant of the mounted Indians. Hawke had initially arrived with a party of five Indians, those formerly stationed at the California mission, San Pablo. These Indians had been taught to cultivate land and to perform other tasks set for them by the mission fathers, and all could speak and understand at least a smattering of Spanish.

Sutter took avid pleasure in his small private army. All his life he had pictured himself as a dashing military leader, and now at least he had a detachment of troops obedient to his commands. Life at the fort was conducted with the austere discipline of an army post, but Sutter knew Hawke would not stay long enough to help him keep order, for the man was in search of someone. Sutter was convinced that Hawke's search had something to do with the Benningtons.

Chaka peered askance at Hawke, but that one never turned a muscle, just kept his gaze trained straight on his dusty boots stretched out on the ground in front of him. Chaka had come to know this man and his black moods, to understand him like a brother. In fact, they had both had brothers who had disappeared, and so their causes had been linked together. Chaka knew Hawke would stop at nothing to discover what had happened to their brothers, but in the back of Chaka's mind he knew he would never set eyes upon Chino again. Something very bad had happened to Chino, he felt this in his bones.

Together, linked by their mutual bond, Hawke and Chaka had searched for Jess and Chino. Their investigations and inquiries had ultimately ended at the mansion Temloc; both men had last been seen there, a certain Indian maid named Maya had covertly told them after Chaka had sworn that she would have his undying protection, and Maya had found a steadfast friend in Chaka.

Chaka sighed softly, not wishing to disturb Hawke's dark reflections. Chaka imagined it would become very unpleasant for the young woman, Monica, if Hawke should discover Bennington had done away with or harmed Jess and Chino. Maybe the pretty *señorita* knew nothing of Bennington's villainous deeds; Chaka hoped, for Monica Bennington's sake, this was so.

The silence stretched on maddeningly until Chaka could stand it no longer and spoke up, modulating his voice to a low pitch. "Did you find out anything from the girl, *amigo*?"

"No."

"Ah, that is serious."

Steven sat woodenly, but his face was hewn from granite. "She definitely knows something."

Chaka's interest was whetted. "Did you mention any names?" he asked the stony figure.

"*Sí*. Only Jess's."

148

"Ah, that is risky, *amigo.*"

"I asked her once before, disguised as the Indian. Do you recall that I told you?"

"*Sí, sí!*" He laughed. "But she does not know this *sargento* is the same man."

Suddenly restless, Hawke sprang to his feet, running fingers through his coarse black hair. "I visited some friends outside the fort today. Fremont is staying in the area and he is busy signing up volunteers in order to strengthen his ragtag army for the expected showdown with the Californians." He grinned slowly. "Now, you and I are going to make some plans."

"Do these plans have something to do with the stolen horses, *amigo?*"

Steven grinned even wider, the squint lines in his eyes deepening. "Ah, Chaka, you are getting smart, do you know that?"

"*Sí, jefe, sí.*"

Monica lay weary but sleepless. She wondered if she would ever sleep again, ever forget the happenings of this night and the feel of Sergeant Esteban's hard fingers biting into her flesh. He made her feel so pluckless, she thought as foolish tears sprang to her eyes and ran down her cheeks in tiny rivers.

Finally, exhausted, she began to sink into a sleep she prayed would be deep and renewing. Search her memory as she might, Monica was hard put to think where she could have seen the sergeant before the fiesta, before this awful night. She had long ago put away her girlish dreams of becoming involved with the likes of *his* kind. Though she ransacked the recesses of her mind, she could not—dared not—recall where she had looked into those eyes, obsidian and black. And it had been more than once. . . .

Monica came fully awake as soon as her eyelids parted. Light flooded the room as she gazed through the window at a summer-blue sky, her arm crooked and her head resting on her hand. It would have been such a beautiful day, if not for . . . oh! she would not let the memory of *him* spoil her day!

Suddenly there was a commotion, and a flurry of excitement outside the walls of her room told her that men were rushing to the main gates. Drawing herself up she sped to the window, her legs bare, her nightshirt sliding up and down her thighs.

"My Lord," she gasped.

Santa Fe wagons were coming in, drawn by eight or ten hard-laboring mules, some driven by Spaniards, some by Americans who resembled Indians because of their long, straight black hair, and some by Negroes. The dilapidated and muddy condition of their wagons, and wagon sheets, and the sore backs of the mules, all bore witness to the length and hardship of their journey.

Then Fremont made his appearance before the gates of the fort with his entire army. Among the men were Merritt, Carson, and a great many settlers—a total of about one hundred men.

Puffs of dust seeped under the door and window,

and Monica held her hand over her eyes and coughed.
"And I thought all this was going to be exciting—
ugh!" she gasped with a hand around her throat.

Just as she was turning from the window, Tina
burst in carrying a bowl of pungent-smelling meat.
"You are lucky I got this here in one piece. Lord,
there's some mighty hungry-looking dudes out
there!" Then she added, "It must be midmorning,
and here you are missing out on all the excitement!"

"I do not welcome either the morning or the
'excitement' as you call it," Monica said.

"What?" Tina couldn't believe her ears. "What's
gotten into you?"

Monica caught her breath, then replied sheepishly,
"Nothing."

"Ah," Tina said, thinking she knew. "You'd
rather not face the day and just want to reach the end
of it somehow?"

"All in one piece, thank you!" Monica exclaimed.

"You just want to get out of here and return home,
eh?"

"Home?" Monica thought about that. "If you
could even call Temloc 'home.' It cannot be much
worse than this awful dusty place, though."

And Conners, where was he? He would just have to
bring back those horses if he wanted to appear even
half the hero to her.

And what was bothering Tina? Had she seen the
sergeant again?

Narrowing her eyes as Tina hummed about the
meal, Monica wondered what could be making her

maid so happy. Her mood had altered so since yesterday. Gone were the questions she'd asked the previous evening when Monica had returned from her "walk" in the moonlight, questions regarding Monica's whereabouts.

At Tina's urging, Monica sat down to eat. But it wasn't long before she grimaced at the highly seasoned fried meat and the beans smothered in greasy onions, and pushed the bowl away.

Hiding a grin, Tina said, "We can always pick some wild grapes when we—ah—go for a ride. . . ." She went on despite the incredulous look crossing Monica's face. "We should have gone a long time ago, but the horses won't disappear. They're still waiting."

"Riding?" Monica said, disbelief written across her awakening features and Tina's words dismissing the gloom of a few seconds before. She shot out of her chair. "Really?"

"Uh-huh, of course 'riding'," Tina repeated happily. "Lieutenant Conners thought you might enjoy a ride and it will give you a chance to steal away from all the commotion."

"What about clothes?" Monica said, a little breathless.

"We can rig up some makeshift riding clothes." Tina shrugged, finishing her meat and beans. "Whoever said women were unimaginative and uninventive was dead wrong!" She stood, dusting off her skirts. "C'mon, drag out a needle and thread and some old duds and we'll rig up some costumes fit for a king."

Monica laughed mischievously. "I am not sure how we'll look dressed as the sex that fathers young, but I am willing to give it a try. Anything," she sighed loud, "to go for a ride."

The horses chafed at the bit as the party prepared to mount. Even the dark-fleshed Spaniard, wearing a sharp conical hat with a red sweatband and holding the horses, only made Monica shrug her shoulders in abandonment when he informed them he must go along on the outing. Even when he feasted his shining dark eyes on her "outfit," she was calm, her eyes placid as a mountain pool.

Mounting beside the ladies, Santino thought to himself, "What a woman! And such a smile, so brilliant, like the sun itself." He turned to flip a grin at her then and was rewarded as she smiled audaciously making Santino blush hotly and think, "*Dios mío!*" The peasant blouse she wore was cut exceedingly low, displaying creamy golden mounds at the top of her youthful breasts. The breeches . . . *breeches!* Santino flushed twenty shades of heightened red, peeking down at his own slender form, then up again. "They are my own, my breeches!" He eyed the older woman with suspicion and, seeing her airy expression, knew what had happened to his other pair.

But then Santino's eyes widened with a pleasant shock at the taut backside, firm thighs, and long slender limbs, Monica revealed as she moved out, and he told himself the woman's confiscation was well worth the sight before him! "Ahh," Santino murmured, *"Dios mío,"* and crossed himself, praying that God would give him the strength not to swoon over so much femininity.

The gates were flung open wide and the women had no idea where they were heading, but for the moment it mattered not to Monica. The countryside widened enormously as they left the fort behind. Already it was scorchingly hot, but just the same a glorious day, with finespun clouds scudding in from the west, and an azure-blue sky above the patchwork green of the countryside, the songbirds' music idyllic.

To be free like a bird to roam about the country; Monica felt alive as never before. Not even on her outings at Temloc had she felt this unfettered spirit soar in her. She tossed her head and felt the wind thread her hair and touch her cheeks in a sultry kiss of warmth.

Grapes swarmed in purple hordes on the banks of the American River and Santino allowed them a brief stop to pick some of the wild profusion of delicious fruit. Juice ran down Monica's chin. Tina squirted Monica in the eye as she bit into a plump morsel and together they laughed like happy children, Tina tossing her head way back, Monica adding tears of joy to the grape juice.

"We will ride now, *señoritas*," Santino said, sharing their happiness with a warm smile of his own. But his smile was mostly for the young *señorita*.

Monica understood some of the Spanish and most of the intermittent English Santino spoke so he informed her she would be free to visit her father when they returned to the fort. She would have been able to visit him before they left on their ride were it not for Fremont wishing to question the Bennington men.

"And, Señorita Bennington, there was no reason for your presence." He shrugged then, adding, "I mean you did not have to be there for the questions."

Monica shrugged back. "Of course, Santino, I quite understand." In fact, in this instance, she was more than relieved that her presence was unnecessary.

Again Monica wondered about those stolen horses that were to be used in a campaign to turn the settlers out. Now, who in the world would be so nasty as to steal those horses and keep them hidden? Who was so land greedy? Her stepfather and Alex were, weren't they? And who would be so full of fire as to snatch them back before the settlers were turned out? Perhaps that would explain where Conners had disappeared to; he might be a hero after all.

The three continued on their jaunt down the right bank of the river, traveling for a time over a wooded upland. Their bird's-eye view of the landscape and the fort was indeed breathtaking, a sweep of gorgeous emerald verdancy. As they began to descend, Santino held up his hand and they stood, unmoving, while he rose in his stirrups.

Then, across the dead level of the prairie a black smudge appeared against the sky, apparently moving at a great speed toward them. A cloud of smoke appeared on the horizon and a distant rumbling reverberated.

"What is it?" Monica asked their guide.

"A storm?" Tina wondered.

Only after the roar remained unbroken for some time and the cloud of smoke grew did Santino speak. "Horses. Many horses."

Monica's heart lifted. Conners! He was bringing the horses in!

The rumble grew, became louder still, until it matured into a deafening roar. Shrill, yipping cries rent the air despite the pounding of many hooves, and just then a high-pitched whistle echoed in the air. One hundred or so gallant horses came with the cloud of smoke, the undulations of their backs in the moving throng as regular and easy as the rise and fall of swelling watery waves.

"Hey! Esteban!" Santino bellowed. "The horses, hey, you brought them in!"

Monica gasped, and catching Santino's line of vision, she whirled her mare about. "Wha? . . ."

Her eyes widened at the sight of Sergeant Esteban astride a great black, motionless but with sides heaving. He sat near the edge of the wood, waving his Indian companions along to guide the horses into the fort. Hawke set his big black easily back into motion with his knees and reined in alongside Monica, a deep scowl sweeping his lean, dark face.

"What in hell are you doing out here joy-riding?"

Monica drew her mouse-colored mare away from him. "I think it is none of your business, Sergeant

Esteban!" she said, highly piqued. "And Lieutenant Conners gave permission for our *joy ride* for your information—sir!"

Only Steven's steely black eyes showed a reaction, vivid blue sparks, enhanced by the dark tone the sun and wind had etched into his already coppery features, and rendering him much like a savage, with his shock of Indian-black hair.

Steven ignored her remarks. "Take my place, Santino," he ordered tersely.

Santino shot ahead immediately, not questioning but only obeying. Esteban was well respected by all of the men and Indians, especially for his savage skill with the bow and blade, and not one questioned his intelligence when he doled out an order—Indian or not. In two short weeks the sergeant had come across strongly, and there wasn't a man, no matter how big or strong, who wished to tangle with the tall, swarthy man. Only this young woman dared talk back to him in such an insolent manner, and she had much to lose if she were not more cautious in the future. Yet, Santino knew that Esteban wanted only one thing from Monica Bennington—information.

Disturbed by the stern look in the sergeant's eyes, Monica eased her mount away from him cautiously and urged the mare forward at a quick pace. She had no desire to speak to him for he made her feel tremendously ill at ease. She had hoped to avoid an encounter with him this day, especially after the frustrating return of the dream. Even now its memory made her shiver.

But the mouse-colored mare was no match for the huge black steed although she urged her mount on. She turned aside, surprising the sergeant and throwing him off balance with her expertise in handling a horse. Steven swore under his breath and in a rapid movement lunged his black toward the mare. The mare reacted by shying violently when he made an attempt to grab for her reins. Then she fled like a frantic deer, dashing off across the grassy plain and disappearing into the woods, leaving Tina to stare in chagrin after Monica and Sergeant Esteban who rode close behind in her stormy wake.

The sharp command to halt surprised Monica as it rang through the primeval silence, resonant in the hushed stillness of the ever-thickening glade. Only the soft thudding of their horses' hooves could be heard now, the din of the one hundred being muffled now. But Monica could not bring the mare to a halt even if she wanted to, for the horse, given her head, was running wild and free.

Monica braved a quick glance over her shoulder and bit a trembling lip. His mount was nearly overtaking hers. With a frightened shriek she veered off and headed for the densely thicketed pines. These being too narrow for the speedy passage of his larger mount, Steven was forced to slow the black to a walk that merely minced between the trees.

Monica strained unmercifully at the reins causing the bit to cut deeply into the mare's soft mouth. Finally she brought the quivering beast to a halt, in the heart of the rank, dense, silent woods. Time crept by with measured slowness before she decided to dismount. She heard the sound of water trickling, a stream nearby.

As she stroked the nervous mare and murmured to soothe her, it suddenly struck Monica that she was lost. She whirled her head this way and that. But, of course, she was heading north . . . or was she? Had the sergeant given up his foolhardy pursuit? Perhaps he had decided to teach her a lesson and leave her to find her own way back to the fort? She hadn't known him for very long, but it seemed to her that it would be his nature to leave a woman to fend for herself!

"Well, I will find my way, *sir!*" she thought angrily. But a tiny voice niggled at her, repeating: *You want him to find you, even if you do fear him.*

Bah! She already had discovered it would be dangerous to spend more than a few minutes in *his* company.

Sunlight flooded warmly through the woods as Monica led her weary mare toward the bubbling murmur of nearby water. She hoped to find a cool stream. How welcoming the sound was to her burning ears. The warm, spicy earth odors which the heat liberated from the carpet of pine needles surrounded her. She listened for a time to the mellow bass of bumblebees, the finer chord of adventurous honeybees, seeking store for their empty combs. How beautiful it is here, she thought, at peace for the moment. One could surely spend the day here, content to roam about inspecting the lovely wild-flowers in their moist, cool shady haunts . . . if one were not lost.

Monica kept going. Hopefully the stream was the same one which she had spotted between the branches earlier. If she followed it she would surely come out near the fort. She had nothing to worry about, after all.

Only a few minutes had passed since she had dismounted when a startled gasp escaped her, for she could dimly see the shadowy figure of horse and man as they emerged into the open sunlight from the dark shadow of pine. Now she could clearly see the sergeant. His cold, insolent eyes were fixed on her shocked face. His white shirt was dusty and travel-stained, open to his waist, and a medallion dangled from his neck but she couldn't make out the carving on it. His fawn-colored breeches were tucked into soft black boots and he led the black by the bridle while the powerful horse tossed its narrow head, snorting, its wild dark eyes rolling at the discovery that strangers had invaded the glade before them.

Methodically Steven stroked the stallion's powerful satin neck as he approached the woman who watched him, entranced, while he wiped the flecks of foam from the horse with the gentle motion of a steady, sure hand. Time seemed to stop, yet an eternity to pass before he spoke.

"Awww, if you don't look lost, little girl," he said mockingly. Then, "It did not take you long to discover *that*, did it?"

Traces of her hectic ride remained on her pink,

flushed cheeks, and her hair had come loose and hung about her in wild disarray. "No," she ceded. "But I can fend quite well for myself, in fact as well as any man, no thanks to you." Her tone was tart-sweet but her sun-spiked countenance was determined.

Steven quirked a dark brow as a derisive grin broke out and displayed pearly white teeth against his dark face. "Is that why you are wearing breeches, *milady?*"

She glared hotly at him, knowing he was right. Still she primed the only weapon her feminine pride could allow her—her tongue with its waspish tone. "You are quite imaginative, aren't you, *sir*, with your cold, cutting remarks meant to hurt a woman."

"Woman?" He looked around as if he couldn't find one there to speak of. Then his face changed. "Be careful, kitten, your sharp claws are showing and I just might be tempted to show *you* what a real man who hasn't had any sport for a few weeks is like." Then he added, "Even if you are, ah, sporting breeches." He chuckled deeply, mockingly.

His boldness infuriated her. "If you ever so much as touch me again, I will surely become violently ill!"

With a toss of her haughty head she prepared to mount again, lifted a heel, and cried out.

"Oh—*no!*"

In two whiplash strides he had reached her and violently jerked her to him. "You little *bruja*."

She turned on him with a little sob, her only weapon now.

"Oh, Monica Bennington, don't give me that wide-eyed innocent look. It won't work with me!"

161

Her breath caught as he gazed deep into her vulnerable eyes; they had altered to a deep jungle green which imparted to them a strange fluorescent beauty, and her wild tresses made her delicate face appear much smaller than it really was. Almost heart shaped, not quite, but almost, Steven thought.

His arms went about her, pulling her to him, and suddenly his lips came down to sear across hers, his tongue, hot as a brand, exploring and penetrating with unexpected urgency. Monica bombarded him with tight clenched fists, twisting and battling against his overpowering strength, but to no avail. He kissed her again and yet again, raining hot kisses down her pulsating throat as he crushed her soft frame to him painfully. Finally she relaxed as the first true awakening seeped through her and her responses took over.

"Let me go!" she begged when he took a moment to gaze down into the heightened green of her eyes as if to see if this woman were real.

"Ah . . . sorry, Mona," he said softly against her hair.

He paused, studying the challenge of her pink, moist lips, but only for a moment before he took charge of them again.

Warmed by his passion, the scent of horse and leather intermingled with his own masculine odor, her senses came alive. Spurts of flame coursed through her body like wildfire, and trickles soon became torrents of sensation as new meaning was given to her woman's body.

Desire spread through Steven's throbbing loins as

he pressed his knees between her clenching thighs. "Damn you, *bruja*," he said softly, almost inaudibly.

His renewed possession of her lips altered and became sweet, a gentle ravishing like the swish of a bird's wings. She could not understand this, how he could bring a sudden lump of happiness to her throat. Her sense of urgency deepened, but she was unable to break away. Her body, with a will of its own, yearned to love the kisses he was raining on her very soul. Nothing in Monica's wildest imaginings had prepared her for what was happening to her, but this was not because she had lost all fear of him. She still feared this new awakening he was arousing in her inner self. Suddenly she became as apprehensive and shamefaced as the most skittish of maidens experiencing passion's first kiss. Maybe, her mind was roiled by the thought, maybe it was because the mantle of forest made it all the easier for her to forget her innocence and to yield like the bold woman she sometimes fancied herself to be.

Now, as she moaned deeply, his searing lips moved from the pulsating spot on her throat to the first upper swell of her chest. His hand took bold liberties, roaming over her waist and hip as if he had never caressed a woman before and he needed to memorize her every soft indentation.

Bewildered by her own abandoned response and her loss of self-control, Monica's shocked eyes flew open to see the black, curling nape hairs on his dark neck. He was hugging her close—much too close. Then, to her even greater shock, she felt him boldly reaching down her blouse.

"What—just what do you think you are doing, Sergeant!"

He drew back sharply and groaned as if she had kicked him in a vulnerable spot, his eyes gone angry—blacker, if that was possible. He stared hard at the slackness of her lower jaw. Then, a mocking smile spread over his taut countenance. He leaned back and it was clear that he was greatly pleased with what he had purloined.

"It was pleasurable, ma'am, while it lasted."

An inner rage took possession of Monica, and settling her hands on her slim hips, she looked at him, deep scorn etched into her lovely features. "I am not subject to lecherous authority, Sergeant!"

He caught himself up short. What was the matter with him? He had almost forgotten why he had come to this place, this damnable fort, the motive behind his endless meanderings, the diversion being *her*— revenge for his own brother's possible death. This, he decided, would never do.

He mocked, "But there doesn't seem to be anything you can do about it, *Miss* Bennington."

"Oh? Your many mistresses may think that. I for one am not content to stand by and do nothing!" Her voice was torn in half by emotions she couldn't begin to even fathom. "Can't you see that I would never . . . that you could never force me into submitting to you?"

"And," he taunted with Indian-black eyes, "will you fight earnestly next time?"

"I am willing, yes. But, Sergeant, there will be no next time," she said flippantly. "I—I've hated you since—"

He cut in. "You've never been known to shy from a fight then?" he asked with a half-smile, his eyes lazy, lidded.

She thought this over for a moment, then: "I am looking forward to standing my ground, sir. I've been known to fight like a wildcat if the need arises."

He laughed at that. "It would mean sure deflowering, Monica, not an honorable venture I might add."

"Huh! One you have never undertaken I suppose? And what do *you* know of the laws of chivalry?"

"Nothing," he said, "and I don't mean to learn them any day soon." His tone was completely matter-of-fact.

Monica's heart seemed to tighten in her chest. The near future would prove to be a heady adventure, but Monica knew she might not come out of it unscathed, nor the winner. She frowned, unaware that she looked quite worried.

"There's no need to look so disturbed, Miss Bennington. I won't go hungry until that time arrives." He grinned at her cheerfully. "I keep women. The kind that welcome me with open arms. *Sociable* ones, Mona."

"Hah. The questionable kind you mean."

"It's a cruel sport, I know," he drawled without reserve, "but I cannot stand to see all that beauty going to waste."

"Waste?" she said, holding back her next thought

165

and giving it no voice. Instead she taunted, "You must live a very crowded life, Sergeant."

"No. They always sleep on the edge of my bedroll." Again he grinned. "Afterward."

"Well, Sergeant, I hope for *all* their sakes it's a mild winter!"

"No, Miss Bennington. I'm afraid I always make nights heated enough for them so they will not freeze." He eyed her narrowly, noting her embarrassment and mortification. "Or go hungry," he added to the first.

"You are an *ass*, Sergeant and I—I hate you!"

"Silence!" he interjected. "You did not hate me a few moments ago, and for your information I was not going to force you to endure my lovemaking. It is quite evident now that you are only one of those inexperienced, quivering-thighed virgins, seeking thrills and knowing nothing of the dangerous outcomes of such behaviors. I've no time for your kind, Miss Bennington. You see, I've never had to force a woman, ever, they always come to me willingly." He tossed her a sneer meant to intimidate. "You had better keep those breeches on, Monica, just in case you make me forget I never force untried maids. Excuse me now. I have an important assignment back at the fort."

She snapped up the reins viciously. "Why you—you conceited *bore*!"

Over his shoulder he said, "Tsk, tsk, Miss Bennington, your claws are emerging again."

"Go straight to hell, Sergeant Esteban!"

He chuckled deeply. "Sorry, kitten, but that won't be a new experience for me."

Monica bristled all the way back to the fort. For certain, it was not going to be easy to sleep this night, perhaps not for many nights to come, she thought, shivering with a pure loathing she could not repress.

13

After the smoke of battle had cleared somewhat, Monica was almost her old self again. But one thought remained to nettle her. Why, oh why had it been the sergeant who had brought in those blasted horses and not Conners?

The latter was waiting impatiently for Monica to finish her visit with her stepfather. Conners's face darkened at the fresh memory of Sergeant Esteban and Monica riding in one after the other. Her cheeks had been flushed and flaming, her lovely face contorted with what he had assumed was displeasure. Conners gritted his teeth. What had caused Monica to appear so ill tempered? If Sergeant Esteban had so much as laid a hand on her . . . He wanted more than anything to have Monica as his own, for he had fallen hopelessly in love with her, he knew that now.

Ever since the fiesta when she had gazed at him in open admiration with those deep, ever-changing green eyes. Damn that Esteban! Who did he think he was bringing those horses back like some damned hero! He was incredible, in the most aggravating way.

It was hot and humid when Conners finally escorted Monica Bennington back to her quarters. A distant rumble of thunder vibrated in the uplands, and clouds were already beginning to gather to blot out the sun.

Monica smiled sweetly at the lieutenant. He thought she was especially beautiful today, even though she hadn't bothered to pin her hair up and tendrils of finespun strands curled softly at her temples. She seemed deep in thought.

"Monica," he cleared his throat to begin, "if Sergeant Esteban has done anything to offend you, I'll . . ." When she said nothing he went on quickly, deciding to ask her point-blank. "Why did you come back alone with him?"

"Alone, Lieutenant?"

"I mean first Santino Estrada came in with those crazy Indians, whooping and hollering, and then Tina told me you were out there with the sergeant. She was terribly worried, you know. I was just getting ready to saddle up, when you came riding in right after him."

"Him?" Monica said coyly. "Who do you mean, Lieutenant?"

"The sergeant!"

Monica caught the naked look of jealousy in the lieutenant's eyes and shrugged. "The mare, she shied, because I guess the horses scared her. Anyway,

169

when the sergeant finally caught up with me, the mare had carried me deep into the forest—"

He cut her sentence short. *"Forest?"*

She hesitated and quickly looked aside, avoiding his frantic gaze. "It does not matter anymore. He thought to bring me back, Lieutenant, that's all."

He did not believe her, for he was certain that was not all that had taken place out there. But for the time being he would drop the testy subject, and let her believe her story had convinced him. Right now he was thinking unpleasantly of another matter he had to contend with. The United States and Mexico were at war, and that meant he would soon be leaving the fort. Monica, not knowing what was going on, was greatly surprised at this news.

"Does this mean you will be going into action?"

Lieutenant Conners frowned unhappily. "Yes, I'm afraid so. With the Stars and Stripes flying over Northern California and the movements of General Castro unknown, we have received orders to march down El Camino and engage the enemy. We must complete the occupation of the southern part of the province." He went on, a lighter note in his voice. "The flag of the United States will be hoisted later this afternoon. There'll be a flag-raising ceremony, and the cannon have been made ready. I have been asked to forewarn you and Tina not to be near any windows at that time."

"Where is the danger, Lieutenant?" Monica spread her golden-fleshed hands.

"Oh, just a precaution. The discharge blast from

the cannon is so powerful it is possible all the main building's glass windows will shatter and I certainly would not like to have you receive even a tiny cut!"

Just then Santino appeared to inform the lieutenant that Fremont was bellowing, "Where in hell is Conners?" Santino shrugged at Conners's dark frown. "That is what he say, I just repeat this to you."

Santino was just an aid to Sutter, but Santino liked the Capitán Sutter and felt sorry for him right now. Fremont's action in taking over the fort and stationing his detachment of troops there was proving a heavy blow to Sutter's pride; besides he was using all of the best men at Fremont's own disposal.

"*Perdôneme, Señorita,*" Santino said stepping aside. He watched covertly as Conners gently squeezed her shoulder in a familiar fashion before following Santino to Fremont's quarters.

"I must speak to you later of a matter of much importance. Could you manage to take a walk after the ceremony?"

Monica peered into Conners's guileless blue eyes. "Yes, of course, Edward."

Though she replied her mind was too full of other ponderings, disturbing to say the least, for her to worry over a mere meeting later. She just hoped Edward had nothing more serious in mind than lasting friendship. Marriage to him, or anyone for that matter, had become entirely out of the question to her way of thinking lately.

Conners walked quickly away and was so preoccupied he failed to notice Sergeant Esteban leaning

171

against the buttress of the blacksmith shop. Steven's eyes crinkled at the corners as he took in Monica Bennington standing there, almost peacefully he thought, watching Conners leave. He could almost discern her contemplative thoughts as she stood dreaming of the pretty-faced lieutenant.

He is such a gentleman, Monica thought, so polite, and he is more than just a little interested in me, I am certain of it. He is so unlike that devil sergeant. Why, discounting Edward's little error in taking liberties, when he kissed me it wasn't so fiercely savage, so exhausting emotionally as it was with *that* one.

"Where are your breeches, Angel?"

Monica gritted her teeth, thinking that voice could only belong to the *savage*. Monica steeled herself and turned slowly to view him standing there, as bold as you please, and staring at her, up and down, with just his eyes roving. No other muscle of his pantherish body seemed to move. Not a flick of a lash. Not a twitch of a cheek.

"Ah, you are blushing, *señorita*. Is it over your handsome lieutenant?" he asked around the cigarillo between his teeth. "Eh, *muchacha*?"

"Don't, I say." She took a long breath. "Do not . . . ever . . . ever . . . touch me again!"

He spread his hands, breaking the laconic pose. But she was already snatching up her skirts as she whirled and then marched, nose in the air, past the sergeant. Infuriatingly his deep chuckle followed her all the way to her room, where she slammed the door with a violent, resonant thud which caused Tina,

172

who was sewing, to start and prick her finger.

"Bejesus!" Tina exclaimed.

Whirling angrily from the door, Monica crossed the room and stood looking out the window. The rain had begun and pattered forlornly against the pane. Finally the moisture had come, after all the dry arid weather.

Monica caught her wavy reflection in the pane. She saw before her a beautiful woman, one who seemed to have been transformed overnight from girlhood to glorious burgeoning womanhood. The woman who gazed back at her was not herself, but a seductive and fascinating creature, innocent and inexperienced though she was.

Through the silvery threads of moisture she saw Sergeant Esteban hastening toward the administrative offices. As he approached the rear entrance he paused, shot a look at her window and disappeared inside.

Monica nibbled her lip in contemplation. Why had he changed so abruptly from violent interrogator to such a lecherous bore? She prayed fervently that they soon would be leaving this place. When? Her thoughts were interrupted as Tina's voice came from behind.

"If you will permit me, I should like to put a question to you, Mony?"

Monica had almost forgotten about Tina who had patiently sat, her embroidery across her lap, when Monica had entered, not even saying a word as she went to the window. How unkind she was being to her beloved Tina.

"I am so sorry, Tina, what is it?"

Tina came right to the point. "Which one is it that makes you feel this way? I hope it isn't—" She bit off her next question.

Tina observed the deep flush that had suddenly filled Monica's cheeks. Was it caused by anger? Or something more serious? Tina wondered but dared not pose the question.

"I feel nothing," Monica shrugged, adding, "Which way do you mean?"

Sighing, Tina finally emboldened herself to ask, "Is it that nasty sergeant? Does he mean anything to you?" Tina looked aside hastily. "I mean—is he a part of you?"

"Tina! Whatever *do* you mean?"

"I could see that something bothered you terribly. Did he . . . he didn't? . . ."

"He did not touch me, Tina, not in the way you are thinking."

"Oh."

"Why did you ask if he's a part of me?" Monica wanted to know.

Tina slowly came to her feet, putting the embroidery aside. "Oh, I thought maybe you were falling in love. . . ."

"Tina! Please," her voice softened, "no more of this."

Tina pushed her chair back to the table. "I'll fetch us some of that hot soup from the kitchen now. It is a mite tastier than that meat drowned in beans and onions you wouldn't touch earlier." She went for her shawl, draping it over her head to keep the rain from drenching her. "I helped make the soup myself and I snuck in some of your favorite herbs."

"Oh drat!" Suddenly Monica couldn't stand the seclusion of the little room and she took down her own shawl. "I'll go with you, Tina. You know, I think I am starved and could eat ten bowls of soup right now!"

Monica and Tina stood quietly, expectantly, as did the others gathered for the flag-raising ceremony. The glory of the sunset shone through the soft, misty rain creating the most awe-inspiring spectacle they had ever witnessed. As many rays of light drifted upward through the blazened sky, a beautiful tricolored rainbow appeared to the sunward side and just as it reached its most dramatic hues of gold, lavender, and rose, a twin rainbow appeared alongside it, seeming very much like a shadow of the first.

The military men, the settlers, the prisoners, the workers, and the savages, all felt as if they were blinded of a sudden, unable to capture all the beauty of the final phase of the sunset, so fleeting was the phenomenon of the rainbow.

Against this spectacle was set another equally dramatic performance. The Star-Spangled Banner rose slowly on the flagstaff and fluttered at the gateway to the fort. The cannon began, continuing until nearly all the windows, as foretold, were broken. The cheers and cannon fire in salute to the new flag spread from Monterey to Yerba Buena, Sonoma to Sutter's Fort, as seventy years before, on the Atlantic Coast, tintinnabulation and loud cheers had welcomed the Declaration of Independence.

"God bless our land!" went up, and Monica, standing apart with Tina, knew this day marked the end of her stay here.

A blue-clad sergeant stood alone, his dark face lifted to the misty spray. Tears swam in his eyes, but no one could see them clearly. It was raining.

14

The wagon and the outriders managed to reach Temloc by nightfall of the next day without incident. For some reason the journey had been shorter traveling back to the Valley from the Rio del Sacramento. So it had seemed to Monica. But then the underlying edge of expectation was missing on the return trip. Monica knew this to be the reason she had often dozed—boredom. It mattered not that she missed most of the beautiful scenery along the way this time, for she was much too absorbed in ponderous imaginings to be observant of other things.

Branville Bennington was in an ugly mood when they reached the mansion. He ordered the servants about, thundering all the way to his salon. Word would eventually get around of his imprisonment, short in duration as it had been. Who would want to have dealings with him after he had been accused of stealing and harboring the horses? Ranchers certainly wouldn't. He did not know who had accused him in the first place, but he had a feeling that pretty-countenanced lieutenant had had something to do with it. Conners must have had his own personal motives, and moping in his salon, Branville began to believe they might have something to do with his stepdaughter.

Upstairs Monica sat quietly, a bit depressed, before her dressing table while Tina brushed out her hair which fell in long, shimmering waves to her waist. What she saw in the mirror was herself, yet inside Monica knew she had changed drastically during the last week.

Pondering her last meeting with Edward Conners after the flag-raising ceremony, when he had proposed marriage suddenly and much to her surprise, Monica's eyes widened as they had back then. Her first inclination was to answer in the affirmative, but in all fairness being wed just to get away from Temloc would be terribly unfair to Edward. She didn't love him in the least, and love remained foremost in her mind after living so long in a house without it, though she seriously doubted she would ever fall in love now. It was just too risky an undertaking to give yourself wholly to another human being.

Monica tilted her head. Still, Edward had been a gentleman—but for the one drunken liberty—and his kiss had stirred her gently in contrast to the sergeant's, which had set her body repulsively aflame. Conners's had merely evoked in her a blush and a reluctance to think that the kiss had been preparatory to what followed. Conners had accepted her inde-cision about his proposal and had promised to make a visit to Temloc as soon as circumstance would allow, begging her to decide on a firm commitment before that time.

"One hundred!" Tina said, putting the brush down on the dresser and then beginning to braid Monica's silky hair.

Monica pulled away. "No, not tonight. I am so bone-weary and to tell the truth, Tina, all I can think of now is that nice fluffy bed waiting over there for me."

Monica stood up and stretched, her youthful curves under her cotton nightgown silhouetted in the glow of the lamp. She placed the porcelain water pitcher and a glass on the bedside table, then turned and smiled. "Mmmm." She eyed the bed. "It will feel good after that disgustingly hard bunk."

Tina smiled and folded her arms across her chest as she stood back and watched Monica reenact a scene from her childhood. Monica backed up several paces and then broke into a small run, leaping and quickly burying herself beneath the patchwork quilt.

Tina smiled again, but this time with nostalgia. Victoria had sewn together the patches for the quilt herself and now Tina watched as Monica lovingly reached out and fingered the colorful squares while she stared forlornly out the window at the quarter moon.

"Good night, Mony."

"Good night, Tina."

Monica was asleep when Tina brushed away a lonely tear from a dewy cheek and then she went quietly to her own room after closing the door on Monica's peacefully slumbering form. Tina shook her head as she made her way along the dimly lighted hall. Poor child, all merry and optimistic one minute, then crushed and full of care the next. What, dear God, would become of her, Tina wondered as she closed the door to her own room.

Early in the morning the house was quiet except for the quiescent twittering of bird song permeating the thickness of the walls. But for the faint glow of rose beginning in the east, the house and grounds were still a deep twilight gray. A dog barked somewhere far off.

Monica came awake instantly. She stared up at the gray ceiling still bathed in dark shadow. She wondered if a sound somewhere in the hall had awakened her or if it was just her imagination. Usually the maids were not about until the morning light struck their rooms. Branville himself had demanded they conserve as much as possible and rely on natural resources, using candles only to light the way to the privy. He had an intense fear of fire.

Now she was certain someone stirred in the hall. She sat up with a start, listening while the scuffling sound halted abruptly outside her door. The knob turned ever so slowly and Monica watched in horror as a dark form filled the portal, her eyes seeking to identify this early morning intruder. He, yes, *he* moved toward her clumsily after shutting the door firmly behind his tall frame. She caught the potent odor of brandy fumes when he came ominously close.

"Branville!" she cried in alarm as he staggered toward her.

"Victoria," he mumbled, studying the challenge she posed, then tripped toward the bed and reached out, not for Victoria but for Victoria's daughter. But how would he know, befuddled as he was? Monica thought, feeling desperate.

He was quick despite his alcoholic stupor, and though she would have torn herself from his groping fingers, his hand caught and held onto a fold of her nightgown. She heard a rending tear and felt the threads of her bodice give way. He grasped her arm then, and flinging himself awkwardly across the bed, he pinned her half-naked form beneath his body.

"Oh dear God, spare me!" Monica prayed. She tried to scream but the shriek died in the tunnel of her throat when his coarse fingers clutched the nape of her neck, his wet lips smothering her protests.

Branville was breathing so hard that Monica thought she would surely faint from the stale odor of brandy and cigar smoke combined. Her senses began to reel. Sickened, she allowed him to pull her closer to him. Then her mind began to clear a little, and when she realized the horror that was about to take place, she renewed her battle with frantic haste, tearing at his sweaty flesh with her sharp little nails.

"Oh no, Vicky, not this time," he muttered thickly, "you won't get away so easily from me, this night you are mine."

"I am Monica! Your stepdaughter!" she said violently, choking on her fright now as the horrible moment drew closer.

He was laughing drunkenly now, excited by her futile struggles. Branville splayed both hands on the circles of her breasts, grasping them painfully. Since he had freed her shoulders and was much too intent upon his fondling to notice her change of attitude, Monica seized this opportunity to escape.

She heaved herself off the bed but tripped on the rag that had been her nightgown. She whimpered defeatedly, but nevertheless crawled toward the door that seemed miles from her. She moaned as she looked back over her shoulder to see if he was coming after her. Haltingly, he groped his way toward the door, and her terror drove her to her feet.

"C'mere, Vicky!"

She lunged sideways with the swiftness of a young doe, darting to the other side of the bed, but now his presence at the door made it impossible for her to get out. She backed against the night table and Branville chuckled at her trapped position. Monica knew what it must feel like to be a little animal ensnared in a steel trap, quivering in fear while the burly hunter came forward to claim his spoils.

"I have you now, you little bitch. Always have been evasive . . ."

Unintelligibly, he blabbered on, tripping over his own bare feet as he reeled toward her. Still he came on, and Monica felt as though he would always ruin her life.

Before Monica could scurry across the bed, he again had her in his drunken clutches. Monica tried to scream, but just like in a dream the sound died in her throat and would not come forth. Nausea rose instead while he grasped and pulled at her torn nightgown. In panic she summoned forth all the reserve strength she could muster and shoved him backward. He stumbled for a moment and in that instant Monica remembered the porcelain vessel that stood behind her on the nightstand. She grasped the handle and when he came at her again, she swung the jug with all her might. The heavy object struck his temple with a sickening thud. He groaned, losing his balance, but she struck at him again and again. He grew weaker with each blow. Blood trickled down the side of his face and finally his eyes glazed over while she stared down in horrible fascination at what she had done.

In the tentative light slanting over the sill Monica could clearly see his nude form, the blood running down and dripping onto his chest, into the black hairs there. The scene was like a grotesque nightmare, unbelievable. He had slumped to the floor, with eyes wide open and staring right past her.

Monica's heart thumped a tumultuous tune in her breast. Oh, dear God in Heaven, this could not be happening! Had she killed him? she wondered, beside herself with shock. Had she?

"No. Just could not be," Monica whispered to herself, but she knew it to be. A hard, cold truth. Still, after tossing the vessel on the bed, she hastened to kneel down beside the inert form. She felt for a heartbeat. There was none. Branville was indeed dead.

"Oh God . . ." Trembling, she bit her knuckles as she rose. Her heart was racing so fast.

She looked around dazedly and suddenly she began to cry, her body quivering with broken sobs. What was she going to do? . . .

As she stood there staggered by the enormity of her trespass, a tentative knock at the door sounded like thunder in Monica's too-hot ears. She whirled shakily to fetch her robe. Donning it, she went to stand before the door, praying that it was only Tina.

"Wh-who is it?" Monica pressed her back against the door, her breath coming in tiny gasps while she listened for a reply.

"Monica? May I come in? I heard something and . . ."

A whimper of what sounded like pain came through the wood to Tina. Casting a glance, fleeting as the wind, over the sprawled body, Monica whirled and plied her trembling hand to the knob.

"My, but you are up bright and ear—" Tina bit off the word. "My God, child, you look as if you've just seen a ghost!"

She stared at Monica who stood like an inanimate object, frozen in time, and then Tina suspiciously eyed the heavy vessel tipped carelessly onto the quilt. Afraid of what they might encounter next, Tina's eyes flew down to the bloody mess that was Branville Bennington.

Self-possessed, she soothed Monica with a few softly spoken words and then went to secure the door against any unwanted visitors.

The house was silent when Tina and Monica dragged the dead weight down the back stairs. Wrapped in an old blanket and tied like a sack of flour, the body thumped heavily on each step.

Tina silently thanked God that Alex wouldn't return for a few more days from his trip into Monterey. She had cautiously sent all the maids into the farthest garden and into the chicken coop to gather eggs. Not knowing if it was quite ethical to do so, she nonetheless thanked God that Monica still had her wits about her and hadn't collapsed under all the stress.

As Tina shoved and heaved, she thought: The dirty old man, the bastard had it coming! Over her dead body, she vowed, would any soul learn what had transpired here today. Tina had it all neatly planned. She was going to inform everyone that Branville had just up and left, couldn't stand up under the strain of losing the respect of all the ranchers. She would say he had said that before he disappeared! She had finally convinced Monica this was the only course, just take him way out back under cover of the trees and bury him. Otherwise that malicious Alex Bennington who hated everyone—his father being the only exception—would make no bones about killing Monica himself in vengeance. God only knew how many others he would destroy if he found out!

Monica's thoughts were totally of a different nature, after she had recovered enough to think. Terror, then shock, and now a blessed numbness overtook her as she aided Tina in lowering her stepfather into the crudely dug grave. The pain in her shoulders had become so unbearable that Monica nearly fainted from it—that and the sick feeling that caused her stomach to heave and turn every time she touched the still-warm body. After their ghastly chore was completed the two women swiftly made their way back under the cover of trees and bushes.

"Monica, I think it wise you go away for a time," Tina ventured slowly, then quietly calculated Monica's response. Monica could only nod numbly. "It would do you good, and I have heard news of a man in need of a housekeeper in Yerba Buena. Seems Maria heard about it while she was there picking up supplies for the kitchen. She thought about taking the position herself, but then she decided against it, having been here at Temloc for so long. The job wouldn't be as hard as a kitchen maid's, more like a housekeeper's. I happen to know the housekeeper there now. But Mrs. Anders is getting too old and Maria said she's taken ill. The new owner, a merchant captain, is away so much of the time that he's left the hiring up to Mrs. Anders and the major-domo."

Her head spinning and aching badly, Monica could only nod again. Why not? Anything would be preferable to remaining in this horrible place.

Hopefully she would forget she had ever lived here or had ever become a part of the Benningtons' lives.

It was as if Tina had read Monica's thoughts. "You will have to leave immediately." She looked thoughtful and then went on. "And there is one more thing: You will have to go by a different name. It will be a while before Alex goes looking for you. He's going to be so busy searching for Branville he won't give your absence any mind—at first. Anyway, if he did go looking for you he'd be tracing Monica Bennington, not another."

Part IV

Return to
Yerba Buena

15

"Miss Simmons. I understand from Tina Maller's letter of introduction that you wish to take over the position as housekeeper here?"

The older woman sighed deeply as she pushed her eyeglasses back up her thin nose with a blue-veined finger. She took in the worn cotton frock of the young lady seeking position and waited for her to speak.

"Yes, that is correct, Mrs. Anders. You need only introduce me to the others and I will take over from there," the young woman said politely and with much confidence. "Oh yes, you'll have to show me around the house." She smiled sweetly. "It is so big."

Mrs. Anders lifted a graying eyebrow. "So you would take over that quick, mmm?" Then she smiled, her faded brown eyes crinkling at the corners. "Good, lass. I like spirit in a woman, young or not, and so will that rogue that owns this place. Not that you'll ever be seeing the likes of that one, mind you. Only spoke with him once myself when I first come here. Guess he's always down at those card palaces of the town, gambling like crazy. Hear he's just like a professional gambler, but I've never seen him coming home late at night but once. Still the younger maids sure have." After she shot up an eyebrow with what appeared to be disgust, she went on. "You are young and too pretty for the likes of that rogue. Anyway, I don't think you have to worry much from what I've heard."

Monica blinked confusedly at this, but Mrs. Anders only went on in her monotonous undertone.

"Few women there are in this town, and the men outnumber the women. That tall, handsome rake seems to go for the older ones, though. Ah, you know the kind." She took in the shake of the girl's head. "You don't? Well you soon will see some of them, mark my words. You can't miss them, there's only a few really. All painted up, some Mex and Indians too, hanging around that hovel they call the "Saloon" and them tents they set up for the same ungodly reason. I swear them bold hussies even play a few hands themselves."

Mrs. Andres sighed wearily and stood, patting hanging wisps of hair back up into her tightly coiled gray bun. "Oh, Miss Simmons, you'll be wanting to know where the store is. Actually you can't miss it as there aren't many here in Yerba. But this one's just down the hill apiece and very limited in stock too. Course, they got sugar and flour almost all the time and then the ships bring in fresh foods, eggs, and other produce every couple weeks. You be watching out for *those* men too." She missed the rolling of the young woman's eyes. "Deserters from the army, they are, and runaway sailors and the like, or"—one eye squinted in warning—"the ones who are always running away from the law." Her eyes returned to normal. "Well child, you just plain tuckered me out with your chattering, so I think I'll go up and rest a piece after I have introduced you to some of the maids and we've had a bite. You met the major-domo already?" She didn't wait for the golden brown head to finish nodding. "Yes, yes of course you have. He said you'd do just fine, he did."

Shaking her head, Monica followed the prattling woman down the hall. She hid her amusement over the woman's quaint actions. She liked Mrs. Anders and already she was beginning to relax and enjoy her surroundings. Yes, she thought, she was going to like it here and be free from worry. Her fear of being found out was overshadowed by excitement. A brand new adventure was beginning for her since she had never known independence. Now a whole wide berth lay before her.

As they rounded the turn at the end of the long hall, Monica took in the lemon scent of freshly waxed floors. The bare parquet was a delicate pattern of differently colored woods set in squares and octagons. She noticed the great carved oaken doors, left open to air out the huge room, and the excited chirrups of birds could be heard coming from the long, open windows.

"Come along, Miss Simmons. I'll show you to

your room and then leave you to wander about the house if you want. But after your journey, and on that horrible wagon at that, you should be taking a rest in your bedroom."

The housekeeper gave Monica's attire a minute inspection before mounting the long staircase with the younger woman trailing close behind. There was a strange aura in the house, Monica thought, but one she could not put her finger on. It was as if someone had lived here before that she knew personally, or as if such a person lived here right now.

"The master has paid me for the whole month of May," the housekeeper was saying, "though it's not the first yet. Sort of a bonus, you might say. I can say one thing for him, he sure is a generous sort. Says I can hire on a whole damn army if I choose, and I'm quoting him so don't think I go about cussing." She smiled.

They went along a hallway and then entered a large, airy bedroom. "For now this is yours. Later this will be the master's after he has it decorated to his liking. He has a daybed in his salon now, anyway." Mrs. Anders quirked one side of her mouth. "Oh, the salon is locked and the only room you must not enter, as those are . . . ah . . . those are his orders. He is very private about his affairs, see."

"I understand."

"Miss Simmons, is this your only baggage then?"

"Yes."

With a shake of her head the housekeeper stared down at the carpetbag and the small reticule. "Seeing

as I've such a large bonus, Miss Simmons . . . Mona
is it?''

"Yes, Mona Simmons."

"Seeing as I've such a large bonus, Mona, it
wouldn't hurt if I loaned you a few coins."

After a moment more of chatter, the kindly
housekeeper went to her own room and Monica
sighed, looking down at her old cotton frock. It was
indeed in poor condition, as were the others. But she
had never been able to beg, it just wasn't in her to do
that.

Walking across the room, Monica drew back the
old velvet hangings, and in great puffs the dust
escaped from their inner folds. Monica coughed and
opened the floor-length window to stare in sudden
awe at the beauty of the blue bay stretched out below,
just beyond the small village of Yerba Buena.

The bay was dotted with ships of all kinds coming
into and going out of the harbor. It was almost
surrounded by the hills of the peninsula and was
guarded by the rocky entrance. She counted twenty
vessels swaying to and fro at their moorings, their tall
masts pointing to the powder-blue summer sky.
Monica took note of one in particular, a trim, square-
rigged ship with three tall masts. With her topgal-
lants filled, Monica thought, she would be magnificent to behold!

It was too far for her to decipher the lettering on the
side, but she imagined the ship bore an excellent title.
For all her ignorance of seaworthy vessels, she judged
this one to be superior. Later, if she found time she

would go down and take a closer look. Maybe even walk about town, what there was of it, and that wasn't much, she could already see.

With a deep intake of breath, Monica smelled the fresh salt air in the light breeze from the ocean, and it made her think of adventure and daring. That strange emotion again seized her as she stood there gazing out the window, that thrilling fascination that she had experienced all the way to the fort, a premonition tingling and dancing on her nerve ends. She felt lightheaded and laughed in sudden gay abandonment. Perhaps she was only breathing too deeply, but she felt something, definitely, that she was powerless to deny.

Something was about to change the course of her life. Some daring excitement was very near, like a flame being fanned to life.

Mrs. Anders left that week and the following ones Monica found herself busy with her endless duties as housekeeper. But she loved every minute, she thought now as she took down a volume of Shakespeare and blew the dust from its cover. She could see that she would have to get busy in here, too.

This room, the library, was one of her favorites, for it held a small selection of novels and the complete works of Shakespeare. She wondered about its mysterious owner for a moment and then brushed the thought aside.

Monica was very proud of her new position and got along well with Bartholomew, the major-domo, and all the household maids. How wonderful it was to be able to come and go as she pleased and not have to answer to a soul. She was content when her tasks were finished and she could slip away to her bedroom to overlook the bay from the windowseat. Here, she stitched new dresses from the material she had purchased and watched the ships coming and going all day.

What pleased Monica most was that the very first dress she had sewn in years had turned out nicely, a bright pink muslin with beige trim adorning the bodice and sleeves. Too, she had fashioned with her needle a work apron of white starched cotton to complement and go with the dress. The major-domo had complimented her the very first day she wore it.

The major-domo was a dark-skinned Peruvian who had lived in Yerba Buena since he was a lad of sixteen. The town held perhaps seven hundred folk and a great majority of them had the same dark skin.

Monica remembered the first day she had gone down to purchase some material. The fog had been gathering all morning out on the Pacific and by late afternoon the sun shone hazily through. On her lips she could even taste the salt that the lazy fog captured, and she smelled the delicious scent of the sea that traveled on a slight breeze. She had stood silhouetted against the background of Yerba Buena's grassy hills.

Earlier that same day she had climbed to the peak of Windmill Hill, where the coffee grinding mill had been erected years before, to watch the arrival of a ship carrying merchandise from the East. The wind puffed up her skirts and tugged at her shining mass, making small golden wisps escape around her pinkened cheeks. She couldn't know it but her sparkling sea-green eyes actually glowed.

Today, in rapt fascination, Monica observed the ships that were being unloaded as the townsfolk stood close by gawking at her as if she were a princess who'd stepped from a fairy tale. Monica felt uneasy as the somber women snickered under their sunbonnets at her and the sailors winked boldly into her flushed face. A dark-skinned lad sauntered up to her.

"Say, sweetheart, where do you come from so's I can come and visit you sometime? Must be up on the hill, eh?"

He kept admiring her. Monica finally told him politely that she was betrothed and that her fiancé awaited her in the saloon just in case he was of a mind to follow her back up the hill. He looked so determined, however, that Monica stretched the falsehood a bit. Not that she didn't long to have gentleman callers, but not now and not randy sailors.

"My fiancé is very handsome," she said, then flexed a muscle for the persistent sailor to see, "and he is *very* strong!" The lad backed off and let her be on her way.

Monica moved along. She purchased several yards of fabric in various colors, mostly muslin and a few yards of a coarser material for petticoats. Then she selected a handful of brightly colored bows and trimmings. She gazed dreamily at the exotic silks, soft velvets, delicate linens, cambrics, and lacy eyelet flounces, all too costly for her purse at the time. It would take her months to hoard enough for even a few yards of the finer stuff, she mused, admiring these luxuries for a few minutes more before turning away. She paid for her purchases and made her way through the curious crowd that had gathered to gape at her.

"Look, Ma, that there lady's pretty!"

"Hush, son. She's just another person."

But Monica smiled down as the family passed by and the boy beamed brightly at her and then hid his blush behind his mother's skirts.

Monica spent the next few days cutting, basting, and then finally fitting and stitching the muslin dress. The stiff white aprons were quick and simple, taking only one afternoon to assemble.

Just as Monica was placing a volume back into its slot on the shelf after dusting it off, one of the maids walked in all flushed and pretty from excitement.

"Excuse me, mum," Terri said, "but I was wondering if you'd like to come with me down to the bay tomorrow morn. My beau is coming in on a ship and well, with all the rowdies down there"—she shifted her feet—"well, would you be maybe too busy? Or, maybe not?"

"Why of course I will accompany you. Anyway there's something I want to take a look at myself."

Monica smiled saucily to herself and went through the double doors with a jaunty swing to her hips. She'd had the same thought deep in her mind for many days, to have a look at that ship she had admired from afar. And now she would, for she wouldn't be all alone down there with so many randy sailors and merchant men.

16

The bay was smooth and glassy under the lambent rays of sun. Monica could now read the title lettered on the stern of the ship. On the "bum," Tina would say.

Terri and her beau had walked, arm looped in arm, to the hovel called Al's Saloon. They are so happy, Monica thought and sighed wistfully as she watched them leave her to herself for a time. Then she returned her attention to the ship.

"*Mañana*," she said out loud, trying to pronounce the Spanish word correctly. The sunlit hair that hung beneath her bonnet blew softly in the wind.

"Howdy, ma'am." A deep voice reached her ears and a hearty chuckle followed as she started.

Monica whirled to see a great hulk of a sailor standing not five feet from her, his sea-blue eyes as watery as the ocean itself. He wore a striped shirt, open to the waist, from which his great hairy arms and bold chest protruded.

"I—" Monica did not know whether to speak to

such a man or remain silent. She was embarrassed at being caught standing there seemingly talking to a ship.

Amusement was written all over his bearded face, and the man's massive chest lifted and fell in hearty laughter. "She's not for sale today, ma'am, or on any day for that matter. The captain of 'er would slit yer throat if he caught you looking at her thataway."

Monica made haste to be away, not even staying long enough to explain why she had been looking at the ship, why the sleek, merchantman made her emotions come alive somehow.

Monica turned quickly to see if he had followed, and when she did she heard laughter as she glanced at the smiling faces of the sailors crowding around her. This was no place for a woman to be unescorted, especially when these men had all been out to sea for so long. To these men a woman came here alone for only one reason.

With relief she saw the seamen go back to their tasks. Then she turned just in time to see the broad-shouldered frame of a tall, well-dressed man saunter-ing into Al's Saloon. His attire was impeccable. She noticed the black broadcloth suit, the white silk shirt and the rakish black hat atop his dark head. She caught a glimpse of his hawkish profile and then he disappeared into the saloon.

Of course she would not go, even if Terri and her beau were still in there!

Monica hurried now, quickening her pace, and not once did she glance back over her shoulder. To do

201

that would be inviting trouble, the very last thing she wanted to intrude on the comfortable little web of contentment she had woven about herself. For now, she wanted no more unpleasantness.

Monica trudged up the hill, the sun beating down around her. The more she climbed, the more intense the heat grew, until the few tall houses on the hill shimmered in waves like some white tropical furnace.

As she walked, something tugged vaguely at her memory. The man she had glimpsed speaking to the burly sailor, the very same well-dressed man who had walked casually into the tavern was strangely familiar to her. Come to think of it, a number of things were becoming a puzzle to her—like the man she worked for. She had never seen him and more puzzling was the fact that even his name was unknown to her. Only one thing had made her aware of his presence and that was the light she had seen seeping out from beneath the salon door when she had crept to the kitchen at night to have a bite to eat.

Bartholomew met her at the front door, and she was just about to question him when she heard angry curses and vituperative words coming from the library. Bartholomew shrugged his shoulders, and without warning a strange woman appeared at the library door. She wore much sparkling jewelry and expensive French traveling apparel.

"What have we here?" she asked the man with visible annoyance, looking Monica over. "Ah, another one of *monsieur*'s lady friends?"

Juliette, Duchess of Fitz-James, did not wait for an answer but continued in a demanding tone, dismissing the younger woman as if she had not appeared at all.

"Monsieur Bartholomew, I take it Étienne has left? You did not say—before this young woman intruded."

"Étienne?" Bartholomew asked her.

"*Oui*! Steven!"

"Yes, madam, he left a quarter of an hour ago."

Juliette stamped an expensively shod foot. "Oh, he told me he was going up to change. Liar! Did he say when he would return?"

"No, madam. Now if you will excuse me, I must go out back to make certain the boy cleans the stalls before he returns."

"Yes." She waved him away with a glittering hand. "But let me know immediately when he returns. I shall await him in the library—for a time only. Then I shall return to my stateroom aboard the *Cynthia*, ah, if *monsieur* should ask."

When Bartholomew turned to exit, he took in the thunderstruck expression on Monica's lovely face. Mistaking its cause for his neglect to make an introduction, he turned back to clarify her presence to the older woman.

"Pardon. This is Juliette La Chapierre, Duchess of . . ." he cleared his throat having forgotten the title.

"Fitz-James," Juliette supplied, coming forward. "And you are Mona. Ah, let me guess . . . mistress?

Not his wife, for that is doubtful knowing Étienne. Oh yes, I do mean Steven Hawke."

Monica started at the familiar ring to the name. She whirled to face Bartholomew. "Steven?" she said. "Bartholomew, do you know the name for such in Spanish?"

"Of course, Miss Simmons. That would be Esteban."

So! She had been living under the same roof with *him*. Still, she could barely credit the fact. And of course, he was the captain of the *Mañana*! Damn him! She knew she had seen that pair of broad shoulders before. Was he to be trailing her everywhere, forever? Would she never be free of that one? He had been around ever since her disturbing dreams began. What did it all mean? Whatever, she meant to be gone from here at the first opportunity. She prayed fervently that the fullest portion of her dreams would never be realized. But she knew, now that she had seen him again, that her dreams would return this night. She would try to stay awake as long as possible, at least until the morning light. Then he dared not come to her.

Monica was bound and determined not to allow this woman—one of his many mistresses, of course— to become aware of her unease.

"My name is Mona Simmons and my position here is that of housekeeper. But not for long, you see, I am going to seek employment elsewhere this day." She swished her skirts. "Now, if you will excuse me, *Duchess*, I have duties to tend to before making my departure!''

Bartholomew's eyes widened for a moment and then he continued on his way, going down the long hall and out the rear entrance.

Monica was just about to climb the stairs when Juliette's voice interrupted her. She turned about slowly to watch the dazzling woman make her way toward her. Monica noticed for the first time that the elegant middle-aged woman seemed to acknowledge her presence. Her expression was becoming one of genuine interest now. Monica steeled herself for battle with the duchess.

"Mademoiselle Simmons, will you join me in a drink?" Juliette was smiling thoughtfully now. "I could do with a little refreshment and conversation. Perhaps some sherry?''

Astonished at this sudden change in behavior, Monica could only stare at the other woman. What could be going on in her mind that she wanted Monica's company of a sudden? Monica was suspicious, to say the least.

"I do not care for a drink myself and I am not even sure we have any sherry about, Miss . . . I mean, Duchess.''

"Please, just call me Juliette, *ma chère*. We will have something else then. But please join me as I have had such a boring time on my long journey here and I could do with a little female conversation. Please?''

Monica gritted her teeth, but sighed outwardly. What could it hurt? It was apparent Steven Hawke

205

wouldn't return for a time, and she could be packed and away before he did. But where, she wondered, just where would she go? Perhaps she could seek employment at one of the ranches as cook or maid. Yet, she shivered at the thought of doing so.

"All right. But just for a few minutes as I have much to do and I will be leaving before late afternoon," Monica told the duchess. "I will see about refreshments and then I'll join you in the salon."

Juliette watched the young woman make her way down the hall and then she whirled about. A knowing smile etched Juliette's full red lips. Her green eyes glittered. There was no doubt in her mind now. That young woman could only be Victoria's daughter, the child she had left behind in this stinkhole called California. *Mona*. Monica, of course! The many lights in her hair and those bright green eyes, not to mention Antoine's golden complexion. She was really very beautiful, come to think of it, just as Victoria had been—but so ill and out of her mind for years after the fall from her horse that only Juliette had knowledge of. No one had been able to find out where Victoria had secreted her lovely daughter—in California!

A notion crystallized in Juliette's mind while she sat waiting for Monica to bring in refreshments. Now she knew she must confront the young woman with her offer—one that the young woman would not refuse, for it was apparent she wished to be away from this place.

"Ah, Mona. That looks very refreshing, my dear."

Monica, her back turned, wrinkled her nose, knowing Juliette could not see the smirking gesture.

Juliette stood after sipping the lemon drink, walking about as if examining the *objets d'art* and peering out the window several times. "It will be dark soon," she said.

"Yes." Monica frowned lightly at the woman's strange behavior.

Suddenly Juliette whirled about and spoke in a hurried tone, her emerald green eyes sparkling like a cat's in the dark. "How would you like to come to France with me, Mona? I am in need of a lady's maid and you will do nicely," she rushed on, "*ma petite.*"

Monica's pink mouth opened soundlessly and her eyes widened. "France?" Her heart fluttered against her bosom while she clasped her hands tightly together. "France?" more softly this time.

Juliette wound her beringed fingers together. "What do you say?" Her eyes flashed. "We could leave before *monsieur* returns and he will never know what happened to his little housekeeper, *non?*"

"Oh, no. I—I just couldn't. You see, I have only a few coins left and I—"

Juliette smiled reassuringly. "You do not need any money. I will take care of everything and you will even have your own francs when you begin to work for me. You will see, *petite*. Ah, you will love France! New clothes, balls—oh, and many *beaux*! Yes, you

207

will attend the affairs with me. Let me see, I will introduce you as my ward if there are any questions. *Voilá!*"

Monica, in her great excitement failed to note the woman's extreme nervousness and the fact that Juliette was being overly indulgent and solicitous.

"Ah," Juliette began, "how well do you know Monsieur Étienne?"

Monica was abruptly alert and on guard. "We—I have never met my employer, you see, because he always comes in very late. I have only been here for two weeks now. I did not even learn his name until this day."

True, Monica thought, she has just today learned it is Steven Hawke, Sergeant Esteban, she works for!

Juliette was surprised at this bit of news, but not overly much. Ah, how well everything was turning out. How nice. This little chit was just what she had in mind for her crafty scheme. They would sail together for France in the morning, for she could see that Monica Lyons had no other choice.

17

Steven Hawke's bellowing rage echoed throughout the halls of his house. The maid Terri peered nervously about the corner, and she shivered with a fright that permeated her bones. Bartholomew came skipping breathlessly from the back entrance to see what all the commotion could be about, and espying Hawke, he came swiftly to stand before his employer, still wiping the garden dirt from his dark brow.

"Sir? Back so soon? The *Cynthia*? . . ."

"What the devil! Can't a man come to his own home without the whole household setting up a frenzy?" His brows knitted together darkly then. "The cursed ship has sailed!"

"You *were* bellowing quite loudly, sir, loudly enough to put all the maids in a tither, not to mention myself."

"Yes. So I was." He ran his lean fingers through his wind-ruffled hair. "Sorry about that. Bartholomew, fix me a brandy in my salon and await me there for I have a few more questions to ask you. I'm going out to wash and I'll be back shortly, so gather your wits about you, man."

Bartholomew nodded meekly, wondering what this was all about as he watched Hawke bolt down the hall, shedding his white shirt en route and tossing it onto a piece of expensive Louis XIV furniture. The Peruvian servant wrinkled his forehead in serious contemplation. He wondered how much the duchess's visit had to do with Hawke's peculiar manner and his rage. Ever since she had arrived in California, there had been many changes, one being the perplexing and sudden shift of mood that had come over Mona Simmons. From what he'd observed, Mona had been completely happy and her presence in the house had been a joyous occasion each and every day. He had enjoyed her pleasant smile and her melodious humming as she went about her duties. In the two short weeks since her coming, she had transformed the dreary house into a sparkling home, and not once did the cheerful maids dally under her supervision.

Why had Mona Simmons up and left with that fancy duchess from France all of a sudden?

At the moment that he asked himself the question, the doorway was filled by a tall frame. His master's wet hair glistened jet-black, in the light from the lamps Bartholomew had lighted in the salon. "Sir." He acknowledged the presence of Hawke who carried a towel draped over his dark granite arms as he strode into the room as quietly and smoothly as a black panther.

"Now, tell me about this vanishing housekeeper, my friend," Steven Hawke demanded, but more gently this time. He snatched up his brandy and settled himself comfortably in a huge leather armchair.

Bartholomew unfolded the tale, asseverating his earlier thoughts he had harbored of the housekeeper. He was startled when Steven Hawke sprang out of his chair and paced restlessly back and forth while he listened, relentless puffing on a slim cheroot. Suddenly the younger man stopped suddenly to whirl about.

"Which room did she occupy while here, Bartholomew?"

"Why, the one the old housekeeper had, the bedchamber in the front overlooking the bay, sir."

"Thank you. You may go now, Bartholomew," Steven said absentmindedly. "Oh, one other thing. Please see about my dinner."

"I was going to, sir."

"Something light and not too filling?"

"It can be done, sir."

Steven was left to ponder this puzzle alone. Damn that Juliette! What could she be up to this time? How she had found him was beyond his comprehension. Not really, knowing Juliette, he reflected. How ironic, though, that they had all come together—well, at different times—in this house, here where he thought he could have kept to himself for several months out of the year with no one to bother him. This was to have been his sanctuary, a place to renew himself—and to grieve over his loss, but he would not dwell on that for now.

He had given strict orders to his servants to speak of him only as "Mister" in his absence from the house, just in case there was any upheaval over that horse affair. He should've left those beasts where they were, holed up at Tom Hunter's rancho. And what earthly good had it done really to go and free the Benningtons? They had all disappeared shortly thereafter and he had been in no mood to go chasing after them—no, not even if one of them had turned his insides out and had caused this implacable feeling to hang on relentlessly.

Then Juliette popped up, right here at his house as if he lived down the road apiece from her, demanding to see Monsieur Hawke. How cunning to order Bartholomew to fetch him because she had an "important appointment" with him and if he delayed, well, she had said, "Steven will be quite angry with you!"

Damn, how could the servants have perceived that she was the very last person on earth he wanted to have an appointment with! Of course, it was true that Juliette would try to follow him to the ends of the earth, motivated by nothing but her lust and her greedy pursuit of riches and more jewels.

Steven ground out his cheroot in the huge ashtray and downed the remainder of his brandy, his eyes widening at the strength of this stock. He placed the glass aside, knowing he'd had enough for one day.

So! He was convinced this Mona was none other

than Monica Bennington after speaking with his servant. It didn't quite make sense, however. Why the false name? She had disappeared from Temloc about the same time this demure housekeeper had shown up at his house seeking employment. Mona Simmons! Still, it baffled him that some of the ranchers had informed him that her stepfather was missing also and that Alex Bennington was out looking for his father but had been unable to find a trace of him.

There was more. A few of the Indians released from Temloc had made him acutely aware that Monica Bennington had ridden out the same day Jess had been murdered. *Murdered.* Steven had almost choked on his anger at learning of Jess's death, but no one seemed to know just who the murderer might be. Or else someone just wasn't talking. He felt that he was butting up against a brick wall. But if he were perchance to find out who his brother's murderer was, he would impale him—or her—to the nearest tree and walk away gratified by the deed.

What did Monica know? he wondered. He should have choked the living truth out of her when he had the chance. Not that he was in the habit of beating defenseless women. But Monica was different, purely infuriating and such a schooled liar!

Now to make the situation worse, that made-up twit Juliette had snatched Monica up and carted her off to France! Odd, that after their distasteful little *tête-à-tête* she would depart so abruptly, allowing him to put her off. He could not believe, not after all this time, that Juliette would finally come to believe that he was through with her—for good. Maybe she did. But what in hell did Juliette have in mind for Monica? Or worse still, what did they *both* have in mind for *him*?

That, he would just have to discover for himself. He was getting his fill of this place anyway. There was nothing to hold him in California now that his only living relative was dead. He shook his dark head. Oh God, when would the pain end? When would he find that which he sought? If only this infernal emptiness in his gut would disappear, he thought, groaning softly from deep within.

There was nothing here, and he was weary of running around like a savage at night, draped like his Indian brothers; working at his ledgers during the day; and making love with whichever woman suited his fancy in between. He was bored as hell again. Would the cycle ever end? He thought not. Happiness was just not to be for Steven Hawke.

Abruptly, Steven vacated the salon. His footsteps resounded on the stairs, and when he reached the upper story he entered his old room overlooking the bay. Once inside, he closed the door softly and walked around this room that he knew Monica Bennington had occupied such a short time ago. It smelled of misty roses, but otherwise was devoid of any evidence that she had ever been present.

Ah, Dieu, she had been right above him all this time. *Monica.*

Steven sauntered over to the windowseat and gazed down over the bay. Small lights twinkled below, the only sign that there were humans in the bay area; and the tall masts of ships were dimly outlined in the yellow aura of growing moonlight.

He wondered what thoughts Monica had pondered as she stood here gazing down as he was now. How lovely she must have been standing in this same spot, silvered by the moonlight, gilded by the early sun, and illuminated in its rays by day. And on dark moonless nights, had she been forlorn with longing as he was now?

Steven's face darkened with a scowl and he could almost feel the silky texture of her skin beneath his fingers. He could almost, yes, could almost feel her as he had in the woods. Her breath would quicken when he lowered his lips to hers, and she would gasp when he finally captured those dew-pink lips. Ah, her arms would come up to wind like white tentacles about his neck. His hands, they would be like crystal spikes, shooting through her as he manipulated her body to electrify her soul with shimmering brightness. He would draw her to him, provoke a wistful longing in her long-lashed eyes. She would come to his deep summons. A cry would come to her lips at his touch, a cry of wonder. He would stroke her soft hills and her most secret golden mound and excite her until she was ready with the dew of her womanhood. He would hold back no longer, but plunge deeply, deeply, until she arched against him and . . . Steven shook his head to clear it of the hot, erotic vision and just caught himself before final physical release came.

Perspiration dotting his upper lip and his ardor over his daydreams beginning to cool somewhat, Steven picked up his thoughts where he had left them before losing himself in a vision of Monica and himself ardently making love.

His servant had said that she had been happy, like a ray of sunshine in an otherwise dull and methodical life. A muscle worked hard in Steven's cheek. Bah!

He was just about to turn and go, when something on the windowseat caught his wandering eye. He turned up the jade green lamp, then snatched up a dark blue dress, unfinished by the look of it. He knew the material, having worked with the textures for months now. It was muslin. Possibly overlooked in Monica's hasty departure. Bows of light blue, cornflower perhaps, embellished the bodice running down the front in a neatly spaced row, carefully and lovingly—

Holding the dress up to his face, as if he were mesmerized by the bit of cloth, Steven caught the light scent of rose petals as vague and mysterious as the delicate female that had meticulously stitched on it. To think that she had lived here right beneath his own roof for almost two weeks, without his having had this knowledge, without his knowing who paced softly back and forth above his head in the middle of the night, made his senses run rampant. He recalled something which Bartholomew had said in the salon before he had gone off to see if the *Cynthia* had sailed.

"Miss Simmons appeared awfully strange upon

hearing your name mentioned, sir. All of a sudden she was in the greatest hurry to seek employment elsewhere. She was more than glad to go off with the high-class duchess to France. That duchess even offered me money to keep my mouth shut about her taking Mona with her. At last, I had to promise her just to hold her tongue. But as I see it, sir, promises are made to be broken. Didn't you say so yourself, sir? Always turns out that way somehow. And anyway, she was foolhardy enough to believe that I would keep her secret from my own master. Hope you're not angry, sir?''

No, he hadn't been angry. Not with Bartholomew at least. He flung the sweet-smelling garment aside, thinking that something was truly missing in his life. What could it be? *What*? Something more than his need to find permanent roots. Women, he had aplenty and they were all the same, boring and incumbent. Some were passionate, true, but he had never loved one of them despite his many affairs of the heart. In fact, the only woman he had ever really trusted had been his mother, beautiful beyond comprehension, just like ... Damn her! That wheaten-haired vixen!

He should have made love to her that day in the woods, then he would surely have forgotten she ever existed! Just as he'd overlooked all the others—poof!—who had been fool enough to be ensnared by his male charisma. Not a foolish virgin that one, however, he laughed bitterly.

A great longing stirred his blood. Whatever he was

searching for in his restless and unfulfilled world, when it came into his life he would know, and it would be like a breath of fresh air, like soft sunlight after the storm cast into his befuddled and bitter soul.

Steven could feel his pulses beat rapidly when he thought, as now, of the sea opening to him while he gazed out over the moon-silvered waters. It poured into his blood, this brash excitement, leaving him eager to feel again the salty spray on his face, his ship rocking beneath his spread legs, rocking and riding the waves into the wind. Nothing in the world could equal that desire and satisfy his soul as much. But then, one other thing might.

Revenge, he would have it—on Monica—and oh, how sweet it was going to be.

Part V

La Masque

18

Crystal spikes shot through Monica, electrifying her soul with shimmering brightness.

It was at the hour of midnight that her phantom lover drew near once again, stepping out of the lavender webs of her dream.

Hypnotically, sinking deeper into it now, Monica found herself walking toward him, hearing his deep summons. A wistful longing swept over her face, and a curiousness as to what this passion was all about invaded her. He drew her, like a magnet, into his waiting arms and a cry of wonder escaped her parted lips at his touch, achingly familiar from the last times she'd found herself in this erotic dreamland. Eyes, black as thunder, fixed down on her and she caught a glimpse of what was in them.

She knew this man—she knew his name now!

With a sudden jerk of fear Monica came awake, slowly realizing that she was alone in her bed. Lambent tongues of flame still coursed through her blood and the network of her nerves. Feelings of a great loneliness washed over her, bringing tears to her eyes and a choked emptiness within. She sat there as if in a trance, for a brief frightening moment wondering if she had really been dreaming. She must have been, she told herself, for there was no reality like that in the world she knew.

Monica gasped as heat lightning flashed in the dawn sky. The curtains stirred as if a wraithlike figure slipped between their folds and then vanished without. The haunting traces of sensual pleasure, of his imaginary possession, had begun to ebb from her body moments ago and now she wondered what madness had bound her to that one again.

Lust! That was all it could be and she wanted nothing to do with the shameful feeling!

But morning was no better. The memory of the dream—no nightmare—and of his unseen presence lingered with her making her believe her life had been thrust into chaos ever since that devil had come along. She had even kill— No, don't think of that!

Monica blinked her bleary eyes and shook her head, spilling her golden brown hair about her face and trying to shove the dark vision far back in her mind.

Monica slowly descended the stairs, following the delicious fragrance of steaming coffee and the clinking of china. Now, suddenly, as she cast her cares behind her, she embraced the morning happily, carried along by a wave of excitement and expectation.

France! She could scarcely believe that she was

finally here after the many weeks at sea. Where Juliette had found the crossing distasteful, Monica had loved every moment on the east-bound ship. The song of the tall sails singing in the wind was music to her fledgling ears while she stood on deck with the blue-green waters spraying her flushed cheeks.

Today Monica wore the old blue damask gown Juliette had given her the evening before, one that Juliette's maturing figure had outgrown. The full skirt was trimmed with silken flounces and bows of ribbon of a lighter shade of blue, while a petticoat of a honeycomb pattern peeped out in front. She had artfully arranged her hair in the current fashion, parted in the middle with soft, front curls dangling at each side, and her tresses glowed with sun- and sea-kissed highlights.

Monica reached the dining room and found that although coffee and cakes had been set out, there was still no sign of Juliette or of any other this morning. It was no wonder then that she started when suddenly the grim-faced butler appeared to pull out the chair she stood by, while a French maid bustled in to pour steaming black coffee.

Monica smiled but felt a bit embarrassed at having so much attention come her way. Even though it had been this way since she had arrived at the luxurious château the week before, she could not get used to the butler, nor to being pampered and lazing about every day.

"Good morning," Monica said cheerily.

Obviously the butler could speak no English, but

the busy little maid returned her greeting. She poured the strong French coffee laced with *chocolat* from a silver pot while asking with a soft accent, "Mademoiselle Simmons will have her breakfast now?"

"I will await Lady Juliette, and coffee is fine for now, thank you," Monica said, feeling uneasy about the etiquette of her situation.

The maid smiled kindly and then left Monica to stare about the lavish dining room. Her nostrils twitched at the scent of mimosa stealing in through the long glass doors that had been thrown open much earlier. Her gaze wandered about the room. The walls were covered in rose-colored paper and the curtains were of a beige damask with delicate green threads embroidered at the edges. This was one of many lovely rooms in the medium-size château. Juliette had informed her there were many châteaux and villas much larger than this one, and her eyes had misted over strangely as she said this.

For the first time in weeks, Monica had time to ruminate. In spite of her life in this thrilling world of the French, a burning question had remained at the back of her mind, dormant until this moment. Actually, one mysterious question had led to another even more mysterious question. She could not help but wonder if she had done the right thing in coming here. Juliette had befriended her, true, but that in itself was strange; for the duchess at first had only sought to employ her as lady's maid and now she treated her as if she were an honored guest.

Another matter puzzled Monica. She could see why Juliette had desired to get away from Steven Hawke. What woman in her right mind would not? He was abominable. But then, why had Juliette gone to California in the first place? Gone through all the months of traveling on a ship when she so detested sailing?

Monica fidgeted with her cup. True, Juliette had made her aware of the fact that Steven was an old acquaintance and that she occasionally had met him on a business basis while he resided in France. Juliette had gone on to add that she found Monsieur Hawke intolerable time and again. Was this then the reason for her hasty departure from California, to get away from Steven as quickly as possible? Oh! it all just did not make much sense.

But, Monica recalled, it hadn't been Juliette who'd evaded the confrontation. No. Steven had been the one who had rudely shunned Juliette. Did he treat all women like lowly creatures then? She was truly beginning to think this was the way of it.

Monica was shrugging on this last thought when a sleepy-eyed Juliette glided into the room, clad in a scarlet silk dressing gown with red velvet slippers peeping out. Her green eyes clashed wildly with the ensemble.

The maid cracked the door leading to the kitchen and Juliette laconically gave an order in French which sounded something like omelettes to Monica. Juliette turned her attention to the younger woman then, eying her curiously while she took a seat opposite her.

"I do hope that my servants have seen to your needs properly, *chèrie*?"

"As a matter of fact," Monica began softly, "they are all so pleasant and absolutely kind that I find it hard to believe that this place is real sometimes. How can I ever repay you for bringing me into your home and employing me as your lady's maid?"

"Please," Juliette frowned and smiled at the same time, "do not rattle on so, child."

Monica, suddenly feeling alone and lost in this vast golden world, hung her head in despair. Juliette reached over to lift her dejected face and smiled again.

"Someday you shall thank me, dear child, someday you shall." Juliette's green eyes sparked with mysterious glints in their depths. "But for now," she sighed, "I just want you, my dear, to get used to your new surroundings and way of life. The—ah—maid part shall come later. I want you to enjoy yourself, have fun, ride, swim, buy lovely clothes and all at my expense." She laughed artfully. "Although I—ah—am *nearing* forty I love having younger people around and you are quite young and charming, *Mona*. You remind me of a young woman I used to know. We had great times together, her and I." Juliette sighed as if saddened, lifting her dainty coffee cup while her breakfast companion waited in silent curiosity.

"Sad, the woman passed away not too long ago, as did my husband, the Duke of Fitz-James. Since he passed away, I have been very lonely and have needed a friend like you to come along, Mona. So—let us not worry about this maid business for now, as my previous one has returned and will probably stay on for quite some time again.''

Monica blinked. "I'm sorry to hear about your husband, and your friend, Juliette."

Juliette waved aside Monica's concern, but she looked as if the memory and burden of her losses weighed heavily on her mind. Monica made a mental note never to speak of them again in the woman's presence for it was plain to her that the duchess suffered greatly over the death of her dear husband— and that of her friend.

Later, Juliette looked down from the tall window in her bedchamber as Monica strolled the green lawns decorated with lush, overgrown flowerbeds, watching her with narrowed eyes while weaving her plans. Juliette was determined to triumph over all obstacles. She barely resembled the bereaved widow she'd seemed a few hours ago as she smiled a wicked smile.

Juliette, from above, scrutinized Monica with cold calculation. Monica's cheeks were flushed a pretty pink, and sun-kissed, pale honey tendrils curled about her smooth temples. She seemed very small and insignificant to Juliette, just a mere child. Ah, but what a beauty, like a wild nymph in a green forest, unaware of the dangers that lurked all about her.

She will be like putty in Étienne's pliant fingers,

Juliette told herself.

Étienne and Antoine would become lasting enemies, and Juliette would make them finally pay for causing her to look the fool. Imagine, her own dear cousin Antoine commenting to her own friends that she was "no good" for the likes of Étienne. Pah! If she were no good, Étienne was then the scum of the earth.

Revenge—her eyes glittered—she would have it and Antoine would not keep Étienne away from her after he had learned that his young friend had amused himself with his virtuous little daughter— his long-lost daughter! Why . . . the little chit had never even so much as had a single beau. She had told Juliette as much during one of their lengthy conversations. A virgin, ah, how very convenient.

That horrible scene that she had had with Steven Hawke in California didn't trouble her a bit for Juliette was certain Étienne still desired her. If her memory served her right, he had once declared, as they lay pressed together in intimacy, that she was the most desirable woman in France.

Then Juliette recalled the liar's words a few months afterward.

"It is all over, Julie." He had replied in answer to her question of why it had to end. And then:

"Why you continue to pursue this relationship is beyond me. You knew yourself that our little liaison would never last. You said yourself you enjoyed many lovers, not just one, dear Duchess. Then when my wealth increased and I became sought after, you were willing to be my one and only paramour and to forsake all your other loving gentlemen. But"—he had sighed wearily—"I am afraid it *is* all over, and to be blunt I no longer desire you. The flame has died, Julie, and the sooner you realize this, the quicker you will be able to return to your illicit love affairs. All your many others.

"You know, if I were you I would look to my husband. He needs you, Julie, the poor fool, you know how ill he is. All the more reason why you should go back to being a nice little married duchess."

Juliette stared, looking back in time and reflecting on how she had spat back at him, "You cannot ignore me, you roué." Her breathing had become irregular and then suddenly her lips parted over gleaming teeth. "I do not believe you, *mon amour.* Let us not argue, and I will not question you again regarding your other women. You are just angry now because I have confronted you with the fact that you keep so many mistresses, true?"

Étienne had left her standing there, her mouth sagging, while he strode briskly out the door without so much as a kind word, as if he had renounced her forever.

Now, watching Monica who was strolling at the far end of the garden, Juliette realized she could commence her plan sooner than anticipated. "Six months," Étienne had said. He would be returning to France soon to check on the progress at the factory.

Ah, but just today one of the servants had brought news from Blaye that the *Mañana* had been moored at Bordeaux and that Étienne Hawke had been seen patronizing the shops and stores there! Perhaps then, he was now of a different frame of mind concerning her. He was apt to be inconstant where she was concerned, so things hadn't changed all that drastically—yet.

Now, at last, she would set her plan into motion, be rid of this unwanted friendship, and have her revenge. Now that her time for mourning was ended, it would be quite proper to have the ball of the century, one the very wealthy would not soon forget nor would the bourgeoisie.

Without entirely excluding the cheering effect produced by the sun's rays, the transparent material of the curtains served to break the strength of the light stealing in through the tall window in the boudoir.

"What remarkable beauty," Philip Bouillet remarked to Juliette who sat in a green velvet chair opposite him. She had changed from a pink dressing gown into a gold-printed satin dress adorned with full flounces.

Philip took a pinch of snuff and delicately placed it to his thin nostrils. Philip Bouillet was splendidly turned out, foppish to a degree. His tight olive-green trousers fitted his thin frame immaculately while a lace handkerchief adorned his short-waisted coat that fell in long, narrow tails. His high black boots were polished to a glossy sheen, and his graying hair was cocked in a hairdo almost too young for a man in his early fifties.

"Still, she is an ugly duckling when it comes to knowing how to dress and present herself." Juliette spoke, hiding with a lace hanky the smug look that crossed her face.

"Ah, but some day she will become a swan and perhaps sooner than she realizes," Philip said. "Where did you ever come across such a lovely companion? Surely she comes from an aristocratic family, with those high cheekbones and uptilted eyes."

"I agree, Philip, she is a unique beauty and hers is a long story. I will tell you one day all about her, but it must remain a secret between us. For now, she is only to be known as my companion, do you understand?"

"Thoroughly, dear Julie." Philip, however, eyed her suspiciously. "Why all the mystery? Is she with child? Perhaps a runaway from a well-to-do family?" He loved a scandal.

"No, Philip, nothing so tragic as all that and no more questions, please. You must swear you will not bring up Mona's mysterious background to a soul. She is an orphan for now and my companion, that is all if any should ask. Now, how long will you be staying?"

"For as long as you wish, *ma chèrie*, and as for my services? Well, you know how my reputation as a couturier has grown." He went on quickly. "But for you and your lovely companion I will produce the most elegant of gowns. It will be a pleasure of a *certainemente* to transform your ugly duckling to a ravishing swan, one that the trousered wolves will fall short of forgetting!" He sniffed pompously.

"I am quite sure you will, Philip," Juliette smiled in anticipation. "Now, what do you think you can do in less than two weeks?" Then she added quickly, before he could answer her question, "Oh! I have forgotten something of great importance. It will be as a masquerade ball, with the masks and perhaps dominoes for a part of the evening! What do you think, *mon cher?*"

The invitations had been sent, yards of flowing transparent material had been transformed into gowns of character and elegance, and all the while Juliette was ill tempered. She was fearful that Étienne would appear at any moment to bring her plans to naught. Of course, she knew Monica and Steven had never met, but nevertheless she preferred that Étienne not meet her revenge-child until the eve of the masked ball. There was a possibility that Étienne might have learned that she had whisked away his little housekeeper, even a chance that he would be aware of Monica's real name. And then, Antoine must not decide to come back to France. Otherwise, what could be so bad about taking a companion, even if she had been employed by Hawke himself? He didn't care about such trivialities anyway.

On the morning of the festivities, Monica was so excited she could barely eat, though she forced upon herself a cup of *chocolat* and a buttered croissant. Philip entered the dining room in the hope of finding her there, and when he sat down beside her he noticed she could not suppress the obvious merriment she was feeling.

"Oh Philip! Do you think they will like me?" Pure excitement was singing in her veins.

"Like you, my dear? They will absolutely love you. You shall be the belle of the ball. Take my word for it, *ma petite*." Philip selected a croissant and buttered it lavishly.

Monica sighed. "This will be the first ball that I have ever attended and I will try to remember everything that you have taught me, Philip, all the social graces and the fashionable manner in which to conduct myself. My own mother tutored me on all this long ago and I was taught how to speak and dress like an elegant woman of fashion, but I took none of it seriously back then, for my thoughts and my attentions were elsewhere, off riding a big white stallion or walking through the woods on a lovely summer noon. Still, some of the schooling has returned to my memory, of course with your help, Philip." Monica sat straighter when he indicated that she was leaning her elbows on the table.

Monica smiled. An explicable feeling of confidence always came about when she conversed with the arrogant couturier. After all, he had seen her in a state of undress while he had taken her measurements, yet he hadn't blinked an eyelash. Instead Philip had remained very businesslike despite her agonizing embarrassment, and she recalled him saying to her:

"Come now, Mona darling, you must remove your clothing and not just down to your petticoats, either. You must strip completely. Otherwise how do you think I can manage to secure a true measurement, *ma petite*?"

"Oh, all right then. If I must, I must. But turn around for a few minutes, please."

A week later, with the gown made and only a few remaining touches to be added, Monica stood, her hands on her hips, hiding her radiant smile from Philip who paced back and forth behind her adoring his princesslike creation.

But Monica pouted. "I don't like it, Philip, I just don't like it!"

"What is this?" He frowned.

Laughingly she whirled about like a sparkling sugar confection atop a music box. "I *love* it!"

Now, today, Philip sat speculating on what Mona had just revealed to him of her past and her mother. She was fast becoming an enigma to him and a marvel, both at the same time. He had the strongest feeling that she harbored some deep dark secret within those strange jewel-colored eyes.

"Now, remember to lower your eyes, blush, and flutter your lashes becomingly at all the gallant swains you encounter this evening." He held up a beringed hand. "But, don't overdo it, darling, be a little evasive and never dance with the same one more than twice. Unless, of course"—he smiled a warn-

234

ing—"unless you are prepared to face the consequences. The men in this country take these affairs quite seriously if you so much as give an inch, *petite*."

Monica gave him a feigned genteel expression, making a *moue* at him. Her voice rose an octave. "Will someone please explain to me the mental and moral value of such training?" She grinned mischievously then. "Is it not shocking that innocent girls should be instilled with the notion that there is a reason why they should not look men frankly and simply in the face?"

Philip, who had begun to giggle, now laughed heartily for the first time since Monica had known him.

"I once heard a tale of a girls' school in France. They, the young girls, were strictly forbidden to lift their eyes to a man's face."

He broke out in a grin and she begged, "Go on, Philip!"

"If any of these girls happened to be about when the old professor of eighty passed through the private courtyard there was an instant cry of alarm, '*Du monde! Du monde!*', which always meant 'the wolf in trousers and coat,' and invariably the girls trembled, blushed, and lowered their eyes in the *dreadful creature's* presence. Perhaps it was a convent, *non*?"

"*Oui, monsieur*, but of course," Monica said smoothly and fluttered her long lashes.

19

Was there some subtle magnetism in the air that night? Monica was to wonder later. She had certainly sensed something as she had descended the long staircase to the admiring looks she was receiving.

Those in the crowd milling about at the bottom of the stairs stopped whatever they were doing to stare at this vision of loveliness. The almost transparent golden gauze floated about Monica like mist from some mysterious lake and the gown did very little to conceal the firm, feminine curves of her slim, youthful body. Her hair which was done up *à la Grecque* looked like finespun silk and shone in the light of myriad candles. She exuded the sweet, yet musky fragrance of spring roses.

At the same time, Monica studied the crowd she was descending to meet. At the last minute, Juliette had decided against the dominoes, at least until later in the evening. For now the men and women wore provocative little masks, some matching the color of their wearers' gowns, but most of them were black.

Monica's mask, however, was pure white as were her shiny satin slippers. White, for the lamb led to slaughter, Juliette had thought with nasty cunning, for this was the name of the game.

"Ah, how lovely you look," Juliette complimented her unknowing victim.

The incessant music throbbed in Monica's veins as Juliette swept her along through the milling crowds, stopping often to introduce her new companion, and then moving along through the dancing couples.

Monica caught glimpses of herself in the long gilt-framed mirrors lining the halls and the lavishly decorated dining room. She was reflected iridescent gold, and her eyes were a bright silver-green tonight. Little tendrils of shining hair fell softly about her glowing face. Monica could see Monsieur de Toneau's bright green coat reflected in the mirror as he came through the throng of gay, laughing people. His glance had lingered on her when Juliette had introduced them only minutes before, and now, she just knew he was going to ask her for a dance.

"Mademoiselle Simmons?" He held out his hand and bowed stiffly, haughtily, like the pure Parisian that he was, and then taking her arm, he guided her to the center of the dance floor.

Toneau flirted outrageously with Monica while he danced divinely, holding her so near his chest that Monica thought he would surely crush her pretty bodice. The whole room seemed to be spinning as they glided expertly across the twinkling floor. All present stared, especially the young bucks and soon

Monica had become the center of attention while one male after another swept her across the floor, each fixing smoldering eyes on her gently swelling bosom. Out of the corner of her eye, Monica saw Juliette approaching. Across her arm she carried a white domino. Gold threads were embroidered throughout its encompassing folds, and they winked like stardust in the light from the long, tapered candles.

Monica had been dancing with the Baron von Haughen and he stopped when Juliette whispered to Monica.

"My dear Madam, you are not going to hide this lovely creature under that dreadful cape?" Von Haughen demanded of Juliette.

"Why yes, of course, Baron," Juliette answered sweetly. "This is, after all, a masquerade ball and it is time for a little mystery, *non*?"

"But everyone here has seen the *mademoiselle* without such a costume!" Baron von Haughen persisted, leering at the younger woman's attributes of face and figure.

"No, not all. As you well know yourself, the dashing young swains always arrive a bit later and there will be a rowdy crowd coming in shortly from the salon in Bordeaux. Come along, Monica."

The baron sniffed disdainfully and gave a stiff bow while he watched Juliette guide the lovely creature away from him. It was shocking, he was thinking, that Juliette always invited that repugnant bunch to her parties.

The dashing young swains finally made their entrance and in a short time Monica found herself maneuvered into dancing with emboldened, mock-chivalrous characters who had imbibed to excess and who muttered covetous, obnoxious endearments into her flushed face. One especially, Monica found intolerable. His breath reeked heavily of stale wine and his free hand kept roaming about her back until she glared a warning at him through narrowed eyes.

"So, they are green!" he said of her eyes and spun her about until she was dizzy.

Monica noticed while she was being whirled that many of the distinguished ladies and their husbands were taking their leave, going out with scandalized expressions on their aristocratic faces. Monica was wondering why Juliette's acquaintances ever came in the first place when they knew the company the duchess kept was not entirely up to par. Monica could not deny that she was somewhat surprised and shocked herself by Juliette's friends—most of them trousered at that.

It was obvious to Monica that Juliette was more than just a bit friendly with the raucous males and seemed to encourage them overly much, flirting and tossing her head back to laugh at the obscene tales drifting among the dancing couples and drinking men.

Philip came to Monica's rescue just as she was about to be swept away again, this time by the obnoxious Joseph Coderre with the wandering hands. She smiled in relief as Philip led her away to a distant spot on the edge of the dance floor and gratefully accepted the glass of pale champagne he proffered her. She was very thirsty, but she tried not to drink the wine too fast, because her head was already spinning. She was not used to spirits. Still, she finished her glass quickly and Philip plucked another from a footman's tray for her.

"Well, what do you think of Juliette's gallant young friends, Monica darling?"

"They are perfectly, mmm, what did you call the wolves in trousers?"

"*Du monde?* Yes, they are more wild than that, though." He cleared his throat. "I care what happens to you, dear Monica, and I want to warn you, these gentlemen—hardly that—are not beyond attempting to . . . ah . . . ravish you if you so much as bat an eyelash the wrong way, especially one as tempting as yours have proven to be. I should have forewarned you, but I was certain they would not be present at this masquerade. Juliette must have decided to invite them at the last moment, for I'm sure their names were not among those on the list. I made most of the invitations out myself."

"You have been so kind to me, Philip, and whether you are aware of it or not, you give me some self-respect." She smiled sadly. "I was beginning to wonder for a while if I had lost that capacity, until you came along and—and thank you for warning me, Philip, but I'm quite sure that I can handle the *wolves*. I promise you, I will not bat an eyelash at a single one of them for the rest of the evening. I'm

enjoying myself immensely and I shall not let a few
roués spoil my evening!''

"*Touché!*" Philip said. "Shall we dance, *mademoiselle*?" He bowed elegantly.

"Oh yes, Philip. Let's." She smiled at his handsome aristocratic look. "I was beginning to wonder if
you would ever ask."

Despite all the women Philip had been in love
with, he believed that if he had met Mona sooner, she
might have become his one and only true *amour*. But
he was nearing middle age, and Mona, to him, was
only a child-woman. Although he felt a growing
passion for her, marriage was the farthest thing from
his mind. He believed her to be unsullied, for she
never spoke of men or of certain other topics most
young women were in the habit of chattering about.
Stifling, that's what they were, the young demimondaines who frequented his shop in Paris. Their
powder was an inch thick and their teeth were
already showing brownish rot. A few came close to
being as lovely as Mona, yet they were either
enamoured of themselves, or were chattering mag-
pies who killed his admiration the moment they
opened their silly little mouths.

Mona was different. She was lovely, yes, but above
all she had a passionate warmth flickering inside and
just waiting to be torched by the right man. Philip
sighed. If he were only a little younger. Still, he
believed he would call out any man who would dare
to hurt her or disgrace her, even in a small way.
Juliette certainly was not good company for her, but

241

then Mona had a mind of her own and she wasn't about to become promiscuous; he had already witnessed the warning looks that she had shot a few eager young bucks.

Glancing over Philip's shoulder just then, Monica noticed a tall, darkly clad man enter the ballroom. He stopped, glancing quickly about as if he meant to single out someone in the crowd. After his regard raked the dimly lighted room, he moved slowly to claim a dance with a lovely blonde by the name of Michelle.

Monica knew she hadn't been introduced to this man, for she would have noticed him at once. He was at least a head taller than the rest of the men in the room, and his attire was in the height of fashion. Like a royal prince's, she thought. When he flung back the domino, as he was doing now, he revealed a white silk shirt, a black evening vest, and trousers. Other than that his identity was concealed by the high-collared domino and the black silk mask. She noticed that he danced with several women and that Juliette's gaze seemed to follow him wherever he went.

"My dear Mona, do you realize you have danced with me four times now? Recall what I told you earlier? Not to dance with the same man more than twice?"

Monica laughed, breaking her trance. The champagne she had consumed was making her slightly giddy. "Oh, but you are different, Monsieur Bouillet, or might you be playing me false, sir?" She tickled his chin with her forefinger, and he smiled down into her youthful face, alight with merriment, flushed with wine.

"Mona, soon I shall miss your happy, smiling face which has made me almost a young man again these past few weeks. What will I do without you and your youthful charms to pleasure my soul?" Philip looked almost sadly at her, but Monica didn't notice. Suddenly she felt very strange, just as she had on the night of the fiesta when Steven Hawke had rudely raked her with his dark eyes, looking much like a *bandido* in his black charro suit.

Monica smiled up at Philip. "You have become a dear friend, Philip. I hope that you will come to visit me often, but I know how far Paris is from here and . . ."

Philip had been smiling, but suddenly his expression altered. He was looking over her shoulder. Just as Monica turned to see what held his rapt attention, she encountered the tall stranger in the black domino, coming face to face with them. He finished nodding an acknowledgment to Philip, and before she knew what was happening he was sweeping her off into his strong arms, unrelenting, even as she stared in utter amazement while the haunting strains of the waltz picked up.

The handsome intruder held Monica in a stiff circle. He guided her with mindful expertise, until she felt as if she were nothing but a marionette. She was very conscious that he held her none too gently, and a muscle twitched along his jaw tensely, or was it angrily? She wasn't sure.

Her partner did not speak and was almost prudish in the way he held her, but she was becoming acutely aware of his masculine scent. He smelled strongly of brandy and tobacco. The combination was making her head reel dizzily. Beside that, all Monica noticed was the long, straight bone structure of his nose, his flared nostrils under the black mask, and the arrogant way he tilted his head.

Over his shoulder, Monica noticed Joseph Coderre. He was watching from the sidelines until Juliette sidled up to him and whispered into his ear, and then they began to dance, edging to the far side of the dance floor.

"You are frowning, *mademoiselle*."

A glance, fleeting as the wind, swept by her, as did the deep sound of his voice, for suddenly a great commotion broke out, causing the couples to come to a standstill, the music to halt, as a murmur passed through the cluster of astonished faces, whispering and looking at one another. Monica, shivering from some strange emotion sweeping her, aroused herself from her languor to wonder what all the clamor could be over.

The man Monica had been waltzing with bowed stiffly and soon disappeared. Bewildered, Monica blinked and gazed through the slits in her white mask to watch him move swiftly in the direction of the rumpus which was attracting all the males while the women remained where they were.

Monica overheard the Baroness von Haughen speaking to her husband as they brushed past her.

She swept her mask off, revealing the shocked expression on her haughty face.

"Utterly shocking. Imagine. Fisticuffs and practically all of the finer families of Bordeaux present at such an exhibition of outrageous behavior! Oh, I just knew we should have been out the door when that bunch of riffraff made their entrance. Whatever has gotten into Juliette . . ." Her voice died away as they hurried past Monica.

Monica noticed that some of the obvious courtesans were laughing excitedly, enjoying the uproar and smiling with garishly painted red lips. The musicians glanced at one another and then shrugged, settling back to wait for the incident to exhaust itself. Philip was nowhere in sight and Monica was becoming highly nervous. Only eager young swains and the painted courtesans now seemed to be present. An almost pagan atmosphere took hold, and it made Monica feel stifled and fearful. The elegant ball was being borne into a ghastly nightmare from which she had to escape.

Monica spun about to make a hasty retreat, pushing past the laughing faces, promiscuous comments trailing her. She was just about to mount the stairs when Juliette caught her by the arm and unceremoniously drew her aside.

"Where do you think you are going, my dear child?" Juliette murmured thickly. "Come with me, I wish to speak to you." She flung out her arm. "Here, in the drawing room."

They entered the dimly lighted room where Monica all at once became aware of a couple involved in a heated embrace—and more it was revealed as they drew apart on the corner sofa where they lay. Monica gulped softly and looked aside with a swift lowering of her eyes.

"Ah, Zoe and the Duke of"—Juliette waved her arm—"whatever. Would you mind, dears? My companion and I wish to have some private conversation before we resume our festivities."

The couple pulled themselves together while Juliette smiled impatiently, and they exchanged snickering glances before they departed. The duke winked at Monica and threw her a sidelong leer, both of which she missed completely as her eyes were trained on a delicate china vase. Busily a maid entered, bearing a tray containing two glasses of dark red port. She then bustled out the door as quickly as she had entered.

Juliette, Monica noticed as the maid disappeared, was showing signs of becoming befuddled. She was intoxicated. Weaving, Juliette made her way to the drinks, dismissed the maid—who had already gone—with a clumsy wave of her hand, hesitated a moment, and then returned to Monica.

Monica could only blink, confused. "Now," Juliette mumbled, offering the red liquid to Monica, "what do you think of my little masquerade? Exciting, is it not?"

Monica took the port, though she did not really wish to drink it. Well, what could one more hurt? Perhaps it would help her to sleep. She would certainly need the rest for suddenly she was experiencing the exhaustion that comes from frustration and disappointment, nothing more. Monica swallowed a bit of the liquid before she answered.

She tried not to grimace at the first sip, but found it hard not to for it was very bitter. "Yes, exciting," Monica answered in a monotone. "I was so exhausted that I only wanted to go to my bedchamber to seek repose from—from all of . . ."

Indeed she was suddenly so tired that she had to stifle the yawn that would have occurred right in Juliette's lowered face. Why was the duchess smiling at her like that, her green cat's eyes, slitted and evil?

"I never knew your eyes were so green. . . ."

Juliette smirked. "What is the matter, darling?"

"Oh, I do think that I'd better go up and lie down . . . if you will . . . pardon me?"

"*Oui*," Juliette purred. "I was just about to suggest the same, *ma petite*. Here, let me help you. I will give your apologies to the others. Some will spend the night, so you can meet them in the morning when you are wide awake and fresh."

"Spend the night?" Monica stammered, taking Juliette's outstretched arm that looked like a watery tentacle to her. "All of them? Those out there?"

Suddenly Monica was wide awake, but only for a moment before she slumped against Juliette's side. Juliette purred in a voice meant to soothe.

"*Oui*, of course. But do not worry, pet; not a soul shall bother you in your sleep. I promise. Believe me?"

"Oh . . . yes." Monica looked at Juliette, like a lost child, bewildered and confused by so many strangers about.

Before Monica could prevent Juliette's quickly moving fingers from removing her clothing, a strange languor like none she had known took hold of her. She felt the silky sheets brushing her exposed breasts sensuously.

Monica's eyes flew about the room. Bed? How, how could she have possibly gotten upstairs and in her bed so quickly? Was Juliette a witch and she, Monica, in her spell?

Juliette peered down at the languid form, glistening with sweat in the moonbeams flooding the bedchamber. She almost hated her then, for her youth, her firmly pointed breasts, her firm thighs, but most of all because she would become the object of Étienne's passion in the long hours before the break of dawn. Still, it must be done if her plan was to succeed.

He would come, Juliette was confident of that. Étienne was not one to dismiss a proposition readily. Especially when she would have Joseph inform Étienne that the beautiful vixen in the glittering white domino awaited his pleasure in her bedchamber, with nary a stitch on. Étienne enjoyed a slight amount of mystery in his women, and Juliette was certain that he had glimpsed Monica's lovely figure between the slit of her domino and the transparency of her gown.

"*Touché*," Juliette hissed before she sailed out the door, closing it softly on the immobile figure in the huge bed.

20

Downstairs in the crimson salon, Steven Hawke smoked a slim cheroot and drank sparingly of the brandy Joseph Coderre had declined, opting for more champagne in its stead.

Over the rim of his snifter, Steven peered askance at the arrogant youth, disliking Joseph for the asinine conversation he strove to hold and the proposition to which he haltingly referred. Insolently curt, Steven spoke in gruff undertones.

"Get on with it!"

"Monsieur, I am speaking of the so-luscious creature with the *ravissement* of a figure and the sweet pink mouth, like a rosebud. You know," he said as the other sat without blinking a lash, "I watched you and she dance. She had on a white domino with gold threads running through it. She looked like she would seduce that old couturier, Philip Bouillet."

Hurriedly, under the dark regard of his companion, Joseph polished off the champagne as if it were cheap ale, and Steven grimaced, revealing his thorough distaste for the young man's lack of social graces.

Steven's eyes narrowed and his nostrils flared as he blew a puff of smoke right into Joseph's coughing face. Joseph wondered if the wary silk merchant was preparing to strangle him right then and there. This was just not his cup of tea—except for the gold he'd been promised. He was hard put to face Monsieur Étienne Hawke and his infamous temper nonetheless.

"Is that all you have to say?" Steven questioned the young man who seemed to have sunk between the red cushions.

Joseph stared down as the other toyed with the gold tassel of a pillow. Then he gulped before he spoke. "Monsieur, if you d-don't I-I will have her!"

"Who the hell is *she?*"

"Ah, Mona Simmons, M-Monsieur!"

Steven was on the man in an instant. Joseph, for all his stockiness and strength, could not hold his own with Steven who was quicker by far and deadlier because of his Indian upbringing.

"I dare you to carry out that statement, Joseph"—Steven shook him like a rattle—"whatever-your-last-name-is."

"I-I really didn't mean it, I-I . . ." Joseph sputtered, looking up into the blackest orbs he had ever seen.

"It matters not who crawls into this vixen's bed, is that what she told you?" His long fingers choked the truth out of the other.

"N-No," Joseph stammered, his bloodshot brown eyes vacant and dull. "She begged solely for your pleasure, *monsieur*, and went up just a few minutes ago. Ah! I swear!"

By the collar and waistband Steven hoisted Joseph up and over to the door, Joseph's feet merely brushing the floor, his fat belly protruding because of the pressure about his middle. "Now," Steven began, "if you breathe a word of this to anyone, I'll not hesitate to blow a hole in you about the size of your fat head. Do you comprehend?" Steven ground in the other's ear.

Joseph's head bobbed up and down. Just before Steven released the wretched lad, Joseph felt something pressing against his rib cage, something hard like a pistol hidden beneath monsieur's black domino. He blanched and came near to swooning.

After Joseph scurried out like a scared rabbit, Steven peeled off his domino and, straightening his waistcoat, drained his snifter with his other hand. He then quit the crimson salon and mounted the stairs two steps at a time.

At the bottom of the staircase Juliette's gaze followed Étienne. Her eyes glittered and she rubbed her hands together, satisfied at last that her plan was coming to fruition.

Upstairs, Monica felt strangely disoriented. Her breath came quickly now, and she could not sleep no matter how hard she tried. She kicked at the silken sheets listlessly, trying to escape the unbearable heat washing over her. A persistent pounding in her head was making her skull feel as if it were splitting in two. Trying to rise to fetch a glass of water from the bedside table, she found herself too weak to complete the effort. She fell back to the bed and groaned softly.

"Oh . . . I must have had too much to drink, too little to eat." She thrashed about weakly, her voice husky. "God, am I in a heat—"

"Indeed you are, sweating. I, too, am running a temperature. . . ."

With some effort, Monica jerked her head across the pillow, fear piercing her to the bone. There was a man in her room! She struggled to sit up but found the movement more than difficult. She peered up at the tall dark figure looming over her bed.

"Who are you, sir?" When she received no answer, she said, "You have come to the wrong room. . . ."

"No mistake," Steven answered, looking down at the naked glistening form bathed in moonlight, lovelier by far than any other he had seen before. "You are not going to send me away after I have come this far, Mademoiselle Simmons."

His last words sounded definite and Monica squeaked out, "Get out of here this minute, you rake, or I shall scream."

Monica doubted she had the strength to scream, but she threatened to do so just the same. Dear God, he was removing his mask and clothing, and laughing softly, mockingly. Monica lifted herself up to lean on one elbow and stared at his naked outline with virginal awe—the first male she had ever seen nude . . . well, what she *could* see of him in the dark.

"So lovely," he murmured, "so achingly lovely."

His eyes sparkled then as the moon came out from between the intermittent clouds. He sat on the bed while unceremoniously removing his boots. "You do not seem to be in a rush to escape my passions, *ma petite.*"

He turned abruptly then and Monica thought he looked like a leering devil when his white teeth flashed boldly into her terrified face. She came out of her trance but all too tardily. She squealed as she slid to the other side of the huge bed, the effort exhausting her, but he snatched her back before she could go any farther.

"Oh no, my dear sweet Mona. You will not escape me now. You asked for me and here we are, just the two of us," he whispered into her ear, causing Monica to shiver.

His hard fingers massaged her shoulders and then he was exploring her silken body, his touch stealing her breath away. Now she was terrified by something else, the sweet tenseness between her thighs; and her face flaming, she felt a tightening of his belly as he hardened against her.

Was this the touch that had filled all her dreams? Monica wondered.

What was he talking about? Her mind whirled. Was he truly Satan then, come to gloat over her because she had murdered her stepfather? Maybe she was, in truth, dead. Oh Lord, forgive me for murdering my stepfather. She thought, desperate for absolution, but she realized it was too late. She should have begged forgiveness beforehand, months ago. I will never be the same if he does this, she told herself.

Determined that he would not, she struggled and lashed out at him, but in vain. He was covering her damp face with ardent, flaming kisses while she groaned aloud in his ear. She was just about to give in to her fate when she caught the scent of brandy fumes and the odor of tobacco. He was her stepfather all over again!

"Let me go, Branville!" Monica sobbed, trying to slap at his face but he was too quick. Could this be the ghost of her stepfather, he who had never moved so fast?

"Do not play the innocent with me, Mona. It's much too late in the game for such feeble statements," he said, his breath a harsh pull. "I'd much rather you be the lovely coquette that you really are."

If Monica had been more alert she would have noticed something familiar in his deep voice and in his free use of her name, but as it was his voice remained unidentified by her dulled senses. She suddenly braced herself for the worst, it was coming, it was inevitable, it was ugly. Would she survive it? she wondered dazedly.

Rigid as iron, his arms held her prisoner while a hand lambently palmed her breast, caressed the swell, stroking, turning a pink tidbit, causing shivers to course up and down her spine and her body to suddenly be one licking flame of fire. Then his touch changed. His hand searched downward, and against her renewed struggles the firm, strong fingers found their way to the silken crevice between her aching flesh. White-hot nibbles tugged at her ear and she cried out for him to cease, not the caresses of her ear but the other.

"Too late," he rasped, brushing her frantically beating hands aside. Then, in a somnolent whisper she could never hear, "Mona the Cat, I've wanted you for so long. . . ."

His lips fastened to hers again, he kissed her in a deep, ardent fashion that carried her almost to the point of abandonment. Almost.

"Oh God, I need you," he breathed in a tightly strained voice. "Would you have me choke from this torture, sweet?"

"Y-Y . . ." she stammered and then blurted, "yes!"

"Ahh," he murmured with a low groan of frustration, "you are cruel, woman, oh so very heartless."

"Just go away—please."

"Would you have me pay you then?"

"What!" she was outraged, but her protest exhausted her.

"Money buys a great many things," he said as if he were running quite fast, "or haven't you heard?"

"Another tried to do what you have in mind, *monsieur*, and he is not among the living today."

Now he laughed like a mischievous rake as he pressed her deeper into the smothering folds of the bedcovers, his thighs hard and intimate against her own.

Monica felt herself weakening under his ardent attack to her senses, and her breath was snatched away as a new quickening sent a tingling ache through her belly. She was past the point of struggling or caring, only aware of his hard frame bearing down upon her softer one and causing pangs to surge through her like shock waves, while his lips held hers captive.

The pins seemed to fly out of her hair then as he tangled his fingers within the softness of her tresses, freeing the long, flowing silk. He raked his fingers through her locks while continuing to kiss her deeply and very thoroughly. Then his nostrils flared, taking in the vague scent of spring roses that he remembered so well. In the deepest corner of his mind Steven knew her, but he would not allow revenge to steal from him this sweetest moment ever. He must make her part of him or forever be in torment, though she would not assent.

"Be still!" he ordered his niggling inner voice. "I must—do this." He parted her thighs and met that first blockage with his burgeoning strength. "My body feels as though it will explode!"

Her maidenhood gave way, as if a blade slashed through silk, through silken inner folds that yielded to each branding burning thrust of his bold member. She mewled softly in his ear, pulling him tighter against her, against her will. For all her preparatory moisture, the burning ache still spread through her groin into her belly, but the pain changed swiftly to sweet lapping sensations that became very bearable to her tender insides. He gently thrust himself deeper and deeper within until he became part of her body, and she responded, arching her back naturally, gathering, thrusting her slender buttocks to meet the bold strength of each plunge and pull, then missing beats as she grew weaker and sank further into the confusing mist of Circe's cup.

Monica cried out at his last thrusts, deeper and rougher, and as she felt his contractions surging through her. Finally he stopped, his passion spent, and he lay back, sighing raggedly but contentedly. He heard her tears come then as she brokenly sobbed into the pillow. His hand groped out through the dark to find her trembling shoulder damp with a moisture soft as nightmist.

"Why do you weep, sweet Cat?" He reached out. "Did I hurt you?"

"N-no," Monica lied. He had really hurt her in more ways than one. "Whoever you are, *monsieur*, just go away, I beg you."

He sighed. "That which you begged for, sweet, that is what I gave, for it was you, yourself, who desired first this liaison." Anger grew in his voice. "It is much too late to play the innocent with me. *Mon Dieu*, you and I both know you are not that."

"Please," Monica whispered imploringly. "Leave me now. You have done enough damage. Leave me with at least a shred of respect. . . ."

Her voice trailed off into nothingness and soon Steven heard her breathing evenly, tiny heartfelt sobs escaping only now and then. She was asleep.

If Steven didn't know better, he would have believed her suffering to be in earnest and her overly dramatic act authentic. But as it was, he had played Juliette's charade to the hilt. Perhaps, though, he would learn the meaning of this masque too soon.

It was now time for the unmasking.

Once again the pale moon drifted out from behind the gauzy veil of cloud and Steven peered downward at the dark specks staining the silken sheets.

A virgin!

She had remained so since he had first watched her play the little coquette at the fiesta, watched those flashing green eyes hold every male captive with her youthful charms.

His slim golden limbs swayed sinuously. Idiot, ah what have you done?

Steven put out his hand to tenderly push back a straying lock of hair that had fallen over her tear-stained cheeks, but he snatched his hand back quickly as if burnt by her baby-softness. He scowled blackly, disgusted by his dark deed this night. He had allowed the fire in his loins and his male curiosity to get the best of him.

Monica Bennington. He should have known this would come to pass one day. That first time he had looked upon the golden girl in California, she had been firmly engraved in his mind's eye and would be forever—but not in his heart. Never that!

Without delaying any further, he donned his clothes, hastily and with exact movements, minus the swagger he had affected upon entering the room earlier.

"Damn that bitch Juliette!" He swore as he closed the door softly behind him and, at once, heard the drunken laughter floating up through the halls from below.

21

Monica came awake with her teeth apprehensively set on her bottom lip, and a smattering of moisture dotting her forehead.

Monica's eyes opened onto a new sun-drenched day. Although the chamber was bathed in a topaz light that should have been comforting, to Monica it was dull, like old used coins, and lacking in spirit as she was feeling this morning.

Why? Monica wondered. Why was this morning so different from any other, as if she were a stranger to the world?

Dreams again. The troubling ones, yes, that was it. And dreams with nightmarish people, but one individual particularly had stood out monstrously clear. As he was now.

Her mind retraced the events of the past evening, and suddenly she knew who the stranger in her dream had been. The big man in the black domino, of course. She remembered dancing with him, the fight, then Juliette in the drawing room, pressing a drink into her hands, and after that a total blank! She must have passed out and dreamed of him, Steven Hawke. She shivered to recall his name.

That was all she seemed to remember now as she sat up, her eyes wide, and glanced down at her naked form. Juliette must have helped her to her room and removed all her clothing.

If only she could put her finger on more. She rubbed her eyes and grimaced suddenly from the dull pounding in her temples. Struggling to rise, Monica blanched, observing the flecks of blood staining the sheets.

Monica put a hand to her mouth and screamed softly. She jumped in horror to the edge of the bed, but the spots mesmerized her and she continued to stare at them with horrible fascination. How . . . how had they gotten there?

Gradually the nightmare took hold again. She relived that night. Monica shook uncontrollably while tears coursed down her flushed cheeks and ran over her slightly bruised breasts. Her tangled, tawny hair hung in limp strings over her puffed face and she shook her head back and forth. Ah, such misery! she thought. Then:

"No dream," she said as she remembered the intimate searching of her thighs; a liquid fire burning. She had been kissed before but never so completely devoured. The searching out of the curves of her body; the almost possessive way in which his moonraked eyes roamed to make her soul come alive with passion; his eyes filled with questions . . .

always more questions . . .

But why, why would his eyes have been so questioning? Why?

Monica knew she had been changed forever. A pervading warmth deep inside her drew her body toward something she had no real knowledge of, but she knew that she would someday.

"No, no dream at all." Her voice echoed her thought. The red specks attested to the fact that she was a pure maiden no longer.

She rested her chin on the heel of her hand. The repulsive beast—I hate him! She expelled breath and, looking up at the white ceiling, pounded bunched fists on the bed.

"He will pay for this, and dearly . . . ahhh, ahhhh yes!"

To think that she had murdered to keep her virtue intact, and to have it all come to this. Nothing but a toss for a lecherous beast! Indeed, how could she have enjoyed that haphazard intercourse herself? She had been intoxicated.

Monica flung the top sheet over the bed to shield the signs of her lost virginity from her sight. And in frustration she bit her lip and tasted salted blood just as Juliette swung cheerfully into her chamber. She stopped short, however, and taking in Monica's disassembled appearance, rushed over to her, deliberately avoiding the rumpled appearance of the bed.

"Darling, what has happened to you?" she gasped, concern lighting her eyes as she took the slim girl into her arms and crooned into her ear.

Juliette peered obliquely at Monica's close, damp face. "Please tell me, poor child, you look so distraught. What has caused you such unhappiness?"

When Monica's sobbing had ceased, she straightened while Juliette held her at arm's length, a pretense of worry etched on her freshly madeup countenance.

"Nothing."

"*Faugh!*"

Juliette pushed the tear-jeweled tendrils from Monica's face and pouted with red lips. "You will not tell me then?" she sounded wounded by Monica's evasiveness.

Juliette rose suddenly and, walking over to the commode, pulled out a blue dressing sacque from one of the drawers. Coming back, she placed it about Monica's quaking shoulders. She couldn't stand to look at the slim, youthful curves any longer, knowing what had taken place between Monica and Étienne.

"Juliette?" Monica whispered. "Who was the tall stranger in the black domino, the rakish one who had all the women beating after his heels?"

"That one! I should have used more discretion when I sent out the invitations," Juliette said, nibbling a corner of her red mouth. "But what could I do when I learned of his presence in France? Monsieur Étienne would have invited himself if I had forgotten—"

"Étienne!" Monica cut across her words. "How do you say this name in English?" She asked but was sure she already had her answer.

"Why—Steven. He is Steven Hawke to the Americans."

Juliette watched Monica's face go deathly pale. "If he has done anything to you, dear, I want you to tell me and I shall take care of him—the arrogant blade!"

"Steven Hawke? Here, in France?" Monica felt the blood crashing against her temples.

"But of course, *chérie*, did I not tell you? His business is here and his villa. It is quite a distance from here"—she shrugged—"but in France nevertheless. He is a silk merchant, one of the best, not to mention one of the richest." Juliette patted her dark curls lovingly. "He sails the seas from here to California, bringing more wealth than you could ever dream of." Juliette paused, then went on. "One reason he purchased a house in California is that I have heard he has a brother there. But I would not know about that." Juliette paused, her green eyes glittering. "Now, tell me what Étienne has done to you to make you so sad?"

Composed now, Monica shrugged. "I am not sure. He forced me, at first against my will—if I had any last night." She sighed. "Everything that happened after that was a blur. It happened so quickly." She flushed. "I—I only recall a little d-discomfort." She coughed, affectedly and fiddled nervously with her fingers. A sudden thrill thrummed in her blood.

"Ah, Mona, he defiled you and took you against

your wishes!" Juliette held up her hand. "Now, say no more. I will send for my cousin Antoine and he will know what to do with Étienne. The roué! It is time someone put an end to his puss-and-wolf games anyway. In truth, you are not much more than a child and you are my ward. He will pay for this disgrace!"

Monica stared at Juliette, frowning her confusion. "But what can he do?" she sighed. "It is over and done with and I wish to forget it ever took place."

Juliette knew a moment of indecision before she replied slowly. "*Oui*, I know you do, *chérie*. But you hate him and wish to put an end to his monstrous escapades. Just think of all the other unfortunate girls he has ravished—and will continue to ravish if we do not put a stop to him! My cousin Antoine has quite a bit of influence in France and he could ruin Monsieur Étienne!" She noted the pallor in Monica's green eyes. "Do not worry, he shall not get to you again.

"Now I will fetch a maid to prepare you a bath," Juliette went on, a placating note in her voice. "In a few days Antoine will come and we will fix that roué!"

"But—" Monica felt the startling sensation of pins and needles.

"Hush now. It is settled."

From the window of the hired fiacre Steven fixed his stare on the road winding through the meadows, on pine copses springing up now and then; and he listened to the soft trotting of the horses' hooves on the moonlit road. Patches of farmland appeared at intervals, and in the lifting indigo of night, rankled dogs barked at the unexpected rumbling of the carriage.

The distasteful masque he had quit a short time ago had left him with a sour feeling inside. He shifted uncomfortably, unused to the small fiacre. He muttered a strong oath. His mood was ugly, he was impatient with his life that seemed to have no direction, and angry because one of his prize, high-stepping bays had suffered a broken leg and he'd had to end the beast's misery. But mostly he was nettled because for the first time in his life he had taken it upon himself to deflower a maid a few hours ago!

Incongruous as it may seem he still had enjoyed her immensely, almost to the point of ecstasy. But she had not come there with him. She had not yet realized the full meaning of her womanhood. He recalled the soft feel of her beneath him, moaning as she clutched him to her thighs after he had awakened in her a tiny spark of desire—a spark that had burned out because she was a maid untutored in the ways of love.

Ah, Dieu! She wouldn't remember a thing. It was obvious she was either intoxicated or dead tired. One of the two. But still there was a motive behind it all and Juliette would approach him in time. He would sit back to await the outcome of this charade; it would come soon enough.

Faint streaks of dawn were watercoloring the late-summer sky oyster gray, coral, and Tyrian purple as

Steven alighted from the hired carriage which had halted in the lee of a dingy gray building on the quay. Sea birds swooped and shrieked in the cool gilded morning. A small weathered sign hung above a door: French Atlantic Enterprises. Steven noticed that another carriage had drawn up and in the early morning mist the russet horses appeared somewhat familiar to him. He stood watching for a moment, the wind ruffling his feathered hair at the front.

A tall, gray-haired man bounded out with zealous vitality for a man of late middle age. A wide grin broke out on Steven's face, displaying his delight.

"Monsieur Hawke! Now what the devil would a merchant captain be doing here, of all places and at such an hour. Tsk, tsk."

The gray-haired man jested with his good friend and business partner.

"Antoine, you old sea dog. When did you come in?" Steven laughed in genuine delight. "Let's go inside and warm our backsides. What do you say?"

With this Antoine followed Steven into the building to examine the silks that had been damaged by high water seeping into the warehouse.

Vaguely, Steven recalled something, call it a twinkle or a spark. It was there in Antoine's eyes. But why did this make Steven think of another just now?

Steven shrugged, following Antoine to the open crates of silks waiting for them.

Part VI

Steven & Monica

22

Monica sat staring out of the tall, many-paned windows at the garden below. Wilted flowers blew in the wind, the grass was turning yellow-green, and there was not a single, pretty flower in the vases now.

The felicity of the weeks preceding the masque was gone, and in ever-menacing dread, Monica awaited the moment when Juliette's cousin would appear.

Monica shivered and hugged her shawl closer about her shoulders. At times she felt so lonely, sitting in the bedchamber in boredom as she did now. Philip had gone back to Paris and a cheerful Juliette occupied herself with a few of the hangers-on from distant towns, like Boulogne.

One thing Monica felt a bit of consolation over was the fact that Steven Hawke was nowhere in sight and hadn't been around in several days. *One* consolation.

Monica paled at the thought of meeting him again, her eyes suddenly becoming aquamarine. The coward! But she knew he truly was not that, not really. What he was didn't matter to her anyhow, and if the opportunity ever arose she would enjoy thoroughly slapping that beast across his arrogant face!

Monica stood and, peering out the window, pressed her forehead against the platinum coolness of the pane. All at once something in the distance caught her attention.

A speck of dust was moving on the road and as it raced closer she could make out a pair of high-stepping thoroughbreds, their coats winter-apple, followed by a gleaming curricle.

Monica did not linger a second longer at the window, but went straightaway to the wardrobe. Much to her dismay she found only the pink muslin hanging there. The yellow one in her traveling bag was much too wrinkled.

The pink drooped limply and was in a disheveled state. Where were the bright gowns the duchess had given her? As if in answer, Juliette entered the bedroom unceremoniously, decked out like a queen.

Jewels dripped from her arms and neck, she reeked strongly of eau de cologne, and her dark hair was done up in an elegant fashion.

Juliette stared hard at Monica and, with a critical gaze, turned to peer into the wardrobe. Monica followed Juliette's crafty glance.

"Never mind about that now. Just put the pink one on." Juliette snapped the order, one finger outstretched. "And hurry, Antoine is here!"

Juliette stood there a second longer, watching Monica remove the dress from the wardrobe. "Shall I send Marie in to help you dress?"

"No," Monica said. "That won't be necessary." She was feeling so empty, of everything. "There is not much to do, and I would like to be alone. I—I would like a ribbon, though, if you have one to tie back my hair."

Monica was having second thoughts as to punishing Steven Hawke. Something was not right; she could feel it.

"There." Juliette pointed to the white French commode in the corner. "There is an assortment left in the drawers by Philip. I do hope the maid remembered to put them in there yesterday as I ordered. Now! Do hurry! It is not as though you are going to meet Louis Philippe, king of France!"

With that Juliette rustled out the door, leaving Monica to wonder about her cold unfriendliness of late. What had she done to bring about this sudden indifference?

With shaking uncontrollable hands Monica dragged a brush through her tangled mass of golden brown hair. She hastened to fetch the bit of cloth and, trying to create some semblance of neatness, chose a soft pink, gauze ribbon.

When that was done Monica donned the pink muslin, and running her hands down its length, she tried to iron and smooth out the wrinkles. Finding that impossible she peered at her reflection in the mirror. Color—she had plenty of that, even in her embarrassing situation and her nervous, flushed state. Only her sea-water eyes lacked their usual luster because she had been merely vegetating and idly lying about. She hadn't even gone swimming, not for over two weeks, and besides, the stream she preferred, the one behind the château, would be chilly by now.

Now it was time to face this dreadful contretemps, she thought as she straightened her spine, and shortly she stood downstairs, trembling, before the door to the salon. The footman opened up the double doors and Monica, her chin held high, swept in.

Juliette swept down over her in a second. "Antoine, may I present Mona Simmons, my ward and companion."

Juliette gently pulled Monica further into the room and guided her into the dimly lighted salon. "The poor, unfortunate child I told you about." She clucked her tongue noisily.

Monica blushed hotly and watched as a tall, handsome man struggled up from the low settee and, placing his drink on the sideboard, turned to face her.

"*Ma foi,*" he said with pent breath.

As he slowly walked around the young woman, a stunned expression crept over his thin countenance and he tried desperately to speak again. His whisper, "Victoria," was inaudible to those present.

Juliette said, "What did you say, Antoine?"

Monica, moving ever so slightly, could not know that the yellow light caught the fine-jeweled sparkles of her hair nor did she realize she fumbled nervously with the folds of her crumpled dress, a slight frown creasing her lovely brow.

Antoine stepped closer to view the girl better and Monica could smell the manliness about him. He gave her the impression that he had sailed off to see every port of the world and there was nothing left undone in his life. But she noticed a deep emptiness in his eyes, where a tiny spark flickered, and was it true or was she seeing things, was that spark coming to life right before her very own eyes?

"*Mon Dieu,* Juliette." He gasped. "Who is this girl?" And then peering down into her flushed face, he continued to study her features.

"I have already introduced her, dear cousin, she is Mona Simmons, from California." Juliette said these words with much pleasure, waiting for the startling repercussions.

"What is your mother's name, child?" Antoine Lyons said, great emotion in his voice. He already knew the answer to his question but asked it to verify his suspicions, nonetheless.

Monica stammered, groping for words. "I—I have not seen my mother for years, sir. Whether she is alive or dead, I know not." Monica paused timorously, not thinking of the consequences as she blurted, "Her name was Victoria Clivedon Bennington, sir."

"*Lyons,*" Antoine snapped in a hasty moment of sheer jealousy, unmindful that he said this out loud.

"*Mon Dieu!* Unbelievable!" Juliette cried out.

Someone in a dark corner of the room muffled a cough. Monica narrowed her eyes to peer into the shadows and then blinked from mild shock. She was suddenly oblivious to everything and everyone except *him* and his dark staring eyes.

"Monica," Antoine cried softly. "My baby, *mon Dieu, ma petite.*"

Starlight shimmered down, pulsing about Monica as she began to slip to the carpet. Strong hands found her just in time for her knees had begun to give out at the discovery that this handsome middle-aged man was her father. The arms holding her were familiar as she was being carried to the couch and a piercing sweet pleasure coursed through her, due to the discovery or the man holding her so tenderly, Monica could not tell at this time.

The man set her down and the warm sense of life left her. Tears were welling up inside of her and finally the dam burst forth. She gave vent to choking sobs as if all her glorious dreams were being realized at this moment. It seemed to be the beginning of forever.

Still, Monica felt confined by the new, conflicting emotions that battered her. She wanted to release them, give them the life they sought; she looked up into her father's handsome face.

"You are the image of your mother, did you know that?" Antoine murmured softly and guided her shoulders upward to seat her gently beside him on the couch, his arms still about her slight, quivering form.

Juliette, looking like the cat that swallowed the mouse, came to stand before them, father and daughter, so sweet, and then she lifted her gaze smugly to Steven Hawke who had moved back into the shadow but had not sat down again.

"Fetch my daughter a glass of sherry, two fingers, Juliette," Antoine ordered. "We have both had a pleasant shock, have we not, my dear?"

"Y-Yes," was all Monica could manage to murmur.

Antoine lifted her fine chin gently. "Why the surname Simmons, my darling? You are not wed then, are you?"

Monica thought for a moment and then answered slowly. "I ran away from my stepfather's home, b-because"—she hesitated, hearing a soft snort from behind, but went on—"because I hated it there, Father." It felt strange calling him that when he seemed such a stranger.

"Why?"

"The name?" she watched him nod and swallowed a gulp. "Fearing that he would search for me I took the name Simmons to hide my identity."

Juliette clucked in sympathy, but the man behind her blew breath through his nose disgustedly. Only Juliette heard this. If she had chanced a glimpse at him she would have seen that his face was hewn from granite, his eyes for one only.

Antoine's dark complexion became one of blackened, angry rage. "Why? Did he beat you?" More softly then, seeing that she moved in alarm. "Did he?" Antoine lifted the quivering chin.

"No," Monica answered softly, tearfully. "He did not beat me. I just had to—to get away, that's all!"

Antoine sighed, not content with her story. "We

275

will speak no more of it for now. I can see it troubles you to talk of the past. You are here now and you will not have to return." He paused. "Bennington. Was that the name of the man your mother married?"

Monica said a small "yes", and glanced down at her fingers clasped tightly in her wrinkled lap.

"From now on your name is Monica Elise Lyons, as it should be," Antoine said gruffly. "Let no other change it"—he smiled then—"unless of course someday you wish to marry and change it."

"Not with Étienne she won't!" Juliette was thinking as she brought them the drinks and peered over the couch past them at that remark. She received nothing but a shadow-blue look, cool and remote.

"Now," Juliette broke the momentary silence. "About that other matter. Have you forgotten, Antoine, dear cousin?"

Antoine Lyons placed his hands on his knees and looking as if he had just recalled something quite distasteful, he frowned distractedly. He glanced at Juliette and then returned his gaze to Monica and sighed deeply.

"Now what is this you tell me, madam?" Antoine asked without paying Juliette any regard, still studying his daughter as if she would vanish from the room. "I do not believe my friend Étienne Hawke has ravished my beautiful daughter." He tossed an arm over the back of the couch. "Étienne? Tell me this is not so?"

Antoine spun slowly now to face Steven, and Monica gasped softly, not daring to turn around and

276

be confronted with one of his dark looks. She hadn't realized until she had swooned that someone else occupied the room with them, seated in the darkened corner—like a huge black bat.

Juliette put on a smug, satisfied expression. "*Oui*, Étienne, tell Antoine you *did not* know that this charming *mademoiselle* was his daughter and how you—"

"Be still, Juliette!" Antoine ground out between large white teeth. "Let *him* speak for himself. Étienne?"

Steven stepped out from behind the settee, smoke curling up around his black, cropped hair. He wore a single-breasted Earl of Chesterfield topcoat with a green velvet collar reaching nearly to the firm contours of his chin. His white silk shirt contrasted with his deeply tanned complexion and he looked like a splendid male animal, impeccably attired, who made everyone in the room look dull by comparison. All but Monica. As she gawked at his finery, her cheek color became high and her body flushed with erotic tingles of pleasure.

But Monica was embarrassingly aware of her own ruffled appearance as his eyes rested on her with a sinister caress. She was finding it very difficult to even breathe with his eyes on her like that. She felt a warm flush cover her body again at remembering what had happened between them. She could almost feel again his hard body pressing her softer one, molding her to him. She swallowed the hard knot in her throat. Every inch of her body was pricked with hot points of fire, as his bold perusal raked her face. Finally his eyes flicked away and she breathed a bit easier.

Blinking black lashes once, his gaze slowly slid over to catch Juliette's glassy-eyed stare. She had seen something, and it was an exchange she did not much care for, especially not at this moment.

"Juliette is correct, *monsieur*," Steven drawled. "I could not have said it any better than the duchess."

Steven nodded toward Juliette and gave a mocking bow. "I knew only that she had a stepfather, but this, let me tell you, comes to me as a surprise much as it does you."

Steven nodded once, saying, "Yes, I took her against her will. And now I am prepared to make amends, *mon ami*. If you will permit me to ask for your daughter's hand in marriage, I will be more than kind and generous to her—as my wife," Steven finished in a dry voice.

Juliette's mouth fell agape and she appeared about to be the second one to swoon. Monica looked as if she, too, were about to faint once more as her mouth formed a silent *"No."*

Planting his hands on his knees Antoine shook his graying dark head. "*Bon Dieu.* Such a predicament!"

This being too much for Juliette, she bolted upright and snapped at Steven. "This is a matter best left for Monica to decide, is it not?"

Now all eyes rested on Monica and she felt her scalp bristle, her hands sweat. She was fully aware of the impact of Steven's intentions. He must have wanted her all along, for his prey, for revenge. She toyed with the muslin dress absentmindedly and glanced over to Juliette, trying to summon strength, but there was no help there, for the duchess only smirked.

It—it would be the proper thing to do, Monica was thinking unhappily. What would become of me if I were with child and without a husband to care for it? And what would my father think of me if I declined the proposal?

Monica could not know that she was unbelievably alluring as she kept her eyes downcast and gave her consent.

"What did you say, daughter? We could not hear you, you spoke so softly."

Antoine lifted her chin and stared into her tearful eyes. Monica sighed, a deepfelt sound.

"I said 'yes,' Father. I accept monsieur's proposal for ma-marriage. What else can I do?"

Shrugging, Monica spread out her dainty hands in full defeat.

Steven peered up at the ceiling and sighed. "*Comme il faut*," he muttered to himself. He strode over silently to the sideboard and poured himself a generous snifter of brandy, his back to his audience.

Monica glanced at his broad-shouldered frame, so cold and indifferent, and shot up abruptly to run out of the room. They watched her go, a flash of pink, and heard a tearful sob echo in the salon. Antoine stood up to follow, halted, shook his head, and decided it was better to leave her be for now.

Juliette's shrill voice followed the last note of Monica's tearful sob. She was in a shrewish, frosty mood.

"Well, well, *comme il faut*, eh? As it should be? Faugh! If this is not the most nauseating occurrence in the history of France, please tell me then what is?"

Juliette spoke to the bright-papered wall, she might as well be speaking to it, she thought and then spun about, her countenance nasty.

"Étienne! Surely you are not going to go through with this little charade and marry that silly chit?"

"Juliette, I think this matter does not concern you—or your petty jealousies," Antoine spoke harshly. "Of course he is. Monica could turn up with child and then what? I respect him for doing the proper thing."

Smiling unpleasantly, Juliette flashed back at him, her eyes blazing green fire, "Respect him! Proper!" Juliette shrieked. "Pah! He cheated her out of a proper and respectful marriage. He blackened her name and robbed her of her virtue. Don't you hate him for it?" She asked desperately. "Look at him, how he grins now!" She tossed an arm in Steven's direction.

"Juliette, you have not considered the fact that Étienne might find my daughter very attractive and not hard to fall in love with"—he cleared his throat in embarrassment for taking it upon himself to speak for the other man—"in time," he added as Steven turned slowly about.

Juliette seemed about to have a fit of the vapors.

"They are young," Antoine continued. "And as a rose slowly opens, so may their love blossom forth to full maturity." He heard one person snort and the other hiss, but he went on. "It happened to me, but alas much too late for me to do anything about it."

Antoine stared into his glass, at the amber liquid. He was thinking that he had completely forgotten to mention the death of Monica's mother, but this surely was not the time—nor the place. In fact, he might not tell Monica for months, years, until he thought her strong enough to hear it.

"Oh-hh," Juliette groaned. "Since when did my cousin become a soothsayer? And a dreadful one at that, I might add!" She threw her bejeweled arm toward Steven. "How indeed, could such a child ever be of interest to *him*? And how could she ever aspire to gain the *love* of such a man as Étienne?"

"I think, *mon ami*," Steven interrupted in a cold and hard voice, "that we should take our leave now. I have to be in Lyons by tomorrow afternoon. There are some silks that I must inspect." Nonchalantly then, he lighted a slim cheroot and exhaled the smoke slowly. "Juliette, prepare Monica for the journey. She travels with us to El Corazón. And see that she has something a bit more pleasant to wear for the journey, would you please?"

Juliette's mouth hung open in shock and disbelief at what he had ordered her to do, in her own house. She stood there, glaring at him repugnantly, and then smiled hastily. "That is all she came here with and all she shall leave with. *Not a stitch more!*"

"Why, Duchess," Steven said charmingly. "I believed that you had a special place in your heart for the girl. Ah, perhaps I was sorely misguided by your generous display of kindness." He casually measured her shocked face.

"Where is the gown that she displayed so elegantly the eve of the ball?" Steven ground out harshly.

Juliette remained speechless while he drained his snifter slowly. Antoine rose, stretched his long legs, and then prepared a fresh drink for himself. He waved an arm before he unstoppered the bottle.

"Never mind the gown, Étienne. My daughter shall have many of her own soon, I will see to that!" He chuckled, in rare humor this day of all days.

"Oh, of course she will," Juliette hissed. "Well, I can see that this conversation is getting nowhere fast!"

Juliette made to quit the salon, but was halted by Steven, his body a huge, stalwart barrier before her.

"Why? Where did you think she would end, Julie? In the gutter like your so-called delightful acquaintances? Or did you hope to gain something else by all this, this masque, this charade it has come to?"

"No." Juliette stiffened, made a gesture of defeat. "I will go and make Monica ready to depart."

"I'd rather see to it otherwise, Juliette," Antoine broke in demandingly. "Have the footman send Marie up to prepare her belongings. She will not stay here any longer than is necessary, and it is best that you do nothing to further excite her. Monica has had enough excitement and confusion for one day."

That was the end of the conversation, Juliette knowing she would never see her cousin again, at least not in a friendly fashion. It seemed that Étienne had again been one step ahead of her, as he had in the past. But she had plans, oh yes, she would not stop here, nor would they see the last of this charade as he had named it.

A short time later they were in the curricle, and Monica could barely breathe or move because her father and Steven Hawke were taking every inch of available space, their huge frames crushing her slighter one.

Monica kept her eyes fixed on Juliette standing behind the gate, so vexed at their sudden departure that she could scarcely even look at them as the curricle rolled away, tooled expertly by an elderly Englishman.

The lengthening shadows followed the curricle across the rutted and dusty road winding through the meadows, the farmland, and the darkening pine copses. Starlight began to shimmer down and the earth pulsed with twilight gray as it awaited the darker hours of night. The moon was nascent, lifting inch by slow inch above the treetops. The black coolness of night began to cloak their passage and Monica permitted her mind to wander with the sway of the curricle.

It took every bit of concentration and will power for Monica to keep from showing her frustration, and her mild discomfort at having Steven's thighs pressed so intimately against her own. His hard knuckles rested between their thighs where he had casually placed them at the onset of the journey. It was as if he sought the warmth of her tender young flesh.

Monica remained aloof and restrained, indulging in no conversation. As time went by, however, it became increasingly apparent to her that her father and Steven Hawke were more than just mere acquaintances. Indeed they seemed more like father and son because of their easy camaraderie.

Steven and Antoine spoke of business associates, "Canuts," ships and the sea, a place called El Corazón which needed a woman's touch to brighten it up; and on the last topic Steven peered obliquely at Monica with his dark brooding eyes. For a moment Monica thought that she caught a tender look on Steven's face when she happened to glance up at him, but he carefully slid his gaze from her at that second to peer out the window, leaving her to shiver at the abrupt way he turned his shoulder to her.

Antoine put his arm about his daughter then. "I am sorry we did not include you in our conversation, my darling. But Étienne and I always have much to catch up on when we have not visited for a week or two."

"That long?" she wanted to drawl shrewishly, but she let it go. Instead she murmured, "I do not mind, Antoine, I mean, Father. I am very weary, anyhow."

Steven brushed her ankle with his hightopped boot and she squirmed and pulled that leg tighter against her other one. Antoine drew her closer.

"Are you cold, my child? You are shivering like a leaf in the autumn wind." His eyes caught the soft glints the moonlight angling through the hazy, dusty window made in her hair—fine-jeweled sparkles.

She looked up at her father. "Just tired, and yes, I suppose I am a bit chilled, probably overexhausted, and pleasantly shocked, I might add, at discovering my own true father is once again part of my life— after so long." She was unable to halt the flow of emotions coursing through her, emotions which had lain dormant so terribly long. "It is more than wonderful to find that I have living and breathing kin instead of just unrelated people who seem to come and go, appearing and then disappearing just when I thought I had found someone special I could truly care for."

"I know, my dear."

She said tearfully then, "Don't ever leave me, Father, now that you have made me so happy. Please don't call me child anymore, either; I am nineteen now."

Monica pressed her tear-stained cheek against the roughness of his coat and emitted a heartfelt sigh from the depths of her breast.

"Nineteen," Antoine exclaimed softly. "Has it really been fifteen whole years since I last saw you as a babe? You were only four then, if my memory serves me correctly. But even then you had a crop of wild tawny hair and bright sea-water eyes in a plump little cherub face. You were your moth—" He cut his sentence short, looking down at her cautiously. He looked up to see Étienne nodding.

Her eyes were shuttered by her flaxen lashes beneath which tears sparkled, and her breasts rose and fell evenly in slumber.

Steven just stared at some distant spot on the darkening horizon, recalling his own memories of a time long ago and almost forgotten. He half-remembered standing on a hill and clutching his mother's hand in mutual love and respect. Or hunting with his father, a tall handsome Frenchman who called himself Chief Black Hawke, and Jess, a small lad who often tagged along discreetly and remained undiscovered until nightfall found him among the mesquite. They were all gone now, every last one. And soon he was to wed this little wisp of a vixen that had come into his life, ironically because of his brother. To say the least, it was ironic.

Steven shifted, staring out at the moon-dappled lane. Would he ever go back and continue the search for his brother's murderer? Unlikely, he thought, but it was not in his nature to give up the fight so easily.

At this point in Steven's reflections they clattered up to the Newcastle Inn in the ancient seaport of that name set upon the little Isle River. An unusual gray chill hugged the air now that the sun had vanished, making one think of early autumn, and Monica recalled that she didn't have a shawl when she opened her eyes and shivered from the crispness surrounding her.

Antoine, after searching the contents of Monica's threadbare carpetbag for a shawl, came up with only a questioning look on his tired face.

"*Mon Dieu*, Monica, don't you even own a shawl?" He blustered noisily.

Monica smiled slightly at his flabbergasted face, rubbing the sleep from her eyes. "I had one. At least a tattered remnant of one. But I found a friend behind the château who was in dire need of its comfort and warmth"—she smiled—"a feline mother and her litter of eight newborns."

Antoine smacked his high forehead with his hand. "Ah *Dieu*!"

Steven peered up into the curricle from where he stood, looking darkly virile in the descending moondust as he waited to help his fiancée down. He couldn't help but smile as he looked over her sleepy face into Antoine's puzzled one. He held the lantern higher over the door.

"Daughter," Antoine was saying, "you should not be so charitable where your own warmth is concerned. But never mind, we will fetch you one in the morning."

Urging her forward to be handed down to Steven, who was nowhere in sight now, Antoine frowned, wondering where the lad had gone off to. Monica glanced around for Steven as she was stepping out unaided, and catching sight of him, she observed his easy conversation with a pretty French girl standing between the courtyard and the inn. He was handing her something and Monica felt her heart sink as he bent to buss her hand, gallantly, lightly, and then turn back.

"Ohh-hh," Monica raged silently. "He just could

not wait to seek out a maid to warm his bed for the night, even paid her right in front for the whole world to see!"

Monica was fuming. Because of the tears shimmering in her eyes she failed to notice that Steven carried a bright shawl draped over his arm. She flew past him in a huff, leaving both him and her father to stare after her in puzzled fascination.

Then the reason for her display of temper dawned on Antoine. "I think, Étienne, that my daughter is indulging in a fit of jealous rage, be it ever so subtle. *Mon Dieu*! Already I have counted so many different facets in her personality. She is so like her mother that I find it unbelievable that two can be so alike, and it is quite sad at the same time."

Antoine sighed deeply, knowing Victoria was lost to him forever. Her cruel death had come as a shock. No, he would not dwell on the painful scene of Victoria's and Juliette's friends, Juliette herself in the party as she had sadly informed him, and how riding to the hounds Victoria had slipped from her loosely cinched saddle to her death. An oversight on the horseboy's part. Juliette had been near angry in the telling. Oftentimes he had wondered . . .

Steven ignored the incident, Monica's huffiness, and walked off to the left of the courtyard to hand the shawl to a young tavern maid. He left her standing there staring at the shawl with wide wondering eyes while he strode swiftly back to Antoine. Antoine shot him a look that was part troubled and part skeptical, "I do hope you know what you are doing, Étienne."

"I do."

23

Monica sat alone at a large table near a red brick fireplace built into a corner and darkened from years of use. A corner of her mouth lifted as a furry-tailed dormouse scurried into a safe nest in the corner and whirled, twitching its tiny ropelike tail, sniffed the air, then turned in a sudden dash to disappear into the hole.

Monica shifted, wishing suddenly she hadn't been so hasty as to come on ahead by herself. A few young blades of the *haut ton* stared at her with covetous openness and were just about to approach when they espied two tall gentlemen coming toward them, the younger one giving them a stare-down of careful admonition. All three went back to their ale, knowing the man to be dangerous despite his casual stride and attitude.

Antoine acknowledged his daughter's seating arrangement and then excused himself. He left the dining chamber, intending to make inquiries about lodging for the night.

Steven curled a corner of his crisp mouth. "*À votre service*," he said, "at your service, *mademoiselle*."

He eased his tall frame onto a bench opposite the furious Monica who acknowledged his presence with a look that immediately skittered past him to watch the serving maid weave her way in and out amidst the tables. Heads bobbed above plates, while hands lifted tankards of ale, and conversation flowed all around. The maid paused for a moment in her duties and then came to stand before the handsome couple seated at the back. She glanced from one to the other and then smiled suddenly when her lazy eyes came to rest on the roguish gentleman.

"Monsieur Hawke," she declared when she leaned forward, exposing generous mounds of flesh that spilled out from a low-cut bodice.

Monica emitted a snort of irritation which the serving maid ignored totally.

"I knew it was you, *mon cher*, what other man has such beautiful and thick black hair, *naturels*." She glared down her long, straight nose when the young woman—to her it was questionable if she was a lady or not—groaned softly at her sugar-sweet words. "What brings you here at this time of year? Such a surprise!"

Monica tapped her foot beneath the table as the serving wench bent downward to whisper in his ear, then she gasped upon viewing so much flesh as the low-cut bodice sagged.

Steven chuckled low, enjoying himself at his fiancée's expense. "Nydia, would you be so kind as to fetch my fiancée and myself platters of that famous plate of partridge and truffles? And quickly? We are quite starved from our long journey." He ended with a polite smile.

Monica was drumming her fingernails on the top of the oaken table. The gesture matched the ill-tempered look on her face. Steven peered askance at her, a wicked grin smearing his countenance.

"Fiancée!" Nydia expostulated and then quickly shut her mouth when she caught the innkeeper eying her suspiciously. Nydia at once became businesslike as she straightened her white apron with a snap. "Would you like the same brandy? And perhaps a light white Chianti for the little lady, *monsieur*?"

Steven nodded and the serving maid sashayed away, drawing glances to her partridge-plump bottom. Monica tore her narrowed glance from the sight abruptly, giving Steven her full attention now.

"Another of your secret *amours, monsieur*?" Monica questioned, tart-sweet. "My, but you do move around quickly and efficiently, don't you?" She flipped her napkin briskly. "What did this one promise you when she whispered in your jaded ear? That she would join you with the other *mademoiselle* when the moon is full?"

Steven studied her intensely for a moment, tearing down her defenses with one brutal swipe of his night-black eyes.

"Promises, my sweet?" he ground out harshly, leaning forward so that she could see the perse flecks swimming around in his irises. "You dare to speak of promises? What did the dear duchess promise *you* for that little charade you pulled back there at the château? Jewels? Perhaps a chance to meet a rich young duke? Or maybe she promised to find your father! Very cute indeed, to have you clothed like a pauper and playing the poor, meek little innocent when you met your long-lost father."

He snatched her wrist and tweaked it when she would have pulled away.

"Did she have it all neatly planned to expose me as a ravisher of gentle young darlings? You couldn't have changed all that much since we first met so unfortunately in California. Then the teasing flirt; the shy, young vixen; ah *Dieu*, and the railing virgin. What happened to all of those *pleasant* traits, my sweet?"

His look, raw and unappeased, swept her.

"Strange, that since you showed your pretty face in France you have discreetly demonstrated the character of *timid* virgin and then lastly deflowered, tearful daughter. Your father was exact in enlightening me on the fact that there are numerous facets in your personality. Too bad he failed to unearth your phony act of jealousy as a fraud."

He smiled derisively and flicked his lacy cuffs with indifferent vexation, letting go of her chafing wrist.

Unblinkingly, Monica had stared at him throughout his fiery tirade, and now having had enough she sought retaliation.

"You go too far, Monsieur Hawke." She glared with jade-dark eyes. "I shall never marry you now . . . you sarcastic, misinformed beast! I would drown myself in the Isle rather than share your bed!" She returned Steven's angry glance.

"Marry me you shall," Steven said smoothly. "But share my bed you will not."

Monica blustered, opening her mouth to toss back the soundless words, but instead she turned a mottled beet red. She caught sight of her father then and with great relief saw that he was coming to join them. He had Nydia in tow, bearing their dinner on a huge steaming tray laden with dishes fit for nobility.

Smiling sweetly at her father, Monica, in her peripheral vision, caught the ill-mannered smirk Steven aimed at her profile.

"Ah, my pet," Antoine sighed in displeasure. "I am so sorry, but I must leave you in the hands of my future son-in-law. You see that man over there?" He nodded in the direction of a well-dressed man standing just inside the entrance to the inn and pacing impatiently. "Important business calls me away."

Panic hit Monica and she stared across the room, terror shafting through her at the thought of being alone with Steven Hawke.

"What? . . ." she began, but became silent when Steven stood to excuse himself. "Where is he going now?" she wondered out loud.

"To speak to our man," Antoine furnished for her. "He has been chasing us across the whole country-side and finally managed to intercept us when we stopped. He has just informed us that there has been trouble of a serious nature aboard my ship," he spoke rapidly, being in haste to depart. "I must survey the damage and see to my man who has been injured in the raid."

"But," she said quickly, "can Steven not go in your place, Father? Surely?"

"I'm afraid not. The mate is well past his prime and I must speak to him before . . ."

"You pause, Father, why?"

"It is impolite to speak of such matters at the table, my dear."

"Such as death?"

He smiled endearingly. "You are very bold for one so young and charming, my darling Monica. You must have grown up fast." He waved a negligent hand, apologized, and then went on. "Étienne will escort you to his villa and then return to assist me in whatever unfinished business needs be performed."

"No," she began in near panic, "I will go with you, Father. Don't leave me here with—with him, please."

Monica made a move to rise, but he pushed her back down gently. His fingers moved over her pouting chin. "Now, Monica"—his eyes flashed determinedly—"do not be a silly chit. Étienne will soon be your husband and you will spend the rest of your life with him—alone. You may very well be carrying his child at this moment. You see, it is much too dangerous for you to come with me at this time, and speed is of the essence in such matters."

"Child!" Monica croaked, blanching.

"Monica"—Antoine looked at his daughter as if she had gone daft—"that is usually the case when a man has implanted his seed into a woman and it takes hold."

With a swift intake of breath, Monica cut across his words. "Father . . . *no more!*" She fanned herself with quick swipes of her napkin while Antoine only smiled ironically at her prim and proper manner. "I have decided that I do not wish to wed Monsieur Hawke and spend the rest of my years with a rogue such as he!" she snapped, her tears gone. "I hate him, Father, and . . ."

Antoine held firm against her railing. Within moments, Steven was striding back across the room in their direction, a dark expression on his countenance. She made a helpless little gesture in her endeavor to plead with her father, but he remained steadfast in his decision.

"Monica, whether you become his wife or not, you must go with Steven and await me at his villa. You have my solemn promise that nothing to which you are unreceptive will occur from now until then. When you arrive at El Corazón, Dazie will see to your comfort and your needs."

"And who just might Dazie be?" she questioned as she felt her heart give a sudden lurch at the feminine name.

"She is my housekeeper," Steven interrupted casually, but politely enough. "No worry there, my love, as she is a lovely gray-haired Frenchwoman who is well past my idea of a carnal seduction."

Steven gazed down at her, letting his stormy eyes mesmerize and measure her with cold calculation as she permitted his regard to fall like icy fingers to her quivering bosom. A wolfish smile brought out the deep slashes from his nose to his lips.

Monica's hand flew to her breast. Exerting every bit of her will to tear her eyes from his hypnotic gaze, she caught sight of her father striding into the far reaches of her vision, then out the door of the inn to leave her with the man she so detested.

It was close to the witching hour when Monica focused her weary eyes on a struggling shaft of moonbeam filtering its way through the half-closed shutters.

Finding sleep hard in coming, she bounded from the sagging bed, its springs creaking ominously in the darkened cubicle.

Tearing a quilt from the cot, she snuggled her naked, shivering form in its folds and, hugging it to her tightly, tiptoed on bare, icy feet, like a wraith in the night, to stand before the fire dying in the tiny hearth.

She stood staring with big, lonely eyes at the glowing embers for what seemed an interminable time. Finally the footfalls in the halls waned and then diminished altogether, giving her to believe she must have lingered there forever while time, behind and beyond, had passed her by.

Monica sighed as she looked out into the clear chill

night at the random scattering of stars. Her honey brown curtain of hair swung around her shoulders, the brass hairpins having come out in bed.

"A navigator could pick out a pattern on a night like this, one that could enable him to steer a ship," the captain of the vessel had told her on their journey to France when she had stood on the deck staring out at the moon-dappled sea and the huge starry sky.

It all seemed so long ago and far away now, for it had been truly a joyous adventure then, and now the future foretold only gray doom wedded to a man she had hated from the first moment he had stepped into her life. Not only that; it was plain to see that he despised her. He had made that shamelessly clear by his earlier harsh words and his lack of conversation throughout their otherwise delectable meal.

Long ago, it seemed, she had dreamed of love; yet whenever she clutched some semblance of that treasure, like a thief in the night it quickly left her, fleeing as if she were contaminated. Like her dreams fled upon arising. Oh yes, it was almost inevitable that her father would again leave her.

It never occurred to her that someone could fall in love with her someday; not like Edward Conners who merely had lusted after her body, but real, true love. And Steven, he was worse than Conners, for his lust nearly suffocated her. When he was present, it was as if sharp talons encircled her throat and pressed a little harder each time they met.

Sighing in boredom, Monica returned to her bed and prayed that nothing which might take her father

SONYA T. PELTON

from her would befall. With that she fell into a fitful
and impotent sleep during which Steven's disturb-
ingly handsome face hovered above her pillow,
grinning and mocking her like a ghost. The dreams
returned drawing her body to his imaginary possession and evoking unfulfilled desires.

Downstairs in the smoke-filled room restricted
only to men who were wont to idle away the hours in
gambling and playing cards, Monsieur Claude
Sinclair shuffled the cards. He was eager to win back
the staggering amount of francs he had lost to none
other than Monsieur Étienne.

"One more?" Sinclair questioned, though in-
censed by the deflated condition of his earlier
moneyed state. He hadn't believed all the rumors
circulating about Étienne's notorious winnings
across the country; even in the most lavish salons
Étienne frequented gentlemen were known to come
out grumbling over their losses to the cunning, slim-
fingered expertise they had witnessed.

"Sure, why not?" Steven drawled into the smoke he
had just released from his nostrils and mouth. "If
you're game then so am I, gentlemen. But one more
thing before we begin, Monsieur Sinclair. Let's have
a look at that delightful little gem you purchased for
your bride-to-be, *non?*"

The huge clock ticked away the early morning
hours and the room was almost vacant but for Claude
Sinclair, and Nydia sleepily clearing away the
overflowing ashtrays and empty glasses, and the
innkeeper dousing the oil lamps.

298

"Monsieur, shall I leave one lit for you?"

"No, that shan't be necessary," Sinclair spoke harshly. "I shall be leaving in a moment." *And almost in the poorhouse*, he was thinking.

Minus one precious ring bedecked with diamonds and centered with a priceless emerald, Sinclair indeed felt poor and bested. So, it was true that Étienne Hawke, merchant captain dealing in silks, definitely lived up to his reputation as a devil-may-care gambler. Those smiling slashes in his cheeks as he picked up the gem and deposited it in his waistcoat, Sinclair was not soon to forget.

Sinclair had plans for Monsieur Silk and his fiancée. He was certain that Nydia would follow the man to his room. So it was with great surprise and disappointment that he observed the serving wench going out the front door, and not to Étienne Hawke's room as he had suspected.

Sinclair continued in the low light of one lamp to muse on his play of revenge. But of course, none other than the *demimondaine*, Michelle de Medicie, she who had been Étienne's paramour on and off for the last two years. Who could forget that tall, slinky, promiscuous blonde? He would rather have her than the mousy little Frieda he was to wed come Saturday. But alas, Frieda's father was a land baron, and her dowry was plentiful and large.

Michelle would be insanely jealous to find Monsieur Étienne had decided to take for himself a fiery-blooded American—monsieur had said offhandedly, that she had a temper to match the subtle fires in her tawny hair—the one who had sat alone earlier and had looked as demure and innocent as a maiden. Apparently she was without funds, judging by her disheveled appearance, but still young and beautiful beyond words. Like a little white dove. What would monsieur want with such a pauper? Perhaps her innocent countenance belied her ability to entertain such roguish gentlemen in bed. Dressed in fine raiment, she would be a sight to see.

Sinclair bellowed loudly and in a few moments the sleepy-eyed innkeeper peered around a wooden beam. *"Monseigneur?"* He yawned and blinked several times.

"Send a boy for a carriage as I must leave posthaste for Paris!" Monsieur Claude Sinclair demanded.

Ominous dark clouds began to gather above the inn, and as Steven moved quietly, cautiously, so as not to awaken Monica from her exhausted slumber, he noticed that the room had become chill, the embers having gone out long since. After replenishing the logs and lighting a new fire, he went to stand before her bed.

The flames in the hearth sent forth a lazy glow that penetrated the shadowy darkness, and Steven could see her now. The quilt had come away as she moved in her sleep, and as she turned over, Steven caught sight of white, rounded breasts before she presented him with a smooth curving back on which pale gilt-tipped lengths of hair twirled and twined in seductive profusion.

Steven felt his blood rise, and much to his surprise, upon seeing her in such a state of undress and

300

languid vulnerability, Steven desired her so that he was quite frustrated. It would be easy to slide in beside her and take her against her will, he was thinking, but that would only be going against the pact he had made with himself to leave her alone. Unless, of course the idea of having children should ever arise and that would come from a mutual agreement between them.

Then, he thought, she could well be with child at this very moment, but time would tell the truth soon enough. He was only marrying her to keep his friendship with Antoine Lyons, he told himself, and there would come a time when her father would see what a beautiful and conniving daughter he had. Then Steven could be rid of her for good when Antoine discovered that she was anything but a sweet young lady; and if there was a child to consider, it would be solely his, he would make certain of that. There were ways for a man to eliminate and condemn his wife in France.

The engagement ring in his waistcoat reminded Steven that Monica would soon be his wife and he walked carefully to the opposite side of the bed where he reluctantly slid it onto the slim third finger of her left hand. She stirred slightly in her sleep, and peering down at her face softened in repose, Steven thought she appeared most angelic, if not for the wicked slant of the long lashes that fringed her eyes. He checked himself then and strode swiftly from the overwarm chamber.

*   *   *

In the moonlight the hawk again came to Monica.

But the beast of prey was different, much different this time. Now he was a man, a real flesh-and-blood man. Still, Monica knew he was only a dream conjured up by her weary mind and as such she felt safe succumbing to his magic, her subconscious mind drifting, dreamily drifting into its arms.

Come, sweet dream, do what you will, there is no danger here—come, beautiful man . . .

Steven, hoping that his potent whiskey breath would not jolt Monica to full wakefulness, stripped and carefully slid, naked, into the bed beside the jewel of his desire, the woman he so craved, to the point of madness.

He had sat below in the taproom, the bottle he had purchased cradled between long, stretched-out legs, replenishing his cup each time he saw it empty. True, he had promised himself to leave her alone, had told her as much. But each time he had stared down into his cup, the amber liquor spreading like the motion of liquid sun, radiating into his eyes the jewel-like tones of her hair, his desire grew apace with his everwarming mood.

Steven found his body and soul wanting her, each thought one of desire, each breath released from his lips a tongue of flame so that no matter his condition by the time he set his half-finished bottle down on the rough-hewn table and stood to his feet, he knew he would go to her. He would be gentle.

Steven mounted the stairs, paused on the landing and then went on more determined than ever, his body like hardened virile leather, his whirling mind as if sick with the fever of first, greenhorn love.

Unable to resist the ever-heightening temptation, Steven surrendered to it while midnight whispered through the shadowy curtains and his head reeled giddily like a schoolboy's.

Now he held her as if she were a precious work of art, a newly painted canvas and he must take care not to disturb its delicate melding of colors. With sensitive fingers he explored the glorious contours unfolding beneath his careful manly touch, and he was attuned to her faint writhing movements that resembled those of an exotic butterfly emerging from its chrysalis. She was, Steven understood, bewildered even though she dreamed on and on. . . .

Monica's dream lover kissed the most integral part of her soul and she was transported back in time, into a misty dream haven that somehow seemed so very real. She walked on a moonbeam, exposing her wings to the air, soaring, and before her arose black twinkling eyes, arms held out to her. She drank him in with her eyes. He appeared older to her. Tiny lines were deeply etched around his eyes, and he seemed to be suffering from some strange malady. But peace and love flowed into her and in this strange mistiness there was content and ease.

A thousand suns were pouring through the open windows of her soul. She was light and buoyant. She was enslaved. She flamed with passion when his lips, moving with such gentleness, swept from her own to her throbbing throat and cherished her taut, blue-veined breasts and delicate-hued nipples.

"Precious jewels . . . ah, *chèrie*, you are. I want to fill you with honey."

She could hear him now. His voice resounded in her soul and Monica opened first like a sweet rosebud and then like a wanton rose spreading itself to the incandescent body of radiating sun, in warmth, in brilliance, splendor. The masculine voice urged her forward. It was the language of summery flowers, of pink things just being born; and her own soul was emerging, expanding upward. Her sexuality was coming into a flowering state. My God, was she dreaming? If so, she would not open her eyes and come awake to shattering reality. No, not yet . . .

The arrow of love pierced her then as the virile cheek pressed her own softer one. From afar, Monica could hear herself panting as the flame came alive in her belly.

Consumed with the beauty of sexual love, Steven sighed deeply as he entered her moist haven. With fire and fury pounding in his blood, the puissance inherent in a man, his passion towered and he made powerful thrusts. And Monica was pleasured beyond her wildest dreams. Her dream lover drove, a restless roaring tide of savage ferocity, to the integral part of her quintessence, drawing her to an end she would always remember but would defy until reality delivered her.

Steven roared to a spellbinding climax never before known to him in such pure white ecstasy, ecstasy which lit his very soul. He moved away and slipped quietly from the wondrous creature sound asleep in the mussed bed. His heart pounded, his nerves quivered with the exertion of having fully tasted her sweet nectar and of having filled her to overflowing with his own warmed honey.

Monica had not been just a night's pleasure to him, he found himself agreeing when his conscience spoke to him in a soft, gentle voice and then chided him for taking her while she was again vulnerable and bone-weary from her long journey. He had not abused her tender parts, but had been a gentle lover though he admitted now that he had been too hasty—and yes, he had been selfish in his ravishment of her.

Steven slipped from the room, closed the door softly, and made his silent passage to his own room across the hall.

24

Morning dawned dark and gloomy with a light, intermittent rain falling softly against the window and urging Monica to wake to its trickling tune which pervaded the stillness of the room. She had had the dream again, and this time the hot, voluptuous sensation had stayed with her. Monica blushed hotly against the cool sheets.

It had been a dream, hadn't it? . . .

Monica hugged the quilt closer about her nakedness to hide from the expected chill and then, finding it warm as toast in the room, bolted upright wondering who had rekindled the fire during the wee hours.

"Who indeed!" And just how much had the stranger witnessed during that time. Hah! No stranger at all, but that one who trailed ever after her, hounding her, never giving her one moment's peace!

Monica cast the quilt off in a huff, and throwing her long, slender limbs over the side of the high bed, she caught sight of a dazzling jewel surrounded by lesser gems, which were also breathtakingly beautiful and obviously expensive.

She held out her third finger, left hand, letting the gems twinkle and coruscate, their brilliance oddly out of place in the murky interior of the ancient room.

"Who, indeed!"

But of course it could have been none other than Steven Hawke. How sneaky and cowardly of him to steal in here, undoubtedly to catch a glimpse of her as she was now. Monica wanted to tear the gem from her finger, but for a moment only, as if by that gesture she broke any bond between them. She merely slid the ring to the tip of her finger, and then carefully pushed it back, loving the feel of its richness weighing down her slim hand.

A timid knock fell on her door then, and she hastened to cover her body with the quilt as a servant girl hesitantly entered the room at Monica's bidding.

"Monsieur Hawke," a girl murmured, speaking with a heavy French accent, "he is ready to leave and he asks me to give you this shoulder capelet, *mademoiselle*, and to bid you to hurry. He awaits you downstairs and he looks so angry. You had better come quickly!"

The girl smiled and then, handing the green capelet to the bemused young woman, turned, and left the room. Monica wondered where Steven had procured such a lovely feminine garment. No doubt in the blink of a dark lash, or perhaps on a secret moonlit tryst as payment for his notorious services.

She made a feminine snort. She was no novice to the likes of his lust-craved appetites. It was becoming all too clear to her that he must have mistresses strewn all about the countryside. Last night bore witness to that fact, as did Nydia's swelling bosoms flaunted right before his leering eyes!

Dressed and cloaked in less than ten minutes, Monica was descending the creaking old staircase, delighting in the fact that the capelet hid her rumpled gown and the matronly bun atop her head.

Ha! See how he likes her now!

In the dimly lighted inn, Steven's velvet gaze caressed her from head to foot as she came forward to greet him stiffly, her cheeks flushed because she knew he had seen more during the night than he was looking at right now through the opening in the cape.

"You look like a lady of questionable virtue concealed mysteriously in that capelet this morning," Steven laughed softly into her shocked face, adding, "pet."

"The gentleman who presented it to me is certainly not of any questionable sort. *He* makes himself well known to all of the swishing skirts."

She threw the taunt back into his arrogant, smiling face.

"Touché, mademoiselle!" He bowed low, looking up at her laconically. "Or should I say 'Madam,' for you shall soon be my wedded wife and what treats I have in store for *your* swishing skirts."

"Oh but, Steven," she replied, her voice tart-sweet,

"just last night you let me in on the secret of not sharing your . . ." She blushed then.

"Bed," he furnished for her.

Sharp little darts of pleasure pricked her flesh in the most secret places and she damned her senses for allowing them to be felt.

"That is not what I meant." He leaned over her, whispering in her ear because of a couple just coming in to breakfast. "I meant that I would treat you to a *thrashing* now and then, well deserved I might add."

Her eyes widened in terror as he pulled her along with him to be seated at a table. The steaming hot breakfast fare rested on a side table and she smelled the luscious odor of *crêpes suzette* minus the flaming brandy.

"Well?" He smirked tauntingly. "Are you going to break the fast with that cloak trailing in your food? Or will you permit me to help you out of it? I'll try to be good and not touch the delicate shoulders of my bride-to-be."

Monica's stomach rumbled with a hunger she could not deny, for she had nibbled only lightly the night before, but the rumpled appearance of her gown made her reluctant to remove the cape. However, before she could protest Steven came around and removed it.

"That settles that," he said, ignoring her distress.

Monica was embarrassed by the curious looks they were receiving, looks that made her wish she had remained cloaked. And as if that wasn't enough,

Steven peered across the table at her in disgust, Monica thought. The bun she had hastily arranged with only two brass pins now sprawled down her back.

Determined not to fuss or make a scene, Monica gave full attention to the meal placed before her, nibbling only lightly whereas Steven attacked his food with great relish and washed it down with *café au lait*.

"When we arrive at my villa," Steven began, avoiding her accusing eyes across the table, "we will have to see about fitting you with more suitable garments. I will not have it known about the countryside that my fiancée has the appearance of a waif in rags."

Monica held her tongue at his crude remark and the remainder of the meal passed in silence. The heavy oaken door opened now and then as travelers trickled in and out, causing the occupants inside to shiver and moan. All present had qualms about traveling the slippery, muddy miles this morning.

Nonetheless, soon they were off, with Monica nestled in a corner of the carriage, hugging her capelet thankfully, as they climbed to a rise in the road from which they had a panoramic view of the river not far from the inn. At this point Monica suddenly realized she had forgotten to put on her precious ring after her clumsy ablutions.

"Steven!" she gasped, causing him to lurch and peer at her angrily. "Oh, Steven how stupid of me! I have left the ring in my thoughtless haste!"

Monica was afraid he was going to strike her, he looked so angry.

At once he ordered the driver to halt and backtrack off the muddy summit. Steven muttered an oath as the horses gained footing in the slimy muck in which the wheels had almost sunk.

On returning, Monica had only to wait seconds before Steven stepped back outside, looking for all the world like a harbinger from some dark pit, and shaking the dampness from his black cloak as he climbed back into the waiting carriage.

He thrust the ring at her, and she timidly accepted the precious jewel she had so lovingly cherished from the first moment she had viewed it upon her finger mesmerizing her with its glorious richness and beauty.

"Steven . . ."

She heard him grunt in reply. He looked like a brooding cliff beside her, his dark, impenetrable eyes the caves.

"Thank you. I love it and shall cherish it forever. I have never owned or even laid eyes on anything quite so beautiful. I promise I will never lose sight of it again as long as I live."

There was a soft shyness about her now. But an embarrassed silence followed in the wake of his dark scowl and it continued for miles as the rain splashed on the roof and the gloomy gray sky glowered down on them.

Boredom reigned after Monica had gotten her fill of admiring the gem because their progress was painfully slow, the wheels rising and falling into deep ruts and the horses neighing low in distress at their constant overexertion.

Soon the carriage was traveling in a northerly direction where the roads proved an improvement over the latter route and the horses, breathing easier, picked up speed. The gentle rocking motion of their vehicle was peaceful and calm, and the softly golden sun peeped out and slanted into the carriage to gild its interior and its occupants. Birds came out to display their colorful rain-sparkled plumage in the lukewarm rays of late September sun, and frisky, curious squirrels sat up to twitch their bushy tails at the passing conveyance that gleamed impressively at its woodland audience.

The swaying of the carriage gradually overtook Monica, and soon she grew drowsy. Her head nodded and the cowl of her cape fell back to release her abundant locks. Murmuring contentedly, she let her hair fall as it would and snuggled back against the seat of the carriage, giving in to her travel weariness.

Suddenly the carriage executed a sharp turn, and the resulting jolt broke her peaceful slumber. Vexed at this, Steven reached out a long arm and pulled her against his side. Roughly, he pushed her disheveled head down onto his shoulder and his long, lean fingers rested on her tiny waist just above her belly.

Monica came fully awake then, and as she pulled away from him, he marked her intent, only to crush her to him harder still. At that, she relaxed but her muscles remained rigid and alert to any move he might make.

"Be still," he ordered, whispering raspingly in her ear.

Sleep was entirely out of the question now. Rest of any kind, or composure, was unattainable while her cheeks felt the roughness of his dark coat and she was surrounded by his masculine scent, while she felt his firm, muscled thighs pressed intimately to hers. A strange kind of warmth was spreading right through the layers of her garments, and his. Her eyes fell to his taut trousers and she was at once sorry she had permitted them to stray.

Monica quickly lifted her gaze to his brown fingers, but she found no help there either; for the long leanness of them lying warmly against her small waist caused her to shiver.

"Cold?"

"N-no."

His eyebrows rose. "What then?"

No answer was forthcoming. She thought if she had to stand up just then her limbs would turn traitor and barely support her own lean frame.

Where his hand rested, a warmth grew in her flesh, permitting strange sensations to spread down into her swirling belly. Pressed to his left side as she was, Monica felt the bold pounding of his heart, and much to her surprise, it matched her own telltale thumping. His free hand rested lightly on his thigh, sliding up and down in restless abandon.

Steven stared down where the cape had fallen away, at the pale gold mounds revealed to his bold inspection. From this vantage point he could almost glimpse the rosy points where the material stretched taut. He felt fire flare in his loins and almost heard the fervid beating of his heart. His eyes shifted to the smaller gems on her finger, the diamonds glowing with a pure white brilliance.

Finally he could stand it no longer. He lifted her chin and forcing her lips to meet his, he parted her lips with his fingers. Her whimpering protests were accompanied by his own deep groan. He stroked her open mouth with his tongue and was possessed by a wanton demon when he tasted the inner sweetness of her lips.

Monica felt him crushing against her, felt the suffocating demand of his kiss while both of his arms pinned her back against the seat, and then the kiss became deeper; penetrating, touching her with the art of an experienced lover, probing sweetly, forcing fires she never knew existed. Until she had no will she could call her own. She began to sway to his erotic music and shivered unconsciously when his hard fingers undid the buttons on her bodice and searched out a firm, ripe breast.

It seemed as though his fingers were entering her body as he teased the taut, pink tip to hardness. Monica panted as his lips burned and scalded, then momentarily lifted, giving her the chance to flee danger. His darkened eyes were engraved in her soul.

"Steven, no more," she said, her breathing uneven.

She pushed energetically at his hand, but he paid her no mind and continued to probe relentlessly.

314

"I'm completely bewitched by you, Mona," he said in a slow voice.

"Steven, don't do this," she said in an angry voice that sounded as if it were caught in her throat.

But he went on to nibble her ear and to kiss the long column of her neck down to the throbbing pulse in her throat. She pulled away from the burning revelation of his passion and pushed her head forcefully against his chest, viewing as she did so the tumescent bulge of his manhood.

Seeing no escape, she closed her eyes tightly against the storm raging within and without, against everything he was doing to excite her. Then her situation became clear to her. She was merely to be a possession of his, nothing more. Another woman for him to toy with and then cast aside when he became bored with her.

Steven's hand left her breast to slide up and stroke her hair. As if she were a child, he sought to stay her pitiful tears. But Monica was now determined to show him that she was a woman fully grown and not just another of his bedtime *amours*. This would be the last time he was going to make her cry.

Monica tore herself from the steely circle of his arms, and much to her surprise he permitted her to seek her lonely corner of the carriage.

"I should have known better," he said sarcastically. "I suddenly realize what a child you are, Mona. I find it hard to believe that you will ever really grow up, even though you are still quite young and have years ahead of you in which to mature. If

315

perchance you do and I am still around, you will be a highly prized possession."

"Possession!" Monica exclaimed. "I knew it! Everything, human or otherwise is just that to you—a possession! I'll wager that you do not even love your brother—the one that I heard tell lives in California!"

She went on despite his murderous expression. "And, Monsieur Hawke, if I am such a child then how is it that you desire . . ." He wasn't listening and the murderous look on his face deepened as his obsidian eyes narrowed, became icy, while the details in his face stood out blackly, ominous and threatening.

Steven was now reminded of unfinished business, long forgotten in the heat of the moment and of his lust for this girl.

He was on her in a flash, shaking her energetically until her head snapped back and forth and her hair fell about her in golden-spiked disarray.

"Yes, Monica Lyons, I once desired you." He watched her eyes grow wide. "Are you perhaps a murderess?"

Shock waves hit her with full force, and she blanched. How could he know of her stepfather? He could not, just could not!

"What do you know of my brother Jess?" He gritted his teeth in full-fledged anger. "I'll bet you even had a part in my brother's murder."

"I-I . . ." she stammered, in her mind's eye watching again in horrible fascination the murder committed by her stepbrother.

Jess! Dear God. It dawned on her then, the reason Steven, as the sergeant, had struck her as familiar, when he'd stood close, even in the moon's full light.

She felt the walls of the carriage closing in, engulfing her in blackness. It was all about her and she kept hearing over and over, "An eye for an eye . . ."

25

When Monica came to, Steven was leaning over glaring at her. Her flesh still tingled where he had been touching her and her heart was pounding so hard she could almost hear it.

"Well, Mona? Did you think I had forgotten?"

"Oh, Steven," her voice quavered. "Why didn't you tell me that Jess was your brother? It would have saved so much grief."

"Grief? For who, you or I?"

She could not go on, she just hadn't the words to answer him. His face reflected the pain she, too, was feeling, and her mind was a whirling mass of confusion. Then she found her voice.

"But Jess, he—he was an Indian. And you are French, are you not? How could? . . ."

"Doesn't it dawn on you, Mona, that many of the French in America have Indian blood in them?"

How terribly naïve of her! he thought.

Then she set out to tell the whole story, leaving out the horrible near-ravishment by Branville Bennington. She also left out the murder scene, the one Alex Bennington had made come alive in her worst nightmares—Jess's death; she was afraid that Steven would drag her back to face the consequences of the murder *she* had unwittingly committed in a moment's madness.

"What is it that you have left out, Mona?"

He leaned back against the rocking seat, releasing a bitter, grief-filled sigh. She couldn't know that he was again remembering that he had not a trace of kin and that his heart ached with a wild longing. He looked out the window of the carriage, saw nothing but torturing visions, then looked back to her, a world's sadness buried in his eyes.

Her heart went out to him then, but she could not reveal the fact that Alex Bennington had been the assassin. That would leave her open to exposure for her own misdeed. Oh, she groaned inwardly, what was she to do?

"I have left out nothing," she said, eyes lowered.

He kept silent, letting her think that he believed her, for now.

A day and a half later, after stopping at one inn to sleep and several to eat, they were deep in the heart of Lyon, passing through picturesque scenery and crossing many bridges, then finally driving onto a narrow tongue of land between the Rhône and Saône rivers.

The sloping banks were lined with a sparse sprinkling of attractive villas. Monica saw that the green horizon was bordered by distant mountains, almost all the way around. She also had noted that in the town they had just passed the inhabitants were morose and inhospitable, giving her to believe that every outsider was an enemy against whom they sedulously barricaded their doors—until they recognized Steven. Then their glances indicated that, to them, the prosperous silk merchant was the pick of humanity, the cream of the crop; and they waved to him, smiling generously wide.

The lazy silver-white ball of moon hung low when they crossed the last arched bridge, the decreasing tattoo of the horses' hooves clattered and announced that El Corazón loomed up just ahead—journey's end. Monica drew herself up, and when Steven spoke up suddenly out of the dark, he caused her to jerk in her seat, for the light, inconstant conversation that had been the case throughout the long hours and miles that stretched somberly behind them had made a dull and lethargic mood prevail.

"These are my estates," he said quietly, pointing to a house up ahead. "The villa, El Corazón, and your home for as long as you wish it to be."

The huge villa, milky white in the moonlight, seemed to beckon to her. It was awe-inspiringly vast, and as they crunched up the drive to halt before the white stone steps, Monica felt a strange contentment begin to grow in her. She had seen, on the east side of the house, a tower thrusting into the moon-washed sky, and it had seemed a harbinger of a new beginning. Now she stared, wondrously warmed by the yellow rhomboid of light greeting them thanks to the lighted lanterns.

Huge dark brown doors swung open, as did Monica's dark eyes when she viewed the burly man who so covetously had guarded the *Mañana* in the bay, that time seeming long ago to her now. Taking in his fine red and gold raiment, she thought that he looked terribly out of place without the sea and ships around him.

Pitt Dailey saw her and gaped, taking Steven aside with a "'Scuse me, ma'am," and a bob of his large head.

After a few words with Dailey, Steven's dark brows shot up in quiet contemplation and then all at once he was at her side, guiding her over the threshold to the entry bordered on both sides by large, light- and color-filled rooms.

A flat-arched, timber-paneled ceiling of Tudor design greeted her gaze and all about she glimpsed furnishings in the French taste of Louis XV.

A very agitated Frenchwoman, perhaps in her sixties, came to stand before them, and with a heavy French accent she spoke to Steven in a prudish manner, looking from Monica to Dailey to Steven.

"Monsieur Étienne," she began low, "I do not understand . . ." She jerked her head upward and they seemed to share some private knowledge Monica could not even begin to guess the meaning of.

Steven shushed her at once, saying, "Please, Dazie, no questions. Take Mademoiselle Lyons upstairs at once." He paid no mind to her nervous manner. "I have no time for proper introductions and explanations at the moment."

With that he turned and strode swiftly back out the door, leaving Monica to the flustered housekeeper who immediately ushered her up the stairs and into a huge bedchamber where lovely, old, velvet drapes and red curtains fell in ponderous folds of crimson and deep gold about the many-paned windows.

The house was splendid, but Monica was thinking that it bespoke unfinished and delayed improvements here and there, uncompleted touches that had been directed at brightening and enhancing the old natural beauty of the place. She started. Just like the home he owned in California. Yes, he seemed to be the type of man who never finished what he set out to accomplish, be it women or houses. He left them both hanging in the balance.

The keen-sighted housekeeper stared at Monica for a moment longer, her hands clasped primly in front of her stiffly starched white and black apron, embellished with lace *à la bobine*.

"Ah, that man," she spoke half in disgust, half in devotion. "Will he never settle down?"

Dazie was asking herself these questions. So, another woman to warm his hearthstones. Obviously this beautiful young woman knows nothing whatsoever of monsieur's reputation with the demimondaines, otherwise she would not be here. Tsk, tsk. She looks like a common wench, with an otherworldly look about her, dressed the way she is, with the looped braids caught at each temple. But even so, her golden sheen of hair bespeaks loveliness unblemished, and her soft pouting lips look like tiny rosebuds.

Dazie tilted her head. What would monsieur want with such youthful innocence? Dazie wondered. His wolfish tastes usually ran to females a bit more mature, indeed much more experienced. What would the tall, cool Michelle be thinking right now if she knew that Monsieur had this pretty little thing stashed away here. Dazie did not especially like Michelle, but she knew the older woman would eat this pretty little morsel alive in one swallow.

"Would you like tea sent up, *mademoiselle?*" Dazie was asking politely of the young woman who looked as if she were suddenly quite lost in the huge bedroom.

Dazie, for now, could not tell if she liked this one. So many others had been sweet and charming at first, and then had turned into demanding shrews. If monsieur had lived in Biblical times, she swore he would have been like Solomon and taken himself many wives. Yet, wives—even one—were not what Monsieur was after. In fact, she doubted he would ever become a husband to a sweet young thing such as this girl seemed to be.

Monica was becoming horribly aware of the fact that Steven wished to stash her away because of her disheveled appearance. She couldn't remain hidden until proper attire was prepared for her, although perhaps that was what Steven had in mind—that she stay locked up in this room until her father came.

"Yes," Monica replied belatedly. "I would like

some tea. But first I would like to bathe if you would be so kind as to direct me."

Dazie, undecided, hesitated for just a moment as she wondered if Michelle had remembered to remove her personal articles and toiletries. What a time for that demimondaine to show, making herself at home as if she owned the place. And how was monsieur going to manage to keep the two of them from meeting?

Dazie sighed wearily, knowing that was bound to happen sooner or later with Michelle occupying the room just down the hall and right beside Étienne's.

A short time later, preparing to bathe, Monica disrobed quickly while permitting her eyes to roam about the large expanse of mirrored walls. She was fascinated by the lavishness of the bathing room. Yet, she was not surprised in the least at the feminine articles on the shelves—vials of cosmetics and perfumed toiletries.

Picking up a pretty lavender bottle she popped off the stopper and sniffed the contents. "Ugh!" She wrinkled her fine nose in distaste and hurriedly placed it back in its place on the shelf. What, she wondered, would a woman want with all these costly preparations?

Was this the way it was to be then, Monica wondered sadly, being married to a man who openly flaunted his mistresses while his poor wife stood meekly in the background?

Sighing dispiritedly and moving languidly, Monica saw her reflection staring back at her and she was at once horrified by what she saw. An overly thin young woman with unruly autumn-colored hair braided in loops at either side of her temples. Her cheekbones had become more prominent. When had she lost the soft roundness she used to think of as baby fat? And when had the slant of her jade green eyes become more than apparent?

She looked just awful!

Tearing the dusty braids loose, Monica stepped into the water that had become lukewarm while she had dallied. Luxuriating in what she likened to be the water of the gods after the long, tiresome journey, she scrubbed herself with a luscious bar of rose-scented soap she had pilfered from the shelf, rubbing until her skin tingled and blushed with a rosy hue.

Wrapped in a huge red velvet dressing robe bordered with silk, left for her by the kindly housekeeper, Monica tiptoed quickly and discreetly back to her appointed bedchamber, holding the huge robe up to keep from tripping on her bare feet. She prayed that no observant eyes saw her haste—especially dark, mocking ones. Steven would find it hilarious to say the least to see her looking like a child, lost in his large robe and with straggly strands of hair falling wetly to her waist.

Inside the room, she drew the curtains aside and stood, silently staring across the silvered green lawn. Leaning forward, she caught sight of someone in a creamy yellow silk damask gown, someone who moved from the concealment of tall bushes into the revealing moonlight.

"Oh." Monica felt her heart give a sudden lurch as one became two, moving into the shaft of yellow-gilded light that spread from a window just below her. Monica viewed a thick coil of silvery blond hair that was woven intricately and fashionably atop the woman's head. She was almost as tall as Steven and was slanting her face up for his inspection of her flawless white skin and her ruby red lips, lips that anticipated his kiss. But Steven seemed to be regarding her coolly. He was definitely unnerved about something, Monica was thinking.

Feeling the intruder, Monica quickly let the curtains fall back into place, half-sickened at the thought of the lovers. But just for a moment, then she became so irritated she was actually shaking.

Whirling and flying from the bedchamber, Monica heard her own soul whimpering as if it had been struck a nasty blow. She followed the corridor to the stairs, not knowing where she was going or what she was about to do. She only wanted to leave this horrible place as soon as she could.

Stopping short at the top of the stairs she peered down in embarrassed surprise, for at the bottom three pairs of eyes stared up at her with what she thought was cold-blooded collaboration.

Avoiding the collective glares coming her way, Monica returned to the relative safety of her room, blushing feverishly. Seated on the edge of the bed now, with a sullen heaviness she hung her head.

How conspicuously foolish she must have appeared in the eyes of her betrothed, the housekeeper;

and from the frosty, mocking expression on the tall, ethereal blonde's face it was clearly evident that she was amused to see Monica looking like a small, drowned rat.

And Steven, he stared with arched brows as if he had just met her. Strange, but when their eyes clashed momentarily, Monica could have sworn he was mocking her, as the blonde had.

"Oh, father, I wish you would come and take me away from here," she thought to herself. "To be married to this man would be complete hell. How can I stand meekly in the background while my husband openly flaunts his mistresses in my face? I would not and could not stand for it!"

Still, it was a fact that Steven was his own man and did just as he pleased with whomever he chose.

"I feel so weak whenever he is near, and so cowardly, as if I were a mouse and he a savage lion. I must not let him see this in me. I will try to be brave. Can I do it? Can I tame the lion and make him bend to my will?"

Deep in her heart she doubted her strength and a great weariness overtook her. She lay back, and let inevitable slumber draw a veil over her as she lay across the coverlet snuggled in the musk-scented robe. She basked in its familiar redolence all through her peaceful sleep, unmindful that she caressed the robe lovingly about her naked breasts.

The frail, gauzy light of the moon stole into the

bedchamber to cast a nimbus about the white-sheeted bed, and in the half-circle stood a man, half in the dark, half in moon- and starlight.

He walked about the bed while his head slowly moved back and forth and his dark eyes studied her sleeping form. Steven could hardly breathe for the bittersweet pain that was sweeping over him. What part had she played in the ruthless demise of his brother? And what was she doing to him? He had never felt such a greenhorn with a woman, had never experienced a woman's kisses—though stolen, he confessed—in the same way. Never before had a woman's lips tasted so much like honey, nor had her body felt like the finest spun silk to his touch. She was, he admitted, the most fascinating and desirable woman he had ever known.

Steven wanted to search out the curves of her glorious body, but he knew he would have to wait. She would become his wife, and then, only then, would he sate his thirst for revenge and slake the desire that was making him mad.

He left the room briskly then, after he had cautiously tucked her in and felt the burn of her throat's velvet texture sear his fingers, the temptation of her more than his flesh and blood could stand.

Part VII

O Defiant Heart

26

Morning dawned and illuminated the bedroom with yellow rays that stole through the long slash in the curtains. Outside Monica's window, cheerful birds twittered and flew about in gay profusion to broadcast a warm Indian summer's day.

Surfacing from a delightful dream, Monica was feeling invigorated, fresh, and stubbornly determined to make her new life worthwhile. She wanted to make others happy for it had been her lifelong dream to be surrounded by loving people, like her mother had been. Her mother was gone now; Monica had read this in her father's mournful eyes as he had haltingly referred to her.

But a new world was blossoming for her—and what would this life bring?

Being aware that someone had stolen in during her slumber and tucked her beneath the quilt did not bother her in the least. She sat up for several moments, hugging her knees under her chin, and lines from a Shakespearean volume she had snatched from Steven's library in California came to her in the glow of the warming day:

> *Give me that man that is not Passion's*
> *slave, and I will wear him*
> *In my heart's core, ay, in*
> *my heart of hearts.*

Jolted from her lighthearted reverie, Monica's eyes flashed brilliantly when Dazie entered bearing a tray laden with *café au lait* and hot, thin crêpes smelling of cheese and ham. Monica's eyes devoured the delicacies, and then much to Dazie's satisfaction she tackled them hungrily.

"It is good to see a young woman eat so well," Dazie said in that delightful French accent. "Proper Frenchwomen of Lyon frown upon taking more than a cup of hot tea in the morning, thinking only of their trim figures and not of the importance of a hearty breakfast. Myself, I believe it is the most essential meal of the day." She paused for a moment, smiling apologetically before she began again.

"Monsieur Étienne has informed me of his plans and of the forthcoming marriage between you and himself. I did not know of this, and I apologize, *ma chèrie*, for being so rude."

"Dazie. May I call you by your first name?"

"Oh *oui*, please do." Dazie laughed. "Wait. I have something for you that monsieur left before he set out early this morning."

Monica frowned lightly, drawing back from her

cup of chocolate. "He is gone already? So soon?"

Monica fingered the fluffy, feathered coverlet absentmindedly. But before she could further question the maid, Dazie was already out the door with a brisk nod of her head.

Before long, the housekeeper returned, a familiar shade of blue material draped carefully over her outstretched arm. Shaking it out, she held it up for Monica's perusal. Amazement mingled with delight washed over Monica at the sight of the blue muslin she had absentmindedly left behind in her hasty departure from California. And then another thought brought a clearer picture to her mind, sweeping away the cobwebs of confusion.

"He knew! He must have found it was I who was his housekeeper!" Monica said under her breath.

Dazie pretended not to notice the young woman talking to herself. "We shall finish it today, Monica Lyons. All it needs is to be hem-stitched and to have buttons put on, *oui*?"

Engrossed in her musings, Monica had hardly heard Dazie speaking.

"I will be back with a needle, buttons, and thread. You relax and enjoy your chocolate." Dazie turned to leave the room.

"Wait. Did . . . did the lovely blond woman accompany monsieur this morning?" Monica questioned quietly, afraid of the answer she would receive.

"*Non*." Dazie's little eyes twinkled merrily. "Michelle is still here, but preparing to leave, and quite soon now! She was very, very upset on hearing Étienne announce his forthcoming marriage. Pah! Do not worry your sweet little head with the likes of that one!''

Dazie went airily from the bedchamber, black skirts rustling busily, crisp white cap askew.

Staring about the room, Monica noticed for the first time that directly to the right and leading off a path well worn into the Aubusson carpet, a pleasant dressing room was finished in a soft turquoise and appointments of white stood out cheerfully in the flood of morning light. The bed itself was a handsome piece of furniture. With silk-covered bolsters at both ends, it resembled a medieval couch.

Monica sighed dreamily, thinking how lovely it would be to have the curtains match the bedcover and the bolsters, instead of being randomly matched as they were. Her gaze rested on the writing desk, French blue, and situated where one could gaze out the window while penning a letter or writing silly little romantic poems. How wonderful it would be to sit there in the morning with the lemon yellow light flooding into the chamber. Studying, reading, writing letters . . .

Writing letters! Oh, if only it were possible to pen a letter to Tina. Likewise, at her first opportunity a letter to Bartholomew and Terri would be forthcoming.

Leaving her bed Monica went to stand before the fireplace, and placing a hand on the shiny, dark Italian marble surrounding the now-cold hearth, she stared intently for a moment at the cloudy imprint left by her small hand. In a contented mood after her delicious breakfast, Monica moved slowly about the chamber, touching things and running her hand along the back of the blue desk until she paused before the mullioned window.

Looking down she caught sight of large areas of unadorned brickwork, the simple bays with widely spaced mullions; then, looking up, sharp gables and broad uncarved barge boards. A simple brick tower adjoined the house on the east side, unusual for a country villa, she thought. But what did she know of such things, really?

Actually taking into consideration its designer, whom her father had lightly discussed with Steven in the carriage, the design was not so unusual after all. Auguste Charles Pugin, a French émigré and an authority on medieval architecture had designed much of El Corazón back when it had carried an Elizabethan title. Part of Pugin's style was the simple unadorned paneling of the main rooms, and the ruling out all "pagan art," including that of the Georgian period. Pugin's son had just completed the Grange, which also had the basic form of a medieval house, the crisp detail of its stonework being consistent.

Monica's gaze wandered from the grounds surrounding the house, which were in dire need of a gardener's talents, and roamed to the greenish-gold hills, tawny in some patches and orange in others. The hills on either side were crowned by fortifications which provided one of the chief bases of French military movements. Monica had picked up this knowledge from a conversation she had overheard at one of the inns where they stopped for food.

Just then Dazie returned with a sewing basket tucked neatly beneath her upper arm and pins sticking out of her mouth in anticipation of the fitting of the muslin dress.

"Ah, *mademoiselle*. Soon we will have you clothed in something a bit more proper before the couturier arrives. He would be surprised, much as I, to find such a princess of a young woman, *pardonnez-moi*, in such shabby cloth."

Dazie noticed that her words passed, almost unheard, by the young woman, for she only nodded and returned her gaze to the hills while Dazie perched on a chair, searching in her basket for buttons to match. She wondered about a great many things and would have put them into questions, but it was not her nature to be inquisitive as were many servants with whom she was acquainted.

Time passed while Dazie sewed and Monica continued to gaze out the window as if there were something of interest out there for her in the green-gold woods. She stared and stared, as if in search of something—or was she feeling that something was going to happen out there, something that would change her life forever? Or, and this was the strange part, was she seeking the beginning of this new life she had been dreaming of?

"*Voilà!*" Dazie announced as Monica walked

across the room, feeling rather ashamed at ignoring the housekeeper and at allowing Dazie to complete the task she should have seen to herself.

"You are very kind, Dazie. Thank you." Monica smiled. "I do not know how I could have overlooked it in my packing." She did not catch Dazie's puckered frown. "Perhaps the excitement and hasty departure, but then monsieur was kind enough to bring it along."

Dazie thought the young woman's eyes darkened with some mystery and then twinkled merrily when she held up the gown to her. Donning the muslin, Monica stood back to regard her image in the long mirror. Something was terribly wrong. Her hair—what a mess! The pink ribbons were yet in her hair, all tangled, and the curls were awry. No wonder Dazie thought she was a pauper!

"Enchanting."

A feminine voice mocked and laughed from the open door. Monica glanced obliquely toward the doorway knowing who stood there laughing even before she turned to watch Michelle sweep into the room elegantly. Monica gulped, for the woman's ethereal loveliness lit up the room.

"So, this is Étienne's bride-to-be," Michelle quipped. "Where has he kept such a ravishing *child* concealed?"

Michelle did not wait for an answer but went on, "Why, you should be at home, with your mama. Not here, in the villa of a rogue such as Étienne Hawke!"

"My mother is not among the living, madam,"

Monica told the platinum blond beauty.

"Tsk, tsk. I am so sorry to hear this. But please, my dear. I am *mademoiselle* and not *madam*." Michelle sighed in feigned disappointment. "What does one need with marriage anyway? It is far more enjoyable and definitely less encumbering, shall we say, to be unattached."

Showing her back to the arrogant blond, Monica faced the mirror and, tearing the ribbons from her locks, picked up her brush and ran it through the long ripples that fell just below her waist.

"I, for one," Monica began, "much prefer the marriage bed to sleeping with a strange man every night."

Dazie's mouth flew open at such language escaping the lips of one she thought to be shy and naïve. But then, Dazie thought with a smirk, Michelle had it coming for sure. Deciding this was between the two of them, the housekeeper meekly made her exit, hoping the younger woman would come out unscathed from the encounter with the demimondaine.

Michelle watched the retreating form of the housekeeper, and then whirled about to vex the girl once again. She studied Monica's slim back and the flowing abundance of her rich chestnut curls, their ends spun from flax after days in the sun. Michelle's stiffly starched petticoats rustled as she moved to stand directly behind the younger woman.

"If you think that being wed to Étienne will change things between us, you are in for a surprise," Michelle hissed tauntingly. "There is not one

338

woman on this earth who can change him, or his desire for me. Hah! A skinny wench you are, and I suppose he has gotten you in the family way and is forced into wedlock. So! I can see it on your face. This is the truth of the matter. How else could you have bound him to you with the promise of marriage?"

How near the demimondaine had come to the horrible truth, Monica was thinking. Still, she was not about to entertain this woman's haughty assumptions.

Monica turned about slowly, suddenly possessed by dauntless rage. As she faced Michelle her eyes flashed turquoise sparks which made the demimondaine step back in alarm, almost tripping on her full petticoats, as the younger woman sashayed toward her.

"You are in for somewhat of a surprise yourself, *mademoiselle*, for you see in a few years you will begin to shrivel up like a rotten grape while I still yet cling to the vine."

Michelle's freshly painted lips took on the look of a shriveled raisin as she pursed them tightly in a pucker that matched her drawn brows in distress.

"Now," Monica tossed her head, "leave my chamber at once. Or be thrown out on your arrogant backside by Mr. Dailey!"

Michelle had no doubt that Pitt Dailey would do just that. She despised the giant, and he her.

"Just wait until I spread the news that Monsieur Étienne Hawke is living with his unchaperoned bride-to-be!"

Michelle tossed the last barb over her shoulder as she rustled out the door. Perhaps, she was thinking slyly, she would even add that the wench was with child. She was devising such schemes that she nearly walked right into the major-domo who waited at the foot of the stairs, anticipating Michelle's departure from this house.

"Your carriage is waiting, *mademoiselle*," he said in slightly mocking French.

"Faugh!" Michelle said irritably, right in the man's face, and in a loud rustle of silk she stalked out the main entrance of the villa.

Upstairs, Monica tossed herself onto the bed and buried her head under the pillow she clutched. Under ordinary conditions she was not inclined to hold a grudge or feel ill will for long; however, Michelle had angered her to the point where she had become sharp and unpleasant. Certainly, she told herself, these circumstances were not ordinary ones.

Monica flopped onto her back to stare up at the high ceiling. Michelle was right on one account, though, there was not a single woman on God's earth who could change Steven Hawke. He was cynical, willful, selfish, and capable of greatly influencing others with his magnetic personality.

She felt the burden of the future resting squarely on her shoulders. Did she really want to change the man? On the whole, taking all things into consideration, she was beginning to feel a strange need for him.

The monster! she thought angrily.

Running her hand down over her belly, she wondered if she carried his child. Would a babe change things between them, bring about an ideal balance for the two of them? She laughed bitterly—hardly!

There was still the matter of Jess's death to contend with. For at times a savage desire for revenge surfaced in Steven Hawke, especially when she was near him. Too near, she thought as she remembered the hot kisses and fondling in the carriage.

Monica sighed. Life was indeed a cruel foe at times, the carving out of one's destiny oftentimes hewn by a sharp, nasty blade. If only she could pick up that blade and hack her way through the harrying months just ahead. This would be a telling time, one that would prove whether love existed between them. Monica shivered this time. Love would be wonderful with such a man, if only she could wrap him around her tiny finger and bend him to her woman's will.

She went very still then. He had been the man in her dreams who stirred her desire, the promise of his imaginary possession almost tangible each night. But did she love him? Had matters gotten that far yet? She was indeed feeling something for him she had never felt for another human being.

All of a sudden Monica became aware of a presence outside her door. She bolted upright in bed after noticing a pair of thick, trousered legs. Michelle had not shut the door after her, and Monica now felt this was an intrusion on her privacy. Then she laughed at herself, for, after all, she was not the madam yet.

"S'cuse me, ma'am, but there be a gentleman down in the parlor waiting to see you," Dailey announced sheepishly. "Says his name is Philip somethin' or other. . . ."

As soon as he had left his message, Dailey respectfully withdrew to the top of the stairs. "Will you be comin' right down, ma'am?"

"Yes, Dailey! Immediately!"

Shrieking with joy, Monica hurried into the hall, pausing only once to smooth tendrils away from her temples while Dailey looked on in curiosity. Then she was flying down the stairs, her feet barely touching the carpet.

27

Philip crossed to Monica in three quick strides and clasped his arms about her. Then he sat, and they talked and laughed gaily. She felt at ease in his presence, as usual, as if she had known Philip all her life. They chatted about the damp weather, Philip's high-toned compeers, and the gaiety of Paris.

When it came down to discussing her trousseau, Monica fell silent and a cloud of gloom descended over her. She stared hollow-eyed at the gillyflowered wallpaper, the buds clove pink, the background honey-pale, and she tilted her head.

"What is it, *ma petite*?"

"Oh," Monica began softly, with her eyes downcast, "nothing."

"Oh, it *is* something."

"Philip, I do not wish to wed Steven Hawke!"

"Who is— Ah, the American name, Steven," Philip nodded.

"I hate Steven and I will never want to marry him!"

"What?"

"It is true, Philip. I will be happy when I leave this place, not until then."

"Your wishes do not count, *mademoiselle*."

Monica turned suddenly, sensing Steven's presence in the room even before he had opened his mouth to speak so harshly.

Philip unwound himself from Monica's tight hold on his arm and stood to greet Monsieur Hawke. Steven only nodded, dark eyes barely polite. Then he faced Monica.

"It didn't take you long to become acquainted with your couturier," Steven remarked cruelly, spotting the imprint of her fingers on Philip's arm.

"Acquainted!" Monica laughed shortly. "Philip fashioned my gown for the masque."

"Ah," Steven drawled. "Juliette's masquerade of fools."

You were there yourself, fool, Monica wanted very much to fling at him, but she restrained herself.

Facing Philip, Steven let the boom fall. "You see, Philip, *la petite mademoiselle* could very well be in the family way—"

Philip gasped.

"—and so it is highly imperative that she become my loving bride at once."

"Loving!" Monica laughed hysterically.

Steven paid her outburst no mind but only studied the expensive materials with a silk connoisseur's eye, some of the finest materials brought from his own factory. He crossed over to finger a bolt of heavy silk meant for the wedding dress and let it slide through his hand as he looked up and spoke.

"Did I not send for you myself, Philip Bouillet?" Steven said, raising one shapely eyebrow.

"Why—of course this is so, monsieur. But what has *mademoiselle* in such a dither? It is plain she does not wish to marry you." Philip coughed nervously. "And what is this of a *bébé*? Already?"

"Monica was a maiden when I took her, and—"

"You took me without asking first, monsieur!" Monica blurted, and her tone brought Philip's gaze around to rest on her hot face.

"It was never my intent to ravish you, Mona. You were so willing that I only complied."

"Bah! Double-talk." She sent Steven a glare and set her lovely profile against his unusually soft gaze.

"I was wrong, I admit," Steven went on, holding himself severely in check. "And"—he shrugged— "there is no telling what could come from our little liaison. Perhaps a baby. Perhaps not." He addressed a stunned Philip once again. "No matter. She has no say in this and her own father says she must accept my honorable intentions."

"The only thing that could come from our l- liaison as you call it would be a two-headed monster!"

"Tsk, tsk," Steven clicked. "Such faith in your own ability to produce normal offspring." He shook his head. "Mona, Mona."

"Don't call me that!"

Knowing by Steven's darkening look that she had

stretched her role as the poor, wounded virgin too far, she sat and folded her hands meekly in her lap. Steven's eyes flicked over the blue muslin she was wearing and then lifted to fix on her stubborn face.

"We will become man and wife by the first of October," Steven said casually, nodding in the direction of Philip and then the materials for the preparation of the trousseau. "It must be completed by then," he said crisply and turned to leave the room.

"*October*," Monica said softly. "But that is only—"

Philip silenced her by placing a finger over her lips. "I can do it, *chèrie*, not to worry."

"But Philip, can I?"

Monica stood alone on her balcony. Sun streamed through the window and birds sang on the roof, and the very air seemed laden with a golden autumn mist. She could see only one lonely gray cloud on the horizon. She went back inside.

The small pendulum clock on the escritoire showed twenty after one, so she hurried to get the finishing touches to her hair that sparkled like sun-spiked autumn mist. This didn't take very long and soon she was pacing the carpet in search of something to do. She *needed* to do something with her hands, for she was very nervous.

This was their wedding day.

Ten more minutes dragged by with nerve-racking

slowness before Philip knocked at the door and Monica at once bade him enter.

"Ah *chérie*," Philip chuckled, "you look good enough to marry."

Monica smiled, her brightest. Actually she was a tangled mass of nerves, though she tried hard not to show it.

"You are wonderful, Philip," she said, a tender glow in her eyes.

"And you, shining bride, are absolutely magnificent!" Philip checked the clock. "Ah, time to go. Your father has arrived and"—he held up a thin finger—"so has Michelle, let me caution you beforehand."

"Oh no, who invited her?" Monica groaned; then she thought she knew. "Just what I need, a white-haired witch stewing in the pew," she said irritably, while Philip chuckled low at her pun.

"Tsk, tsk, remember you are to be every moment the charming bride this day—one who glows not glowers. *Non?*"

"Yes, Philip," she sighed, stiffening her shoulders soldier-straight. "I shall try very hard, sir!"

Thunder rumbled like a disgruntled sigh in the distance as Philip handed the bride into the carriage that would take them to Tempe of the Woods Church. Monica glanced up at the foreboding gray clouds and experienced a sense of doom before she dipped into the carriage, her bride's gown a creamy billow following her.

Before long the carriage bounced up in front of the

quaint little country church. Ivy climbed in jungle-like profusion over its walls and over the windows, the leaves dark and somewhat lifeless as the first throes of winter hibernation set in.

Monica emerged and got her first look at where she would be joined in holy—or *unholy*—matrimony to Monsieur Étienne Hawke, Lyon silk merchant. *Lying.* Monica smiled, congratulating herself on her sense of humor this day of all days. Looking at the ivy-draped church, haloed by soft falling mist, she took Antoine's arm and gazed up at her father as they sped to the doors to keep from getting too damp.

The church was lovely inside, tall stained-glass windows being the only form of luxury afforded its humble simplicity. Then Monica's eye caught Steven, already waiting for her at the altar. She felt grateful when his eyes rolled slowly upward, breaking contact, to seemingly stare at the dark wood beams arcing above like praying hands.

He was Apollo himself, Monica decided. His midnight hair shone. It was brushed smooth at the sides and back, and even the wild curl at the front had been tamed with a steady hand. He was immaculately fitted in a silk waistcoat with black velvet lapels, and his narrow trousers fitted snugly to his cords of dense, tough muscle. His snowy shirt, without a ruffle, was a splendid foil against his dark bronze throat.

Mechanically she moved forward on Antoine's arm, her father straight and proud, his handsome white smile beaming down on her lace-covered head. Antoine wanted only the best for his beautiful daughter and as he glimpsed her face that was flushed a becoming shade of pink beneath her veil's mist, he knew no silly emotional regret as they neared the alter where he handed her over to the younger arm.

Eyes, like a bolt of black silk, slid over Monica, but she could not know what Steven was thinking. She was only aware of her cold clam-shell hands and heard nothing but the furious pounding of her heart. Steven took her hand in his and she knew a moment of uncomfortable self-consciousness. His hand was unemotionally warm and dry!

Before the emaciated minister opened his Bible, Steven squeezed her hand reassuringly and Monica's heart quit beating to soar to the sky and back. But then she made the fatal mistake of gazing starry-eyed at him. A muscle twitched in his lean cheek and she again knew he was experiencing frustration and a great need for—*for what?* If it was revenge, she wondered how he would go about inflicting punishment on her.

A flash of regret struck Monica. *Alex Bennington, you should be here to take the consequences, not I!*

Steven had been aware of Monica the very moment she entered the church, before he had seen her. Ah, but she was a lovely cream-and-gold sight to behold, he thought as he looked upon the ethereal vision Monica made in her lace-adorned satin gown, glorious and shining in its heavy folds, its cut and style simple. Her veil cascaded down her back and graced the old wood floors, a soft cream cloud that barely shut out the sunshine of her sweetly fashioned tresses. Beneath her veil, her mouth shone like a buffed red cherry, tempting, sugar-sweet, sensuous, innocent, intoxicating him more than several brandies ever could.

Then *le crime passionnel*, revenge like bitter wine, took hold of his heart and soul, and Steven shook himself out of admiring her. A muscle twitched in his cheek and he damned himself for allowing her to see it do so when she glanced up at him.

"You may kiss the bride now."

Oh dear God, it was over! Monica stood dumbstruck as Steven lifted her gauzy veil to touch her frozen cherry lips with his. Monica shivered and looked up at his beautifully rugged face, his mockingly curved lips.

"You are not glowing, Madam Hawke," he whispered as they turned around to face the small admiring group gathered there. Pretending to buss her ear, he said into it, "Paste on a smile, a grin, anything. But don't look as if this is the most unhappy moment of your life."

Monica stepped forward a bit, awkwardly. It was Steven's fault that she couldn't act normally! This was supposed to be a happy occasion, so she forced a smile to her lips but the smile did not reach her heart, nor did it reach her eyes when Michelle sauntered up to congratulate the groom with a studiedly sensual kiss.

Behind them the minister cleared his throat noisily, breaking the embrace that was clearly out of place here in his sanctuary. He gave his grizzled head a few discreet shakes, looked toward the bride. *Poor lass*, he thought.

Monica was furious by the time she and Steven raced down the aisle. He pulled her by the hand, through the rice, while Monica held fast to her veil until they reached the waiting carriage. Monica pressed her face to the carriage window, smiling for the benefit of her father and the others, but her put-on joy soon froze on her lips when through the rain-streaked window she noticed Michelle's look of jealousy, grotesquely evil. A look that promised ill will for the new Madam Hawke.

Monica leaned back against the wine-velvet cushion, striving to push from her mind the spiteful look Michelle had meant expressly for her. She knew she had not seen the last of *that* woman.

In trembling apprehension, she dared to refuse him. But Steven clamped a hand on her arm, and pulled her from the inn where they had supped quietly together with the gentle revelry of *la noce* in the background. Dismissing Michelle's rancor, they had all been complaisant to the bride and groom, waving them off with salutations although one of Antoine's compeers tossed a ribald remark at Monica's burning ears as she left the inn with Steven. Her father's friends left much to be desired in deportment. *How rude they were!*

Not long after, entering the villa, Steven at once led

her up the stairs, the railings of which had been garlanded in red and white hothouse flowers, roses, and exotic hibiscuses. At the top of the stairs, white mimosa floated in a bowl, spreading its delicate sweet fragrance all along the hall to the bridal chamber which was garlanded with roses, their deep green leaves and branches yet intact.

"The smell of love," Steven remarked, burning his wife's ears.

Now Steven lifted her into his arms, as he had not at the front door, and carried her over the threshold. Sprinkled over the floor were velvet rose petals, and Monica flushed to see they were strewn in a path to the bed which was also decorated.

"Not very cute," Steven said, a tenseness about his lips. "I'll have a word or two with Dazie, she was the last one out of here. No wonder she took so long. Do you like roses?"

Monica, still flushed a becoming pink, turned from the bed to vacantly stare at the extended rose. She reached out and took it, hoping he could not feel her awful trembling. "They are lovely," she said, wishing that he wouldn't stare at her so, as if he were measuring her for a portrait sitting.

So long as he doesn't pull out a brush, Monica thought to humor herself and went to the high dresser with the mirror framed above it. He came to stand behind her, and the mirror she peered into showed his manly image beside hers, his dark eyes also gazing up into their clear-cut reflections.

"Man and wife," Steven said against her moist

nape, brushing the veil aside with a tender motion, "finally. Are you happy?"

He used no endearments and Monica began to wonder, with a little disappointment, if he ever would again. It seemed to her that their hasty wedding preparations and now their wedding day had further estranged them. Would theirs ever be a joyful union?

"Yes, Steven." She told a half-truth. "I am a happy wife." *And confused*, she would have added had his frame of mind, and hers, been less set for battle than for connubial bliss.

It has been said that married love is for masculine enjoyment only, and that it is "dirty" or "evil" on a woman's part if she participates. But Monica could only believe that this concept had sprung up in the Dark Ages. How could anyone assume that anything so enjoyable must be evil?

Monica reddened. It must be that for those who were truly wed and blessed by their Creator with love, sexual relations could provide the most exciting experience. Already she felt dutybound in that direction. . . . She glanced toward the huge mahogany bed that was her husband's—and soon would be hers too.

"Eager?" The word was breathed in her already blushing ear. "It's not as if we have never known each other, you understand. So why is your body quivering?"

"Steven, *you* have known me. I-I was"—she faltered and spun away from the mirror—"I don't know what condition I was in!"

She crossed over to plop on the edge of the bed, a sparkling confection of sugar and spice and everything nice. That was what little girls were made of. Were brides supposed to be nice too? Or . . .

What Monica failed to realize in her growing bride's apprehension was that she had just opened up Pandora's box.

Not looking at her, Steven popped the cork from the tall champagne bottle. "Want some? You don't have to, you know."

"I know that, Steven, when to drink and when—"

"Not to," he supplied for her.

The chuckling effervescent bubbles rose to the rim of his glass and Monica stared across the room at them—and Steven. "No toast," he said sarcastically.

Monica blanched, leaving pink flushes on her suddenly white cheeks. He was not smiling; in fact he was the picture of virile hostility. He was not the happy bridegroom bent on jocundity. There was not a drop of cheerfulness in him.

Aha! Monica thought. Back to his desire for revenge.

Suddenly Monica quailed and drew back in alarm. *Already?* Already he was removing his clothes!

"Why, Mona, you look as if I were about to attack you."

"Steven!" she said sharply. "Wait!"

"Wait?" he drawled, having stripped to his lean black trousers, his tan fingers pausing at the fastening. "Resist all you want, dear *Mona*. No

354

one will hear you back at the inn. And guess what?"

She shook her head, not liking these frightening games, and her bridal veil went askew and made her look like a little girl playing in her mother's clothes. Then she knew.

"Steven—you didn't," she said, afraid of him suddenly.

"That's right, Mona. A night spent at the inn, for all of them, at the expense of the cock of the walk, the bridegroom. Food, lodging, wine, and women too, for Antoine's compeers, should they want them."

She stammered, "E-even Dazie?"

"Dazie too."

She had a right to be afraid of him now. Steven without his clothes was a much more dangerous animal, menacing, a tower of strength in prime male condition. The beauty and the danger of this man who was now her husband hit her like a cuff to the head.

As he moved toward her, the soft amber light crept down over his body striking each play of muscle and tendon, waking each sinewy ripple into all its gleaming bronze color, as if an unseen hand reached down into the room—Adam come to life.

He started to pull off his last bit of covering, his shorts. Not yet warmed by desire, Monica felt an icy, tingling quiver shoot through her. The dark trail of hair running down from his waist grew thicker, and where the thickness fell off, Monica could only gape at the timbered reach of manhood.

"I-I . . ." Monica stammered. "Now? Steven, now?"

"My, you are sharp-eyed, aren't you."

"Steven," she whispered as she sank down deeper into the bed.

He answered the thought that gathered in her eyes. "I'll pretend I did not hear that pitiful, pleading tone in your voice."

Monica ripped the veil from her head and tossed it over the bedstead. Coming to her knees she scooted back, but her cumbersome skirts kept her from getting beyond his reach. "I had nothing to do with it," she shouted, "I tell you—*nothing*!"

"Is this yours?"

A tiny thwack hit the bed and Monica, her hand over her galloping heart, stared down at the hawk medallion. My God, no, no, no, not Tina too! First Maya, then Tina. Why had they all thought the thing was precious to her. She thought back frantically. No, it could not have been in her reticule or her carpetbag. How could she have overlooked the one item that seemed to have brought her bad luck ever since she had picked it up after Branville had accidentally dropped it on her bedroom floor? No, this could not be the same medallion!

"Looks familiar, Mona?" He came closer and the intimidating part of him that Monica most feared was speared in shadow, his upper half being lit by the setting sun's orange-gold rays.

"I-I am not sure," she said truthfully. "Jess had one like it, b-but I am not certain this is the one that I found on my . . ." She groaned. "Steven, I don't know what you are thinking, but I had nothing to do with your brother's murder, I-I don't even know for sure"—her voice rose—"*if* he was murdered."

A storm whirled in her brain and she felt danger draw closer and closer.

"You have never been this distraught, Mona darling," he said, reaching out to caress her quivering chin.

"Y-You've never been this angry."

"Who is angry?"

"Oh, no," Monica gasped, her voice low-pitched. "Oh, no!"

For an instant she was suspended in air, having her clothes, such beautiful clothes, ripped from her, the silk-covered buttons popping one by one. She fell toward him, half wild with fear, and there was still enough light for Steven to see the full circles of her breasts he was exposing, as he tore the lovely, embroidered bodice from her already aching flesh. From their pale pink crests and creamy undersides, he let his gaze roam down her delicate rib cage, over her slightly boyish hips to her convex belly. His perusal passed over the golden triangle, the beautifully molded buttocks, the curving thighs, and well-turned legs and ankles.

"My dear wife, you *are* full of pleasant surprises."

"No, Steven," she panted, "not this way, please."

"What other way is there?"

Angry again, she said, "Not rape, surely!"

"No."

"What then?" she whispered, spread out in a pool of ivory and sparkle, like whipped cream with sugar on top. Her on top of that, and him on top of her. "God, Steven, tell me!"

"First I'll have your lips," he said, tucking her under the burgeoning hardness of himself.

He French-kissed her, his tongue whipping and stirring her blood to boiling. Moaning and frightened by this new bold intrusion, she tried to push him away. He continued to kiss her hungrily, no matter how hard her little fists bunched at his chest and tried to heave him off. Her lids half open, she saw the moisture beading his forehead like tiny sparkling glass beads. As he worked methodically at this lover's art, his fingers slowly removed the small golden pins from her hair.

Then, her hair spread about her like finespun amber silk, Steven lifted his hand from her shoulder to twine his fingers throughout the coils and twists, wrapping several lengths of its beautiful coils around his wrist. In the heat of the moment, with him caressing her lips and her hair, Monica dared to speak.

"Are you angry?"

"That has been long forgotten."

"How long, Steven?"

He bent to kiss the ivory mound of a swelling breast. "Since about ten minutes ago when you began to yield, Mona darling."

"And when we are through here?"

His mouth moved lower. "That will be entirely up

to you, love."

"But Steven, I did not have anything to do with Jess's death. I swear that I—"

He pressed a finger to her dewy lips. "Shhh. We'll see."

"I want it out now!" she protested.

He murmured against her throat, "And, love, I want it in—"

"In *what*, Steven?"

"Oh . . . God, are you naïve. Relax, Mona, and come to me."

"I am right here, so—"

"Will you please? Just relax. Not so much talk, love."

Love. Did he mean it? She was on the edge of a great discovery, standing in a silver moonlit tide with her bare foot touching buried treasure. But really, how precious was it, how genuine, how much of it was there?

Now it was beginning. She could feel it. Her eyes, closed for a moment, flew open as his tongue, a bold intruder, slid over her breast and on down her slender hip to her belly and then further, where it stopped. Without wondering what he was doing to her, without ceasing he searched until his tongue found and tasted her sweetness. He probed inward until she arched her back with a small cry, her nails digging into the hard flesh of his shoulders as his tongue began its play exploring, plundering her softness with a blistering soul kiss.

When the rhythm of her woman's body began, he

moved up over her and knelt between her legs. His hands under her slim hips, he brought her up to him and entered the soft golden mound, gently at first, with his hand moving down her slender body. That little bit of her quivered for him and his eager organ plunged deeper. Her hips rose of their own accord to draw him in further and he moved to tutor her as her own sinuous motions quickened with his.

When it came, Monica cried out, and then her breath was taken entirely from her body. It was a total, enveloping, ecstatic absorption that made him master of her body and soul. It was an explosion that held all the world's ecstasy inside it. He joined her then, his body letting all the pent-up honey liquid of love flow into her.

It was over and they lay side by side, still entwined, their hips pressing, her hair a lovely golden cloud about them both. Before she slept Monica thought: If this is revenge, then I want it to go on forever and ever.

"Take revenge, Steven," she whispered, "all you want."

He said nothing. When she was fast asleep, Steven lay awake, a troubled frown knitting his dark brows. He was staring at the hawk medallion that lay on the carpet where it had fallen off the bed. It was his own.

Part VIII

Velvet Black
and Golden

28

Monica became well acquainted with her new role as Madam Hawke. In her lovely, quaint surroundings, the time went by quickly.

When it was not raining, she rode every day, finding a well-stocked stable full of half-Arabians. There was one, a black devil of a horse, that her husband had forbidden her to ride. She did so anyway, when the groom was out, never thinking Steven would find her out. She missed her own horse, Dancer, very much, and the black one's spirit matched Dancer's; she would not settle for a mount with less.

She had penned a letter to Tina and had Steven post it. He had been kind and considerate to a fault, but behind closed doors he wasn't overly passionate with her.

She loved Steven. She knew that now beyond a shadow of a doubt, and she was still shocked by the realization. He must never know how much power he held over her, for that could only make the situation totally miserable for her. He could never love her as much as she loved him. It was sad but true.

Two months after the wedding the nightmares began. Steven had not sought her in bed for more than a week. It was as if he had communicated silently to her that there was a part of him she could never reach and that no matter how she strived she could never win his love. Sometimes she thought he'd only married her for revenge, to keep her always in torment, never knowing his true heart. Even when she awoke bathed in fearful sweat from her nightmares he held something back while at the same time consoling her, and he made love to her as if she were made of the most delicate glass that would break if he handled her too roughly.

Antoine visited often and always clung to her every motion and word, as if fearing that she was just an illusion. All of this, and the nightmares, began to wear on her nerves. Steven would sit there, hurting her with the cold savage pressure of his glances. What was it he wanted from her? He hated her, she knew; and it was becoming more apparent day by day. To make matters worse, she had spotted Michelle's carriage parked down the road and had seen them together in the garden walking like lovers keeping a clandestine tryst. But why, she often wondered, did Steven meet Michelle right under his bride's nose? Either he thought they weren't being noticed—or he didn't care.

One morning, in the shivering grip of cold, Monica dressed for an outing with Steven. Romantically and with a dew-moistened single rose accompanying the note, Steven had *asked* her to join him on a ride to the heart of Lyon.

The ride was short, bittersweet, silent. Wearing a dark topaz velvet town dress, Madam Hawke took her husband's arm as they alighted from the carriage, then again as they ascended the few steps into the shop.

Within, Monica was amazed at the vast array of colors in satin, silk, and linen; and there were even woolens of every texture imaginable. As she looked at a lavender bolt of silk, Steven came up from behind to take her arm. He laughed warmly.

"Would you like me to purchase that for you?"

Shyly she lowered her eyes. "I was just admiring it, Steven."

"What you admire is yours, Madam. Come, I'd like you to meet a friend of mine."

Monica turned, and before she could utter a greeting or hold out her hand, the plump, jolly-jowled Barney was already pumping his meaty hand.

"Glad to meet you, Madam Hawke."

He turned to wink at her husband, and although the exchange that ensued between Steven and his compeer escaped her, she did catch Steven's starry jet eyes rising from her topaz skirts to her velvet-clad bosom.

"Monsieur Hawke is a very lucky man," Barney said, nudging Steven. "Eh, Étienne?"

Monica smiled at the jolly, amiable Barney. "Tell me about Lyon's silks," she said, her eyes flicking down from Barney's head of thick red fuzz, cut short around his ears so that it looked like a halo. He was indeed a comical character, and she tried hard not to laugh when he launched into a verbiage of history. But oh—his usage of intellectual words in between!

"It was first introduced with mulberry cultivation and sericulture in the fifteenth century, you see, from Italy under royal patronage. The silk industry, you know, never recovered at Tours after the persecution of its Huguenot craftsmen." He shrugged. "The silk industry has always, it seems, remained important in and around Lyon."

"The valleys of the highlands that flank the Rhône Valley," Monica supposed out loud, "provide most of its raw material?"

"*Oui.*"

She smiled. "The chief industrial activity must be in textiles then."

Barney thought a moment. "Oh, yes," he said, in an accent full of delightful French harmony. "One-third of imports and one-half of exports."

On going out, Monica said, "*Le bon Dieu,*" and nodded, her eyes smiling heavenward.

He nodded back to her, answering, "*Oui,* the good God."

Back in the carriage with Steven, quiet reigned for a few golden moments of restful peace, despite the bad road. However, Steven seemed moody and Monica wondered briefly where his emotional state would lead.

"Lugdunum was the major route center of Gaul."

She shrugged. "So?" When a smile tugged the corners of his sensual lips, she asked. "Are you speaking of Romans? And what, please, is, or was Lugdunum? Did I say it right?"

"Perfect. Lugdunum, my darling Mona, is *here*." He waved an arm theatrically.

And so, Monica received a brief history of the Road to Lyon, as she named it and would never forget his telling aptitude of transportation.

The Romans, so Steven said, had used and developed the ancient routes of Gaul, including the Greek trade routes that linked Marseilles and other Mediterranean trading posts with the hinterland. As developed under Agrippa, the Roman road system had had as its main feature the great south-north axis along the Rhône-Saône valley toward the Rhine frontier, with transverse offshoots to the Atlantic Channel coasts across the Alps.

"The Roman towns that were the nodes of this road system have in most cases become the provincial towns of modern France, but Paris had no great convergence in Roman times."

"For," Monica took up, "Lugdunum—Lyon— was the major route center of Gaul." She laughed. "And in the north Reims was much more important than Paris."

"Ah, yes. But it was Durocortorum and Lutetia," he instructed fondly, studying the way in which her short hairs curled and spun out glints of gold at her temples.

"Oh, but of course"—she giggled now, fully

relaxed and happy with this new charmingly witty husband—"as Lugdunum was Lyon."

"You are an apt pupil," he said and picked up her hand to unroll the glove from her lily-moist fingers. "As you are in, ah, more intimate instructions?"

"You are asking *me*?"

Husky breath warmed her as he took her petal-like lips with his own, his magical fingers caressing her cheeks and one finger tracing the flowery design of her earlobe. "Kiss me back, Mona. Open for me, darling. . . ."

"No."

"What?"

"I said 'no.'"

She could hardly kiss him seriously after all those happy witticisms so characteristic of the French, and no doubt handed down the line of Capets on his mother's side. They were typical of his people, his neighbors, his own self. Her father— Yes! He was like this too. All of the jokes and proverbs originating in all the Seine and Saône country and in the middle Loire were stamped with the light, lively wit and the often malicious and somewhat bitter irony which were indigenous to these people in whom mystical impulses and skeptical reserve were found side by side.

Steven reached out to touch her cheek gently, and his hand trembled. She felt his thigh pressed hard against her own and realized the tension in him was great. But he stole a kiss, very clinically, and sat back with an offended look. Monica smiled, glancing away from him, a secret of her own stamped on her lips.

As they crossed the bridge, the clatter of wheels and hooves made a muffled din. Monica looked out onto the river and the ridges of woodland, sere now in winter's grip. Occupying extensive tracts north and south of the Rhône where it crossed the lowland toward Lyon were the moraines and the outwash material of the Alpine glaciers. These deposits had overspread the southern part of the old lake floor. And south of the Saône's confluence at Lyon, the Rhône hugged the western wall of its valley and in several places cut into the old rocks of the Massif Central.

Monica saw that despite their dormant state the valley's vineyards and fruit trees were much in evidence. But the characteristic plants of the Mediterranean climate, like the olive, were restricted to the area south of Donzere, gateway to the Midi.

The driver turned in under an ancient stone archway leading into the courtyard of an inn which Steven told her had stood there through the Hundred Years' War.

"That long," Monica remarked and said no more. She knew that was a long time ago, that war in which England had lost all her possessions in France except—was it Calais? It didn't matter, she could look it up later.

With little interest Monica looked at several carriages in the yard, all piled high with luggage. There was something familiar, however, about the tall, somber gentleman dressed in a suit of bottle green who had just stepped into the large room of the inn. She could see hazily through the huge window. He was a mere silhouette as he walked beyond the window, and she looked down at her hands resting in her lap, wondering why she felt a hair-raising chill run through her at the moment. She turned to Steven with the intention of demanding that they leave at once. But he was just holding out his darkly clad arm for her, and the smile he wore made her silly heart glad.

"You look good enough to eat, Madam."

Tawny lashes innocently lowered against her creamy cheeks that began to redden at his Rabelaisian remark. And Steven, who had been watching her closely, was secretly delighted with the high spirits she had been displaying. However, he didn't care much for the dangerous reaction in the region of his own hard-beating heart.

The wood-beamed room received them, a room large enough to have a huge window at the front side and a gallery on the other three sides. Monica tilted her chin up, willing herself to look at Steven. In his eyes there shone a hazy expression, one she was afraid to delve deeper into to clear away the mist of mystery. His eyes did clear somewhat, allowing her a peek into his soul, and she seemed to be on the point of dancing.

"Mona," he said, his tone a husky whisper.

"Yes? Steven?" Her eyes widened as he seemed to be considering the quaint stairs, precarious no doubt, that led to the upper rooms of the inn. Her breath stood still. . . .

"Will you laugh at me," he began, his eyes dancing black crystals, "if I tell you I am thinking to open a mission for the derelicts of Paris to come to and that I'm considering, very seriously the suitability of this place as my headquarters?"

Breaking into soft giggles, Monica gratefully felt the tension pass from her body. "No," she said with a mock-serious face, "I would not even crack a smile." Her eyes a delightful shade of green, she added, "It won't, however, be safe for the womenfolk to venture out-of-doors."

As they sat, Monica glanced around the room and smiled back at Steven. He leaned forward, taking her hand. "A highly romantic touch, wouldn't you say?"

"Magic," she said, her voice near to a whisper. *I've fallen in love with you, Steven.*

Monica looked down at his hands, black hairs glistening at the base of each finger. He hoisted her chin with the tip of one of those lovely, lean appendages.

"I meant the inn, Mona."

She wrinkled her pert nose. "So did I, Steven."

She watched the dark clouds move in his eyes, mysterious, beautiful, whirling slowly against the white suns. Her own green orbs burned into his, and she saw herself through the eyes of his soul.

"You have changed," he said, as the delicious repast was set before them.

In the *feuille mort* shalloon of his waistcoat he

looked very dark and rakish and aquiline, more as if his father had been an Indian than a Frenchman. Monica, remembering reluctantly the brother of her husband, wondered briefly if Indian blood flowed in his veins with the Capet blood. Leah Jeanne, he had said her first name had been. His father, Chief Black Hawke, a French Canadian by birth, and so his mother had called him Jordan.

Monica had thought it rather strange that Jordan Hawke had been the leader of a band of Ute Indians. Someday she would like to hear the whole story of how he had become such a great chief, and their love story—Leah's and Jordan's. She knew they had been very much in love, for Steven had said as much.

His ebon eyes lifted and fastened themselves on hers and she was again unsure whether he possessed a power that bordered on the hypnotic. She always felt that she was drowning when she gazed into his eyes. It must be love, she decided, for what else could make her desire to become one with every fiber of his being.

Only seconds had passed since he had put a question to her, but she had completely forgotten what it was he had asked. She looked at him, half-smiling, half-frowning and shook her head gently.

"You have changed, I said."

"Steven—how so?"

He swallowed a forkful of beef dripping with gravy, and wiped his lips clean. He perused her as, with her fork, she pushed a yellow potato into a puddle of dark, rich gravy.

"That is one of them," he said, indicating her

barely touched plate. "One would think you were in love. . . ."

Her eyes shot to his and held. "I-I'm just not very hungry lately—Steven."

In his soul's eyes she saw the possibility of passion, and of a storm also, a violent storm. He laughed, and the tumult was soon over. "You'll get thin, Mona darling."

Monica now kept her eyes on the tea she was sipping daintily, and Steven thought she seemed to have withdrawn into some highly private retreat of her own. From that point their happy conversation disintegrated. Steven set his cup down while his eyes, moving black diamonds on moon-washed waters, strayed to the pearl clip that held her glorious sun-in-autumn hair back in place.

Gnawing unanswered questions still tore at Steven, but they seemed less dangerous unspoken than set free in words. He had the illogical conviction that, once released, they would feed upon both newly enflamed hearts with a powerful destructiveness.

On a mean and very run-down street not far from the ancient inn there was another building, one which had once been something a little better than a warehouse, although at no stage of its history had it yet sunk to being used as a murderer's "office."

It was not large, but for certain unsavory purposes it would be splendidly well located.

This is it, thought Alex Bennington after having

had a look at it with the former owner. He stood on the other side of the narrow, out-of-the-way road and studied the flimsy timbering of the building and the unreliability of the roof.

He chuckled deeply, the sound rising strangely in his throat. And what, he asked himself, what was there about this old ruin which claimed his interest in this remarkable way?

Who was what he should say to himself. "Who?" Why, Monica Bennington—ah! Madam Hawke, if you will be so disposed as to do away with her. *And so I shall*, Alex concluded, walking away dressed in a suit of bottle green, and making a charade of whistling merrily.

29

Monica discovered, via Cook Pierre, that each region had its own special dishes whose *saveur* was brought out by a great local wine, or even by a *spécial* local wine.

"There are," Pierre said, "dishes which are peculiar to Bordeaux, to Lyon, or to Bresse."

Like houses, it occurred to Monica. In the south there were the winegrowers' houses with the staircases on the outside, in the southwest houses with galleries; there were houses with unequally sloping roofs, tall houses, and the chalets in mountainous regions. Then there were the long, narrow farmhouses so widespread in most regions of France. Monica pictured them all, though she had only heard some of them described.

"I would like to go riding tomorrow," Monica said to Steven who was seated across the long table from her. Then she shouted a little, smiling with humor at the length that separated them, "*On Moses.*"

"You needn't shout." He looked up from his steak

and pearl onions, and smiled. But he grew serious at once. "No, not on Black Moses. He's dangerous. Haymaker, if any horse, he's safe."

He must be angry with her, she thought, no doubt because she had not returned his kiss in the carriage that afternoon. She had desired Steven. But she had turned away from him, while at the same time wanting him desperately. She was afraid of her own deep feelings.

"I ride very well, Steven, if you recall . . ." Oh no, don't say it, not California, not the scene in the woods after he had chased her into a trap. No, don't mention Sergeant Hawke. None of it, for to do that was to bring the subject of Jess's murder back into focus. "Never mind. . . ." Her voice trailed off.

She did not press him further. He would soon forget she had even asked to ride Moses if no issue was made. She would go, however, for she had to get out or she would go stark raving mad.

Late that night, without Monica knowing it, Steven lingered outside her door, almost hoping she would call out in a nightmare. He recalled earlier in the day that he had feasted like a starved man on her profile, after she had asked if she could ride Moses. Damn, he should have let her and had the groom follow to make certain no trouble befell her.

His shoulders slumped as he turned to return to his cold, lonely room. It was cold even with the fire blazing on the hearth, he thought. He was now more than ever convinced of the hopelessness of their marriage, for he still wanted his revenge. Why revenge? he asked himself over and over. She was not Bennington's daughter, she was Antoine's; and that man was his very best friend. He had a bad feeling, though, and it had something to do with the hawk medallion. She had discovered it, but in whose possession? *Where? Who? Why?*

"And where is it now?" Steven softly asked himself, entering his bedroom and softly closing the door.

The next day Monica smugly returned from her ride, invigorated. Since the groom had not been about, she had saddled Moses and taken him out herself. After she had brought him back, her disheveled head had swiveled this way and that as she had snuck back inside the house.

Now she sat in the drawing room with Dazie who was answering some questions Monica had put to her. "His mother came from a long line of Capets, starting with Robert the Strong. There, the painting over the mantel. That is Hugh Capet, great grandson to said Robert."

"They were royal, with lands?" Monica asked, highly interested in anything having to do with her husband.

"Oh, yes," Dazie said, dropping her French at times like these. "The aim of the first Capets was to control the regions within which there were royal lands and sometimes to increase their own possessions by confiscating the land of factious rebels."

"Rebels?" Monica said.

"Louis VI was especially successful in this respect," she added. "It wasn't until twelve hundred and ninety that Philip the Fair laid hands on Lyon, though."

"It would seem that the king had the special right to take action anywhere in the kingdom should he so wish."

"That was generally acknowledged at the dawn of the fourteenth century," Dazie told her.

"*In Regno suo rex imperator est*," Steven spoke deeply from the open door. "*Meaning* that the king has imperium throughout his kingdom—"

Monica broke in, knowing by his dark, dangerous look that he had found her out. "He has the supreme power of giving orders and enforcing obedience or, in one word"—she looked to Dazie who looked sheepishly back—"sovereignty."

Monica faced Steven once again, her chin at an impudent angle. His eyes narrowed as they followed her progress out the door and to the stairs, from which she looked down at him defiantly when he swiftly pursued her.

"Woman, you will listen to me!" he ground out through gritted teeth. "You will not ride that black beast again! He is mine, do you hear? Solely for my pleasure!"

"*Oui*," she said, curtsying and straightening in a fluid motion, then over her shoulder as she crisply descended the stairs, she flung the words "your Lordship!" tauntingly.

Turning about, Steven was just in time to catch Dazie flying from the room, her daisy sampler waving in her wake. He shook his head, talking to the four walls, "Eve, I wish I had been in that garden with you. Oh how you would have learned to listen to your Maker—*and your man.*"

The cold in the room (or the cell if that was where she was) seemed to seize Monica with ice-veined fingers. Huge rodents scurried close by, brushing her skirts while loosing deeply pitched squeaks.

Big rats. One of them loomed tall; in truth no rodent at all but Branville Bennington. He was coming for her, again, and he had a courser tagging behind. Again, no animal that one, but Alex, the human beast's offspring.

Glistening drips of sweat coursed her forehead, splashing her eyes, so that she could not tell if Branville and Alex were still coming for her. Wound on Alex's arm was a coiled length of glove silk, sliding and slipping like a worm—no, a snake. His eyes were extremely wicked, hot, colorless, hostile; an impure glow of hatred pouring forth from them, like refuse or the vomit of sickness.

She shifted her slow-rolling eyes to Branville now. What vile wickedness did he have in store for her? He, too, clutched something in a splay-fingered grip.

Oh dear Lord, how is this possible?

He had—she looked closer—the porcelain jug . . . yes, the very same jug she had used as a weapon to kill Branville!

Father looked at son; then they came for her like

two deadly vipers intent on devouring her soul.

A scream ripped from her throat and she tried breaking loose from her damp tangled bonds.

"Mona . . . be still," a soft voice entered her dream-fuzz. "Hush love, I am here, it is I, Steven."

Opening her eyes that were live terror's looking glasses in the single candle flame held before her, she stared in horrible fascination at Alex's beast-eyes when a gentle hand was laid over her mouth. She looked over the wavering flame, over the dark-fleshed fingers, up the blackthorn-clad form, into orbs of the deepest nocturnal black.

"No . . . no . . ." She shook her head, spilling hair and beads of tears and perspiration onto the hand that stayed her from cringing back into a cocoon of crazed fear.

"Mona . . . Monica!" He shook her gently to release her from nightmare's unrelenting grip. "It is I, Steven. Say my name, love, say it."

"Steven? . . ." she whispered, her eyes a wild green. "I had to kill him, Steven, had to . . . had to. . . . He . . . he . . ."

Cautiously he eased down beside her. "Jess?" was all he said.

"No, Steven, no, not your brother. It was—"

"Mona," he said, stilling her lips, "would you like to come to my bed?"

She was reaching out already for the muscle and coursing warm blood that were Steven, and he was, at the same time, lifting her from the sweat-damp tangle of the bed.

"Steven," she murmured into the strong haven of his shoulder.

A tear crystal remained on her cheek and Steven bent, taking it onto his tongue. "Salty," he said, smiling into her large, rounded eyes. "You are full of salty tears—and is it proper to say sweat?" He smiled down. "Was the dream that bad?"

A moan of anguish gave him his answer.

Wasting no time he brushed aside her long hair, and as he began to unfasten the pink ties of her nightrail, she saw a myriad of sparkles through her tear-spiked lashes. Steven appeared to be an avenging angel with a gloriole about his handsome head. She rubbed her eyes with the back of one hand. He became normal again. Steven. Veiled. Secret. Impermeable . . .

"You are gray," she said, lying still as he covered her with the sheet and began to rub her chilled body down with the ends of it.

"No, m'lady, what I am is a firedrake, a fiery dragon. Do you know, you have a downy covering about your body, like lanugo hair?"

"La— *What?*" she almost laughed, despite the ordeal of nightmare she had just passed through.

"Like a newborn's hair that covers its whole body." He lifted her hand, turned it over, and planted a moist kiss in her palm. "Do you like babies?"

"Puppies; kittens; piglets; chicks—" Her lashes blinked and the stars returned, not as many as before. "What is it?" she asked him after the halting look he gave her.

"Baby *humanus*," he said, studying the flat plane of her belly with a splayed hand. "*Our* baby, Mona."

Already shivering with a great enveloping need, Monica spread her arms to receive him as he laid back the sheet, his intention clear, while at the same time he unlooped the tie of his blackthorn robe. He began by kissing the crystals from her lashes and then moved languidly down to the sheer silk flesh nestling the hollows of her cheeks.

"Yes, Steven, give me your baby."

His manner became urgent now. Like peering through colored spectacles, Monica watched Steven through half-closed lids while he made love to her evoking all the colors of the rainbow. Star shells of light expanded as his expert lover's lips caressed her throat while his hand, like a flambeau, cupped and teased a breast until the rose nub hardened.

"Steven . . . oh yes . . ."

He lifted his head, his lips like rush light as they covered hers and kissed her deeply, drinking in the beauty of her and slanting across her mouth. Her colors changed again. *Couleur de rose*, flesh tint, fireballs.

"I see shooting stars," she said, "and summer lightning . . ."

"And scintilla, Greek fire," he followed, a thickness in his throat. "*Mona*."

He cupped her face on either side, one finger lazily tracing the bruised cherries of her lips. "You have brought light into my life and everything has become colored like the golden sunrise of my spirit." He lowered his mouth again to gently, oh ever so gently, brush hers. "My life was gray before . . . Mona . . . let me love you. . . ."

Two fingers entered her soft mound while his knee gently forced her thighs apart, and he did not go deeply, only found a sweet tense promise as he kneaded her then with the flat of his palm. Now she wanted him with an erotic fire that matched his own, writhing under his hand that was soon replaced by his throbbing length. He paused to appraise the moment when her eyes jeweled with ecstasy and her lips parted, swollen with desire. She cried out and on the last heady note he entered her.

She met him with an open piercing passion, her satin body arching into his maleness. Her pleasure did not diminish as his thrusts became slightly harder and rougher, all male pounding and plunging, hurtling her beyond any pleasures she had known with him before.

When they scaled the furthest limits of ecstasy, they both reached a thousand stars, a universe of light and liquid motion, of opening fluxes, of pistils and thrusting stamens. All that was feminine and masculine, velvet black and gilded white, flowed into each other.

Not long afterward they returned, shivering embers, glowing on the hearth of bliss—but not out, not dying, never that again. As the stormfire of their emotion waned, a glimmer of hope shone in

Monica's love-dewed eyes. Steven had become more to her than life itself.

No premonition hinted at the nightmare about to descend on them both. Only Steven could not sleep. He lay there for long hours and stared at the black void of the ceiling.

30

Wide, jade green eyes flashed mischievously. Beautiful and golden, Monica stood looking out the window at the pubescent oak and the sweet chestnut below. She wanted to dance! She was in love—incredible!

Lifting her eyes, she could see the far reaches of the Saône River. From the stony plateau surfaces that mounted toward the high, heavily wooded Langres, where the birds came for mild winter quarters: ducks, geese, hawks, passerines, starlings, thrushes, wagtails, even some warblers, and a few orange-breasted robins. Even sea birds, like the fulmar, gannet, kittiwake, and arctic tern had the southern limit of their breeding range in France.

"Where do they come from?" Monica asked Dazie, turning cheerily from the window in a swirl of autumnal colors: a velvet gown, fashioned for her by her beloved Pierre with a russet bodice, golden-wheat sleeves, and a brown skirt. Her cherry lips complemented everything she wore, Dazie thought. Even the rusts and browns went splendidly with Monica's cameo-gold coloring.

"They all nest in Brittany, madam. Sometimes, out there in the forest"—she gestured with an arm laden with used linens—"there have been the wildcat and the red deer. But some of them, like the aurochs and the lynx, have disappeared under the hunter's careless hand."

"Hmm," Monica pressed her lips together in momentary depressed thought.

Dazie poked her head around the door as she went out. "I've to see to the starting of the supper."

Again Monica gazed dreamily from the window. Oh, Steven, I have dreamed of you, long ago it seems. You are the one who made me feel real fear mingled with joy in my dreams. Now the fear is gone. But is it really over? What will become of us, Steven? Your dark eyes, smoldering to black. Now I know, you are my torment. Apart during the day, together at night, you have made me realize what a bittersweet flame you are. But it seems so futile to really hope that you care for me at all. Do you hate me so?

Why did you take me like you did, Steven, while I lay so vulnerable to your manly charms? You bade me "come" and I could do nothing but follow your lead, there in the dark, while under some dark spell of Circe's cup. Was it because you truly loved me, Steven, and could wait no longer to have me? Oh, if only this were true . . .

She sighed forlornly. What will become of us, Steven?

Last night had been too wonderful to be true. Was it all a dream? Do you love me? You said you wanted me to have your baby; and did you say you lived in a world full of color now, gray no more?

Monica moved about the room, resigned to her fate—to always run as if chasing an elusive dream, one always out of reach. The brightest stars are always the hardest to reach, but oh, they had reached them, *yes*.

"Madam."

Dazie stood at the door, a note in her hand and a puzzled expression wavering on her brow. As if she moved in a dream, Monica went forward to take the message from Dazie and, opening it, turned her back on the housekeeper to read it. Dazie did not try to see what the note contained but quietly left the room to go back to her duties.

"Dazie . . ." Monica turned, frowning but saw that she was alone in the room. She had wanted to ask the housekeeper who had delivered the message, but it didn't seem all that important now. In fact, it was better that no one knew about the letter or what it contained. She just hoped that Steven would not have returned by the time she got back home herself. Too many lives were at stake. She had to keep her wits about her. But Tina? Tina here, in France?

Crossing to her armoire, she flicked through her gowns and other clothes until she found her warmest cloak. By the time she was ready, her heart was pounding very hard and her palms were dewed with nervousness. Then it hit her. Alex! He was the one who had sent the note. But why was he holding Tina? Dear God, he must have found Bennington's crudely dug grave!

"Where is she?" Steven spun around to face Dazie, harshly questioning the maid for the third time.

"I told you, monsieur, she did not tell anyone where she was going. She— Oh dear"—she faltered—"she, the madam received a note. It was in a man's hand, the envelope had only 'Madam' scrawled across it."

"Leave me now, Dazie."

"*Oui*, monsieur."

After the housekeeper had gone out Steven slumped into the nearest chair in the drawing room, his fingers curling into the gold brocade, his brow a dark bank of thunderous cloud. He brooded into the hearth's licking flames and reddish-purple depths. "So," he growled, "my wife has taken herself a lover in my absences."

Swiftly he quit the room and traced the evidence down to the dimly lighted *salle* where he bent down and lifted a crumb of paper burnt at the edges, the letter *A* barely visible in its curling center. He lifted the poker from its stand and stirred around in the ashes spilling onto the hearth but found no further clue as to who Monica's lover could be. Only *A*.

Again he slumped into a chair, his countenance growing darker and more menacing by the second. Staring back in time, he tried to recall all the men whose names started with the letter, the ones who might have been involved with her. But he came up with nothing. . . . Ah!

Her name is Monica. The bombastic voice from out of the past came to him. *Her last name is not important because you will never see her again. . . .*

Another voice, a woman's: *That one is Alex. . . .*

Jess . . . the disappearance of a number of Indians. They had thought his brother was an Indian.

Another tall, thin, colorless man. Her stepfather . . . her nightmares.

Ah, *Dieu!* What does it all mean?

Monica. Juliette's masque. *Another tried to do what you have in mind, monsieur, and he is not among the living today.*

Which one? Alex? Or the father?

Suddenly Steven's hand paused in its raking through his rumpled hair. Of course! Why didn't he think of it sooner?

If Alex is among the living . . . *I had to kill him, Steven, had to . . . had to. . . . He . . . he . . .*

As Steven shot from the chair, he knew with a terrible certainty that Monica was with Alex, his brother's murderer! And there was no telling if he would find her alive. Now, just when he had come to realize he could not live without her, she would be taken from him.

"I did it, it is true!" Monica screamed out her confession, sobs of anguish and misery following until she could only croak out her next words. "He was going to rape me—my own stepfather. I only tried to knock him out to get away, don't you see?"

"Slut!" Alex ground out between clenched teeth. "I wasn't sure, you know, because of how well your beloved Tina lied for you. But I had a pretty good idea it was you. He only wanted that whoring mother of yours, Victoria. She was evil, just like you."

Alex only laughed cruelly when she tried to push him away after he had fondled her breasts through her cloak. "You enjoy it, you slut."

Monica looked at him sharply. "You are crazy," she gasped as a knot of fear rose in her throat. He was going to kill her, she just knew it. And where was Tina?

It seemed to have taken an interminably long time to reach the address of the ramshackle warehouse in which she was now held captive. As soon as she had alighted from the rented carriage and walked cautiously to the door, a hand had reached out through the opening to grasp her hair and pull her inside.

Foolish, Monica thought now, foolish that she had told the driver not to wait. . . .

Alex had slapped her and then knocked her down. She could feel the bruises on her tender cheeks. When she had asked him about Tina he had only laughed, saying she was safely back where she belonged, at Temloc.

The large room smelled of mold and mildew. Old yellowed papers were stacked in the corners and a myriad of dust motes floated in the rank air set aglow by the setting sun which sifted through the cracks in the wall boards.

What manner of gruesome death did Alex have in mind for her? Monica wondered.

Up and down her shivering form Alex's eyes roved. "Hmm, that dress is very nice, a soft texture. But somehow it doesn't seem right on you." He paced the confines, stirring up more dust. "Yes, I think we shall leave here. My female companion was right. There has been a change in plans." He whirled on her and chuckled when she started slightly. "I brought along some items, just in case my friend's plans seemed the better course to take."

Monica watched Alex kneel in the darkest corner of the warehouse. From a carpetbag he extracted a bundle of what looked to Monica like clothing, a rolled ball of clothing.

"Here." He tossed it to her. "Put these on."

While she was examining the bundle, a hat sailed across the room and landed just short of her lap.

"But they—" Monica faltered. "These are breeches, and a shirt. Men's clothing." She turned the hat over in her hand. "Oh, how awful," Monica cried in disgust. "It is dirty and greasy! I'll never put this on my head!"

Alex stepped up alarmingly fast to stand before her, hissing down at her, "Better the hat were filled with crawling spiders or worse for the likes of—"

"No!"

"Monica *Hawke*, put them on!"

Somehow the emphasis on her wedded name gave her the impetus to go behind the only partition in the room and change into the grubby sailor garb. While she did this, however, Monica studied every means there might be for escape. There was none. There was only one window and one door.

Alex's thoughts were of a different nature. He would terrorize her before he was done. He gave a low growl of pleasure at his plans. He could sense her fear, and he knew he had found a weak spot. She had never liked crawling things, creatures with many nasty legs. Alex felt certain her fear, like a child's, would be her undoing. He would drive her to the point of madness and bring her back again. He would do it slowly, with all the repulsively crawly bugs he could find, and before she drew her last breath these creatures would have intimately touched her body—all of it: her face, her cream-gold throat, her chest, and her long, lovely legs. She is so lovely, Alex thought, clenching his hands while envisioning his planned tortures. From the *djinns*, the witches, he would find out which spiders were nonpoisonous, of course. He would not like to end his sport too early in the game. Monica was going to have to pay for the crime she'd committed against a Bennington.

The schooner lay low in the water. She was an aged, dark slattern that had done her evil deeds well, what with wild sea robbers riding her decks all the way to the Indies.

But the mates of the *Black Pearl* weren't very pleased with the place where this fellow Bennington wanted their captain to take him and the pretty-faced lad with him, no perennial sea scum that boy.

Hughy Dylan, Captain Miles Rumbones's first mate, stepped up to Bennington. "Gov'ner?"

"What is it?" Alex snapped, then thought it wiser to amend his attitude. "I am sorry. What did you want, Hughy?"

Hughy had gotten to know Bennington on the long journey from Yerba Buena to France and Hughy did not much care for the arrogant Californian. But Bennington had promised his captain, and the crew, a weighty purse at journey's end. This mate had thought France would be the last they saw of Bennington, but the rawboned man they had taken on as a passenger had different plans. Sure, Bennington had paid them half and had assured them of the remainder on arrival in Africa. Africa! Hughy could well remember Morocco and the band of raving mad Muslims that had run him off with long, curved blades slashing his backside. And all he had done was come along with his mates and poke a little fun at their chanting. Sweet Mary, but that had been the biggest mistake he had ever made in a foreign country. Actually, come to think of it, every country was foreign to Hughy, except maybe the West Indies isles.

"You say we're goin' to Africa?" Hughy wanted to make certain to say his prayers every day if that was where they were going.

Stepping forward but keeping his prisoner within sight, Alex clamped a firm hand over the yokel's mouth. "Hush." He directed a nod toward the bonny lad he'd brought aboard. "It is supposed to be a secret, mate. You see, matey, the sweet lad is who we will be holding for ransom," Alex lied.

"Wha? . . . Ransom. Cap'n Rumbones ain't said nothin' 'bout that to us."

Alex went on as if Hughy Dylan hadn't heard the word *ransom*. "And if the lad doesn't know where he's going, he can't send a message back to let those know who would come forward to rescue the lad. Not yet anyway."

"So, 'e's rich, eh?" Hughy sniffed through his bulbous nose. "What's 'is name then?"

"Ahhh," Alex paused. "Lad, we shall just call him Lad for now."

"Like a dog?" Hughy blinked up at the reedlike man.

"A dog?"

"Aye. What's 'e? A Welsh corgi or a whippet?" Hughy snorted into his hand, and then looked up with laugh-crinkled blue eyes. "See, 'e looks more like a pussy cat to me, 'e does."

"We shall just call him Lad for now, right, mate?" Alex repeated, but Hughy did not much care for the dangerous gleam in the California dandy's eyes.

"Right, gov'ner." But Hughy frowned as he turned away. From the looks of Bennington, smooth as silk, no one would've known he was going to kidnap this whey-faced lad and collect a ransom. He wondered how much it would bring to old Rum-bones. Rumbones was not his captain's real name. That was Rumford. Hughy smirked at Bennington. That he would *try to collect*, Hughy corrected himself, looking over to the pretty-countenanced lad that was putting up no fight now that he'd been subdued by the rawboned Bennington.

Huddled on the deck with the cold blast of wintry air striking her rosy cheeks, Monica squirmed and tried to scratch the itch in her drawers. Not her drawers but someone else's. She wondered briefly whose they were and what kind of vermin the sickly sailor had picked up. He must have been sickly to have been as thin as she was. But then she looked over to where Alex was speaking with the captain. Alex was thin but certainly not sickly.

Monica rubbed the underside of her breast with her forearm. That this sailor garb was only filthy and nothing else was what she prayed. For her to become ill on top of everything else would be a monumental disaster. How could she ever hope to escape then? Her chances were rather slim anyway, she thought, peering over the side into the dark churning water.

Monica clutched her belly. What was this? She had not gotten sick once en route from America to France. Hunger, she thought, recalling the dainty cake she'd munched for her breakfast. Would Dazie be asleep now, or would the kindly maid be up worrying about where her mistress disappeared to? And Steven, would he be worrying too? She found herself worrying about him, how he was sleeping, whether he ate his meals without her. She asked herself all sorts of questions just to keep her mind occupied with something other than what the dark future must surely hold for her.

Hughy was certainly ugly, Monica decided, but the other mate, the only other one she had seen since coming aboard, looked like something straight out of a nightmare. In her apprehension, Monica clutched handfuls of the blousy shirt she wore and twisted the material into tight knots beneath her fingers, knots that felt just like the condition of her stomach. Hunger pains, that must be.

The really homely one was Zach. Just Zach. And his horrible egg-shaped head was revealed to the round-eyed pretty-faced lad as he swept his hat off in a lecher's salute to her. Oh no, Monica thought with sweeping terror, Terrible Zach must take a liking to bonny lads. She had heard of men like Zach before.

Haughtily, but not too haughtily, Monica snubbed Terrible Zach. He seemed to like that even more. Jagged teeth gleamed against the swarthiness of his skin as he taunted her with what he supposed was a charming smile. But Monica stared into the countenance of this drooling, snaggle-toothed dragon and almost swooned on the hard deck. As it was, she eased herself down in what must appear to be faintness and curled her knees up to her chest.

"Oh Lord, don't let me be sick now."

They had left the harbor hours ago and dusk had already made it impossible to determine where sea and sky met. Gray blurred into deeper gray as the slatternly *Black Pearl* plowed ungracefully through the Bay of Biscay and bore out to sea.

"Queer things 'appen at sea, lad."

Very painfully, Monica bumped her head on a clewline. But she tried not to appear jumpy and fearful as she looked up into the face of Terrible Zach who loomed above her like a horrible apparition. Though her voice sounded vulnerable, she asked Zach, "What? What things?" She made her voice as low and husky, as much she could without creating a betraying croak in her throat.

Chewing a quid of tobacco, Terrible Zach said, "Ye'll see, me pretty lad, what looks good 'nough to eat," he chuckled gratingly, shifting the quid to the other side of his scarred cheek. "Ye'll see, ye will."

"Horrid beast." Unconsciously Monica gasped and the grubby sailor turned to stare at her hard, his greasy braids swinging forth, his rheumy eyes rolling up and down her slender length.

Monica held her breath as Zach shrugged and sauntered away in a bone-clacking stride that made Monica envision a walking skeleton. Monica shivered badly now, muttering under her breath this time, "Horrible creature." There was nothing to do—nothing—but watch the horizon and wait. Someone had to save her, her life just could not end like this. Not yet. She had all this love to give to Steven first.

Toward night, in order to occupy her mind, Monica curled up against the bulkhead and summoned Steven's beloved spirit to her, as she had unconsciously called up her lover in other dreams. Her stare was fastened straight up, as she lay on her back, gazing into the hazy stars studding the black sky. There was no disappointment in this game, for she was rewarded at once by a warm, shivery feeling that changed her bones into liquid fire.

Love and desire possessed her, temporarily over-shadowing her fear, which was one mercy. Monica was surprised to find a trickle of fear creeping in nonetheless . . . *discipline, dream, discipline.*

She smiled. "A discipline dream." She would do this whenever she felt most troubled, as she surely must before she was rescued. She needed to hope; she must never abandon that . . . if Alex permitted her to live into the near future.

"Steven . . . Steven . . ." The dream invading her mind once more, Monica lifted her forlorn countenance and faced the starry heavens.

Part IX

Golden Ashes

31

On the Atlantic coast of Africa, along the peninsula, lay Dar el Beida. The province was situated at the head of a small bay between Rabat and Mazagan. Although its origin was unknown, Dar el Beida was rumored to have been built on the site of a straggling Berber fishing village known in the thirteenth century as Anfa. It had become a base for pirates who harried Christian ships, and to put a halt to these raids, the Portuguese had destroyed it in the late fifteenth century.

The wild province lay lonely and abandoned, in ruins and uninhabited for two centuries, experiencing only the violent battering of the surf. No footfalls walked the maze of narrow streets leading inland from the harbor.

Sections of the walls of its original ramparts remained, and in one area of Dar el Beida ancient whitewashed brick or stone houses still stood. In a few, elderly French, Muslims, or Jews lived. As for the others, only the insistent whispers of the sea rounded their windswept stone walls.

The weed-infested gardens and villas stretched away to the coast. In the unnatural quiet, they seemed to be waiting. Away from the town, where there were no inhabitants and where the sea mists swirled close to shore, there stood one house perfectly intact. But no one went there. It was said to be haunted. Haunted by a beautiful golden-haired siren of the sea. Rumor had it her ship had gone down near there. But some knew differently. . . .

Monica stared down at her feet. They hurt because her overly large boots were hard to walk in. But Alex had said the villa was not much farther now. They had left the *Black Pearl* in the harbor, but Captain Rumbones was to return in a few months, that much she had learned from the conversation she had overheard. Hughy Dylan had begged his captain to accompany Bennington and the lad, to protect their better interests, for more money was promised after the ransom was paid. Besides, Bennington had to return to America come springtime, and there he had even more enticements waiting for his "friends." Bennington had promised them women, beautiful dark-skinned savages that lived at Temloc.

Alex had purchased a donkey to haul the provisions they would need at the villa. Often Monica walked close to the cute, furry brown beast, patting him and whispering in his ear that someday, and soon, they would escape from this mean man. She called him Riskit, and Monica knew he would travel faster at night when the wintry moon would cool his thick hide.

They had passed several, large scattered buildings made of huge adobe blocks as much as five feet thick. The ones not ruined had remained so nicely joined without mortar that one would think them naturally created so. In the immediate vicinity were several mounds and some ruined buildings; and numerous objects made of pottery and obsidian were strewn about.

The lone house stood on a small rise, like a sentinel watching over its fallen neighbors. Beautiful and skillfully fashioned in the style of a Spanish villa, the house stood forgotten. Such a waste, Monica thought. How beautiful it would be to come to a place like this to be alone with her husband. But now, she knew, terror lay waiting just behind the villa's cool white walls.

A melancholy feeling swept over Monica as she stared at the deserted villa. The wind sighed about the hems of her breeches. And then she saw it: the plume of smoke above. Alex was watching her closely before his gaze shifted to the arched door.

A moment later Juliette stood framed in the arch, a horror come to life.

Juliette purred, "Welcome to Cassandra."

Monica's eyes traveled to Juliette. The older woman taunted the younger cruelly, like a witch of the wind with her loose hair blowing back from a seaborne breeze, her emerald eyes piercing and full of unreasoning hatred. The younger woman stepped back, placing a hand protectively over her belly, and Juliette's eyes followed the movement with a narrowed stab of profound jealousy.

"Do you know the story?" Juliette said, staying where she was, the queen of the hill.

Monica remained speechless. Her beautiful dazed eyes moved over the villa while not a muscle in her body even twitched. Juliette must mean the name of the place, she thought numbly.

Finally Monica found the strength to shake her head, giving no voice to her negative answer.

"Come inside while I tell you, child."

Juliette nodded her acknowledgment toward Alex, and Monica could not credit what she was seeing: the two people in the world she disliked and mistrusted most—here together. And she was their prisoner, to do with as they liked. Monica prayed she'd find the strength to see this out for as long as it would take someone to find her.

"Come child." Juliette looked over her shoulder to see if the slump-shouldered girl was following. "Oh, do not grimace. You are still a child whether you know this or not." Suddenly Juliette spun about and lashed out to slap Monica hard across the face. As Monica lifted a trembling hand to the bold, slim imprint on her cheek, Juliette said harshly, "You will listen to me now. I am your master." Juliette slapped her once again, for good measure. "Keep your eyes down in my presence!"

Monica's eyes misted over with hot unshed tears.

She glared at Juliette's back as soon as the older woman turned to lead the way again. She risked a glance over her shoulder to see if Alex followed, but he was nowhere in sight.

Juliette was remembering the last time she had ridden her horse before leaving France and coming to this awful place where Alex had housed her. But now she had several trusted servants and the plans she had made with Alex were coming to fruition. They both had a score to settle with Monica Hawke. But she was more concerned with Esteban. What better way to get back at her old lover than to bring his wife here to torture her until she screamed for mercy?

The last time Juliette had ridden she remembered her horse had stumbled and she had been overcome by anger that was almost ferocious. She had lifted her whip to lash the poor creature until its velvety coat was bloodied. To do so had been easy, for she had imagined her horse was Monica Hawke.

So swiftly did Juliette swing about upon entering the small bedchamber that Monica instinctively fell back against the wall and pressed her trembling frame to the stone.

"A very lovely woman," Juliette began, "whom I shall not name at the moment, christened this place Cassandra. She lived alone—a recluse—this gorgeous, pitiful creature. Of course, she might not have been able to come here to enjoy this seclusion if someone had not come to her aid. Finances, you see. *Mon Dieu*, she was a busy, spirited creature even though she suffered from a broken heart."

Monica emboldened herself to ask, "Who do you speak of?"

"Ah, you are curious." Juliette glared at the red imprints in a crisscross fashion across the girl's cheeks. She turned her back on Monica. "She loved Greek names and her own favorite horse, a sleek Arabian, named Cascara. Of course, I helped her with that name, darling. I was not here at the time. She, my friend, was to see me in France for a brief visit."

"I do not understand," Monica said. "What is this all about?"

"Ah, *ma petite*, we have so much to talk about, *non?*"

Monica silently doubted that they would ever have much in common to talk about. Approaching night was whispering through the shadowy terrace, and a feeling of lonesomeness such as she had never experienced was sweeping through her. Fear, well, that she must try to allay for now.

"Now," Juliette began again. "I will tell you the story of Cassandra. Do you want to hear it?"

"That would be nice," Monica lied.

"Here, sit here, on this bed."

As Juliette plumped the pillows of various sizes and jewel-like shades, Monica picked a corner of the lumpy bed, a spot where she could look out the many-paned window, out to the windswept sea. Rescue me, oh someone, rescue me, the crashing swells seemed to chant for her.

"Apollo loved Cassandra very much and promised

her the gift of prophecy if she would comply with his wishes—no, I mean *desires*. Ah, sly Cassandra accepted the proposal. But once she received the gift of prophecy she refused Apollo her favors. Quite nasty of her, would you not say?" She leaned forward, her eyes coldly glowing emeralds.

"Nasty," Monica readily agreed.

"Apollo then revenged himself by ordaining that her prophecies should never, ever, be believed—"

"On the capture of Troy, Cassandra was ravished by Ajax, the son of Oileus," Alex interrupted, stepping up into the bedchamber. "Oileus, king of the Locrians, in the temple of Athena. While distributing the booty, Cassandra fell to the lot of Agamemnon and was murdered with him."

Juliette sat up from her reclining position on the strewn pillows. "*Mon cher*, you know the story. How clever, how very American of you." She smirked at the younger woman, shifting her viper-green eyes between her and Alex. "We should have known each other sooner, *non*?"

"No! No! *No-o-o!*"

A series of shrieks rent the stillness of the air as Alex and Juliette watched Monica, back to the wall, to splay herself there, her outstretched hands pressing the cold stone as if she could remove it and magically disappear from the room.

Alex smiled wickedly then because Monica had not seen what was approaching her along the wall, and Juliette joined Alex in a malicious smile. Monica thought they both had surely gone totally mad.

A huge brown spider was making his way toward the human arm outstretched on the whitewashed wall. A prickling sensation started on Monica's skin just as a slim hairy leg stepped out to test her flesh before climbing onto it. Monica jerked her head around just as the spider made contact with her. Her face filled with fear as she looked at the biggest spider she had ever seen. Keeping a wary eye on the huge insect, she sprang free of the wall and whirled about just as the spider fell to the floor due to her sudden move and then scurried away.

Suddenly Monica became still and her eyes narrowed as she gazed across the room to the bed where Alex and Juliette still wore their self-satisfied masks.

"You"—Monica pointed a trembly finger—"both of you . . . murdered my mother. Victoria, it—it was she who lived here." Her words ended in a whisper.

"You are very wrong, *madam*. The first one was a good guess," Alex took his time saying, "But Juliette and I have only just met. What was it—three months ago? But ah, how fortunate that we have discovered so much in common." He sneered. "So very much in common."

Incredulously Monica watched the furry brown spider make his laconic path back to Alex. Back yes, for that was where the creature had come from, its master. And now Alex was holding out a colorful, aerated box for his pet to crawl into. Monica shivered, knowing that such a large box must contain several more of these ghastly pets. Alex straightened, putting the lid on the box, and Monica realized she was correct in her thinking when Alex had trouble trying not to squash the spider's legs as he secured the top.

Alex tossed the box up a ways and caught it. "Must thank my friend, the *djinn*, back in town for lending me her pets for a month or so. Yes, Monica Hawke, you might want to swallow hard again. I did say they are going to be around for the duration of your, ah, visit."

Staring a hole in the dusty carpet spread over the cold stone floor, Monica said as if from far away, "One of you—I'm not certain which one—but one of you murdered my mother."

Alex peered over his shoulder and shared a triumphant smile with Juliette. When he looked back at her, Monica was again staring at the floor. But what he said next caused her head to snap to attention and the blood to drain from her veins.

"You will meet the one who did kill your mother— later. But for now we must have our dinner. It will be good . . . you will like it, I promise."

Dubiously Monica stared down at the great big colorful box of brown and black spiders, swallowing a gasp.

32

Morning found Monica alone on the terrace. Alone, but for her guard on the other side of the Moorish arch. Hughy Dylan could only detect her presence by sensing it. He could not actually see her. And he was now a little afraid of the charming creature she had become.

Hughy Dylan knew the lad was a young woman now. He had been embarrassed at the discovery, however. He had come upon her when guarding the Lad as Alex had said for him to, stumbled upon *her* in a "private moment."

Now a deep rose hue broke through the horizon's eastern eye, the great sun at its pupil, suffusing gilded colors over the charming vignette Monica made with one leg slung over the balustrade, her back propped against a stone pillar. A portrait of a lost soul, sad and beautiful, with a kind of forlorn poignancy that would stir the emotions of any gazer.

Monica had been wide awake ever since dawn cracked over the Moorish rubble surrounding the villa. Beyond her she witnessed the sea waking with crescents of pink diamonds shimmering on its surface. By virtue of its deadly power and kindness, the sea could either bring her rescuers safely to her side or send them to the bottom because of the violent swells that crashed along the coast.

All the night long Monica had thrashed in the lumpy bed, nightmares waking her with the sensation of creepy, crawly things brushing her legs. Once she had awakened to sit up straight in bed and brush an imaginary spider from her arm. She would have fled from the bedchamber, but she realized with sudden dismay that the door had been bolted. So she had been happily surprised to find the terrace doors standing open when she rose at dawn to step outside to relieve herself. First she had shed the linen nightgown Juliette had tossed into her room the night before and had dressed in the sailor garb she so detested. With her drawers lowered, she had squatted contemplating the manner in which she would escape, her eyes turned in the direction of the adobe stable she knew housed Riskit, her little donkey, her savior—she hoped.

"Eh?"

At that gruff exclamation of surprise coming from behind her, Monica had shot to her feet jerking her drawers back up to cover her gently curving backside. There was just enough misty gray light for her to make out who the intruder on her privacy was.

Hughy Dylan stood there in stupefaction as he

411

spied first the lovely white bottom and then heard the soft exclamation of surprise, so effeminate that he began to wonder about this *Lad.* He had had his suspicions before, while on the ship, and as he had watched the gentle sway of the lad's hips when the youth walked close to the donkey. The slender form had been hatless this morning, but as the lad straightened with a soft gasp and whirled about, all the hair that had been draped in front making it appear short from behind, went flying in glorious honey brown swirls about the pink face that was all agape. As the long hair settled about slim shoulders, its waves framing large uptilted eyes of soft jade green, creamy flushed cheeks, and lips that had suddenly turned a deep cherry shade now that some color had come into her face, Hughy Dylan came face to face with a most startling discovery.

But Hughy said, his voice quavery, "Just knew ye was a young woman." He stepped back from her then, accusing her with his rum-soaked eyeballs. "Ye ain't no lad at all."

"Good morning," Monica said as pleasantly as she could, damning the little sailor for thwarting her near attempt at escape. Then she turned and walked away from him.

"Hold up there." Hughy tried to keep up with her, but her nimble steps over the loose stones and through the sharp, jutting brush kept him from catching up to her. "I want a s'planation of what's goin' on here." He stumbled again. "Damn rum, should've never drunk so much. Aye, me head's achin' and that blasted dandy tells me to keep an eye on the lad. *Lad.* If that there's a lad I'll be eatin' all the octopussy in the seven seas!" Hughy stubbed his toe and hollered. "You jus' stay right where ye are!"

Just as Hughy huffed up to where the young woman stood, hands placed akimbo on her hips, her lovely eyes laughing tauntingly, Monica stepped closer to him and poked his chest with a slim forefinger.

"Wha? . . ."

"When I am out for a 'walk' from now on, little man, you keep your distance." She smiled at the man's ruddy blush. "Even if you are my watchdog." She sat on the balustrade then. "You can watch me then"—Monica pointed—"from over there. You won't be too far away, and I promise to be good." For a while, anyway, she told herself. And then she was going to run for the stable at her first chance.

Hughy Dylan did as she ordered, disappearing behind the Moorish arch with a grumble. From there he could hear every movement she made on the unswept gravelly terrace. He wondered just what he would do if she attempted escape, because he had discovered for the first time in his life there was a cowardly streak in him. She was so charming and beautiful that he was afraid one touch of her flesh would turn him into an enchanted being. And besides, Hughy did not want to hurt her. Still, he would do what had to be done. Surely he did not want to lose all that was coming to him.

Watching from a side terrace, Juliette kept her eyes

trained on the two figures moving wraithlike in the half-light of gray dawn. One she could tell was that creepy little Hughy Dylan. The other Juliette knew well.

At first Juliette had been about to sound the alarm when the familiar figure stepped out, long hair lifted about her shoulders by a seaborne breeze, walking toward the ragged coastline. Then she had ducked out of sight.

She had ordered Hughy Dylan to stick close to the "Lad"!

About to step away from the fat pillar, Juliette caught another movement. A smaller, wirier figure, fading and then reappearing through the fat clouds of fog. Curious now, Juliette watched as Hughy sprang back as if startled by a snake or a huge green lizard.

Unable to keep from laughing, Juliette kept her eye glued to the little sailor who backed up as if held hostage by an unseen presence.

"Wait a minute," Juliette hissed. "Where is she? If Monica Hawke has gotten away, I shall have that little man's blood." Then she growled softly. "Ah, there she is. *No!* This will never do. Never. Never!"

"What will never do?"

Alex came up behind Juliette and, lifting her dark brown hair from the nape of her neck, planted a husbandly kiss there. She shivered, annoyed that Alex Bennington never seemed to be satisfied. He was worse than she was when it came to sexual appetite!

"That odd little sailor has discovered our prisoner

is not a boy but a beautiful young woman, that is what.''

Alex murmured, "Why don't you swear in French. I love it when you do. It excites me, *ma chérie*. Leave them be. Dylan will keep an eye on Monica." He shrugged. "So, he has discovered a female in the baggy britches. So what? Come back to bed. I've some unfinished business with you. . . ."

"*Non!*" Juliette shrieked at him. "Shut up, will you! The only business we have today is Monica Hawke. Or have you forgotten that the little slut has murdered your father. Are you lust crazed?"

"Yes, yes!" Alex whispered. "Come, it excites me just thinking what tortures we will devise for Monica Hawke." He pulled at her beringed hand which dripped with small emeralds and tiny diamonds. At that moment Alex looked out from the terrace. "See there, our lowly watchdog tracks the lovely maiden back to her tower. He'll snarl at her dainty heels and keep her back, so don't worry, my lovely mistress."

"Faugh!" Juliette tossed her head, eying her lover askance. "You mean he will drool at her heels and fawn at her every wish and command. Idiot! He might even let her go. What will you do then, my bright one?"

"Do you suppose Hughy Dylan would like to live the day out?" Alex flipped a sharp blade from out of the sheath at his belt. "Or do you think that the charms of one lovely slut would make him err and take this in his gut?"

Juliette laughed coarsely. "Hah. My handsome

rhymester, your rhyme has no reason." She shrugged. "Ah, so. Well, come and make love to me and then we will enter into the next phase of our entertainment."

Alex followed the generous hips sashaying before him, but as his eyes lifted to her arrogantly tossed head, he was already making plans for the demise of his French mistress. Cascara, he decided neatly, the horse would take care of Juliette just as he had with Victoria. And then, he would be rid of both females. . . .

By now Monica was famished. She had not eaten anything the evening before but a few grapes, and now the growling in her stomach was becoming painful. As soon as she slipped off the balustrade onto the gravelly floor, her legs wobbling beneath her, Hughy Dylan popped into sight.

"I am hungry," she said, stuffing her hands into the pockets of her breeches.

An hour later, Monica was pacing the confines of the musty bedchamber when she heard Hughy lifting the outside bolt of the terrace doors. He stepped forward and set the tray on the floor. Monica fought down an urge to brush past the little sailor and run for the open forest of cork oaks that grew along the sandy stretch of beach. She could hide there until the sky darkened and then make her stealthy way to the stable. First, she decided, she would eat something, and then. . . .

"It took you long enough," she said, lifting the tray and settling it on her lap as she perched on the edge of the bed. Picking the white fish apart with her fingers, she began to eat slowly while Hughy stood there watching. "I know, I know," she said, waving her free hand, "the kitchen is on the opposite side of the house and the servants there gave you a hard time, didn't they, Master Dylan?"

The little man gaped at her. No one had ever called him master before. He puffed up his rib cage, but eyed her carefully. He shifted his booted feet. No one had ever made him feel self-conscious before, either.

Head down, she gave her full attention to the delicious fish and the assortment of colorful citrus fruits. But suddenly the tray went flying, the fruit rolling across the stone floor, as Monica moaned and curled up on the bed.

"'Ey, what's the matter with ye?"

Bent over the moaning, twisting, female form on the bed, Hughy suspected that one of the weird-behaving servants had poisoned the lass's fare. With one hand placed on the bed, the other reaching out to touch her head, Hughy was not prepared when her clasped fists came up against his chin and a swift kick met him right between the legs. Doubled over and clutching his groin, Hughy stumbled back to the wall groaning while a swift-moving figure dashed out the open door. Straightening, Hughy made haste to pursue her, only to step onto the fruit scattered on the floor. One boot slid, then another, as he tried to right himself, doing a balancing act on a ripe pomegranate, his arms flung wide; and then Hughy Dylan, all five feet two inches of him went crashing to the hard stone floor.

Groaning, Hughy struggled to his feet; then he growled, "That's it, I've 'ad it with that winsome wench. Now she's goin' to get what's comin' to 'er."

Monica fled toward the stable, her heart pounding in her throat, her stomach heaving and threatening to give up the food she had just consumed. All types of illnesses she might be coming down with spun about in her brain but she could not place the fault on just one. She was not feverish. She was not ill until she ate something which her stomach rejected, and she could not tell beforehand which foods those would be. Cramps, now those she did have quite often. The ship, on the *Black Pearl,* of course, she must have eaten some bad fish or drunk some bad water. Either that, or perhaps Alex Bennington had already begun the ingestion of poison into her body!

"Riskit," Monica called into the dim corridor of the poorly kept stable. "Where are you, boy?"

Hurry, make haste, her brain kept signaling to her panicky limbs, but she moved as if caught up in the weblike patterns of a nightmare. Her feet would not budge a step farther. And then shockwaves of heat hit her face. Without warning, she found herself nose to nose with the gleam of a velvet brown muzzle. The heat, she found, came from the huge, flared nostrils puffing warm air about her face.

"Ho." Monica gulped, stepping back to make contact with the rolling eyes, liquid and ebony soft, her own eyes suddenly brimming with curious moisture. Backing toward the door, Monica muttered inanely, "I-I was just leaving. D-don't let me d-disturb you, big fellow." She gulped loudly, ducking when a low beam of mud and straw slapped her in her face. "Go," she waved, "go right ahead and eat."

Monica received her second shock for the day. "Oh Lord, deliver me," she prayed as a dark-countenanced lad, skinny to the point of emaciation, popped up before her like a genie with very large, round eyes. He gesticulated, "Cascara. He is bad." He pointed at her chest, saying, "Must go."

"Believe me," Monica said, "I was doing just that."

The lad waved a skeletal arm, partially covered by an overlarge robe. "Arghh. Another bad one is coming." He grinned foolishly. "You may hide. I show you. *Come*."

"Believe me," Monica said, shooting a panicky glimpse over her shoulder, "I am with you."

Pale as a ghost, Monica slipped beneath the trap door and stared into the darkness as the lid closed over her head.

33

Steven Hawke hastened to the inn where he suspected he would find the same carriage driver he'd spoken to earlier waiting outside for a fare. The driver had rushed up before El Corazón hailing Steven. He had thought it strange, this driver, as indeed it was, that a lady of such refinement would be making a visit to a dilapidated warehouse. He had investigated the matter, and had unearthed the identity of the lady.

"In a most ungentlemanly manner a hand reached out from the warehouse to pull the startled young woman inside. *By her hair, sir!*" he had said.

Not waiting to hear more, Steven had taken up the reins himself and driven the conveyance at a mad pace through the town. Dailey made it just in time to catch the carriage before it sped away without him. It was a strange sight for those looking on, to see Monsieur Hawke's servant riding inside instead of Étienne himself. Halfway to their destination, Dailey cried up for his captain to halt, suggesting that it

might be more *convenient* in such an emergency as
this one if the servant took the carriage in hand
himself.

"To leave you free to do what must be done,
Cap'n," Dailey said, eying the bulge of pistols
beneath Hawke's belt.

They agreed this would be the wisest method of
approach, and Dailey took over. He drove the horses
and before he could haul the lathered team to a full
stop, Steven was out and in one great lunge was
crouching alongside the warehouse, one great pistol
at the ready, the other tucked safely inside his coat
should he find the need for it. Dailey held the horses
back, waiting for the next command from Captain
Hawke.

"Alex Bennington!" Steven shouted. A long pause
followed. Steven nodded. "We have you surrounded!" He gestured for Dailey to come up
alongside the warehouse then, and Dailey reined the
team and joined him. "I know Monica is in there
with you and if one hair on her head is harmed I'll
have yours!"

Nothing.

Steven's shoulders took on a slumped appearance,
and he said loudly enough for anyone inside to hear,
"As I thought." But the true nature of the case was
just as he thought, there was no one inside. To play it
safe he looked around and then strode in plain view
of the window, making as if to step back into the
carriage.

He exchanged a knowing glance with Dailey,

hearing himself whisper, "Now!"

With a whirl, then a lunge, Steven went crashing through the door leaving it sagging on its wooden hinges. Dust motes cavorted in the twilight and Steven looked around as he stepped cautiously here and then, poking his booted toe in the rubble of yellowed papers while hoping to unearth something, one tiny clue, to give him a lead as to the whereabouts of his wife.

Steven heaved a deep sigh of regret. His beloved. Where was she? A great heaviness descended on his chest.

"Have ye searched the place out, Cap'n?" Dailey stepped inside, at once sympathizing with the man. He had never seen Steven Hawke so shaken. Suffering, aye, there was that here; love for a lost one hung in the air. That was the prevailing aura here—that and the delicate scent lingering in the air—the lady. . . .

Steven's eyes roamed the area wildly and then came to rest on the partition. He had avoided that corner deliberately. Dailey saw where his captain was headed and prayed the man would not discover signs of a struggle, blood, or worse, a body. Ah, Lord, the pretty lady's sweet body. Not her. Not her. She had been the one to breathe new life into the captain's body and soul, she'd brung him from the depths of despair and loneliness.

When Dailey rounded the partition what he saw took his breath away. He swallowed. There were tears in the captain's eyes. He clung to something, all dusty and soiled from lying in a discarded heap. He was just straightening with it: a velvet gown in autumnal colors. Ah, Dailey had seen the lovely lady wearing it just that day. How happy she had looked too, humming as she inspected the rooms for dust, even smiling sweetly, gently, as she chided a maid for neglecting a corner of the drawing room in her cleaning.

Steven ran a shaking hand over the fine velvet skirt, brown as a berry. He saw again Monica's cherry lips as she had invited his kiss that morning, and her cameo-gold complexion flushed beneath his ardent gaze. He had wanted to take her to his bed, in broad morning light. His loins tightened. He should have loved her, perhaps it would have been the last . . .

"Dailey," Steven said, tucking the velvet bundle beneath his arm. "We'll go to the inn and question the driver. He might have a clue as to where Alex Bennington would have taken her."

"Cap'n?"

"Aye, Dailey. What is it?"

"I've a mind to tell you we'll be seein' the coast of France by the time the week's out."

The winter weather was pleasantly warm by the time captain and mate made their way to the docks. The *Mañana*'s holds had been emptied of cargo and she sat like a sprite in the blue-gray waters, ready to race the wind and head out into the Bay of Biscay.

She would take on no passengers or mail this trip.

There were enterprising companies like the Black Ball line which had instituted regular packet services between the American ports and Britain, and so far these lines had established a monopoly over the transatlantic passenger and mail services. Those lumbering ladies of the sea waited now while the mail was heaved aboard and passengers waved kerchiefs from the rail, saying their last goodbyes and listening to the Godspeeds and *bon voyages* with tear-blurred eyes.

"Aye," Dailey said proudly of the *Mañana*, "she's the most beautiful lady here, she is." He hoisted his burly belly over his belt, and watched the busy folks thronging the docks. His captain was seeing that the last-minute preparations were accomplished in haste, and with the precision of a fine clock. Hawke was worried, afraid that time was not on his side. He was snappish, peevish, and a bear to live with, moping over his supper at night. And strangest of all his captain took no wine or brandy into his system. He was like a clock all wound up, a huge grandfather clock ready to "bong" at any moment and scare the living daylights out of those unlucky enough to be nearby.

"'Ey there, be watchin' where ye be goin'," Dailey gave fair warning to a drunk who had chosen the wrong fellow to walk into.

"Och?" a slurred voice spoke up. "Why do ye be standin' around like yer a bit of a post of the cap'n of the grandest ship hereabouts? Yer a big lug, ain't ya, eh?"

"Be on your way, Spence," Dailey said. "I know ye. What devil's got ye now?" He laughed. "Kill Devil, eh?"

"Nay, just a bit o' wine, P. Dailey."

"'Ey!" Dailey hauled up the scrawny sailor by the scruff. "I told ye never to be employin' my name that way."

"Heh-heh," Spence chuckled gratingly. "Yer name's Pitt Dailey, ain't it?"

"Aye, but I never give you any leave to be usin' my name by its initials."

"So, Dailey, what ye be talkin' 'bout now?"

"P. Dailey, that be my initials. And ye know. What ye be laughin' at now, Spence?"

"Ye just said it yerself," he chortled. "*P. Dailey*!"

"Why you little wharf rat!" Dailey lowered his head then, grasping the man more tightly. "What's that your sayin'?"

"Och, I said take it easy on me, Pitt. Got meself kicked off the *Black Pearl*, I did. Got a coin, do ye?"

"Not for the likes of ye, sea scum."

"Och, the *Black Pearl*'s not as bad as ye say. She be an old lady, that's all." Spence sniffed, wiping his nose with the sleeve of his soiled pea jacket.

"She be a pirate tramp, that's what. Ye don't fool Dailey, no ye don't. I know old Rumbones ain't running tea and tobaccy."

"She ain't now. She be takin' runny-nose brats aboard 'er when I saw 'er off. Old Rumbones must be into somethin' else what he don't want me to be knowin' about."

425

"I don't be wonderin' why, Spence. Ye be the biggest mouth about from here to the London docks, where ye first come from."

Dailey cocked an ear and Spence shoved at him. "I won't be tellin' ye what I do know." He cast a bloodshot eyeball about the docks. "Besides, I ain't et a thing since yesterday morn."

"I'll give ye the price of a hot meal if ye can tell me anything about a certain American by the name of Alex Bennington."

"Holy Jesus, if'n that be what yer wants to know, I got it all up here." Spence pointed to his skull.

Bemoaning the loss of a coin, Dailey nevertheless handed it over to the shaking palm stretched out to receive it. "Aye, now for the most important question of the hour."

"Just name it, P. Dailey. Oops, sorry, mate." He scratched his head. "That Bennington fellow, aye, he sailed away on me lovely lady, 'e did. Oh aye, he be into some mischief fer the captain to be leavin' old Spence behind. Tried to fool me, they did. I knew that American dandy 'ad a little lady with 'im, 'e did."

Spence shuffled closer to the big sailor. "Ter be truthful, mate, that were no runny-nose brat with them. As I said afore, that one was a female. I can tell one from t'other."

"Did ye see her then?" Dailey was almost jumping up and down now as he shifted from one foot to the other.

Just at that second Captain Hawke made his way

toward them, his manner indifferent to those who would block his passage and have a word with him. "Not today, I am in a hurry," he was heard to say to many a captain and to the occasional friendly sailor who would stop to chat a minute or two.

"Eh," Spence was pausing. "That be yer cap'n comin' this way?"

"Aye, it is."

At once Spence again launched into his tale. "That be the *Black Pearl* what 'e took the little lady aboard. I 'eard some tales about that man what calls hisself Bennington." He eyed Captain Hawke. "Ho, Captain, I be tellin' yer mate 'ere somethin' ye might like to be knowin' yerself?"

"I've heard enough to know I would." Steven nodded. "Go on, and we are in a hurry, friend, so be quick about it." Steven flipped the man a few coins which the man eyed, and then taking one shiny piece between his grimy fingers, he bit into it, testing its worth, and nodded. "So, tell us what you heard," Steven went on, more gruffly than he'd intended, "and do be quick about it."

"Seems there's talk on the docks 'at that Alex Bennington fellow 'as taken up with some fancy French duchess." Spence watched while his companions exchanged frowning glances and then looked back at him. "Just met 'er too, he did, Bennington. She's already left for some villa in a place called Dar el—somethin' t'other."

"Could it be Dar el Beida?" Steven asked, rapt concentration creasing his brow.

"Aye, that be the place. They both be real ugly customers, Bennington and . . ."

The Scottish man scratched his head as if he could not remember anything further having to do with the woman. "I—uh—"

"This might help." Steven pressed several more coins into the man's greedily outstretched palm.

"She be the Duchess of Fitz-James, that's who." He stared down, drool beginning to form at the corners of his stubbled mouth as he saw the small fortune. "Mighty kind of ye, Cap'n."

"Juliette," Steven breathed the name while the old salt, already three sheets to the wind, thanked him again and then hightailed to the nearest inn, humming happily.

"He'll be bilious come morning, Cap'n," Dailey ventured in a lighter mood, and he shook his head as the happy man's last snatches of song drifted back to them.

> . . . then shall no soot fall in your porridge
> pot, Cap'n
> With a hoop-dery, dery, dery, sweep!

So, how was the poor sot to know that Captain Hawke's tomorrows were about to be changed into one long and hideous nightmare?

Captain Hawke paced a yard square in front of his man. "Calahan, have you heaved overboard the spoiled stores?" The nod of a genial head was his answer. "Have you loaded fresh water?" His mate kicked one of the many casks heaved aboard. "Overhauled the gear?"

"Aye, aye, *sir*!"

Calahan saluted stiffly, but Captain Hawke did not smile as he ordered: "Let's shove off then!"

Steven watched with pinched face and narrowed eye as his crew climbed the ratlines and each man fell into his assigned spot in the foot-ropes dangling below each yard. The captain had assigned the lads and lightweight men to the upper yards.

"All right men," Steven gave the command now, "make sail!"

Casting off the gaskets, the crew allowed the sails to drop down, then clambered down the ratlines to the deck or slid down the stays. The men then hauled away at the braces to trim the yards. They paused, one and all, looking to their captain for approval.

"That's it, lads. That suits me. Now take up those sheets and tacks!"

Steven's heart swelled with his haste to reach his beloved lady while amidst a thunderous clapping of canvas the sheets and tacks were taken up until suddenly each white sail filled and became taut.

With fresh life breathed into her soul, the majestic *Mañana* was on her way. Steven stared out to sea for a long moment and then, the ache in his chest becoming a live thing, he strode to his lonely cabin.

34

The land mass lay open to the Atlantic's moist winds as well as to the cold ocean current from the Canary Islands which cooled the coast. But the westerlies dripped their moisture mainly on the narrow coastal plain, and the fog rolled in thickly, shrouding the little stable where Cassandra's prisoner shivered within her airless burrow.

"She is nowhere to be found," Alex snarled to the woman slapping a quirt against the palm of her hand.

Juliette's face twisted into a witchlike countenance as she snapped, "Simpleton, where is that jackass? Bring him to me now!"

Shivering in trepidation, the dark-skinned lad hunched his shoulders against yet another blow from the nasty quirt. He flinched as the thing lifted and came down to strike his wrist where a bruise had barely healed from the bad woman's last reprimand. He looked up at her with his wounded, soulful eyes and tried to explain once more.

"Cuddy gone. He run away." He directed a finger at the abominable quirt. "You whip Cuddy. Him sad. He run away!"

"Faugh!" Juliette cursed. "You are full of lies, Simpleton. Dirty-faced fool! Where is the girl? She has fled on the jackass, so do not lie. You helped her get away!" She lashed out at the cowering boy. "I shall flay the hide from your backsides! Speak!"

Cringing from yet another blow, the trembling boy cried out, "Do not know! Do not know! You go away! *Go away!*"

"Why you little bastard, I'll—"

Her heavy hand was swiftly restrained from bloodying the lad's head as Alex Bennington took her wrist in a painful grasp. "Enough." His eyes searched the grounds then, trying to pick out the route she might have taken. He glanced up at the gloomy overcast skies, down to the fog swirling about his legs like a ghostly serpent. "She could have taken the donkey, I say 'could' have. But I think not. The beast the lad calls Cuddy once belonged to an old man in Dar el Beida. This child used to beg scraps of food there before he came to live here as stableboy for Victoria."

Juliette narrowed her gem-hard eyes. "I told you that, how else would you have known this?"

"I realize this, Juliette sweet. I am just going over the facts." His thin face grew even more sinister. "What I am saying is that the frightened beast—you did lay your whip to its hide more than once—has returned to its former owner."

431

Juliette's face hardened into ugly lines. "Where is she then? Where is Monica Hawke hiding?"

The boy cowered even lower and the orbs of his dark eyes went back and forth. He hunkered before the crumbling abode, his manner wary and protective of his home. In his simple mind he defended much more than these two could ever comprehend. He understood this one thing, that the bad people who had come here would never let him have a friend. Cuddy had been his friend, the only company this orphaned lad had ever known. Human companionship was something he had never sought before, not until the lovely creature dressed in male garb had stepped into his lonely little world. There had been another lady, but she had been sad, and she had wanted nothing to do with the ragamuffin in the stable other than to care for her demon horse. Cascara had been good one day long ago, but now he was bad, just like the bad lady who had brought him here, this one who stood before him.

"You should be grateful, simpleton, that my friend here brought the jackass back for you. We will get him back one more time," she said, affecting kindness all of a sudden. "But if the girl is with your Cuddy, you know what you will get, do you not?"

Mesmerized by the whip stroking the woman's leg, the boy looked up after a moment and said, "But you chase Cuddy away. He hates you."

Juliette whirled on Alex then. "And I hate it here. *Mon cher*, why do we not return to my villa? After we find Monica Hawke, certainly." She glared down at

432

the boy. "And we shall find her, I grant you that."
She looked around once more and before she
returned to the house, she snapped, "I have always
hated it here!"

Juliette had thought the only way to keep Victoria
and her first husband apart was to take Victoria to a
place far away, and what better place than Africa.
Better that than to remain in France where Antoine
would surely come across Victoria sooner or later,
Juliette had whisked her "friend" on a tour of the
Mediterranean and it was on that voyage that she had
learned of a villa being sold by an old paramour of
hers. Of course, Victoria's only desire had been to
find her long-lost husband, but Juliette had been
able to curtail that by saying that Antoine had found
himself another woman. With a dejected Victoria in
tow, Juliette had finally convinced her friend that
there was no other way but to come here and begin a
new life. Juliette had left Victoria alone for a time,
hoping that the brokenhearted woman would see to
her own demise. But such had not been the case.
Victoria had pined away but had not seen fit to take
her own life.

Now, on her way back to the house, Juliette smiled
nastily, like the female villain that she was. They
would find Victoria's daughter, and soon, for she
could not have gotten far. Even if she had, Alex's men
would comb the foggy coastline, and Juliette just
knew it would not be long before Monica met the
same fate as her mother. Juliette would see to that!

Two of Alex's Berber servants came running up to

him, Hughy Dylan loping behind them, huffing and puffing. "Aye, sir, we couldn't find hide nor hair of the girl." Then he sat right down on the hard ground, his eyebrows lifting as across from him the dark, skinny lad glared ominously, his eyes an obsidian threat to the short, squat man. "What're you lookin' at?" Hughy asked.

"Simpleton," Alex addressed the mysterious lad who often provoked an eerie sensation along his back. "Go inside now and brush down the Arabian. I'll be needing him to go into town."

His bony limbs unfolded as the lad came to his feet, and over his shoulder he corrected, "Cascara." He pulled his drowsy-dark eyes away from the other man, and then disappeared inside the walls of the adobe stable, his low whistle audible as he warned the huge horse of his entry.

Hughy Dylan snorted. "That devil horse'll kill ya, Bennington." Then he looked away into the fog, thinking, Now that wouldn't be such a bad idea after all. It was in him to get away, to lay up in town with some French gal until the *Black Pearl* showed her sails in the harbor.

But Alex had plans for Hughy, and he said as much, having read the look on the sailor's face.

"Dylan, take the Berbers with you and keep searching until dark. In the morning you will begin again, until Monica Hawke is found."

With the dark came a faint moaning of hollow

434

wind from the faroff desert. It was a lamentable murmur that shuddered over the great spaces, crept through the maquis, that zone of shrubby plants, and swept over the flat-roofed houses to die away at the forest of cork oaks.

"Mo-nee-ka, come out now," the lad called softly. A groan as if coming from one just awakening drifted up to him. "Moneeka, all right? Safe to come up."

Startled by a shriek, the lad jumped back in alarm and landed on his buttocks in the dirt and chaff. "Moneeka?"

A tiny voice shivered up to him. "Are there spiders down here?" Another shriek. "Oh, I think there is one crawling on my arm!" Monica cried. "Please, please, help me up now! I hate creepy things. Hurry!"

A willowy brown arm reached down and the lad surprised Monica with his strength as he hauled her up and, with his hands beneath her arms, set her in the corner of the stall. Then he shoved the square of wood back into place, brushed some dirt and straw over the whole thing, looked up at her, and smiled. He sat cross-legged and blinked at her.

Monica smiled back and whispered, "Do you have any food?"

The lad looked grave as he listened to the wind and the creaking of dried palm fronds as they rubbed against one another. To Monica he was like an animal in search of something his instinct has detected approaching from a distance.

"What is it?" Monica said, her eyes as large as his.

Then the wind came again with a stronger moaning, more tenacious, more acquainted with itself and the crouching plains, the trembling cork oaks, the long sandy stretches.

The slim Arab boy, bronze-colored and serious as an idol, said softly, "Only the wind. No one comes." He stood to light an oil lamp that swung on a beam of palm.

Phantom shadows lengthened and dwarfed as the boy moved about, digging into a makeshift cupboard and lifting two leaves to place the food on them.

"Food. For you." He handed her one leaf and then sat down with his own, his blackberry eyes mesmerized by the shimmering threads of silk dancing like fairy lights in her hair. He admired her as one does his big sister, and never once did his eyes linger on the loose laces of her overlarge blouse or leer at the tantalizing flesh between.

Daintily Monica took a few bites of the dates, swallowed, nodded as he was doing, and smiled. She took the time to study her new friend. He was very thin, nearly a skeleton, and was dressed in a rag that was supposed to be an Arab robe. Through the tattered garment his dark-fleshed body, sharp with scarcely covered bones, could be seen. His face was already worn with hardship and would turn to the likeness of parchment in a few years.

Monica set down the leaf, drank from the gourd he proffered her and handed it back. "My name is Monica. What is your name?" she asked gently, licking her lips as if he had given her the nectar of the gods to quench her thirst.

"Moneeka," he said. "I hear bad one say your name." He smiled again, his whole world lighting up when she did the same. "My name," he faltered, "my name is Simpleton."

"*No.*"

The boy drew back in alarm at the vehemence in her tone, looking as if she had slapped him, stammering, "No?"

"Who told you that was your name?" Monica tried not to grit out the question, already having a pretty good idea who had named him.

"Lady with the lizard eyes." He bent closer to her. "You have them, but I like yours, Moneeka."

Tenderly Monica placed her hand over his. "You mean the color green, don't you?" Her eyes studied his with a great intensity of compassion.

"Green," he tried. He nodded. "I like your green. Soft. Pretty. Not hard like stones."

Monica closed and then opened her eyes again. "I am going to give you a name. Would you like that?"

Sun seemed to pour into the stable and touch the boy's face. "Yes," he said strongly. "I would be happy. No name but Simpleton have I known."

"Benjamin," she said, watching his face closely for a reaction. "Benjie for short."

"Benhamin," he said. "Benhie."

"That is good enough for now. You will learn to say it just perfectly later. Now Benjamin, or Benjie, tell me how it is possible that we may reach the harbor before morning."

Benjie shrugged. "Ships are not there. Not always."

"You mean it can be days before a ship comes in?"

Benjie nodded.

Monica stood and stretched. "We will just have to take that chance." She walked around the stall and heard the horse nicker low to her. "Is he really dangerous, as everyone seems to believe?"

"Cascara was good. Long ago. When the pretty woman lived here. But he was bad when the woman Juliette came to visit. Cascara killed the pretty one."

Monica's eyes misted over and she began to feel a little faint. Benjie saw a strange look come over her face and he wondered about it. When she spoke, her voice emerged softly.

"Victoria," was all she said. She waited.

"The pretty one."

"My mother."

"Yes!" Benjie whispered softly, knowing that he had looked upon the likeness of this angel before. Then the dark contours of his thin face saddened. "Cascara went wild. He killed her."

Monica shook her head, spilling her magnificent tresses all about her shoulders and bosom. "No. Cascara did not kill my mother. Benjie, show me the saddle Victoria used while out riding Cascara. Is it here?"

"The bad lady took it away. There is another here." He shook his head. "Not the same. I will show you."

He went to a wide partition and lifted the saddle,

an English one. Monica examined it by the dim light of the oil lamp, and found he was right. Then Benjie informed her that the one Juliette had taken away had had a broken cinch. Had Juliette taken a knife to it?

"Just as I thought." She led Benjie away from the pale glow of the lamp and back into the shadows. "Benjie, Cascara did not kill my mother."

"No?"

"No." She paused, taking a deep breath. Then, "Juliette, the bad lady, she did the evil deed."

"She beats Cascara. Just as she beat Cuddy. I hate her." He brushed up his sleeve then and showed her his bruises. Monica gasped softly. "She beats me."

"She is very evil, Benjie, a murderess." Monica began to pace the small area, kicking chaff up with her overlarge boots. "We must leave here. As soon as possible. Benjie, do you think Cascara could carry both of us?"

"He is strong. But wild now."

Monica moved cautiously toward the horse. "We will try it. Are you game?" she asked him.

Black eyebrows lifted in a puzzled expression. "Game?"

"Spirit. You know, courage. Are you brave?"

Benjie shook his head sadly. "Not very brave." Then his eyes lit up as he looked into her lovely face. "For you I am this." He squared his shoulders and Monica could see the beginning ghost of the strong, handsome man he might someday become.

"If I have anything to do with it," Monica said

under her breath. "Benjie," Monica said, holding out her hand. "Do you have anything sweet?"

Briskly nodding, Benjie burrowed his hand beneath the hay and come up with a cluster of purple grapes. "I was saving for later. For you."

Gratefully Monica received the gift, but did not eat them herself. She walked closer to Cascara, cooing his name and holding out a gentle hand to him, her tone more sugar-coated than all the sweet fruits in the world. "Come, my beauty. Ah, that's it, love, that's a good boy."

35

The fog had turned to a deep silver by the time the lopsided Moorish moon, ghostly green and blurred, made an appearance. But eerie, clinging mists clung stubbornly in the lower reaches as Cascara, with two astride his wide back, walked as if a ghost without a sound to his step.

Monica and Benjie had made fast work with their preparations to flee Cassandra. From an old and worn saddle blanket she had torn wide strips, eight in all, and then with Benjie beside her they had approached Cascara with oh so gentle movements so as not to frighten the huge Arabian, for Cascara had grown nervous with all the moving about. Breathing a silent prayer, Monica had lifted one sharp hoof at a time while Benjie bent to his task and secured a muffling bandage over each, tying them beneath the fetlocks.

The horse, surprisingly, had stood tame and willing beneath their gentle hands. Monica had felt delight at her victory over this one small, but essential aspect of their escape plan. But mostly her stomach butterflies came from the knowledge that Cascara's actions told her, in the silent language that passed between man and beast, of his trust in this one gentle female.

"You are mine now, Cascara," she whispered to the stallion.

They had mounted carefully, Monica in front, Benjie with his skinny brown arms wrapped securely about Monica's slender waist. At first Monica had not known which direction she should take, but her mind was made up swiftly for her as, from behind, they suddenly heard shouts.

The alarm had been sounded.

Monica touched her heels to the mount and away they cantered.

A witchlike voice carried on a gentle seaborne breeze: "Search the stable again, you fools! They could not have gotten far!"

Cascara, with Monica and Benjie holding on for dear life, entered a huge coil of fog that had lain dead ahead, and they were now swallowed up inside it, safely concealed from those that pursued in haste on foot. All sound of Cascara's hooves had been wiped out completely, however, and as he gained speed, his riders felt that they floated on air astride their fantasy horse. There was an otherworldly look about their passage, the two astride looking like whimsical figures, and if there had been observers, they would have sworn the trio evoked a picture of the happy hunting grounds of Elysium. Spirits of the air. The fairy ring, from which a dainty sprite in overlarge human garb had blown, landing with her brown pixie atop the bark of a huge bole that at once had been magically transformed into a flying horse.

As if he knew exactly where he was bound, Cascara picked his way, more slowly now, down the hill, still moving as if a disembodied wraith floating above the earth going south of the Chaouia region.

"We lose them good," Benjie whispered. Still, he glanced over his shoulder often just to make sure, but all he could see were the swirls of fog stirred up in Cascara's muffled wake. "Good Cascara," Benjie added for good measure.

Just up ahead, the palm grove that yielded coarse dates appeared, bleak and forbidding; for who could tell who was hiding behind the reddish clay of the ramparts that surrounded the medina. The dwellings had been built of the same red stuff, and by day the Place Djemaa Al Fna, a vast square with market stalls and booths, would become enlivened by acrobats, storytellers, snake charmers, and dancers. Just north of the Place was the sook, the market quarter, and just west of that stood the twelfth-century Koutoubia mosque whose towering minaret, decorated with turquoise-blue mosaics, now silver-green in the eerie swirls of mist, dominated the town by night as well as by day.

The medina lay yet asleep as the trio entered the ancient Moorish town. They plodded along on muffled hooves, Cascara's ears twitching at the slightest sound, inaudible to the human ear, and warning Monica of the dangers that could lurk behind the next corner or come upon them from behind. Benjie dozed against her back, coming fully awake every now and then to sit alert and take notice of his surroundings. Now that they had entered the town Benjie sat up straight and searched for the house of his old friend, Youssef. But at night, everything looked so different.

"Benjie?"

"I am here," he said, so softly that Monica smiled.

"Do you think it wise that we pounce upon your friend's door in the middle of night and lay our troubles at his feet while he is still half asleep?"

"Youssef will not mind." Then Benjie paused, feeling embarrassed by his disorientation. She asked him what it was that was bothering him and he answered sheepishly, "His house is not here."

Monica shot a glance at Benjie over her shoulder. "What do you mean it is not here? Is this not the town where your friend Ben Youssef lives? Benjie?"

He had been silent but now he answered. "We have come very far, Moneeka."

Monica pursed her lips. "Too far, you mean."

"We will go to the sook," Benjie said, excitement in his voice. "I will steal our morning meal." Silence. "Moneeka is not hungry?" Suddenly Benjie stiffened behind her. "Again I hear it."

"Hear what?" Monica said.

Before Monica could even tighten the reins, Cascara was coming to a halt of his own and Benjie was already sliding off the rear of the horse. Tossing his huge, gleaming brown head, Cascara spun on his hooves to greet the friendly visitor that had been trailing them, trying to catch up no doubt for the last several miles and failing to do that had just followed from afar. No wonder, Monica thought now, that Cascara had often turned his head in the direction from which they had come.

A winded bray reached her ears, then it seemed to cry out in harsh happy sobs as the beast of burden clattered up from behind and charged in a soggy heap against the much larger bulk of Cascara.

"Cuddy!" Benjie wrapped his skinny arms about the donkey and massaged its long ears.

A very happy reunion ensued as Cascara shook out his mane, and Cuddy displayed grinning teeth and lifted his voice in a roaring "hee-haw" bray, while Benjie squirmed atop Cuddy like a skinny brown worm, and Monica found herself laughing happily at the gaiety of the moment. It was short-lived, however, as one, two, and then three heads popped from different adobe slots, the chests of their white robes plainly visible in the dark, their shadowy arms raised, and their fists waving a warning to be on the way.

Astride the bark-brown horse, Monica led the way with Riskit-Cuddy and Benjamin trailing close behind. They wove throughout the maze of streets, and then at dawn's first eastern twinklings, the foursome slept in a lonely alley at the edge of the medina, Cascara and Riskit-Cuddy standing guard over their masters until the sun rose and burned away the mist.

"Fissa! Fissa!"

A worried voice broke into the dreams of the fair one. Oh how she hated to leave Steven's possessive kisses, Monica was thinking as she climbed to wakefulness. In her earth-shattering dream, the world had ceased to exist, there were no Juliettes and Alexes, no cute little Arab boys, no darling Cuddys, and no magnificent, heroic fantasy horses—only the two of them, Steven and Monica, as they made love. How startling it was that Steven seemed so close to her, as if she could reach through her dream-stuff and accept him into her arms. But when she opened her eyes all she could see was a dark, wizened, old man with a wispy white beard. Methuselah, Monica thought at once.

"Fissa!" he said again. "Hurry!"

His face was like a frosted blackberry, and he had lively black eyes which puckered at the corners, and a wide nose of great length which made him look for all the world like an astonished rock carving in high relief.

And the old man, he, too, stared at the gentle beauty before him just waking up and blinking at the sun in her eyes. Large, elliptical eyes, ever so slightly slanted at the corners, green as Chinese jade but flecked here and there with yellow lights, peeked from a youthful, passionate, and provocative face. The old man saw eyes of profound depth, their irises like iridescent pools, reflective, lovely; and when her orbs met his, they held him transfixed.

446

"Who are you?"

"No matter!" he said urgently. "The place is being searched. You must come, you are in great danger. Your enemies have large numbers searching you out." He gestured to include the whole lot of them. "I have a store where you may hide."

Benjie had come awake and was staring with wide eyes. "What about Cuddy and Cascara? Where can we hide them?"

The old man nodded wisely. "I have a place for them too, where they will be safe. But you must come with me now if you do not want to be found. *Hurry!*"

Mounted atop Riskit-Cuddy, Benjie questioned the man who had been kind enough to come and save them from being hunted down and taken back to Cassandra as prisoners. "What is your name, old man?" he said importantly, waiting for the moment when he could proudly tell the man who he was.

Wisely, the wizened character answered, "If I do not tell you, lad, then if you are caught you cannot give me away."

Benjie saw the wisdom of the old man's words as he clattered down the maze of streets with Cascara and Monica close behind, the horse's hoofbeats pounding strongly now that all but one of the rags had come loose. As they rounded a corner not far from the old man's abode, he saw that there was no time to take them to his house and hide them there. A group of large straw baskets stood against the frame of an ancient stable, and it was here that Monica and Benjie dismounted while the old man led the two beasts into the stable. He made fast work of concealing the larger of the two animals, placing palm fronds over the stall and at the opening. He then began to lead the donkey out, just as two huge Berber servants rounded the corner, with another three following close behind.

Walking slowly, with his obedient donkey beside him, the old man came face to face with the men he had come upon before, and understanding their Berber dialect, he listened agreeably while they questioned him as to the whereabouts of a fair one traveling with a scrawny Arab lad. They would have with them a fine specimen of horseflesh, too, one of the Berbers explained while the other three slashed about here and there, poking baskets, and peering down the street at one end and then the other.

Finally, the old man continued on his way, but was brought up short by one of the Berber servants. "That ass, he is familiar to me. Where did you get him?"

The old man shrugged slowly. "He belongs to a friend of mine. I was just on my way to bring him back. He has run away again."

"How true," one of the men said. He reached out. "We will return him, if you do not mind."

"Ah, but I do." He pushed the younger man's hand aside as if the appendage greatly offended him. "It is not often an old man gets to visit an old friend." He laughed, showing yellowed teeth.

The Berber hesitated, his dark eyes casting about warily. Then, as if he had come to a decision about the matter, he said, "Return the beast then. But I warn you, old man, if you see the ones we have described, you must come and find us to report this immediately."

"It shall be as you say," the old man said, bowing his head in a humble fashion. He watched them go then, and when he was certain that he could hear them no longer, he sidled over to the tallest of the straw baskets, whispering, "You may come out now. It is safe. But you must follow me immediately." He moved away then.

The lids of two of the straw baskets rose slowly, and one peered out with green eyes, the other with liquid dark eyes. Seeing that there was no one about but the old man leading the donkey back into the stable, Monica and Benjie hastily climbed out of their respective baskets, putting the lids carefully back into place and then following the old man into an alley that led to the back of his shop.

All sorts of pottery, tin, brass, and straw baskets of various sizes, were neatly stored inside, and briefly Monica noticed them out of the corner of her eye as she and Benjie were led behind a curtain and then taken upstairs to an upper room. The old man was clad in a plain, brown robe with a hood that he now pushed back from his face. He smiled at Monica and she saw that he had the gentlest of smiles; and his eyes were so kind and compassionate that she was instantly drawn to him.

"Thank you," she said. "We are greatly indebted to you for your kindness." She didn't know what to call him.

He nodded, only once. Then he moved away and set about preparing a barley soup and wheaten cakes and when that was done, he set out a jug of sweet wine to accompany the meal. All the while, Benjie conversed with the old man, gesturing toward Monica now and then, telling of her kindness to him, and of how she had tamed the demon horse and made him fly like a winged spirit away from the evil ones.

Fully satisfied with the repast, Monica helped the old man to clean up before he departed from the curtained room and left them to rest. Out of respectful gratitude, Monica did not question their friend but left him to his own ends. She had never known such a silent human being; but then, she told herself, she had never known one as elderly, or as kind.

Amidst a pile of pillows and covered straw, Monica soon fell fast asleep, to awake when it was late afternoon. Benjie was seated on the floor and stood to his feet as soon as she opened her eyes, holding out an outfit for her to don: a long concealing robe of some rough material, a haik to conceal her face, and a pair of soft slippers. "We will go after you change into these clothes," he said. "To the harbor where we will wait for your ship." He peered into her face then when she hadn't moved. "The ship, Moneeka, it will come in?" He looked at her with his soulful eyes.

"Yes, Benjie," she murmured, "someone will come soon."

* * *

Even at his late afternoon hour, the narrow streets and shops swarmed with activity. Monica thought the frantic din of shouting and haggling in the sook, where all the treasures of the world seemed to be on display, was vivid and exciting as they maneuvered through the crowds.

"Look, Monica," Benjie shouted as he came up alongside Cascara, his legs bouncing against Cuddy's sides. "Ivory, jewels, perfumes, carpets, taspet—tapet—"

"Tapestries," Monica supplied for him, enjoying herself despite this risky adventure, but wishing all the while she would soon be back in the secure embrace of her husband's arms. She just hoped that he wanted her back, that he truly loved her, and oh how she ached for them to be together. More than anything she wanted his love and respect. But would she ever see Steven again?

Benjie's eyes lit up over an exotic toy he had spied, but then he sat ramrod straight, gallantly astride the donkey's back, with the fairest of ladies riding beside him, and he suddenly believed himself to be much too grown-up for such childish things.

At times the people on foot had to press back against the walls to give the donkeys, whose backs and sides bulged with bundles and crates, free passage. The colors and the reeking scent of hot, greasy food assaulted Monica's senses, and she had visions of the lands from which the wares in the sook had been brought by ships or caravan. Then her stomach rolled and she was afraid she was going to be sick.

"Moneeka is well?" Benjie looked over to her, concern in his great dark eyes.

"No," she said weakly. "Monica is not well."

At one side, the narrow street tunneled through the cooler dark rocks where a series of steps, steep and cobbled, unfolded. Monica slid off the great brown horse and sunk down at once, her back against the cool, dark wall of rock, her eyes closing as she gulped down a lurching feeling of nausea. Beads of sweat dotted her forehead, and the dizzying aroma of incense made her head go round and round. The marketplace began to swim before her eyes. Monica could feel Benjie looking at her anxiously as she struggled to hang onto each separate thread of consciousness. She threw off the hot robe. . . .

A shadow fell over her then. Benjie looked up and gasped.

"Well, well," the voice above her sneered, "if it isn't the princess, the rani, and her faithful lackey."

Though Monica tried hanging onto the delicate gossamer stuff that was all that remained of her consciousness, when she looked up and saw Alex Bennington, the dusty cobbled streets behind him seemed strangely empty. And then, he too, disappeared from view.

36

The sea turned sullen, its dingy waves churning and worrying the *Mañana*'s hull. Captain Hawke stood with arms folded, legs spread slightly apart, balancing himself easily against the mischievous roll of his ship.

Steven had been pacing back and forth just forward of the poop ladder, his gaze scanning the set of the sails, searching the leaden sea. At intervals he would mount to the poop deck to check the compass reading and bark an order to the helmsman; then he would return to the quarter-deck and resume his pacing.

Just the night before, he had awakened from a fantastic, warm dream of lovely limbs entwined around him. It had been so real, Steven had felt that if he were but to reach out he could have taken his beloved into his arms. Had he heard her calling him? He had sunk back against the pillow and listened, but no sound had come to his ears save the creaking of the ship's timbers and the dull thud of waves against the hull.

"Steven." Again the sea siren cried, but it was only the thrum of the wind against the stern windows. Just thinking of Monica safe in his arms, warm and loving, of the soft charms beneath the delicate fall of lace adorning the bodice of her nightgown, sent delicious tremors through Steven's body. Her sweet face and cherry lips tormented him day and night, making passionate hot blood surge within him. But there was no help for it.

At such moments as these Steven strove to steer his thoughts into more sober channels and to seek comfort from his soul's pain by contemplating the vastness of the ocean. But here, too, Steven was painfully reminded of Monica: now shadowing wistfully, brooding; then enchanted, serene, all full of charming golden smiles. Her windsong lifted wildly to his ears, ah yes, Monica, with foam like a silvery green ribbon in her hair, her youthful breasts pulsing deep with every wave that washed over her, her hips arching, wanting, wanting more, ever more. As his pulse began to quicken Steven tore himself from his wild, inner imaginings. He looked up and out. Now the ocean was cloaked in a blanket of fog, and the wind, blowing in fitful gusts, was freighted with cold and damp.

Several days later the *Mañana* slipped, like a silent wraith, into the waters outside Marrakesh. They lay two miles off the coast. Early morning, dead calm. The captain strode about the quarter-deck, driving his crew with many a potent sea oath. He wanted to make certain that everything would be shipshape in time for their entry into port. The sailors labored in good cheer though they talked loudly of the carousals they intended to indulge in while in Marrakesh.

Their hasty words, Dailey noticed, had not escaped the captain's ears, for Dailey watched Steven Hawke frown darkly. They would never get as far as the crowded sook, he was certain. But then, Dailey shrugged, one could never tell how far into the medina that villain Bennington had taken his captain's beloved lady.

Hands locked behind his back, legs braced wide apart, Captain Hawke stood beside the helmsman. His keen eyes expertly scanned the trim of the sails, darted toward the blurred outline of land, then back to his ship.

"'Tis awfully quiet, Cap'n," Calahan said.

"Aye."

Something was out of order; it was a feeling he had, of approaching catastrophic doom. But his tone was light as he spoke, "It'll most likely take us another day to get in. This fog is treacherous, to say the least." He yelled below then. "Jacques, break out the sounding gear. I don't want us running into any sandbars on the way in. If"—he stressed—"we even get her in today."

The first call came up: "By the mark—two fathoms."

A hesitation.

"By the mark—four fathoms."

Captain Hawke's whole body grew tense with a

sort of mingled excitement and concentration as he pitted his seamanship and experience against the machinations of wind, tide, and currents. He frowned, though, the feeling in the pit of his belly growing stronger. There were no charts for this area, and he knew that beneath the surface of the waters could lurk treacherous shoals which, unless a captain knew exactly their whereabouts, could rip out the belly of any proud ship, pile her up, and sink her in the twinkling of an eye.

Suddenly a strange, unaccustomed silence settled over the *Mañana.* What was she telling her captain? Why? the men wondered, and the captain now too, Why was there no motion? It was eerie, almost as if a soundless cry was coming up from the heart of the vessel.

"By the 'orns of Satan," one of the crewmen crooned.

Steven Hawke's whole life up to the time of his boarding the *Mañana* seemed forever lost in a distant and shadowy past. "No," Steven cried. "*No!*"

Even Monica's lovely, charming features lost their poignancy in Steven's mind's eye, and it was as if she were but the image of a half-remembered dream, so long ago.

He thought he heard a woman's quick gasp, a scream, and then that awful forbidding silence. At that moment a deadly moan and a cracking of timbers clutched Steven's heart, he was thrown forward to the upper rail as the *Mañana* pitched forward with sickening force, taking the jutting rock in her belly and then rolling back like a wounded beast.

Men were suddenly shouting and scurrying all over the decks as Steven bellowed, "Get below and check the damage!" He whirled about to face a sailor. "Swing a man over the side to do the same!"

It wasn't long before a man came up from below. "Water pouring in bad, Cap'n. We won't be able ta save 'er, that rock tore the bottom out of 'er belly."

"Get ready your personals, men, and make ready to abandon ship." Steven cursed loudly, heading toward his cabin, and ordering two of his men to accompany him below.

There he directed them to bind up two of his trunks as he himself took up his logbooks and maps, knowing that this spot would have to be charted in order to keep others from falling victim to the same misfortune. The longboats were lowered into the fog-swirled waters and Steven appeared on deck with his trunks, which were taken down into the longboats before he climbed down himself.

The once beautiful ship listed to port, and her cannon, which had come loose, rolled across the deck and smashed through the rail to disappear into the greedy coils of the deep.

Steven stayed where he was, on deck, still shouting orders. "Get those boats away, men! I'll be with you in a minute!" he called down. Then he turned about, staring at the tilting deck of the ship. She had faithfully served him, he thought, and he was indeed saddened to lose his first love, his first ship. Choked emotion rose in his throat as his eyes misted over.

With a low growl, Steven swung over the side to the last longboat where Dailey awaited his captain. He shivered as he heard Captain Hawke swear vengeance on Alex Bennington's head. "This would not have happened if the bastard had not taken Monica. Damn the man to hell!" But would he find his wife alive—or dead, like his brother who had fallen beneath the villain's hand?

All four longboats bobbed in the water now. "Put your backs into it, men! Soon we'll have another ship under our feet, namely the *Black Pearl*!"

By midmorning a brisk breeze tore the landward haze to shreds and straight ahead, mysterious and purple in the distance, lay the Moroccan coast. Steven smiled as a wicked gleam entered his eyes. The sight of the peninsula seemed to have added a new measure of energy to Captain Hawke.

The sun was hugging the tops of the hills on the mainland when the longboats sailed past the first of the cork oaks that stood like sentinels guarding the approach to Dar el Beida. Through the spyglass Steven observed the bits of land. "It is sparsely wooded and appears mostly uninhabited." He ran a moist, nervous hand over his breeches, up and down methodically along his muscled thigh.

"Don't have to go far inland, Cap'n, and we're in Marrakesh. Aye, there's plenty of action there."

"Of course." Sullen, Captain Hawke looked

behind to where the fog shrouded the watery gravesite where his lovely lady was sinking fast—or had already surrendered to the Neptunian god of the deep.

Saddened greatly by his loss, Steven turned back toward the peninsula, strengthening his wits and mood in readiness for the search for his wife, perhaps even the battle for her life.

Monica's eyes came open, a wild look in them as they focused on the strange battle taking place in the middle of the marketplace. She blinked twice, and then craned her neck as she felt her own astonishment wash over her face. She steeled herself to rise and aid her friends. However, it did not look as if she were needed at the moment, for her three companions were doing quite well without her assistance. She stared on.

Benjie rode upon Alex Bennington's back, kicking and clawing the raging man, while Cuddy and Cascara contributed to the foray by kicking and biting the Berber servants who tried to draw near to the swooning young woman against the wall.

"Foul-smelling lackey, off my back," Alex shouted, trying to grab the lad by the britches or the hair, anything to get at the wild cockroach who was bruising his backside and ripping his hair out by the roots. "Damn you lad, you are killing me! *Awwww!*" With a wild "hee-haw" the donkey had showed Alex the dark stripe running along his back and then given him a healthy kick in the shins.

Boxed on the ears, pummeled and spanked and pushed around until he was bruised and suffering a hangoverlike headache, Alex fell to his sore knees, kissing the cobbled street as Benjie vaulted onto his back one more time to ride him and pound his head into the ground. Alex Bennington screamed for all he was worth when the grinning donkey grasped Alex's breeches and a good deal of his flesh in his teeth.

"Cascara!" Benjie shouted, running toward Monica and lifting her up before she could even think twice. He shouldered her up onto the horse's back and then shoved her the rest of the way, his palm pushing her buttocks. Wide-eyed at the lad's overfamiliarity, Monica looked down and was about to scold him when she saw him take to the donkey's back. "Go!" he shouted at her aching head. "Go, Moneeka!"

The Berbers were rushing Cascara to take hold of the reins but the horse recognized the danger and reared, his front hooves flashing sharp and dangerously close to their bobbing heads. They ducked out of harm's way as the stallion's forelegs came down in a scissorlike motion and then clattered before the horse leapt into the air and stretched out in a gallop. Rider and beast—both pairs—vanished in the twinkling of an eye.

The turbaned heads of the Berbers sped to and fro in a comical rush to retrieve their fallen weapons. Seated in a childish fashion with his legs tucked beneath him, Alex Bennington moaned and groaned, alternately clenching his fists in the air or massaging his aching backside. As he tried to stand, one of his warriors galvanized himself into action and bent down to give a hand to Alex.

"Don't touch me, you fool!" Alex growled and gnashed his teeth. He felt his tender jaw and grimaced. Assault and battery, that's what it was. Blood trickled from the corner of his mouth onto his chin while Alex took out a hanky to dab at it, snarling to those gawking at him, "Well, fools, don't just stand there. Damn! Give chase and don't return until you have them." He limped after them as they began to move out. "Wait! Find me a horse . . . you damn fools can run as fast as one, anyway, so why should I kill myself in trying to keep up. Hurry and get me a mount! *Fissa!*" Alex grumbled to himself: "Bloodthirsty devils . . ."

It took every ounce of Monica's strength and concentration to cling to Cascara's wildly undulating back. She stood in the iron stirrups to ease the pounding her tender backside was receiving, and with each and every fall of Cascara's hooves she felt the shock go clear to her aching head. Her stomach floated somewhere outside her body as she buried her face in Cascara's mane, her own hair whipping out in a long streak of tangled honey brown banners behind her. She had left the robe behind.

Monica cast a swift glimpse over her shoulder to see Benjie trying hard to keep up with her and clutching Cuddy's erect mane while shouting curses back to the yelling merchants whose market stalls and booths were being disturbed by the dodging donkey. An enraged fruit seller slowed their flight when he grabbed hold of the tuft that formed the end of Cuddy's tail. But Cuddy kicked, sending the angry fruit seller sprawling into the collapsed sides of his booth, his lemons, limes, and oranges flying colorfully in all directions.

Enjoying the mischief, the braying beast picked up the flight once again, and Benjie yelped with glee because they had gained a goodly distance on their pursuers. He could no longer hear their pounding feet. Slowing to a fast walk now, Cuddy came up alongside Cascara and they made their way down the street, now heading in the direction of the wood and adobe warehouses.

"Cap'n, did ye see that?"

Captain Hawke stood still as Dailey put the question to him after they had just witnessed a strange little scene. The crew had scattered throughout the marketplace, having promised to search until the hour when the sun dipped and washed the red clay with its greater vividness. Before Steven could respond to Dailey regarding the commotion that had suddenly broken out, when he had tried to see what was going on over the many curious turbaned heads and over the baskets women bore atop theirs, Jacques was running up to report to him that the *Black Pearl* had been sighted coming in.

With glittering eyes the captain watched Jacques

as he leaned a little to the right, like a ship listing to one side, and even more curious, Steven kept his eye trained on the crew member as he caught an orange sailing in the air, an orange that could have been deliberately tossed over to him. But it hadn't been meant for his consumption at all.

"Take her," Captain Hawke rapped out the order.

With delicious juice dripping from his chin, Jacques gulped down a section and said, "*Dieu*! Now?"

"Now," the captain repeated. "I want the *Black Pearl*. Gather up your mates, Jacques, not tonight, not tomorrow—now!"

With a shrug and a mischievous grin that made the Frenchman look like the devil incarnate, he saluted his captain and then whirled to disappear into the crowd. That same crowd had parted just enough for Captain Hawke to catch the fleeing backsides of the foursome—a lad bobbing upon the back of a braying jackass and a tall, gleaming Arabian leading the way. But it was the streaming mass of honey brown hair that captured the captain's eye, the slender form of the fair one so out of place here, the turn of her head as she glanced over her shoulder to make certain her unique company followed close behind.

Captain Hawke stroked his stubbled chin. "Dailey," he said thoughtfully.

"Aye, Cap'n. What is it?"

"You say that there are storytellers here?"

"Aye."

"Acrobats?"

"Aye."

"Snake charmers and dancers?"

"Aye, all of them, Cap'n." He tried to read the brooding expression before him. "What are ye thinkin', Cap'n?"

"Oh," Steven said, looking toward the direction in which the odd foursome had gone. "I suppose it is nothing. But, Dailey, did you happen to catch a good look at the girl riding the Arabian?"

"Oh, aye, Cap'n. That little beauty had breeches on, though, so—" Dailey groaned then. "So . . . Hell and confusion, Cap'n! Ol' Spence said that there was a runny-nose brat what boarded the *Pearl* with Bennington! Cap'n, he changed his mind quick enough when he saw you coming with coin a'jinglin' in your pocket. He said that lady was no lad, sure as I been standin' here with ye alive and well!"

Captain Hawke muttered an obscenity and whirled on his booted heel. Without any ceremony or respect for the custom of haggling, Steven picked out a white Arabian from a group of five standing about, and with a running leap into the air, he felt himself landing in a perfect seat atop the startled mare. He had her under control in no time, and Dailey watched him detach the white mare from the others and leave the gaping owner to watch him fly down the street in a cloud of dust. The Arab gesticulated wildly as he spoke, jerking an arm in the direction of the crashed stall, then down the street after the fleeing jinni astride his beautiful white Arabian.

37

Along the narrow winding streets Monica and Benjie took to flight once again. The air was growing cooler with the north wind's gusts, but the red clay abodes and the storage buildings sheltered their passage so that they could see the way up ahead without the sand and the pollution from the marketplace flying in their eyes.

"He comes, Moneeka!" Benjie shouted from behind Cascara's floating tail.

"Who is it now, Benjie?"

"Another bad. On a white horse now. You go to hide. Meet Benjie at old man's. I—"

"Be careful, Benjie!" Her voice was snatched up and away by the wind just as Benjie's had been.

We take care of them good. Monica's lovely countenance was filled with bewilderment. Had she imagined this or had she really heard Benjie shout this to her? There was no doubt in her mind, however, that Benjie and Cuddy would take care of the new huntsman who had taken up the chase astride the white steed. Paid well by Alex Bennington, who else! In this respect she could fully trust the boy and the donkey, they would make sure the man would not pursue her anywhere, not for a long time, anyway.

Having positioned Cuddy sidewise, Benjie was planning to head the huntsman off at the next corner. Holding onto a brightly colored awning above his head, Benjie swung into the air at exactly the right moment and landed on the man's back. This was no simple man, Benjie was thinking, taking hold of muscles that rippled and bunched beneath his hands. He must be a pirate, Benjie decided, one who worked for the bad man Alex.

"What the devil? . . ."

It was as if a horde of giant gnats were suddenly attacking Steven Hawke. He couldn't force the boy from his back; Steven had never known a lad to be this wild.

Stubbornly, Benjie refused to let go of the broad shoulders or to unwind his legs from around the man's surprisingly slim waist. The pirate's shouts and curses infuriated Benjie, but he was determined to cost the man enough time so that Monica could make it back to the old man's shop to hide until he showed up.

"Savage little monkey!" Steven shouted, trying to keep his mount under control, but the horse was going wild with all the jumping about on her back. "Wait till I get my hands on your scrawny neck!" Steven ground out, catching a glimpse of the lad from the corner of his eye.

Steven was about to do just that when, wonders upon hellish wonders, the braying ass began attacking him, too, as the boy prickled him painfully between his ribs. Steven did not have to see them to know that the savage, brown-skinned lad had fingernails as sharp and dangerous as a woman's. But Steven's jab caught the boy, and the air rushed from Benjie's lungs in a sob of defeat. Seconds later the lad felt himself being tossed onto his back in the dirt.

Savage, dark wolfish eyes burned into Steven's own, and he chuckled low, not knowing how sinister he sounded to the boy laid out on the ground.

Bending over the lad, Steven grimaced from the stinging little cuts spread over his rib cage. He narrowed his eyes at the lad.

"Didn't anyone ever teach you that it's not normal for a kid your age not to bite your nails?"

"Bad!" Benjie spat upward with all the surging power he could muster in his tongue and lips. But the spittle never reached the man. The flat of Steven's boot had shot out and sent the separating gob boomeranging back. *"Awsh!"* Benjie cried as he was momentarily blinded by his own spittle. He rolled over and felt a boot come against his skinny rear, not very gently either. It stayed.

"Judas," Steven groaned to himself, looking up and down the street. The white horse had disappeared. He eyed the donkey at the same time the lad did. "Uh, uh, uh," Steven clucked in a warning tone.

Now Benjie shivered. Uttering a savage oath, the towering pirate reached down to snatch Benjie about the waist. Benjie kicked out and squirmed and hollered, but Steven easily overpowered him, lifting the lad off his feet and tucking him without ceremony beneath his arm. "*Mon Dieu*, don't you ever eat?" he said.

"Bad!" Benjie screamed and yelled at the top of his lungs. "*Baaad! Baaad!*" He proceeded to pound Steven's hard thighs with his fists, but found he was only hurting himself.

Steven sighed dispassionately. "I'm beginning to think, kid, that you and your ass are related. Could it be you are not a boy after all?"

"But I am not a Cuddy!" Benjie protested, stung by the pirate's words.

"Granted you are not," Steven said with a mild shrug. "Whatever a cuddy is. And I am not a *baad*."

"Riskit-Cuddy!" Benjie shouted and the donkey did a flip-kick and then went clattering down the cobbled streets at his master's command.

"Now I see what you mean," Steven said. "So, you are not a cuddy."

"I am Benjamin!" the boy said proudly. "Benjie for short. My lady will adopt me someday. She means to give me her last name, too." He ended on a note that dared anyone to step forward and challenge that!

Holding the boy in a secure grip about the waist, Steven lowered him and hunkered down beside him. He shifted the pistols in his wide belt while the lad looked downward warily, a new light lurking in his eye, however.

Their eyes, man and boy's, met and held. The big man was so close to Benjie that he could see anger and bittersweet pain moving fluidly in the shades of black. "I am not a mean man, Benjamin," Steven softly said.

"You aren't?"

"No. I am just searching for something, someone very precious that I lost."

"But my lady says—"

Steven placed a gentle finger over the boy's quivering lips. "Benjamin," he said, "who is your lady and what is her name?" He lowered his hand to the boy's shoulder.

"The little bitch!" Alex Bennington panted, his colorless eyes blazing for once with a touch of blue. "We'll get her now." With demonic vengeance, he slapped the butt of the huge mule, cursing because the animal was choosing this moment to become stubborn. "Get this stupid ass going for me, will you, you pack of fools!" he gritted to the Berbers standing about and hiding their grins at the strange sight of the dandyish American astride the mule. "That's it," he said to one who had stepped forward to whack the mule a good one with his scabbard. "We'll just cut off to the left here and head her off. Come on men! I knew there was something fishy about that old man back there at that shop you men were snooping around in. That furry jackass just shows up in too many places to suit me. We'll just beat her back to the place."

Monica had finally gotten Cascara to slow down but she still cast tired glances over her shoulder to make sure she wasn't being followed.

Up ahead loomed the cluster of warehouses and storage buildings, and she could see the corner of the old man's shop now. She breathed a sigh of relief, telling herself she would have need to be more cautious now so that Alex Bennington would not catch up to her again. Her main problem now lay in getting safely to the harbor and smuggling herself and Benjie onto the *Black Pearl*!

Wearily she hung her head, and feeling lulled into safety she plodded the stallion over to the alleyway. Cascara hung his head, too, and dozed in the weak beam of the lowering sun. The heat felt so good to her, warming, gentle, as if she were wrapped in Steven's arms, so secure. . . .

"Oh, Steven, Steven, will I never see you again, my love?" The kindling of their love, which had only just begun to flame, now lay in ashes. It had flamed, hadn't it? Wistfully she prayed that he had loved her as much as she loved him, even now. What they had shared had been theirs for so little time that Monica found herself questioning the chance that it might have had for survival. Had it been, on Steven's part, mere fleeting lust? How like paradise it would be if those feelings had had a chance to mature into true love.

All of a sudden Cascara was jerking his head up, his iron-thewed hoofs drumming on the cobbles. His pricked ears and flaring nostrils told Monica that danger was near. Her soft green eyes narrowed.

"Cascara!"

Instantly she was surrounded by shouting Berbers and rough hands were seizing her and the horse. Her own fear and the sharp smell of sweat mingled as Monica felt herself being hauled off Cascara's back, yanked by her hair until she thought it would come out by the roots. For a panic-stricken moment she visualized herself being ravished by each and every one of these foul-smelling men whose tongue was totally foreign to her, but she knew their crude conversation had to do with the clothes she was wearing, and she also realized that two of them worked for Alex Bennington.

So when a curt command came from a man just dismounting from a mule, Monica was not surprised to see Alex striding toward her. He paid her no mind, so cool and deadly was he, but rapped out an order to the three dark-skinned men who held her.

"Take that devil horse to the *Black Pearl*." When they hesitated, he shouted at a hook-nosed man wearing a black robe, one that appeared to be their leader. "Immediately!" Alex shook his head like a bull enraged by a red sheet. *"Fissa!"*

They gathered together and laughed at Alex's pronunciation of the word, but the hook-nosed leader demanded sharply that they do as the lean American ordered. What Alex did not understand was that the leader explained in their tongue that if

471

everyone did his job well there would be a weighty purse for each of them, the American had promised. Hadn't he already given them a box of magical spiders that would bring them a small fortune in Rabat?

Monica, though still wearing the dusty, worn breeches and baggy shirt, looked stirringly beautiful and oddly vulnerable, despite her wind-blown hair and flushed countenance. As Alex Bennington thought these things he also realized that the young woman possessed a rare courage and a free spirit despite her delicate beauty. It would be sad to see such a lovely and fragile flower crushed so early in its blooming, but it must be done. Monica must pay for her sins.

Alex's keen eyes shifted from the old man standing worriedly by, wringing his hands and peeking around a corner in the alleyway, and swung to Monica. To the remaining Berbers who understood his own language, he gave an order. "Take the woman inside the warehouse and be sure you tie her up so that she cannot escape." He slapped the quirt on his rawboned thigh. "I'll be with her shortly," he warned.

The old man had left his place at the corner and was scurrying down the alley to his back door when, shooting a glimpse at the corner he had just vacated, he saw the ugly foreigner coming after him, his long strides eating up the distance with a deadly swiftness that caused the old man to shiver uncontrollably. He shot around the door, moving surprisingly fast for one his age, and took the bolt up into his quaking hands.

A helpless cry rose in the old man's throat when he realized he could not bolt the door, and that door was now being pushed inward and was carrying his weight along with it. The old man heard the door close and began to back toward a low table piled high with various items of merchandise, his eyes blinking away moisture while they stared straight ahead. He looked up then but did not cower. A brass kettle was overturned and fell to the floor with a loud crash. Then all was silent.

Unconsciously, Steven's hands began to caress the ornate handles of his pistols as he contemplated Alex Bennington's demise. His thoughts turned to Monica then, and he swallowed, feeling cold perspiration beading his forehead.

"Captain, please!" Benjie cried, stepping before the man to break his fixed concentration. "You must come. Now. Must save Missy Moneeka." The boy grasped Steven's coat sleeve and gazed at him searchingly. "No time to lose!" He eyed the man, more suspicious now. "Is true you love Missy Moneeka?"

Steven blinked down at the boy, the murderous blood lust suddenly wiped from his eyes. "Take me to your lady then, mate!" He looked up to see the donkey clattering down the street, doing flip-kicks now and then. "Cuddy is fast. You like to ride?" Benjie asked, smiling at the picture the tall captain would make seated on Cuddy, his long legs nearly touching the ground.

Lunging forward, Steven brandished an imaginary sword. "Ready now, let's go!" He stepped back a few paces and then threw himself onto the donkey's back.

"Hiyaah!"

At first a little surprised and affronted when the boy sailed onto the donkey's back, taking the prime seat up front and forcing Steven back, he was soon smiling, and he announced to the world as they clattered away in all haste, "Ah, the lad is every inch a king!" Then, regarding the boy's slender back, Steven realized he had swiftly grown fond of this brave little ragamuffin whose unflagging devotion to his wife—Moneeka—moved him.

Benjie was gulping hard as he called back, "We save her, yes, Captain? We be in time?"

"Oh, I assure you that we will, Benjamin."

The pale shaft of sunlight no longer filtered into the alley where not long before it had beamed accusingly on the man just leaving by a back door, cold-blooded determination driving him to his next act of blood lust. The next one would be special—the one Alex Bennington had long been awaiting and working himself up to. He felt dizzy from his need to snuff out the life of that lovely flower.

No sooner had Alex Bennington vacated the alley than it was occupied again, this time by a very concerned neighbor of the old man, another shopkeeper of Marrakesh, a man who had prospered in the batik trade who had dealings with the East India Company.

Hakim took a tentative step toward the old man, once he was inside the door. "Simon, old friend, are you well? I noticed that you had very strange company not long ago?" He went to kneel beside Simon and took up the leathered hand, deeply concerned now when he saw blood trickling from Simon's head. "The man hurt you." A sob caught in Hakim's throat, but he was soon singing Allah's praise when the old man's eyes finally opened.

"Hakim, my friend, what brings you here at this time of day?"

By the time Benjie thrust himself through the door, Simon was seated at the table, albeit not too willingly, and nodding responses to his neighbor's questions. But Hakim would not allow Simon to rise.

"I have not yet finished cleansing this wound on your skull, my friend. Do you want to die, Simon?"

Benjie skidded to a halt at Simon's feet, taking the old man's parchmentlike hand. "Old man!" he cried. "Who has killed you?"

Simon chuckled, but Hakim frowned down at the boy as if he were a bothersome gnat that had flown in when attracted by the smell of blood.

"Shoo," Hakim said. But Simon told him, "Let him stay."

"I am not dead yet, my boy," Simon spoke low. "I—I only forget things sometimes—matters of importance." He looked up then to see a tall figure of a man framed in the door. "You have brought company with you, Benjamin?" He observed the man warily. "Your large friend has dangerous weapons. Does he mean to use them on us, lad? Or another more unfortunate?"

"He is my friend. Moneeka's too!"

"Simon, hold still."

Taking the old man's hand, Benjie held it against his cool cheek. "Simon. I won't tell anyone your name."

"Ah, lad," Simon said, feeling proud. "You are learning to speak very good English. The—the Missy—" Simon blinked, and then his eyes widened and he tried to rise to his feet, but he couldn't make it all the way so he sat back down. Groggily he went on, "You must hurry, Benjamin. Hurry. The Missy Monica is in great trouble from the evildoer. Take your friend here with you." He looked up then as the man stepped into the room, his pistols hanging loosely in his hands. "No," Simon said suddenly. "Benjie will wait here for you. Down the street to the first warehouse on the right, she is there . . . go quickly!"

"Monica," Steven breathed the name, gripping the pistols to his chest while turning from the room.

"Yes. Go now!" Simon urged. Then he shouted at the piratical figure going out the door, "Watch out, young man, beware the thin man with the terrible lash in his hand." He looked down at Benjie and then up again, muttering, "That one is *shaitan* himself."

38

A bitter wind harried the storefronts, rattling shutters and setting the warehouse signs to creaking. Inside one of the thatch-roofed buildings, Alex Bennington hunkered above the dirt floor, his quirt methodically tapping the straw baskets that stood between him and Monica Hawke.

Alex's colorless gaze measured the young woman as if to gauge her worth. "So, we pick up where we left off before, Monica *Hawke*." His cold eyes roved the cracked red clay of the walls, then rested on the pile of discarded straw baskets and other sundry unwanted articles no longer suitable for sale or use. "Perfect," he muttered, slapping his quirt on the floor while Monica coughed, "a perfect dusthole for what I've in mind for you, *madam*."

Monica said nothing, just stared past the sin-laden countenance of Alex Bennington.

"You must be in love. Is that why you look so forlorn and lost? Pining for your husband, Monica Hawke?"

Why was he asking her all these questions? Monica wondered with a desperation born of weariness and hunger. She was in fact starving.

Alex was muttering something and Monica stared at him as if he had gone quite mad. "'. . . In this kingdom by the sea, A wind blew out of a cloud, chilling My beautiful Annabel Lee; So that her high-born kinsmen came, And bore her away from me, To shut her up in a sepulcher, In this kingdom by the sea. . . .'"

Alex's smile was unnervingly evil. "Know it?" he asked, then went on to quote Edgar Allan Poe: "'. . . In this kingdom by the sea, That the wind came out of the cloud by night, Chilling and killing my Annabel Lee. . . .'"

"You're mad," Monica said softly, but her mind went on to pick up the next lines of the poem: "'But our love it was stronger by far than the love Of those who were older than we, Of many far wiser than we; And neither the angels in heaven above, Nor the demons down under the sea, Can ever dissever my soul from the soul Of the beautiful Annabel Lee. . . .'"

Aloud Bennington skipped ahead in the poem, his eyes glittering as he quoted: "'In her sepulcher there by the sea, *In her tomb by the sounding sea. . . .*'"

Her heart gave a sharp leap then. *Steven.* Alex wants Steven. She had the most uneasy feeling that Alex was setting a trap for her husband. But why? Why Steven?

There was no way she could warn Steven if he

should happen to discover the scent of the trail and come for her. Now she had another great fear to torment and plague her: What if she had not destroyed that note thoroughly enough and Steven had discovered a clue as to where she had gone? Still, how would he know where to look? The carriage driver, had he become suspicious and, discovering her identity, gone back to report this to Steven?

Monica had no way of knowing, indeed, she might never know anything after this day. Like love—what it would be like to have a man love her in return.

She had promised Benjie that their ship would come, that *someone* would soon come to save them. She hung her head in dejection. It was too late. Where is your indomitable spirit now, Monica? she asked herself.

Alex fished in his vest pocket for something, and Monica watched as he extracted a large envelope and then untied the string around it. Shivers racked her, and drawing a deep breath, she experienced a forbidding feeling of disaster.

There, before her rounded eyes, Alex dangled the hawk medallion. He snickered. "A woman like you only loves a man when he is touching her. But you'll never have Steven Hawke again! Believe me!"

"No!"

Monica shook her head, letting her hair fall over her face to hide her distress from Alex Bennington. She would not tell this evil cad that she had loved Steven even before he had come upon her so ruthlessly at the fiesta. He had been in her dreams, had been an intrinsic part of her way before she had looked upon his beautifully virile face and form. It had been inevitable that they should love . . . but did Steven really and truly love her?

Her hair fell to curtain her tear-stained cheeks. She would never know now.

Looking at Alex, knowing what kind of person he was, Monica realized Steven's worth as a man. Alex Bennington had been a cheat and a liar, and had never once set a good example in his life . . . like his father. And now she realized something else. She had never truly been like her mother at all. Mother like daughter? Daughter like mother? They had all said this of her and Victoria. But her mother had gone after life and all it could offer with a vengeance, never caring who she hurt in the process. One man had not been enough. Her child had not been enough. She had not even taken that child away from a man who had been monstrous to her while she was growing up. Victoria had always desired more; but in the end she had lost everything. Suddenly Monica did not want to be like Victoria at all, although she still loved her.

Was it too late for her and Steven? What was he thinking now? Where was he?

"Why are you in such deep thought?" Alex growled, setting down his quirt for the moment.

"I was thinking of my husband and of how much I love him," she said, lifting her chin higher. "And of how much I hate you." She frowned at what she had said. "No, I do not hate you, Alex Bennington, I feel very sorry for you. You'll never know what it is to love, for it isn't in you to love, only to hate. You grab what you can from life, from others who owe you nothing, never caring how much you hurt people along the way. You are one of those who thinks that life owes you a living. But I, for one, do not owe you anything, Alex, not a single thing; for I only protected myself from your father who was as evil in his heart and soul as you are."

"God bless you, Monica, you are so very observant." He came to his feet. "Now, as God deems it, you are going to pay for your sin. Sins, for you have committed more than one. You are a slut, just like your mother, Monica Hawke, and for driving my father to lust after you, you shall have to pay. No one will ever lust after you again."

He now caressed a length of rope, slipping it through his gloved hands. Monica was quickly reminded of her dream, the nightmare in which Alex was coming at her with a weapon in his hands. Branville had been in that dream, too.

"What are you going to do?" she said, hating the cowardly tone that had entered her voice. He dropped the hawk medallion at her feet, and she stared at it in horrible fascination.

"You shall see," he sneered across to her.

Hoisting herself to her feet, Monica made a dash for the door, but she could not open it before he had her hands behind her back. Alex whirled her about and backhanded her across the face, coiling the rope about her shoulders, her arms, and then finally her hands. He kneed her in the ribs and she fell groveling to the dirty floor, looking up at him with intense loathing in her eyes. Blood trickled down from the right side of her cut mouth, but she did not even try to wipe it away with her shoulder.

"There it is, Monica," he snarled, kicking the hawk medallion close to her face, "see if that Indian witchery can save you now."

"It is not witchery," she spat upward, a drop of her blood staining the medallion. She knew something else now; Steven had the other medallion in his possession; there were two of them, and she guessed out loud where the brothers had gotten them: "Those medallions are gifts from beloved parents, something you, Alex, never knew. They were given to two sons, two tokens of love. Love, Alex, you do not even know the meaning of the word."

He snickered down. "There are two? Yes? Ah. Then your lover has the other. . . ."

"He is not only my lover. He is my *husband*."

"So," he went on as if she hadn't said a word. "Steven Hawke has one too. Too bad he will never see this one again, for it is going to burn with your body, Monica Hawke." He shuddered. "Gad. *Monica Hawke*. I do feel sorry for you, trollop. At least, I would have. But that is over for you now, for I am doing you a favor because I have spared you from a life filled with deception, lies, and an unfaithful husband, you understand? What could be more devastating to a woman than to discover that her husband was stud to every available wench in the country? Would this not drive you crazy, Monica Hawke?'' And so he finished, an evil leer on his face.

"No! No more," she cried, closing her ears to what he was saying now. Steven was not like that, he was not!

"You are crazy!" Monica hissed up at him.

When she looked up finally, Alex was setting fire to the dry, dusty objects in the room as he backed toward the door. "Now, murderess, whore, you shall die a death worse than my father did!" he shouted to the ceiling, no longer looking her way.

But before Alex could reach the door, it burst open, the frame filled with the avenging spirit of Steven Hawke. In his hands were a pair of dueling pistols, and they were aimed directly at Alex's heart. His eyes shifted once, quickly, to her, and Monica's elation was unbounded. A strange weakness seized her with such strength that she almost fainted where she lay on the floor. She was giddy with joy and at the same time afraid for Steven.

But Steven looked so different that he seemed almost like a stranger to her. His body was leaner and he seemed dangerous—cool and deadly.

Alex spun, wielding a nasty blade in one hand. Bending, he snatched a bludgeon from the floor. He had weapons in both hands now.

Before Steven could react—in the moment when he stole a concerned glance in the direction of his wife— Alex leapt forward with the speed of a panther and hit Steven a blow on his head. Steven's weapons spun across the floor to be lost in a pile of refuse. Smoke,

483

coiled like standing cobras, the flames hissing now and then, and roiling toward the treacherously weak ceiling.

"Steven!"

His knees buckled and he went crashing to the floor while Alex stood over him kicking him in the ribs. But Steven only moaned. Monica screamed again, but Alex only kicked Steven all the harder. Alex looked down at the hurt man and said in a sneering voice:

"I'll not put a bullet in your head like I did your brother Jess's. You'll just burn in hell with your slut!"

Alex stepped over Steven who was hunched up in a hurting ball and made for the door, casually closing it behind the occupants who would be engulfed by flames along with all the stuff in the warehouse.

"Oh God, Steven . . ."

Monica could now feel the searing heat from the fire, and the smoke was choking her as she screamed softly for Steven to wake up. But he could not help her, for he, too, was unable to move.

But Steven, bleeding from a deep gash in his forehead, somehow found the sheer will power to force himself up onto his knees, shaking his head to clear it, blood trickling down the side of his face and his neck, and staining his white shirt a deep crimson.

Steven now seemed to be moving through a dense fog, not of the smoke but of his consciousness, as he heard Monica scream for him again.

But she was so far away . . . so far away. . . .

Like one in a misted dream, Steven reached down and drew a knife from the scabbard in his boot; then he walked over drunkenly and cut the ropes that bound Monica.

"Steven, oh God." She coughed, choking. "Oh thank God, Steven . . ."

Monica gasped, falling to one side as Steven reached down and caught her up against his chest and, weaving across the littered floor, hurrying as best he could, headed for the door.

Staggering along with his precious bundle, Steven managed to fling the door open.

Oh, how sweet was the rush of crisp, cool air that at once began to revive the couple. Fresh tears made clean paths along Monica's soot-stained cheeks and she hugged her husband's neck, thanking God that the one to be her hero was Steven Hawke—her husband, her love, forever and ever.

Away from the burning warehouse, Steven laid Monica gently down on the opposite side of the narrow street, then turned in time to see the brilliant red flames and black, smoking devil's horns lifted to the angry sky. Flames leapt from every crashing timber joist, and the sucking infernal orange demons seemed to collapse the weakened clay walls from within.

Benjie, clutching a frightened Cuddy he was trying to calm, stood wide-eyed beside Simon and his gaping neighbor. As more and more curious folk began to gather, Steven looked up and saw Dailey running toward him, and without thinking Steven ordered Dailey to take charge of Monica. "See to her." He coughed. "Please. I have some unfinished business to take care of."

For something had caught Steven's hawk-keen eyes. He had spotted his prey darting down a side alley and looking confused about which direction to take.

Like a wild deer startled from a thicket, Steven sprang to his feet and with a swiftness that surprised even Dailey—especially after what Steven had just gone through—he seemed to hurtle himself bodily along the street.

Within a few blocks Steven spotted his prey running between two tall buildings that had fallen into a state of dilapidation.

Alex, unaware of his deadly mistake, had gone into an alley with no way out, a dead end, and he was caught now, like a wild stallion in a box canyon.

Steven chuckled—there was a nasty ring to the sound—and he felt new strength surging into his powerful frame. Excitement pounded throughout him.

Madly spinning about, this way and that, Alex searched frantically for retreat, but found only the menacing figure of Steven Hawke bearing down on him. The man was laughing, laughing at a time like this! A piratical laugh . . .

Alex skipped aside swiftly and slashed out madly with his blade, but he was not quite fast enough. Steven lashed out to grab Alex's wrist with one hand while yanking the bludgeon with his other. "Ha. I've got you now, you skinny bastard," Steven said, surprised at the power in the man's thrust and pull. "There is no way out for you now, Alex Bennington," he taunted.

"I'll see you dead, Steven Hawke," Alex rasped, "and before I leave this alley!"

Alex forced his knee up and caught Steven in the thigh. Steven fell back against a dingy clay dwelling that came alive with the cries of hungry rats squeaking their protest from inside.

Steven propelled himself away from the wall. This was a fight to the death.

Like two demons they crashed each other, rolling down into the filthy, odorous gutter, cursing each other; Steven's grip on Alex's wrist became a vise, and he seemed to feel each separate bone weaken under the pressure of his squeeze. Now Alex, with his other hand, tried to free his knife hand from that relentless grip.

With a curdling Indian yell, Steven rammed the bludgeon ever forward, driving from his waist with the momentum of speeding shot, jamming into the bottom of Alex's nose, driving the pieces of cartilage and bone up into Alex's brain.

A shudder jerked his long frame three times, and with a stare of wide-eyed wonder, Alex went limp. When he fell over, he was dead before he hit the ground.

Steven rolled to one side, exhausted both mentally and physically, and spat at Alex's dead face: "You bastard!" He gasped for breath. "You will never kill again."

Arching from the ground on all fours, Steven turned to look up, only to witness the bloody scene mirrored in Monica's eyes.

"Steven . . ." she breathed, her face white.

When Steven saw that his wife was badly shaken, he moved slowly to his feet, dragging himself inch by painful inch, at the same time commanding his man:

"Dailey, take her away, away from this." He waved an arm in a downward stroke. "Away from this ugly sight."

"The men have taken over the *Black Pearl*, Cap'n, just as you knew they would. Should I be takin' the lady there now?"

Steven only nodded.

Before Monica moved slowly away, Steven dropped his eyes to her hand. She clutched the hawk medallion in bone-white fingers; two drops of blood mingled upon it, one hers, one Jess's.

Once again Steven lifted his face to the sky, tears shimmering in his eyes. But this time there was no rain to hide them. He didn't care. For Steven Hawke had just begun to live again.

Epilogue

Winter frosted the village of Lyon with prismatic colors, gemming the eaves of houses with cut diamonds and dripping moonstones from window-panes. Harness brass jingled on teams of horses whose steaming breath hung in puffs outside busy shops and storefronts. There was a sparkle in the air, and laughter as well because of the joyous winter holidays. Upon a hill at a place called El Corazón, a willowy lad, beaming with happy smiles, cavorted with a playful donkey that did flip-kicks while a contented Arabian stallion nickered from his stall. A reformed pirate by the name of Hughy Dylan stood framed in the stable's door, watching over his charges while enjoying a bit of the rising sun just warming the rolling hills and streaming into the windows of the villa.

Steven sat beside his bed, gazing down at Monica, waiting for her to awaken. Her long hair was spread out on the pillow behind her framing her in a colorful rainbow of beauty.

When she opened her eyes he bent close, saying, "Why did you not tell me, madam, that you are with child?"

"Steven?" Her eyes widened. "What are you saying?" Monica looked around at the room, at the big bed in which she lay.

"You are pregnant, my love. The doctor has been here and has examined you." He took her hand in his. "I am sorry, but you have been out of it for five days."

"Five days."

"Yes—mild shock, he said. Don't you remember becoming ill on our return to France? Chills and a fever, not to mention all that you had gone through. It must have been terrible for you, my dearest." He smiled sheepishly and caressed her shoulder. "You revealed many interesting items during that time."

"How did you find me?" she wondered, as she had when Steven had burst through the door.

"The carriage driver was very puzzled when a lady of refinement gave him the address of a dilapidated warehouse. Then when she entered he was further alarmed by seeing a hand reach out to pull her inside. 'In a most ungentlemanly manner,' he said. He made an investigation of his own and found out the lady's name, and came up the road to hail me just as I was leaving El Corazón."

He held out his hand then, displaying the two hawk medallions. "They are like a puzzle, you see. One fits into the other. And later I will tell you more of how I found you."

Fascinated, Monica watched as Steven pressed the raised hawk into the depressed one, saying, "My mother made these, one for Jess and one for myself. These are the signs of my father's tribe, the one my mother came into when she became his wife." He pressed her cheek with two fingers, the two medallions wrapped over his hand.

"Steven," she said, caressing his hand with her cheek, "I had nothing to do with Jess's—"

"Shhh, I don't want to hear any more of it. I heard enough while you were in shock. I know it all now." He shrugged. "The story is complete."

She smiled. "But you . . ."

"Long ago," he began, "well, not all that long ago I had a desire for a young woman, a desire that was not only in my body but in my very soul. She had hair like a butterfly rainbow. I saw her first at the grand opening of the trading post. Something began to grow between that young man and that girl."

"Yes, Steven?"

"Love is the flame, Monica." He took both her hands in his. "I am deeply in love with you," he said, the strength in his voice announcing his conviction, "*very* deeply, my darling, *irrevocably*."

"And I with you, Steven," Monica replied, answering his commitment with the full measure of a woman's love, "but . . ."

She broke off. How could she tell him that she had been witness to him and Michelle standing in the garden in what looked to be an intimate rendezvous on several occasions?

He lifted her and hauled her into his arms. "No more of this, Monica. From now on when there is something between us I want to hear about it and from your own lips." He tilted her chin and Monica was forced to meet the ardent flame glowing in his eyes.

"Oh, Steven, do you really love me?"

"*Mon Dieu!*" he exclaimed.

"Say it, Steven, say you love me and—and not that awful woman Michelle."

She lowered her gaze. "What does she mean to you, Steven, can you tell me? And will there always be other paramours for you? Am I not enough for you, Steven?"

"Ah, so it's Michelle." He took a deep breath. "Now I know what is troubling you. Monica, Michelle means nothing to me. The only woman I can profess to loving is you, even though you sometimes infuriated me and you defied me every time I tried to get you closer to me. Yes, I confess to ravishing you"—he grabbed her by the shoulders and shook her gently—"and I used jealousy to make you love me, Monica, don't you know that, even now?" He caressed her. "How slender you are even in your pregnancy. How madly I love you now, and will even when you are huge with child."

"Michelle means nothing to you, truly, Steven?"

"Cross my heart, woman. Dammit, what do I have to do, get down on a knee and kiss your lovely—" He coughed. "Let me rephrase that. Get down on my knees and profess my love and renounce all other women?''

"Yes! I'll have no other women between us from now on.''

"*Mon Dieu*,'' Steven breathed; then he said aloud, tossing his arms wide, "I love you, no other woman, ever, not Michelle. Not even for a minute do I love her, not for a tumble. *I love you, Monica Hawke.*''

He drew her to him again. "I love our baby that is coming too.'' He smiled. "Do you believe that as you grow with child you will become more beautiful in my eyes, even though you may be like a plump watermelon?''

"Yes, Steven.''

After carefully undressing her, Steven made love to Monica, gently, their bodies striving to get closer to the ardent flame in them both, until the shimmering spire wrapped their hearts in a glorious, achingly tender ecstasy. Glimmers of joy and bliss shivered through Monica, and gushes of deliciously hot sensations thrilled her, evoked by her husband's expertise and his tender loving.

Later, after she had fallen asleep dreams came to her. In them she feared that when she woke Steven would be gone. She looked back into the violet night of the past, hearing the faint cries of nightbirds calling from moon-spangled trees. And as the moon rose higher a stream of light, almost magical, fell across the spot she was staring at and the man who appeared there dressed as an Indian. She realized with almost feverish joy that this was Steven. The glory of life rushed over her like a flood of gold in which thousands of tiny sunbeams danced joyously. He was leaving her. Steven! *Don't go*!

Monica whimpered, curling away from the dream. If he left she would surely die!

"Steven! . . ." Her dream made her wake in a burst of fear. "You came to me as an Indian, at Temloc again. Was that real, Steven? Back then was that you?"

"Yes, I was dressed in the fashion of our village, the way I had scouted around as a lad. I hope I did not frighten you?"

"I loved every frightening minute, Steven." She pulled him closer. "Stay with me, Steven."

"I have always been here, sweet love, always in your dreams too, *never* far away."

Winding her slim arms about his tanned neck, she said in a woman's gentle way, "Always and forever, Steven," knowing her love for Steven would never die.

Dear Reader—

   This book is dedicated to you too. I hope you have enjoyed reading FORBIDDEN DAWN. It's always a pleasure to hear from my readers; I would be delighted to hear from you.

New Address:
Sonya Pelton
198 Wells Cove
Giddings, Texas 78942